Advance Praise

"So satisfying to read a volume of new speculative fiction stories centered on women's experience, women's lives, women's choices! You'll find a pleasurable variety here: hard sf, fantasy, ghosts, vampires, horror, sweet lyricism and steel-edged noir — stories from well-known names, and stories from writers you've never encountered before. I guarantee that at least one story in this volume will make you punch the air in triumph, and another will work its way into your dreams, and not let go."

—Elizabeth Lynn, World Fantasy Award Winner

"I'm absolutely blown away. Featuring so many authors who I love, this is a stunning anthology with many different approaches to the subject of bodily autonomy. Readers are going to be captivated by its range and variety. This anthology will be a breath of fresh air in the ongoing fight for the right of women to control and make decisions about their own bodies."

—Chinelo Onwualu, author of "What The Dead Man Said"

"*Adventures in Bodily Autonomy* is a fresh and bold collection. In our current political climate, these stories and imaginings are desperately needed."

—Myriam Gurba, author of Mean

Adventures in Bodily Autonomy

ADVENTURES IN BODILY AUTONOMY

Exploring Reproductive Rights in Science Fiction, Fantasy, & Horror

edited by
Raven Belasco

Aqueduct Press
PO Box 95787
Seattle, Washington 98145-2787
www.aqueductpress.com

Library of Congress Control Number: 2023937931

ISBN: 978-1-61976-250-3
First Edition, First Printing, October 16, 2023

Book design by Kathryn Wilham

Printed in the USA by Bookmobile

Previous Publication Acknowledgments

Nisi Shawl, Queen of Dirt, originally appeared in *Apex Magazine*

Ellen Klages, Goodnight Moons, originally appeared in *Wicked Wonders* (Tachyon Publications)

K Ibura, Pod Rendezvous, originally appeared in *Ancient, Ancient* (Aqueduct Press)

Helena María Viramontes, selection from *Their Dogs Came With Them,* (Atria Books)

Sonya Taaffe, As the Tide Came Flowing In, from a chapbook of the same name (Nekyia Press)

Annalee Newitz, Chapter 10 from *The Future of Another Timeline* (Tor)

Elizabeth Bear, Bullet Point, originally appeared in *Wastelands: The New Apocalypse* (Titan Books)

Editor Acknowledgments

Thank you to everyone at NARAL for being so welcoming to this project.

Thank you to Timmi, Tom, and Kath, for giving it a home and making it real.

Thank you to the deeply talented Jenifer Prince for creating cover art to bring the stories to life on the outside of the book.

Thank you to Maggie for the ass-kickin' Intro.

Thank you to Nisi, Ellen, Kathleen, K, Helena, Cecilia, Sonya, Annalee, Cynthia, Tara, Anya, Jaymee, and Bear for trusting me with your stories and being a part of this conversation.

Thank you to my friends who gave me support in the early days of this, when I was really not certain I could make it actualize, and who encouraged me at every setback. Now we can celebrate together, which is another important part of friendship.

Thank you to everyone who wrote such kind blurbs about this project-of-my-heart.

And thanks to you, the Reader, who has supported NARAL by buying this book. If you bought it secondhand, or got it as a gift, please pop up to their website and give what you can. If you can't do that, please pass the book onto someone else when you're done, or just have some conversations with people about reproductive justice and bodily autonomy. "Pay it forward."

This project would not have and will not succeed without all of you, all of us. Let's keep working together for the basic human right of bodily autonomy.

This is dedicated to every woman who has had to suffer the loss of her bodily autonomy, and to all who have helped in the struggle to achieve that right, and to keep that right.

Contents

Preface

Greetings, Readers!

The book you are holding in your hands right now started back during the time when the Supreme Court was deciding *Dobbs v. Jackson Women's Health Organization.* Everyone could sense that *Roe v. Wade* was going to be overturned, and during that whole time-period there was this terrible sense of dread hanging over me and every childbearing person I knew.

I wanted to give more than the small amount of money I could afford to donate. I wanted it really badly. Just giving a one-time donation wasn't going to help me with this huge ache inside me, needing to *do something*.

What finally came to me was that I knew enough writers who were feeling the same way as me; we all wanted to do more, give more. Being writers, most of us didn't have a bunch of money we could throw at the situation. But we did have words. We had a lot to say, and we could use that to raise more money together than any of us could give alone.

I'd never edited an anthology before, so I dove in with just passion and the optimism of damn-near total ignorance. I reached out to authors, and the ones you see listed in the table of contents were kind and generous and trusted me even though I was just a gal with a goal (and not much else). Then, a dream came true and Aqueduct Press said they would give this anthology a home. To bring it all together, NARAL was warm and welcoming when I reached out and asked them to believe in this project, too.

For over 50 years, NARAL Pro-Choice America has fought to protect and advance reproductive freedom at the federal and state levels—including access to abortion care, birth control, pregnancy and postpartum care, and paid family leave—for every body. NARAL has been at the forefront of this fight since its founding and is powered by 4 million members from every state and congressional district in the country, representing the 8 in 10 Americans who support legal abortion. Find out more at https://www.prochoiceamerica.org/

One hundred percent of the royalties of this book are being donated to NARAL Pro-Choice America to help them continue their vital fight for women's bodily autonomy and basic human rights. Aqueduct Press and I humbly thank our authors for donating their stories, making this anthology and fund-raising effort possible.

The release date of this book is important in the history of women's healthcare rights. On October 16, 1916, in Brooklyn, New York, Margaret Sanger opened the country's first birth control clinic. Just nine days later police shut down the clinic and Sanger served 30 days in prison. She spent her life founding and being involved with myriad birth control organizations, constantly searching for more affordable and effective contraceptives, helping to get funding for medical innovations—such as the birth control pill—and fighting to make family planning available to everyone. Unfortunately, many of the battles she fought and won we are having to refight today.

Raven Belasco

Introduction

Maggie Mayhem

It was chance and good fortune that brought me to the steps of the United States Supreme Court on Jan 22, 2003, where I looked out at a sea of thousands upon thousands of pro-life protestors filling the National Mall for as far as my 18-year-old eyes could see. It was the 30th anniversary of the Roe v. Wade decision, and abortion had been a settled matter for the entirety of my lifetime as a controversial feature of the status quo, but status quo nonetheless. Those who came there to affirm the right to abortion access as a part of healthcare were few and far between. What all the anti-abortion protestors held in common was an ability to imagine a future with a radically different landscape for reproductive healthcare. They did not take for granted that Roe v. Wade was an immutable part of the law. Not only did they far outnumber us there, they out-imagined the pro-choice majority and were willing to fight to make that imagination a reality. I felt afraid of this coordinated mass movement, and that fear made a lifelong activist out of me.

Two decades later and months shy of turning 50, *Roe v. Wade* was overturned. This was a process that has been unfolding over time beginning from the moment that ruling was first delivered. The negative impact of the Dobbs decision cannot be overstated. Though my entry into abortion access activism was motivated by fear, my experiences as a sex, birth, and death worker fighting for abortion access created a foundation for hope. As a full spectrum doula (someone who provides emotional and practical support for any possible outcome of a pregnancy) I have learned that the line between creation and destruction is just one of many false binaries. Just as reactionaries have mobilized to alienate us from our own bodies, so too have those fighting to secure a future where reproductive decisions are respected, not regulated. The future is not yet realized.

As people of conscience who believe in bodily autonomy and self-determination, it is incumbent upon us to commit to the task of imagining a new future for reproduction together. This task cannot be underestimated in its importance, and the framework of Reproductive Justice is vital to guiding this process and expanding upon what we believe is possible. Going beyond the rigid limitations of "choice" within the reproductive rights movement, the BIPOC scholar-activists of Sister Song conceptualized outside of the pro-choice/pro-life binary to pursue a vision that confronts the structural oppression that regulates reproduction. Reproductive Justice affirms our right to create and raise healthy families alongside our rights to prevent, decline, or eliminate the potential for pregnancy. It reminds us that we all have a right to primary pleasure, whether this is engaging in sex or refusing it. Reproductive Justice refuses to draw gendered lines around gestational capacity.

The role of stories and narratives as a necessary strategy for pursuing these rights has been highlighted by the Reproductive Justice movement. Storytelling has the power to drive connections within individuals, their communities, and the world that are not possible with abstract theory or policy briefs alone. Stories, not statistics, are what truly drive movements because they lead us to the reasons that motivate us to fight.

As we face the disorienting wake of the Dobbs decision with its regressive reanimation of the past and the uncertain future it presents, it is perhaps all the more necessary to step into the supernatural contexts of the stories in this anthology to radically reconsider our own social locations and question the elements of our self-determination. This anthology brings the principles of Reproductive Justice to light by striking at its central premise that not all choices are made from equal liberties or consequences. The characters here are faced with circumstances that compel them to identify and act in defense of the vision they have for their lives in unconventional settings that unburden readers of any thought-terminating expectations about the absolute meaning of sex, death, birth, breath, or blood.

In these pages you will companion a space traveler experiencing an unprecedented pregnancy on a mission to Mars, consider conflict between sisters about strange and mystical reproductive technologies, contemplate the role of death magic in sustaining life, and weigh the decision to exchange gestational capacity in favor of alternative and more everlasting bonds. A woman sizes up Las Vegas after the apocalypse as well as the as well as apparently the other remaining human and his notions for saving their species, and a time traveler reconciles with the past. Werewolves, vampires, witches, the Fae, and more all speak their piece from perspectives as alien and familiar as any one person you might ever meet. The collection has been curated to include established authors and icons such as Nisi Shawl, Elizabeth Bear, Annalee Newitz, and Cecilia Tan as well as powerful emerging voices.

I hope that you will enjoy reading these stories as much as I did and gain insight into how you will orient and find your own true north in the years to come as we labor collectively to make way for new possibilities and pursue the path to Reproductive Justice for all.

Queen of Dirt

Nisi Shawl

Brit lowered her wooden sword and sighed. She loved her students. But the girls kept hesitating, getting hung up on the moves, lagging behind. The three boys in the class of nine had stayed with her through the form, but when they thought she wasn't looking they whaled at the ground with their weapons like taiko drummers. Could they be any more clichéd?

Bees buzzed over flowers blossoming in scattered patches of sunlight. That was all right; none of the kids were allergic. And not all bees stung. From the pond beyond the trees a cool breeze blew, drying the light sweat coating her arms. "Everybody siddown." The rustle of the blue plastic tarp rose and fell as they obeyed. It stilled as they looked up at her, their faces so earnest. "You learnin fast," Brit told them. Not a lie. Little kids did learn fast. Way faster than adults, or even teenagers like herself. "But not countin Sunday we got five more days before the show. That all. An we ain't even come up with our routine." Sunday was unscheduled. A lot of kids and teachers went to church.

Tanzi raised her hand, though Brit hadn't asked the class a question. "Yeah?"

"Can we figure that part out in our wing meeting at the dorm tonight?"

Grey barely waited to be called on to object. "But we're sleepin in different wings."

"Okay, in the cafeteria at dinner. If we all sit at the same table —"

"Other teams could hear us!" Grey's cousin Jazman was the most competitive kid in camp. "They'll steal our ideas!"

"The cafeteria's big," Tanzi scoffed. "Let's all sit by the window farthest from the serving line. You could hold it for us, right, Mizz Brit? Make the other teams stay away?"

"Sure." Brit slid her blade into its beaded scabbard and pulled her watch out of her front pants pocket. "We got enough time to meditate. Anything you wanna ask me before we start?" On the first day of camp she'd told the kids she would answer anything.

The smallest girl peered up from underneath a rolled and knotted turquoise bandana. "Did you ever, you know, ever hurt somebody really bad? I mean like —"

"You mean have I ever kill anyone?" Brit had promised herself she would learn all her students' names in the eleven days of Experience Outreach, even the ones in the big morning classes. She had most of them, and just about every kid on her afternoon concentration team. Was this Denighta? Denesta?

"I never kill no one." At least, she'd never killed another human being.

"Now shut your eyes. Let your breath come an go slow — slower — slower — like shadows movin with the sun, like the turnin of the world..." The smell of peace, green grass and water, calmed her mind. She liked it out here with the kids. Quiet, compared to the city. Calm after her work clearing out nests of entities.

So far she'd been able to stay away from the abandoned bunkers up the hill, site of the park's mysterious string of suicides. So far she'd ignored the feelings they gave her.

The hour before mealtime was unassigned. Brit led her team along the overgrown walkway to the dorm entrance where their chaperones waited. She assured the kids firmly that exploring the bunkers would take too long even if they left immediately. She barely had enough time herself to get back to her cabin, shower, and read a few pages of *Return to Nevèrÿon*. But she did manage to beat them to the kitchen building, joining Mr. Crofutt and the other six instructors on the porch outside five minutes before the line opened.

"How's my little half-pint of cider half drunk up?"

Brit thought he was creepy when they first met: an old white guy, ponytail and flamboyant purple shirt marking him as a liberal like her mom and dad, trying no doubt to "relate to the youth"...but he'd helped her figure out her some important stuff. He'd never hit on her or done anything else inappropriate, either.

"I got them students eatin outta my hand. Specially my concentration team."

"They think you're cool because you're just about their size." Mr. Crofutt peered back to where the students were gathering along the porch's fieldstone wall, more or less by the dorm wing. "Have you worked out your routine yet?"

"Tonight." The line began to move. Brit took a plate of spaghetti and meatballs from behind a sneeze guard, and a bowl for the salad bar. "I'm spozed to make sure we have a table by ourself. You mind?"

Mr. Crofutt dropped behind as they entered the high-ceilinged dining room. "Not in the least. Want me to run interference with Lisa?"

"That be great, yeah." Experience Outreach's Language Arts teacher Lisa Plowden was fascinated with Brit's assumed dialect. Her attention had started to feel like stalking.

Brit could talk Standard English whenever she wanted. She'd proved that in her job interview. First day she told her classes not to copy her; they promised, and her Ebonics ceased being an issue for everyone except Mrs. Plowden.

Mr. Crofutt headed off on his mission as Brit speed-walked to the room's far corner on hers. She picked a window table with a close view of a row of fluttering, silver-leaved poplars.

Boys and girls came to the table separately and sat far apart. Sixth graders.

"You were right, Mizz Brit," admitted Jazman. "The drummers only went to Battery Vicars and they still aren't back! We never woulda made it in time."

↞

After dinner, though, Brit's excuses for avoiding the bunkers ran out. Predictably, the boys wanted to base their team's presentation on a war story. Tai Chi was a martial art, after all. Less predictably the girls did, too—if at least one of the two sides fighting were zombies. Much enthusiasm for Tanzi's plan of blocking out their routine on the site of one of the abandoned gun emplacements. Brit would have looked weird vetoing it. Other instructors didn't have the heebie-jeebies over visiting the bunkers, and Experience Outreach was supposed to be about connecting art with the environment.

Curfew wasn't for another two-and-a-half hours, and the sky was plenty light at 6:30 on an end-of-June night. So as the sun drifted down toward the hazy horizon, touching with pale gilt the white clapboard sides of Fort Worden State Park's museums, halls, and dormitories, Brit climbed the hill, surrounded by her charges. It was another idyllic moment. Kids were great. If only you didn't have to have sex to get pregnant with them.

Over the gentle slope of the daisy-sprinkled lawn. Up the crumbling asphalt road where no vehicles were allowed. Brit's heart jumped as a dark, humping shape scuttled behind an empty cabin—but it was only an otter. Onto the sunken timber steps, then the gravel drive circling the hill's crown. Sweeping around to every obsolete battery the stupid soldiers had built.

That wasn't fair. Brit knew it. Experience Outreach's staff orientation had included a brief history of the Fort. Most of it was constructed so long ago air war was no more than a wild-eyed sci-fi concept involving zeppelins and ornithopters. 1897. Nearly a century had passed.

They came to an open field and stopped a moment. Clouds had gathered overhead with typical Quimper Peninsula swiftness. Between them sunrays shot out to backlight a line of firs. Grey and Jazman argued about which way to go. Grey won. They followed the road's bend to the right. Toward Battery Tolles and the bad feelings.

Mr. Crofutt called Brit a "Visioner." He had found her a couple of years ago, running away from home, and helped her understand the weirdness of her life. Said she translated "non-physical entities" into "concrete, manipulable analogies." When Mr. Crofutt offered to recommend Brit for this gig teaching with him at the Experience Outreach camp, he had mentioned there was some sort of problem with entities on one area of the grounds. People kept killing themselves: soldiers, then a couple of local "troubled teens," then an annual average of one camper — usually retired RVers. Not an epidemic, but over the years it had added up to about twenty.

Brit ignored that and accepted the job because it was with kids, young black kids, kids like she used to be and wished she could someday have. Also, it made a nice excuse to spend less time with the rents and their impossible "realistic" expectations. Like how they wanted her to talk "proper" English the way she did in elementary and middle school. How they kept on expecting her to go on dates.

Besides, one little problem spot in the entire park hadn't seemed too much of a challenge. Hadn't she rid a whole city of an infestation of spiritual tent worms?

Under the firs' shadows it felt an hour later. And colder. Brit clasped her hands around her upper arms and zipped her hoodie. None of the kids acted like they noticed. They laughed and hit each other playfully with springy, green-needled branches they picked up from the side of the road. "Hey!" she warned them. "None a that!"

"But Mi-izz Bri-i-i-it," Tanzi pretend-whined. "You let us hit each other with the practice sticks. What's so diff—"

Brit halted. "Stop right there." A ragged wave of obedience. "Turn aroun an look at me while I talk to you." All nine students turned to face her.

"They ain't sticks. They swords. Ack like it. Believe it. You believe, your audience gonna believe too." She and Mr. Crofutt had talked a local supplier into lending the wooden practice swords in exchange for a free ad in the performance night program.

"Also." She stared as fiercely as she could. "How you movin in the form? Whatever routine we put together for Thursday? It gonna be slow, and directed. Purposeful. That's what so different. Unnerstan?"

Every head nodded. "Go on then." She started walking again and the kids, subdued, bunched up, went with her.

Soon the low bowl of Battery Tolles spread to the road's right. A trail spun down its sides. Blank darkness filled the doorless entrances to the concrete shelters at its bottom. They reminded her of giant skulls. Dead eyes and open mouths gaping like the heads of half-buried trolls. Brit shook her head to empty it of that idea. If she thought too hard about trolls, there might be trolls for real. She wasn't sure exactly how Visioning worked.

Grey and the other two boys headed up the stairway to the decommissioned gun carriage on the bunker's roof. "What about if we attack from up here?" That was Byron according to the attendance sheet, but his friends called him Skinny.

"You can't be a zombie, Skinny—only girls!" Tanzi yelled from the bowl's floor. "And we have to hide down here. Right, Mizz Brit?"

"Let's vote." Her favorite way to delegate. It was a landslide victory, six to three. The boys grumbled, but quickly got into the rehearsal, looking relaxed and innocent as they descended the battery's steps, assuming exaggerated poses of horror and surprise as the girls staggered out of their dank lairs. Brit forgot her foreboding in the work of choreography. The feints and disarms and deliberate stumbles she helped them choose drew closely on the forms she'd taught, but there was a nod to MJ's "Thriller," too: "Stomp, stomp, stomp, rear! Stomp, stomp, stomp, rear!"

When Brit thought to check her watch it was fifteen minutes to the 9 o'clock curfew.

Delighta — one of the boys had settled that question by yelling at her when she accidentally flipped his precious ball cap into the blackberries — had been at Fort Worden last summer. She knew a shortcut.

From the trail's head they walked a few feet back along the way they'd come, then took a narrow path that looked like it was going to bisect the main road's circle. As the class discussed how to transfer their routine's blocking to the theater — warrior boys on the stage, zombie girls rising from seats in the audience — Brit did her best to ignore her growing unease. Why did she have to notice this sort of feeling? Why couldn't she be like everybody else? According to Mr. Crofutt, making entities visible and palpable was something she did to fight them. To win.

But why did she have to know evil entities even existed, let alone sense where they gathered? Why couldn't she be like everybody else?

So dark, so early. Maybe the gathering storm was the cause. Looked like it would rain hard. Could even be some of the Northwest's rare thunder and lightning. Ahead of her in the gloom little Delighta paused. "This part's spooky!" she announced. "It'll get so you can't see." Delighta glanced at the student right behind her. "Maybe we should hold hands." She grabbed Jazman's. Both girls giggled.

And why not? They were only eleven, twelve years old, but kids had crushes all the time. Everyone did.

Everyone but Brit. Unless you counted Iyata, who was really just a friend. Really. Despite her mother and father's delicate questions, and their reassurances that it was all right to be gay.

Brit didn't know what she was. Not gay, though.

Delighta and Jazman took a sharp turn and she lost sight of them. For a moment only, she thought, but then she made the turn too and they stayed invisible. She heard their footsteps continue, but they echoed oddly. Following the sound, Brit found out why: the two had entered a low tunnel. Short as Brit was she could touch the ceiling when she reached up with one hand. She let her arm fall to her side. "Hold on!"

"It doesn't go far, Mizz Brit," Delighta said. "We're already out."

"I'm tellin you stop! Now!" Her voice reverberated hollowly off the tunnel's walls.

Then the reverberations ceased.

She pulled her sword. Wanted to. Tried to.

Nothing happened. She was frozen in place. Couldn't move. Paralyzed.

No! Could she breathe? Yes—but when she gasped in a big gulp of air she felt something crinkle and tighten against her skin, a film of thick plastic like the tarp. Panic prickled over her and she puffed out hard and fast. The tightness eased. Brit experimented. Slow, shallow breaths kept the plasticky film from snugging in on her. She had to control her fear.

What else? She could roll her eyes, blink. "Can I talk?" she asked herself. The words sounded flat and dead, but she heard them.

She flexed her toes, the muscles of her calves, thighs, butt, stomach. She already knew her hands wouldn't obey her, but her fingertips twitched. Her mouth opened wide though her head wouldn't nod. Nostrils flared. Eyebrows raised, forehead wrinkled.

So partially paralyzed only.

Why? How?

How long?

Best guess, this had to do with whatever entities hung around here. Was this how they drove the suicides to take their lives? Or was it something else? Maybe if she could figure out what they'd done she'd be able to free herself.

By when?

She was hungry. She had to pee. The air suddenly smelled stale — was she breathing the same stuff over and over? She'd suffocate! She'd — Slow down. Slow. Down.

She should meditate, the way she'd shown the kids — the kids! What were they doing? What had happened to them? Complete darkness filled Brit's eyes, even when she opened them wide. That was magic of some kind, the work of this new crop of entities, but evening had been settling in fast, and it must be night by now. How would her students find their way? They'd gotten out of the tunnel ahead of her. Were they wasting time looking for Brit first? Eventually they'd get back and tell the chaperones, who would organize a fruitless search — What was going on?

Again she took deliberate control of herself. In. Slow. Out. Slow. Gradually she wiped from her mind the useless chafing about her students. Nothing she could do to help them except get out of here. They'd shown no signs earlier of being disturbed by the entities. They'd show up at the dorms without her, and things would proceed according to established policies. Pointlessly. Though maybe Mr. Crofutt would have some idea what kind of trouble Brit was in. He knew about entities and how to fight them.

Meanwhile, what could she do? Without access to the sword at her side or any other weapons — except her mind. Her memory.

Minus the usual immediate sensory distractions, Brit's mental movie of what had gone on before her paralysis reeled past in lucid detail: the giggles of the girls holding hands ahead of her, the gritty sweep of the tunnel's wet cement ceiling against her upheld hand, the slight mound of dirt beneath her feet... Wait. That was new. She'd felt the low mound at the time, but till now it hadn't registered.

Brit reviewed the sequence over and over in her head. Nothing else stood out and she finally got tired of thinking about it.

And no one had found her yet. Hours must have gone by.

A textbook on the sociology of interrogation she snuck out of her mom and dad's library had a chapter about sensory deprivation as a torture technique. Supposedly it worked pretty well. Supposedly it produced horrible hallucinations. Over the course of days, she reminded herself.

So what was that crawling sensation on the top of her head?

Not real! Not not not! It felt heavy, wet, warm, runny, dripping down to her eyes so she had to shut them as it poured faster and faster over her nose and cheeks and if she opened her mouth to scream she'd taste it but she couldn't help it couldn't — "Help! Help me! Hel —"

Sweetness?

She choked, spat reflexively only to get the spit right back in her face, saliva dribbling off her chin mixed with the —

She told herself it was not blood. Not vomit. Forced herself to lick out her tongue and try another taste, try to analyze it.

Like nectar. Spicier, though. Perfume.

It was good. She sampled it again. Yes. A bit of an acid edge, which only made it easier to eat more.

The feeling of having to pee went away.

Realizing that brought her crashing back down to scaredness. She had swallowed some random emission of an entity. She didn't know what the stuff represented, what it did. She didn't even know what the entities themselves were like—they'd be something she was familiar with, but what? What had she shaped them into—Visioned?

Another cascade of liquid flowed over her, sticky and smooth as when her grandmother filled jars with her homemade—

Jelly. Royal jelly. She'd read a description of its flavor that matched. And her prison fit.

The entities were manifesting as bees. And trying to make Brit into their queen.

She couldn't wipe the jelly off. She let it dry on her skin, blinking hard so her eyelids wouldn't stick shut. Lips pressed firmly together; no way was she consuming more, no matter how hungry and thirsty she got.

Why bees? Because she actually knew a lot about them, that was why. She'd researched them last quarter for a Poetry of Biology paper. She understood the differences between solitary and eusocial species, and between primitive and evolved eusocial swarms. Not all bees stung. Not all produced honey. Some lived in hives provided by humans, some in dead trees.

Some nested in holes in the ground marked by low entrance mounds, lining them with secretions that hardened into natural polyesters.

Apparently facts about various kinds of bees had mushed together in Brit's unconscious mind to create these entities' manifestation. The way she'd made the ones in town into giant invisible tent worms. These were giant invisible bees.

Very nice. Now how did that get her out of here?

Maybe she could just be rescued? Left to his own devices Mr. Crofutt should be able to track her down—Locating was his superpower, the way shaping entities by Visioning them was hers. As long as she didn't breathe too deep or fast the air would probably last. Probably. The entities seemed to want her to live. Plus if they could pour royal jelly into her cell it probably wasn't completely sealed up. Probably.

Her face began tingling. Softly at first, then harder, like the vibrating of a million tiny alarm clocks. Her neck and shoulders got in on the act too. Her upper arms and chest. Everywhere the jelly had touched her.

Hadn't her mom said something about how women used to rub bee jelly on themselves for beauty? How they absorbed its activating proteins directly into their tissues —

"Hnnnngg! Mmmmmvvvv!" Brit shrieked with her mouth shut. Did she still have a mouth? "Hmmmmnng!" Panting through her nose, she felt the cell's plastic lining shrink tight like a too-small rubber glove. "MmmmmMMMMMMM!" Thrashing around only made it worse. Made it impossible to move. Soon all she could do was shiver and shudder and sob. Without daring to open her lips. Tears ran from her closed eyes; mucus threatened to stop up her nose.

She would choke on it and die, choke on her own snot. She would die here, buried underground. Nobody would ever see her again.

Unless she got it together. Unless she immediately quit freaking. Unless she surrendered and opened up her mouth. Of course she had one. The substance might trickle in. But how else to get air? She breathed in. Out. In. Out. Slower. Slower.

She felt the plastic wrapping her relax. For the second time. The buzzing tingle kept going, though, got worse —

Screw the tingle. She might lose her shit again unless she igged it. She'd think straight while she could. Until her brain turned into a bee's — No. That was not an all right idea to have in her head.

The entities wanted to change her. Maybe because she had changed the entities? She never knew what she was doing — or she hadn't anyway with the tent worms, the only entities she'd dealt with so far. What happened had only made sense afterwards, when Mr. Crofutt explained it.

So. If worms ate leaves and the worm entities ate the leaves of people's dreams, what did bee entities eat? Some nectar analog. Something harmless, most likely, since bees didn't hurt flowers.

They hurt people they stung. If they stung.

Did these entities hurt people? Yes. Or made them hurt themselves. Especially people who were allergic.

Most bees died after stinging once. Not queens. If the entities transformed her as she suspected they were trying to do, she would be capable of triggering mass waves of suicides.

Though the main function of a queen bee was to breed.

That started her struggling again. She yelled and tensed her muscles and pushed at whatever kept her pinned in place. Got nowhere but she didn't care she would rather die than lay six million eggs, six million fertilized—

A glob of royal jelly covered her face. She sneezed and coughed her nose and throat clear. And gulped some down. Had to. More kept coming. It puddled around her ankles and crept up her calves, climbed over her knees, drenched the bottoms of her shorts, making her legs buzz madly. Halted just below her crotch.

For the moment.

Based on her research, Brit expected that soon the cell would be filled completely. Then...then she would drown. Or worse.

But she was supposed to win. That was what her Visioning superpower was for. Entities real enough to touch were real enough to kill.

How did you kill bees? Tent worms you crushed or smoked to death, and she'd figured out how to poison the worm entities using cigars.

Beekeepers used smoke to soothe their swarms to sleep. If she had her cigars with her here…they'd probably be useless. She couldn't light them if she couldn't move.

Anyway, she didn't want the bee entities to fall asleep. Maybe she didn't even want them dead. Not right now. Right now all she wanted was to get herself out.

But how?

The quiet of Brit's underground cell had slowly shredded apart. Whispers, squeals, and bursts of piping cries built up in the velvety silence, from ones and twos to a steady thrum of sound. The music of the hive. Almost she could make out individual voices. They felt like they came from very close. Almost she could see the members' individual dance steps, see them bow and shake their tail ends, neon gold on black. Almost she could understand their instructions.

Any queen had to go on at least one flight, to mate. Eventually they would let her out for it.

She didn't want to wait that long.

Another torrent of jelly. Viscous and faintly fragrant, the growing pool lapped up to her navel, her nipples, her armpits. Everywhere it touched came painfully awake, like circulation returning to crushed arteries. Then there was another break in the deluge. It had to be the last.

What did Brit have to fight with? Her memories had helped some, helped her identify what shape she'd given the entities. What else was she made of? According to an old hippy album song of her mom's she used to play when she was little:

"Earth, water, fire, and air,
Met together in a garden fair…"

Earth was all around her, holding her in. Earth was part of what was wrong. Water she'd never had much use for. Air was scanty, most of it far away—but fire—fire! Fire could burn her out of any jail. If she could strike a flame—didn't sparks fly up from flint and steel? But all she smelled outside her cell was plain old dirt.

Except the dirt was not exactly plain. It was charged with energy—lines of fire! Like lightning—which leapt to heaven from the earth. Could she call the fire to come through her?

Brit searched for the energy's pathways. She heard them? Felt them? Knowledge of the fire's routes came in by her ears, but not as sounds. More like pressure. As if someone were reeling in a bunch of knotted scarves, squeezing them in through holes in her head. Scarves stretching out around her miles and miles and miles and miles.

The feed rate of the bumping knots sped up to match the buzzing pain. The buzzing pain got brighter, brighter!

Power! Glory! Blazing up, onto her feet, into her veins, her nerves, her brain, along her hair, the fire, the flame was burning hotter! Higher! Whiter! Channeling itself into her, burning faster! Hotter! Higher! Burning higher! Bursting through her skull up to the sky!

KRRRAAAKKKKK! BABOOOMMM! Thunder tumbled out of the clouds. Rain fell with it. The jelly thinned, washing away as Brit clambered out of her lidless cell and stood laughing and free in the wild night. She could move! Wind whipped the brief storm away. She could spin in and out of it and twirl around and she could run all she wanted—beneath her flying Spiras the road's gravel glittered wetly in the light of the emerging crescent moon.

Mr. Crofutt and the two East Wing chaperones met her on the stairs leading to the road behind the dorms. They'd been looking for her for an hour, finally deciding she must have hit her head and been knocked out in an inexplicable collapse no one had yet found any trace of. She let them take her to Mr. Crofutt's van. He drove her to Urgent Care and didn't ask any questions she couldn't answer. He didn't ask any questions at all.

The drugs they gave her at the clinic slowed the buzzing way down but didn't stop it. Brit told Mr. Crofutt as much as she knew about what she'd been through. He said he'd sleep on what she said, figure out what it meant in the morning.

↚

Brit tuned out the ever-present humming in her bones and focused on how things looked: pastel green walls, polished wooden floors, dim hanging lamps, and padded stacking chairs laid out in sixteen rows of eight each. No curtains hung before JFK's primitive stage — or anywhere else in the theater building. How things sounded: the babble of eighty-five Experience Outreach students echoed off hardness on every side, bounced back and forth and became so confused she couldn't make sense of what anyone was saying. Not even her parents shouting politely inches from her face. Something about how difficult it was to come all this way on a weeknight ordinarily, but the holiday tomorrow helped. Brit nodded, her eyes darting side to side, seeking escape.

Oh no. Here came Mrs. Plowden. Grinning insincerely, Brit introduced her to Mr. and Ms. Williams, aka her dad and mom. Kids began taking their seats, which cut the noise enough that even with her head turned away she could hear her parents being complimented on their extremely articulate speech.

Please. Half the reason she talked the way she did was so she didn't have to hear this sort of "compliment."

The other half was to piss off the rents, which usually worked well enough. Though they'd surprised her by showing up tonight. Okay, she'd surprise them, too.

Someone flipped the lights on and off a few times fast. In front of the stage Mr. Crofutt cupped his hands to his mouth and called "Out!"

"Reach!" responded the crowd of students. A couple more calls and responses and pretty much all the ambient chatter died away. Except Brit's mother's. "— her whole life! We're proud of how different our daughter has been —" In the sudden silence Ms. Williams stopped midsentence.

Proud? Of Brit? First time she'd heard of that. She hurried to the seat in the staff section where she'd left her sword.

This afternoon the staff had met and decided on the order of show. The opening number was an all-camp rendition of a modified Balinese monkey chant led by the Movement Arts team, who remained onstage afterward and segued into what they called their Tidepool Dance. Then the Visual Art Team's slides played while the Percussion Team (the drummers' official name) set up; after Percussion came Martial Arts to end the first half.

The artillery-mimicking boom of the taikos nearly drowned out that buzzing hum. Not quite so painful anymore now Brit was getting used to it.

The Martial Arts team's girls had spaced themselves strategically among the unsuspecting audience members. Yesterday — far too late — Tanzi had asked her to help their "side" of the mock battle but Brit declined. She stuck to her teacher role.

She mounted three of the stairs to the stage and looked back at Mr. Crofutt, who'd gone to stand by the light switch. The building's shades, lowered for the slides, had been left that way, as she'd specified. So when she raised her sword and swept it down in the signal they'd agreed on, total darkness descended.

And then not quite total. The braided strand of roses and stargazer lilies she wore around her neck began to glow. At first softly. The vases of iris placed where footlights would normally sit filled with shimmering color and overflowed. The shadowy forms of Grey and Skinny and Slaydell shuffled hesitantly into that spectral light. No dialogue, but the boys moved scared, weapons at the ready.

From their chosen spots the girls stole forward, glitter-dusted faces beautifully ghastly in the shine of the white gardenias Brit had pinned into their hair. They stumbled through the steps she'd lifted from "drunken" Zui quan forms. She called translations of the steps' names in cadence: "Swaying Hips! Pour the Wine! Spill the Soup! Tripping on the Trailing Hem!" The zombie girls crept and leapt and crawled around and above her, wooden swords carried in deceptively slack hands. They surrounded the hapless warriors and attacked! The boys yelled the names of their defenses as they fought. Though valiant they were outnumbered two-to-one. Of course the zombies defeated them.

Good guys didn't always win. Something every kind of artist had to learn.

The boys stopped writhing around and the girls sat back on their haunches, showing their faces. Their mouths and chins were covered in a paste of mashed red petals: dahlias, peonies, glads — whatever Brit had been able to buy at the Port Townsend farmers' market. Blazing smears of blood red streaked their cheeks. They lifted crimson hands to gleam like torches in the hushed dimness.

The audience began applauding prematurely.

Grey sat up jerkily, as if he was strobing. Brit hadn't been able to convince any of the boys to paint their faces with crushed flowers, but she got them to carry bags of bee pollen from the food co-op — expensive, but when they'd rubbed it on their sweaty faces under cover of the girls' feeding frenzy it became possible for her to provide their skin with a nice yellow-green luminosity.

The freshly undead got unsteadily up, and now all nine Martial Arts team members did the MJ moves in unison, complete with crotch grabs. And it was over, and the audience was on their feet, hooting, cheering, and whistling while they clapped, loud and hard and long.

A show-stopper, exactly as Brit had expected. She slipped out of the handicap access door stage right as the house lights turned up for intermission. Milky clouds covered the sky, reflecting back the town's and the park's streetlights, but Brit no longer needed them to see the lay of the land. It swelled and dipped before her, curving fire lapped by the wine of the sea.

The volume of the audience's murmuring increased for a few seconds as the door behind her opened and quickly shut. She turned to face her ally, Mr. Crofutt. "So anointing them with flowers and nectar and pollen like that made them yours?" he asked. "Your kids?"

"As much mine as the women's they was born to." New queen, new hive. New rules. New reproductive techniques, not involving sex.

"And they won't die? Won't kill themselves?"

"Prolly not." Brit frowned. "You say them suicides was like allergic reactions to the entities. Rare."

"Better keep an eye on them anyway."

"Yeah." Or a sensory organ of some sort. She closed her eyes and checked just to make sure. Everyone was fine.

Goodnight Moons

Ellen Klages

I'd always dreamed of living on Mars. From the first time I went to the library in Omaha and found the books with rocket ships on their spines, discovered Bradbury and Heinlein and Robinson. Later, I heard real scientists on the news saying it could happen — would happen — in my lifetime.

I didn't want to stay behind and watch.

A big dream, but I was disciplined, focused. I took physics and chemistry, ran track after school, spent my evenings stargazing from the garage roof — and my nights reading science fiction under the covers. I graduated valedictorian, with a full scholarship to MIT and got a doctorate in mechanical engineering, then stayed on for a second degree in astrobotany. We'd need to grow food, once we arrived.

My husband was an electronics genius, but a small flaw in Pete Morrison's left eardrum grounded him early in the NASA program. We lived outside of Houston while I trained: endurance, microgravity, EVA simulations. I even survived the "vomit comet" with flying colors.

When they announced the team for the Mars mission, I made the list. Four men and two women: Archie, Paolo, Rajuk, Tom, Chandra, and I were overnight celebrities. Interviews, photos, talk shows — everyone wanted to know how it felt to be the first humans to go to another planet.

Our last public appearance was at the launch of the *Sacagawea* with her payload of hydrogen and the gas extractor that would fuel our trip back. She would be waiting for us when we landed, in another thirty months. Once she was up, we disappeared for two years of training and maneuvers in Antarctica and the Gobi Desert, the most extreme conditions Earth could offer.

Pete and I said our farewells the night before the launch team was sequestered for the final countdown week. Champagne (for him), filet mignon, red roses, and a king-size bed. Then I was isolated with the others at the base, given so many last-minute shots, tests, and dry runs that I felt like a check mark on an endless to-do list.

But I made it. On a sunny Tuesday morning, the *Conestoga* roared up into a bright blue sky. Billions of people watched us set out for a new world.

Free fall was a relief after the crush of the launch. We'd be floating in zero-g for seven months. Archie and Paolo were a little green around the gills at first, but they got their sea legs soon enough. For me, it was as easy as swimming.

The tedium of a long voyage set in once we established our routine. Cramped quarters, precious little privacy, and not much to do once we were past the moon. I checked my instruments, sent data packets back to Mission Control, took my turn in the galley. Then on day 37, I tossed my cookies so suddenly there wasn't even time to grab a barf bag. Everyone laughed, no one harder than Paolo and Archie.

For three days, nothing wanted to stay down. Didn't feel like zero-g effects. More like a bug. Chandra, the medical officer, took my vitals. No fever, blood pressure normal — for these conditions. When she took an EPT stick from the supply closet, I laughed. "No way. Brand-new implant when we got back from the desert."

"Just a precaution," she said. "By the book. Anything abdominal I can rule out is a plus."

The only plus was the symbol on the stick. The second one as well.

"Jeez." Chandra whistled through her teeth. "Protocol says —"

"I know." Pregnant personnel are restricted to ground duty. Pregnant personnel assigned to flight missions are immediately reassigned. That was why we both had the implants. A one-in-a-million chance, but mine was defective.

Human error? Technical glitch? For two years, we'd gone over every phase of the mission, tens of thousands of parts, maneuvers, systems — anything could go wrong at any time. We had reams of contingency plans. Every snafu had some kind of backup. Except this.

I zipped up my flight suit. "You have to tell Tom," I said. Another protocol. Information that might affect the crew or the mission had to be relayed to the captain.

"Yeah."

"Wait 'til tomorrow? I need to tell Pete first."

She put her hand on my arm. "Okay." She hesitated. "There's only one option. You know that."

I nodded. If one crew member becomes unfit to serve, the mission is aborted. It had happened once on the space station. Appendicitis. The whole crew had to evacuate back to Earth. And that wasn't possible for us, not in an orbital transit. Earth wouldn't be in the same position as when we'd left, and we didn't have enough fuel to realign. I *had* to be fit for duty.

"Tomorrow," I said.

My bunk was the only private place. I pulled the curtain across and leaned against the bulkhead, my hand on my still-flat belly. Chandra was right. And, in theory, that was a choice I'd always supported. So why did I feel like I had to pick — my dreams or my future?

This was an exploration mission. Seventeen months on the surface. We didn't have the supplies or the technology or the infrastructure to start colonizing. That was decades down the road, and only if *we* succeeded.

When the communication window opened, I sent a message to my husband. I told him what had happened and what I had to do. The fourteen-minute delay for his reply seemed endless. And when it arrived, the words on the screen surprised me.

"Can't let you do that, Zoë," it said.

Before I could type my reply, the next message arrived. That one was from CNN, asking for confirmation.

Then all hell broke loose.

Tom and the rest of the crew stared at me as the queue backed up with message after message. Mission Control was furious. Two different generals sent conflicting orders from millions of miles away.

But the public response was instant and overwhelming. News sites headlined WELCOME FIRST MARTIAN BABY! Within an hour, I was the hot topic of blogs, newscasts, and water-cooler discussions all over the globe. A contest offered a million dollars for the person who named "The First Citizen of Space." It was a circus — and NASA had never been so popular.

The furor showed no signs of dying down, but at least Earth continued to rotate, and we lost the comm signal after a few hours. I went to my bunk, but didn't sleep much. When I got up, the screen held a terse communiqué from Mission Control: "Seventh crew member authorized."

I was relieved. I was scared. The rest of the crew did their best to hide their feelings. An order was an order.

The Surgeon General issued a statement. Barring any complications, the likelihood of transit-oriented problems in the next six months was low. The fetus was in a water-filled sac, exactly the sort of environment the crew had trained in for zero-g. As long as radiation levels were closely monitored, she believed a full-term pregnancy was entirely possible. Deceleration and landing, however, would require further consideration.

Would I still fit in my landing couch? What about my pressure suit—it wasn't designed to stretch. I'd never paid much attention in home economics, but the suit was just engineering, and I was able to make some alterations.

A few days shy of my eighth month, we began the descent to the surface. The baby kicked the whole way down. Fortunately, the landing was textbook: no system failures, no injuries, no unexpected terrain. And out the porthole, we could see the *Sacagawea* a hundred meters away, plumes of vapor wafting from its lower vents. Our ride home.

That first night, Rajuk broke out the bottle of whiskey he'd smuggled on board, and we toasted our places in history. I drank my share; all the medical texts said it wouldn't make much difference, not at that stage. No one knew what difference cosmic radiation and zero-g had already made.

The baby and the planet were both terrae incognitae.

I had studied Mars for more than twenty years. I wasn't prepared for how eerily beautiful and utterly alien it was. Everything was shades of reddish brown, no greens or blues. The horizon was too close, the sky too uniform, the lighting flat. Daylight was butterscotch, as if it were always afternoon, half an hour before dusk. At night, the two small, lumpy moons rose into the starry blackness, Phobos slowly in the west, tiny Deimos in the east.

I was, of course, restricted to the ship. For two weeks I had to watch as the others took turns out on the dusty metallic surface, kicking up puffs of iron oxide with every step. I could feel the floor vibrate as they opened the cargo bay, unloaded the rover, began to set up a base. It took a full day to anchor the *Conestoga*, turning her from a spaceship into a permanent habitat, for us, for future crews.

We had all cross-trained in the others' fields, so I was busy checking schematics, logging soil samples, monitoring pressure levels and hatch seals. I gave hand signals through the porthole as Tom and Paolo unrolled my inflatable greenhouse and moved the equipment in. As soon as they connected it to the Hab and its atmosphere, I started my own work.

The first seedlings were unfurling in the hydroponic tank when my water broke.

Chandra had set up the medical facility as soon as we landed; everything was ready. Like the Russians' rats, which gestated in zero-g, my labor was long and slow. The gravity of Mars — only one third Earth's — meant less strain, but less pull when I pushed. Finally, on day 266 of the mission, Mars day 52, I heard a loud, strong cry.

"It's a girl," Chandra said a moment later. I saw a red, wrinkled face, then she was on the counter, being weighed and measured and tested. "Only five pounds, a little underweight, but otherwise she seems remarkably healthy." Chandra laid her on my chest.

A few days later, a woman in Indiana would win a million dollars for naming my baby Virginia Dare Morrison — the first child born in the New World. But as she lay there, suckling for the first time, I murmured, "Podkayne of Mars," and we just called her Poddy.

The *Conestoga* had not been stocked with infant necessities, so we had to make do. T-shirts were diapers. Archie made a mobile from some color-coded spare parts and dental floss, dangling it above the hammock that hung in my bunk. A blanket became a snugglie; while I worked, I carried her like a papoose from another, older frontier.

I breast-fed her for the first eight months, not much extra draw on the closely measured rations. She got sponge baths, just like the rest of us. When she was teething, her cries filled the Hab — the bunks were only soundproofed enough to offer a bit of privacy — and the rest of the crew grumbled about lost sleep. But they watched her when it was my turn in the rotation to be outside, and she heard lullabies in four different languages.

Martian gravity is kind to toddlers. At thirteen months, Poddy massed eighteen pounds, but her chubby legs only had to support six as she pulled herself up and began to walk. It's impossible to childproof a spacecraft, but we blocked off the lab and the stairs to the upper level of the Hab, and strung tether cords across the hatchways. She could climb like a monkey.

She bounced and hopped the length of the greenhouse, laughing at the top of her lungs and bounding about in a way no Earth baby could. I sent vids to Pete, and they were replayed everywhere; a dance called the Poddy Hop was the new craze. Plans were made for a homecoming tour the next year: FIRST MARTIAN RETURNS.

But that *was* a problem, said the doctors.

Martian gravity *might* turn out to be sufficient for healthy growth. No one knew. Poddy's stats were being studied by scientists everywhere, and would provide the data for future missions. But travel in zero-g was not a possibility, not at her age. She was still developing — bones and muscles, neurons and connections. She would never recover from seven months in free fall.

Every member of the crew already had muscle-mass and bone loss from the trip out. I'd known from day one that once the mission was over, I'd spend the next two years in hospitals and gyms trying to get as much of it back as I could.

For Poddy, they said, the loss would be irreversible. Mission Control advised: Further study needed.

A month before takeoff, I got their final verdict.

Poddy could not return to Earth.

If she did, even as an adult, she would never walk again. She would be crippled by the physics of her home planet, always in excruciating pain, crushed by the mass of her own body. Her lungs might collapse, her heart might not take the strain.

"We had not planned for children," Mission Control's message ended. "We're sorry."

I read the message three times, then picked her up and kissed her hair. I'd always dreamed of living on Mars.

Future missions would bring supplies, they promised. Clothes, shoes, a helmet, a modified pressure suit with expandable sections and room to grow. From now on, they would carry extra milk and vitamins, educational materials, toys and games. Engineers had begun working on a small-scale rover. Whatever she needed.

The next ship *should* arrive in seven months.

Tom reassigned duties for a five-person crew. By the time the *Sacagawea* was ready for launch, Poddy was talking. Just simple words. *Mama, Hab, juice.* She waved her tiny fingers at the porthole as her aunt and uncles boarded: *Bye-bye Chanda, bye-bye Tom. Bye-bye.*

We would never see them again.

Like my great-grandmother, I was a pioneer woman, alone on the frontier. Isolated, self-sufficient by necessity. Did it matter, I wondered as I heated up our supper, whether it was a hundred miles of prairie, a thousand miles of ocean, or millions of miles of space that separated me from everything and everyone I had known?

I read to Poddy, after the meal. A picture book, uploaded a week before, drawings in primary colors of things she would never see: TREE, CAT, HOUSE, FATHER. For her Earth was make-believe, a fantasy world with funny green grass and the wrong-color sky.

On the first of two hundred cold, black nights, Deimos and Phobos low in the sky, I sat by the porthole and cuddled my daughter, whispering as I rocked her to sleep.

Goodnight, Poddy.

Goodnight, moons.

Ten Tips on Becoming a Ghost

Kathleen Alcalá

> This reporter wants to interview me, but I cannot pick up the phone.

> Likewise with makeup. I apply my lipstick, then my smile floats away before dissolving into air, molecules of lipstick clinging to everything as though I am in outer space.

√ 1. I recommend a sheer gloss.

> I look down at myself and see that my clothes are ruined. I am covered in dried mud and blood and—what is this? ew—my hair is matted with sticks and leaves and more mud. I go upstairs and take a shower. It feels so good after standing in the rain for days. And it smells good.

√ 2. I recommend an apricot shampoo, followed by a honey-based conditioner.

> I put my hair in a towel and open my closet. Everything in it is white.

> When my hair dries, it is long and dark. Had it been long and dark before? I can't remember. The time is always now.

> I put on a long white dress. This won't do. I'm too messy, too clumsy, for white.

√ 3. A camouflage print would be better. I remember kneeling in the mud. I cannot get up.

- But there are all-white boots in the closet, just like the '70s, so I put them on, and feel better.
- Why should a ghost suffer from lack of self-esteem? You should ask my sister. She is still alive. She would say I asked for it—staying out late at night, getting caught running with that boy, having one baby, then another and another.

√ 4. I recommend birth control.

- Typing takes a long time. My fingers sink right though the keyboard. I have to hold a pencil and type with the eraser. As a result, my notes look like this

E s

Pan—nnnnn—

Ta

- Say it out loud. Then say it breathing in.
- Then he ran off with that sin veruenza. I never liked her. I didn't like her whole family. They thought they were better than we were. My agent told me it would be good to do this interview. Improve my image. Otherwise, people just hear his side. That I became a ghost out of spite. Mentiros.

> Should I go scare someone? I am scared. I want to scream.

> The reporter lights a candle. She thinks I will come towards the light. But really, it is the heat that attracts me—the heat of her live body. I put my face just above the candle, so that she can almost see me.

√ 5. I recommend two candles.

> I want my babies.

> I can hear you breathing. I can watch you breathe at night, when you are asleep in my room. What used to be my room.

> My mistake was to think I could keep breathing. The muddy water rose higher and higher around me, mud and leaves on the surface, cold at first, then—cold. They slipped away from me in the current. I didn't mean to let go.

√ 6. I recommend holding your breath.

> What is that noise? It is constant.

> I can touch your hair. For some reason, I can't touch anything else in the room. I can't see the clock. It is always now. But I can touch your long hair and drag my fingers through it. It reminds me of—something. Something important.

> I discover I can go outside. It is hot and cold, wet and dry, but I can't do anything about it. During the day, there are too many people around. They walk

right through me. I can give them a chill, but they do not see me.

> At night, I want to get in my bed, but you are in it. I am always cold.

> What is that noise? A susurration. The edge of a sawblade. I want to go outside and find my babies.

√ 7. Don't let go.

> Fires are almost as good as floods. I can stand by the side of the road, and once in a while, people can see me, when their hearts are racing and they fear for their own well-being. "There!" they say. "Did you see that? Did you see her just then?" They make up stories about me later, most of which are false.

> My arms ache for my babies.

> Name my favorite ghost? An image by that Austrian painter, Gustav Klimt. I'm not sure which one. There is something disturbing about his portraits. Glassy and brittle. I think they were of his sister and he… Well, never mind.

√ 8. Ghosts should be disturbing.

> I am disturbed.

> I am cold. I am hungry.

> I want… What is that noise?

> Where are they? Call them! Let me call them. Did I have two babies, or three? Did I make them all up? I don't think so, I can still feel the cocoon shape in my arms from holding them.

√ 9. Don't forget. I don't know what, but don't forget. Be sure and put that in your article.

> Let me touch your hair. I can pull the strands between my fingers and twist them around my fist. Then I can press my thumb into the hollow of your throat.

> That sound. It's coming from me. I am screaming.

> Say it again out loud:

> Esssssss....

paaannnn.....

taaaaa....

.....

.....

√ 10. Try to breathe.

Pod Rendezvous

K Ibura

During third meal, Laki was fidgety. She shoveled down her food without registering taste. Being part of a large birth group had trained her to eat quickly but, for once, her siblings were not the cause of her haste. Today, she was eating alone. It was an odd sensation that she did not enjoy. She rushed through the meal without any mother telling her to slow down or any sibling asking for her leavings. When her platter was empty, she folded it in half and pushed it into the dish slot in the wall. The slot sealed itself and, with a heavy sigh, Laki left the kitchen.

She walked down the hallway with one arm outstretched, trailing her fingers along the wall. The hallways were incredibly empty, emptier than Laki had ever remembered them. She dove into one of her only at-home pleasures. Laki's house was an economical entity, completely lacking in nostalgia. It never sustained empty spaces for long. When a sibling left home, the house sealed off unused rooms, then cannibalized them, using the raw material to build new rooms. Laki loved pressing on walls in search of tiny patches of recycled material. To her, walls were like stretches of skin; each patch had its own history embedded within. A new room could fuel weeks of ecstasy. She could lose herself, methodically working her way around the new walls, releasing memories and relishing in the company of her beloved siblings, even if only in the fleeting and ghostly form of remembrance.

Halfway to Se-se's room, Laki stopped and turned to face the wall. She placed her palm flat against it and closed her eyes. She imagined there was still a room nestled behind the wall and that her sister Yasla was there, waiting to talk with her. The wall released no memory, so she imagined Yasla smiling at her.

For Laki, Yasla had been a twin spirit, a guiding light, a soft embrace in a world that had begun to show Laki its sharp edges. And her departure had been devastating. Yasla had approached her maturation with confidence. A full year before maturation, she had applied for and won a top-secret appointment in the mesosphere's weaponry and transportation department. Laki would have loved to follow in Yasla's footsteps, but she felt more confusion than certainty about maturation.

Her first experiences with maturation had left her indifferent. Watching her older siblings depart into adulthood never troubled her. There were so many of them that Laki saw them as nothing more than troublesome competitors who ruthlessly pushed each other around in wild ploys for dominance and attention. But by the time the birth group had been halved, Laki began to see her siblings differently. They became more precious to her; she saw them as friends rather than competitors. Yasla's maturation was the most painful to her. It had drawn Laki into a yearlong battle with disappointment, panic, and rage. Without Yasla, Laki felt broken and alone.

Leaving behind the sealed entrance to Yasla's room, Laki walked to Se-se's room. She called out to Se-se, but there was no answer. She wandered on, making her way to the end of the hall where she stopped and placed her ear against the wall. She listened for echoes of the playful battles that had been waged up and down the halls outside her brothers' rooms, but there was nothing behind that wall but silence.

Laki felt as if the emptiness of the house would drive her mad. Even the hallways leading to the pod landing room were vacant. Where had Se-se gone? What could the mothers be doing, hidden out of sight? Laki walked toward the mothers' private chambers, still trailing her fingers along the hallway walls. She was a few paces away from the mothers' rooms when she felt the wall buckle beneath her fingertips. She paused. These hallways were no strangers to her hands. She had poked, prodded, and rubbed every inch of wall that she could reach. She had uncovered and released every memory that was to be found in this quadrant of the house. There should not have been a room there.

Laki held her hand over the spot where the wall had buckled; her fingers tingled with expectation. As she waited for the wall to thin, she closed her eyes, anticipating the bliss of immersing herself in the remembered company of her siblings. A moan escaped from the room, causing Laki's eyes to snap open. She quickly pinched above and below the slit that had begun to part the wall.

She peered through the opening. The room within was full of mothers — more mothers than Laki knew she had. Their bodies were shrouded in veils as always, but none of them were gathered into a unit. They stood as individuals, most in a circle in the center of the room. Dark red orbs hovered over their outstretched hands. Standing around the edges of the room, other mothers watched empty-handed, with their backs against the walls.

The moan snaked through the room again, but Laki could not see who was making the sound. She put her hand over the top edge of the opening and elongated it. She leaned in closer and looked up. There, hanging from the ceiling in a shimmering sling, was a woman. Her head was tilted back, her lips parted in a painful grimace. Laki was so struck by the woman's expression that a few seconds passed before she realized that the woman was unshrouded. The woman grasped the sling and groaned again. She shifted her body sideways and revealed a long purplish tube attached to her stomach.

Entranced and frightened, Laki followed the tube's path downward and saw that it was connected to a large globe that was floating just below the woman. The woman gritted her teeth, and the tube pulsed. In synchronicity, the mothers inhaled and exhaled. It seemed as if the room itself were breathing. Silky white strands shot out of the large globe and attached themselves to the small globes that were hovering over the mothers' hands. The globes filled with light and, for a brief second, Laki could see the curled up forms of embryos within the globes. She let out a loud gasp. A few mothers turned and saw her as the globes' glittering illuminated the room with an explosion of incandescence.

Before Laki could see anything else, a body blocked her view. The small opening she had made parted completely. A mother glided out of the room, the expression on her face unreadable behind her veil. The mother sealed the room, took Laki by the hand, and led her away from the mothers' quarters. She stopped at the hallway that led to Laki's room and turned to face Laki. Laki opened her mouth, but found she could not speak. The mother waited patiently.

"That was one of my mothers, wasn't it?" Laki asked.

"Yes," the mother sang. She took both of Laki's hands and pressed against Laki's palms with her fingers.

"How many do I have?"

"Nineteen."

Laki was briefly shocked into silence. "I thought there were only six of you."

"How do you think we can be everywhere at once?"

Laki heard a smile in the mother's voice, though she could not see it through the blur of the mother's veil.

"What is happening in there?"

The mother brushed her hand over Laki's bald head.

"We received new babies today," she sang. "We are nurturing them."

Despite the mother's calming presence, Laki's heart began to beat rapidly.

"Will I have to do that? Hang from the ceiling…"

"You will not have to, it will be your choice."

"But it's hurting her."

"It hurts, yes, but it's not hurting her. She asked to nurture them."

Laki looked at this lone mother incredulously.

"You will learn, Laki. Mothering makes you want to give, even if it exhausts you."

Laki shook her head.

"You don't need to understand now, Laki, but that feeling will find you. Weeks or months into your time with the babies, it will sneak up on you."

Laki's face was frozen in an expression of horror.

"You're thinking only about the pain, La-Laki. Don't. It is pointless. Every drop of pain is balanced by waves of pleasure."

"Pleasure?"

"Pleasure. Pleasure at your successes. Pleasure in watching the children mature. Pleasure with the other mothers. Emotions you never imagined."

"But what if I never find those pleasures. What if I wasn't made to be a mother?"

The mother burst into laughter. "No one was born a mother, Laki. Yet all of us are able to mother if we allow ourselves to be guided by the needs of the children."

"But the babies…"

"Laki, you do not need to think about babies right now."

"But tomorrow—when I join my mother-unit, will I get babies? Will I have to take care of the wombs?"

The mother shook her head and rubbed Laki's back.

"Tomorrow you will meet with the others in your unit. You will begin the process of melding the cloak. Were you not listening to *anything* we told you in preparation for the mother-unit?"

"You didn't tell me about the wombs!" Laki tried to wound the mother with an accusation, but the rage died in her throat. Every word that came out of her mouth was softened by the power of the mother's love.

"We told you what you need to know before you join the unit. No one learns about the babies until after they join their unit…which you won't until tomorrow. This is your last day at home. Why are you wandering around the house? There's no more training today. Take off your uniform. Enjoy the rest of your time, go see your friends."

Laki didn't answer. She imagined herself hanging in a sling suspended over a huge womb. Panic welled up in her chest; she found it hard to breathe. The mother hugged Laki.

"Go," she said.

Laki turned away from the mother and ran down the hall, choking on the urge to scream. When she reached her room, she waved her hand over the sealed entrance. The wall thinned and parted down the middle. She stepped over the threshold, and a softly modulated voice rang out:

"One day to maturation."

Laki winced. Grabbing the edges of her robe, she yanked the white fabric from her shoulders. Her elbow flung out wildly, triggering the voice to repeat itself:

"One day to maturation."

"Shut up!" Laki snapped. She stumbled toward her wardrobe portal while pulling off the robe and dropping it on the ground. As she fumbled to release the waist of her dress, she caught sight of her reflection. Startled, she fell still. Swathed in mother-unit whites, she could be any girl on the brink of maturation. A young mother, perhaps, anyone but herself.

Just beyond her reflection, Laki saw a message globe float into the room. She looked at it over her shoulder, then turned back to the reflective wall. She squinted her eyes and tried to imagine what she would look like draped in her mother-unit veil. She envisioned a group of faceless women gathered around her. A disgusted hiss spilled out through her lips. She waved her hand over her reflection, and the reflective wall went dark.

When Laki walked to the wardrobe portal, the message globe followed her. She passed her hand over a flat, round disc embedded in the wall. A rod slid out from where the disc had been and presented her with a row of cloths dancing around on hangers. Even her wardrobe had ceased to be an accurate reflection of her. Mixed in with her customary black cloths, were the mother-unit whites, permanently shaped into formless robes and dresses that, after tomorrow, would become her daily uniform.

At the thought of tomorrow, Laki felt a tightening in her chest. The terror that she had been carefully containing flooded her body. She rifled through the cloths, seizing anything white and flinging it to the ground. When there was nothing left but black cloths and empty hangers, Laki collapsed to the floor. Every wild scheme she had concocted to avoid her fate trampled through her memory. Breathing heavily, she looked around the room as if through feverish searching she could find the secret and escape her future. The message globe chirped, and her panic deflated. She let out a resigned sigh. She was powerless to change the thrust of her future, and nothing she did could alleviate that fact.

The globe drifted down to hang next to her shoulder. She blew on it, triggering the release of its message.

"Greetings elder sister," a high-pitched voice chanted.

Laki shifted so that she was sitting cross-legged on the floor and opened her hand to accept the message. The globe floated down to rest in her palm. An image of her sister — cinnamon-colored skin, freckles, a dark mouth — sprouted in her mind. She heard Se-se whispering, "I think it's going to work. We're going to get you out of the mother-unit. You have to meet me later. I'll send another message."

Laki rolled her eyes. Even up to the final hour, Se-se was full of optimism. Laki pinched the message globe and it deflated. She flattened it against the wall with the palm of her hand and watched as it melded into the wall. She took a deep breath and climbed to her feet. She peeled off her white dress and threw it onto the heap of discarded white cloths. She plucked a short length of black fabric from her clothes rod and wrapped it around her body. With the heat from her hand, she fused the cloth's edges to create one seamless dress. She pinched along the waist, the dip of her back, and under her bust to give it shape. She picked out a shorter length of cloth to wrap over her shoulders and melded it to the dress, creating sleeves. There was a lump around her middle revealing the silhouette of a marriage belt resting on her hips. Nothing to be done about that.

She pulled a blank message globe from the wall and closed her eyes. She projected images of a wild party into the globe, purred "the rendezvous-less zone," then sent the thought, "Maturation tomorrow." She opened her eyes.

"Twelve messages," she said. The message globe split into twelve tiny spheres—each carrying an identical invitation. She touched each sphere while saying a name, and they zipped away to deliver her invitation.

Laki walked to the pod landing room with a grim look on her face. She didn't look like a woman going to a party, she looked like a prisoner headed to her execution. In the pod landing room, she stood briefly in reverent silence. *This*, she thought, *is the end of my life.* She decided to savor every second. She treasured the whirling sound of her pod ballooning to full expansion and the whisper of the exit portal opening in the roof. She craned her head back and reveled in the pull of velocity as her pod shot away from home up into the upper atmosphere.

When she had left her domed city behind, she reached for the sound module. With quick fingers, she programmed it to record the sound of friction, a static-like screeching bristling between her pod and the thick weightlessness of space. She amplified the sound, adding an echo, then slowed its frequency to match the beat of her pulse. She flipped through her archives and sampled sound snippets before selecting a loop of her siblings laughing through the hallways at home. She mixed in a distorted recording of her own voice, and the jumble of sound built into an aural assault. At Laki's signal, the sound module found a unifying tempo and tamed the layers of noise into a repeating melody. Laki blended it with one of her preferred beats and blasted the mash-up into her pod — a newly created soundtrack for the moment.

For a painfully short stretch of time, the music obliterated Laki's worries. She turned the volume up until she could feel sound vibrating the soft translucent walls of her pod. She started by swaying her head back and forth. By the time her pod was approaching the twinkling lights of the Velvet Stretch, her limbs were flailing, her hips were swaying, her knees were gyrating. She had given herself so completely to the music that there was no space for anxiety, heartache, and other demons.

At the entrance to the Velvet Stretch, Laki turned off the music. She pressed her palm to the thin wall of her pod to register herself with the concierge. As she waited for him to complete his procedures, images of lovers she had rendezvoused with started to flash through her mind. She remembered the sweetness of her sessions with Pemfi, the hilarity of hanging out with Benko, and one heart-stopping moment she'd had with Asla. She could hear Se-se's nagging scorn ringing in her ears — "Do they even have marriage belts to offer, Laki?"

She responded to the concierge's questions absentmindedly, grinning at the memory of her usual entrance into the Velvet Stretch. Were it a normal visit with a rendezvous awaiting her, she wouldn't be standing there, half listening to the concierge; she'd be flat-out ignoring him, crawling around her pod in search of props to enliven her rendezvous.

"No rendezvous," she told the concierge while in her mind she was remembering placing peacock feathers, a pouch of honey, and a latex strap on the floor of her pod.

He slid his fingers over his data machine. "You only have clearance for the rendezvous-less zone. You must return to the concierge's desk if you wish to enter another level."

Laki indicated her consent with the tap of her finger, then turned away. Everything else the concierge said was useless to her. He cleared her entrance, and she plunged into the Velvet Stretch.

Savoring the freedom of flight, she went flitting through the rendezvous-less zone. Even though the Velvet Stretch was all about connection, she steered clear of other pods. She didn't need a date or even a momentary flirt, she needed a private, remote area for her party.

It had been quite some time since she had searched the Velvet Stretch for anything. Amongst her friends, she acted as if she harbored the same appetites that had defined her pre-maturation stage, but the truth was she had changed. She could no longer sustain the intense curiosity of her early days when she had roamed the Stretch, electrified by her quest to find a sexy someone whose energy was so intense that being together would feel like a desperation, a feverish need.

Her identity was so twisted up in her reputation that she didn't know how to embrace a new facet of her personality. She had spent so much time orchestrating fantastic episodes full of intrigue and mind-blowing carnal consummation that solitude seemed like a foreign language. Who would she be if not voracious and doggedly determined to create magical encounters?

Yet somehow the allure of the Velvet Stretch had faded. Gorging on pleasure and emotional intimacies began to tire, rather than excite, her. While pursuing her fantasies, she'd mysteriously transformed into a woman more interested in the workings of her own brain than the mysteries of a stranger's heart.

Laki found a lone star bar with a dim yellow glow. She lodged her pod right next to it, squinting before turning away from its glare. The way that it seductively illuminated her skin told Laki that it was the perfect location for the evening's festivities. She checked the time module, then cursed softly. She realized too late that she hadn't specified a time in the invitations — it could be hours before the first guest arrived.

She felt the silence of the Stretch invade her pod. If you weren't hopped up on adrenaline or some other intoxicant, and distracted by your frantic search for a rendezvous, you would immediately notice the Velvet Stretch's profound lack of sound. The depth of its silence was stunning, yet it had taken Laki years to notice it. She had been too focused on the pods of strangers, and the anatomy of the people ensconced within them, to take note of the majestic expanse of deep space. Now, she was older and irritatingly aware that she was just a noisy little fleck in an infinite field of silence. The loudest thing in the vicinity was her thoughts, thoughts she had come to the Stretch to escape.

She sat on the floor and flicked the sound module on. Instead of hearing the song she had just mixed, she heard a deep voice say, "Let's do this by starlight." Her back stiffened. A heat sparked in her chest and shot straight down into her pelvis. She looked around, but no one was there. The voice repeated:

"Let's do this by starlight."

"Fogo," she whispered, remembering the owner of that voice — the last rendezvous she had had in the Stretch and, quite possibly, the last rendezvous she would ever have.

She touched her waist, running her fingers over the concealed marriage belt, then leapt up to examine the sound module. She didn't remember making a recording that night, and she couldn't understand why his voice was filling her pod now. She vibrated her fingers in front of the sound module, commanding it to spin Fogo's voice into a faster loop. She rubbed one hand over her body, guiding it downward to grasp between her legs as Fogo invited her to do it by starlight over and over again. With the other hand, she added the sound of dripping water to the background and mixed in her favorite song — a love-laced anthem by Mahini.

A soft smile spread across Laki's face. She no longer felt engulfed by the Stretch, not while lust was tingling through her and enfolding her in its embrace. She lay back on the floor and stretched out her limbs. She watched the twinkling lights around her as she ran her hands over her skin, stopping to apply extra pressure here or an added caresses there. Singing along with Mahini, she shrouded herself in arousal and buried time with repeated, focused strokes.

Time had long since abdicated to pleasure when Laki felt her pod rock. Disoriented, she sat up and looked around. Her surprise melted into delight when she saw that her friend Zaha had arrived. Laki scrambled to her feet without remembering that her cloth was hiked up over her hips and hanging open. With a rueful grin, Laki fixed her cloth.

As her pod fused with Laki's, Zaha shook her head. "You're so predictable," she said into the hole that was opening between their pods.

Laki pushed her hands into a pocket in the wall of her pod. She felt the cool wetness of the disinfectant splatter against her hands, then she felt heat as her hands were dried. When the hole between their pods was large enough, Laki ran over to Zaha and embraced her.

"You're predictable too, you know. I knew you'd be the first to come."

"So that little show was for me?"

"Yes, consider me your maturation welcome committee." Laki bowed with a mischievous grin.

Zaha laughed. "Last day! And you're up here making jokes and playing with yourself. I thought you were going to be a mess."

"I am a mess; why do you think I was half-naked on the floor? It's the only cure for panic that I've ever known."

"Well I hope they're open-minded in your mother-unit, you can't…"

Laki held up her fingers to silence Zaha.

"At this party, we will not speak those words. We'll pretend that I have no date with the veil tomorrow and that you won't have to give everything up in…" Laki paused and looked at Zaha. "I forget. How many days do you have left?"

"Well…" Zaha said, and theatrically pointed to the top of her pod. Laki looked up and saw a thin silver marriage belt hanging there.

"You're saved!" Laki yelled. They both squealed. Laki hugged Zaha, but she froze when she looked at the belt again. Her arms dropped away from Zaha, and she fell silent.

"What's wrong?"

"No, nothing. I'm sorry." Laki stumbled over her words as she stepped closer to examine the belt. "That looks like my friend Pemfi's belt."

"Pemfi's? It is. You know him?"

Laki nodded, but offered no explanation. She was, she knew, an idiot in so many people's minds. Her friends, her lovers, and especially her sister Se-se thought she was sacrificing herself for no good reason. She didn't know what Zaha would think if she knew how many marriage belts Laki had turned down, if she knew that the last time Laki had seen Pemfi's marriage belt, he was holding it out to her with trembling hands and she was shaking her head, telling him, "I can't."

Laki put her hand to her mouth as she remembered his stung response.

"You can't or you won't?"

"What's the difference?" she had asked.

"The difference is if you can't, it's beyond your control. If you won't, you're just being a stubborn rub."

Coming from Pemfi, the curse had sounded like a foreign language, but in his anger he had wielded it masterfully. Zaha looked at Laki, an expectant expression on her face, but Laki didn't speak; she just let out a long slow breath. She couldn't throw off the memory of Pemfi, how she had wrapped her arms around him and spoken softly. "You want to make this hurt? You want to make *me* hurt?"

"You've been hurting me for years," Pemfi had whispered in her ear. "But do you know what's really going to hurt? Getting locked in a mother-unit. It's going to kill you. They're going to take away your pod and your props, and your life is going to change forever."

She had pushed him away and assured him that she could handle it. He hadn't believed a word of it. Not Pemfi, not after she'd spent so many nights telling him of her nightmares. He'd offered her a marriage of friendship, begged her to let him save her, but she had wanted to save herself.

Laki smiled at Zaha, hoping her face looked warm and reassuring rather than shaky and uncertain.

"He's a good man, Zaha. You'll have a good life."

Then she pressed Zaha into a tight embrace.

"But what is this?" Zaha asked pulling away from Laki. She put her hands on Laki's waist and felt the marriage belt through Laki's dress.

"It's..." Laki felt the pods jostle before she could answer. She turned and saw that Benko had arrived.

"Ben-ben!" she yelled.

As the walls were thinning where Benko's pod met Laki's, she said to Zaha, "It's a long story...not what you think."

"So you're not getting married?"

"Who's not getting married?" Benko asked stepping through the opening into Laki's pod.

"I'm not getting married," Laki said.

"But there's something under her clothes, look," said Zaha.

Benko held Laki by the hips and examined the bulge. He pushed at Laki's waist, feeling the belt through the cloth of her dress. "It's thick."

"It's just a loan," said Laki. "Pretend it's like any other belt. Did you bring the screen?"

"What kind of freak gets a thick marriage belt and doesn't get married?" Benko asked.

Laki smacked him on the back. Turning smoothly, he smiled at Zaha and held out his hand.

"I'm Benko, and you are..."

"She has a marriage belt hanging in her pod, and she *is* getting married. Did you bring the screen?!"

"Wait!" Benko held up his hand. He stood in the middle of the three pods and cocked his head to one side.

"What are you looking for?" Laki asked.

"Not looking. Listening. This mix is depressing."

He walked to the sound module in his pod. He sped up the rhythm of Mahini's song, then mixed in a hard, fast beat. Zaha went to her sound module and added the sound of an animal yelping, then punctuated it with intermittent high-pitched tinkling sounds. They looked at each other and grinned.

Laki did a little shimmy. "Nice." She kissed each of them on the cheek.

The pods shook suddenly. Laki, Benko, and Zaha stumbled a bit. They looked up to see two pods joining them at once. Laki waved at her arriving friends then shot Benko a look.

"Okay, okay, I'll go set up the screen," he said and walked toward his pod.

Laki linked arms with Zaha, and they walked over to where Laki's friends' pods were fusing with the party. When the pods merged, the space Laki and Zaha were standing in expanded.

Zaha saw Benko float away in his pod.

"Where's he going?" she whispered in Laki's ear.

"Setting up the screen," Laki said.

"What's the screen for?" Zaha asked.

"Oh, you've never been to any of Laki's parties?" one of the newcomers asked.

Zaha shook her head no. She and Laki glanced at each other before Laki leaned in to hug each of the newcomers and kiss them both on the cheek.

"I see," said the other newcomer. "You met in the Stretch."

Zaha laughed loudly. "No, we met at a mother-unit training."

There was an awkward pause.

"I'm going to go help Beni," the first newcomer said and walked away.

A silence settled over the group. Then Laki slapped her friend's arm lightly. "Don't get all weird. You have a mother-unit."

"I know, but I don't know anyone going into one…except you."

"So what? You think we're contagious?"

"No, it's just that…"

"It's weird knowing you're gonna spend the rest of your life with a veil on," Laki said in a mocking voice.

"Why get to know you when you're just going to disappear after maturation," Zaha added with a high-pitched wail.

"Aren't you depressed? Don't you ever think about escaping?" Laki whined.

There was a dangerous glint in her eye, and her relaxed stance had become combative. Her aggression with her peers had grown over the past year. All anyone wanted to talk about was maturation. And why not? It wasn't a death sentence for any of them. None of her friends would be entering mother-units; they had no need. That kind of work was for girls who were hungry, girls with no choices, girls whose families couldn't afford to have a mother-unit raise their children — girls who were relieved to have somewhere to go after maturation.

"I'm sorry, Laki, I just…"

Laki stared at her friend daring him to say something else that would wound. Both she and Zaha were highborn and fully endowed with the indignation of the privileged. But Laki had been orphaned and Zaha abandoned. Their intended futures had dissolved, making them interlopers among their friends and siblings.

"I'll go help Beni with the screen, too," Laki's friend said and left awkwardly without another word.

"These blocks act like I have some fatal disease. It's not my fault things turned out this way."

Laki was breathing heavily as her mind tossed through anger, shame, and guilt at blinding speed.

"Tonight is not the night for this, Laki," Zaha said.

Outside, Benko flew by again, this time with a long piece of cloth streaming from his pod.

"Tell me about the screen," Zaha said.

"The screen?"

"Yes. What's it for?"

"To shield the party from peepers and crashers."

"Didn't know you could do that in the Stretch."

"Yeah, we look like an empty part of the Stretch with the screen up."

"But then the regulators can't verify you, or anyone else in the party. Don't they come looking for you anyway? Is this legal?"

A slow smile spread across Laki's face. She draped her arm around Zaha's shoulders.

"Well, maybe we're bending the rules a little bit, but I don't think we're breaking any laws." She winked.

Zaha laughed. "So breaking the law relaxes you?"

Laki giggled, then someone grabbed her from behind.

"Okay, screen's up," Benko said, spinning Laki around. "If they catch us and they try to ban you, it won't matter. You'll be in a mother-unit."

"Ban you?" Zaha's eyebrows went up. She turned to Benko, "By the way those words are banned tonight."

"What words?"

Zaha mouthed "mother-unit" to him, and he nodded.

"Right. So back to Laki getting banned, she can't control her parties. Once she gets them started, they just keep growing and growing. The whole level gets packed. Nobody can get in for a rendezvous..."

"But this one won't be that big," Laki interjected. "I only invited twelve people."

"Please," said Benko. "The news will spread like wildfire."

Benko gripped Laki around the waist, and they swayed together. Laki grabbed Zaha's hand and pulled her close. The three of them moved against each other, building up a sweaty heat as they buzzed with the joy of movement. Before long, the sweet vibe of languid ecstasy expanded as more pods joined the party. Once Laki felt engulfed by all the new bodies surrounding them, Laki decided it was time. She lifted her arm and aimed her finger at a pouch that was hanging from the top of her pod. She plucked, and the bag popped, releasing a wet blue fog into the air. Laki inhaled; an intense sweetness burst across her tongue. When she exhaled, her smile was a little wider and her limbs were a little looser.

"She always has the best smoke at her parties," Benko said into Zaha's ear.

Laki threw her head back and let out a long wordless moan. For the next hour, she didn't speak a word to anyone. She was too busy flinging off her troubles and releasing her body in total surrender.

While Laki was slipping into a delicious stupor, Se-se was entering the Velvet Stretch for the first time. Her last three messages to Laki had returned undelivered. The only place Laki could be where Se-se's message globes couldn't reach was the Velvet Stretch.

"No registration on record," the concierge stated.

"First time," Se-se said with what she hoped was a charming smile.

"No rendezvous?" the concierge asked, without even bothering to acknowledge Se-se's friendliness.

Se-se shook her head.

"You only have clearance for the rendezvous-less zone; that's right past the entrance here. There are some basic rules and regulations." The concierge stopped speaking long enough to pluck a message globe at Se-se. The globe floated through the walls of her pod and hovered near her shoulder while the concierge finished his speech. "People who violate these guidelines may be barred from the Velvet Stretch. Any questions?"

Se-se did have a question — where is my sister? — but she knew better than to draw attention to Laki.

"You have been cleared."

As Se-se floated into the Velvet Stretch, she blew on the message globe and listened intently. She learned that pod walls were transparent for regulatory purposes and were intended to support mutual consent, not to invite voyeurism. It was bad etiquette to spy on people. She was instructed on the preferred protocol when approaching a potential rendezvous: hover at a distance until the person you are interested in sees you. Once seen, you may approach slowly, so that the person has the opportunity to accept or reject your advances.

Se-se tried following the protocols as she searched the rendezvous-less zone, but the process was too slow. She wasn't looking for a rendezvous; she was looking for her sister. Stopping a respectful distance away from pods made it difficult to be certain Laki was not inside. In a burst of frustration, Se-se put politeness aside. She swooped in close and peered inside the pods she encountered. She forgave her behavior by telling herself that people would excuse her sudden and aggressive appearance outside their pods if they understood the urgent nature of her search.

After Se-se had peeked into all the solitary and conjoined pods in the rendezvous-less zone, she came to a halt. She looked around and considered her options. Leaving without Laki was out of the question. If Laki was not in the rendezvous-less zone, Se-se would be stuck.

While she was mulling over her next steps, she saw a few pods whiz past her, then disappear. She bobbed in place, bewildered. She was creeping forward to investigate when a few more pods rushed past her. Watching them closely, she saw that, after traveling a short distance, the pods dipped down, then disappeared. Determined to follow them, she snapped into action, speeding ahead, but before she could dip down, her pod rammed into something solid, and she was knocked to the floor.

She regained her footing and tried to nudge her pod forward, but it would not move. What looked like open space was clearly a wall of some sort. She backed up and pushed at the wall again, but it was rigid and wouldn't give way. As she was battling the wall, two more pods approached. They drifted right up to the wall, stopped suddenly, then plunged downward and disappeared. Plunging down through the rendezvous-less zone was not an appealing thought, but she reminded herself of the righteousness of the mission. She took a deep breath and directed her pod to drop downward. Every few seconds, she pitched forward, searching for the way forward.

When Se-se finally got to the bottom of the wall, her pod shot forward and she found herself underneath a gathering of pods that had created a space bigger than all her sibling's rooms combined. Above her the party pulsed with music that she couldn't hear. She could see the bottoms of people's feet and the backs of bodies pressed against the floor of the pods.

She navigated up around the side of the conjoined pods. Through the transparent walls she could see bodies everywhere — arms thrashing, hips rotating, heads flung back with abandon. She edged around the perimeter of the party, trying to drown out the voice that was warning her that it was dangerous to fuse with so many pods at once. After looking for Laki from the safety of her pod, Se-se accused herself of stalling. She closed her eyes and guided her pod forward to join with the party.

When she stepped into the party, she felt it immediately begin to consume her. The air was thick and hazy with an overwhelming wet heat — and with each step, she felt limbs brushing against her. Everyone was skin to skin. She moved forward slowly, pausing periodically to step over arms and legs and dodge people who were splayed across the floor. She had thought searching people's pods was embarrassing, now here she was, sticking her face close to people who were kissing and caressing, interrupting intimacies, in search of Laki.

Having determined that she would not find Laki underfoot, Se-se turned her attention to the dance floor. Scanning the crush of bodies, strategizing a method to locate Laki, a pair of long dark arms rose up in the air and extended above the crowd. Without hesitation, Se-se plunged into the throng of dancers. It was hard going at first. Every space on the dance floor was densely packed and jealously guarded. The cost of reaching the middle of the dance floor was repeated jabs by knees and elbows. Se-se's gift for barreling through the crowd was finally finding Laki.

There, whirling around in the middle of the madness, was Laki. Bare-breasted and disrobed, she enraptured the people circled around her with the undulating contortions of her body. Even as she wondered how Laki could be comfortable without her clothes, Se-se found herself spellbound. This was not the bitter, tortured Laki who Se-se had spent so much time pacifying and cajoling in the past year. This was the Laki of legend, the Laki who had conjured up a social life that was a work of art and called the Velvet Stretch her second home.

As Laki's limbs writhed with furious motion, the marriage belt — radiant and gleaming — added to her otherworldly appearance. On her naked sweaty torso, it looked like a mark of divinity. It's fascinating contrast against Laki's smooth dark skin was mesmerizing. So revealed, the belt radiated an awe-inspiring opulence that promised a life few would ever own.

The first time Se-se had seen the belt, it had rendered her speechless. Laki had been out all night, and Se-se had spent most of the day popping into the launching room hoping to see Laki return. Meals passed, and Laki did not come home. Se-se blew off invitations from friends, helped the mothers, and practiced her debates while waiting for Laki's return. Se-se had watched her brothers and sisters leave home one by one, but Laki's maturation was different. Laki had failed to find a path for her maturation years, and — in the absence of a plan — she had been promised to a mother-unit. Horrified, Se-se had launched a concerted effort to save her sister. The closer Laki got to maturation, the more frenzied Se-se became. She knew that her mission sometimes spiraled into a mania, but she was powerless to stop herself.

When the roof of the landing room finally slid open in the early evening, Se-se had been waiting in the shadows. She had watched Laki's pod land on the launching pad. She had remained silent as Laki created a small opening at the base of the pod and wriggled out.

"Sister..." Se-se had said as soon as Laki stood up.

But Laki hadn't heard her. She stood there gazing up at the sky through the opening in the roof.

"Sister!" Se-se had yelled.

Laki's head had jerked to look over to where Se-se stood. When she saw her sister waiting for her, Laki crossed her arms and pinched her mouth tight. She stole a glance at her deflating pod, then turned back to Se-se.

Se-se barreled toward her. "We've already eaten twice. You sent no messages. You've missed your trainings..." It was then that Se-se had seen the belt. She stopped short. She reached for Laki's waist.

"Where did you find this?" she finally whispered.

Laki had looked down as if she did not know there was a very heavy marriage belt wrapped around her waist, a marriage belt she had not been wearing the previous day when she left home.

"Can't get it off," Laki had said, shrugging.

Se-se had surprised herself by murmuring, "It outshines even mine."

Laki had grinned and kissed Se-se's cheek. "Don't worry, sweet Se-se, yours is more true."

Se-se had put her hand to her cheek as if to hold the kiss there. She felt as if her mind would explode. Laki wearing a marriage belt?! Se-se had masterminded several meticulously planned campaigns to get Laki paired up with a mate. Laki had stubbornly refused each plan. Her excuses ran the gamut from bad breath to inadequate personality to insufficient height. Nothing Se-se had said could sway her. Not even her most logical arguments proposing marriage to several of Laki's friends. Laki was adamant that marriage should be reserved for magical connections. Anything less would not be entertained.

Se-se had followed Laki around the landing room, pestering her as Laki closed the entrance in the roof and flattened then folded her deflated pod.

"Who gave it to you? It must have come from Embankment 5, or Embankment 7 at least."

Laki had paused. She looked down to inspect the belt as if considering its worth. Then she had shaken off Se-se's question and stalked out of the pod landing room.

Se-se had followed, undeterred. "Sisterrrrrrr, who is he?"

Laki had walked to her room and unsealed it without answering.

"Two days to maturation," the voice had said when Laki entered her room.

Se-se had entered behind her and sat on the floor. "Come on, what's his name? Maybe I can find him. You met him in the rendezvous-less stretch, didn't you?"

Laki had bent over to unbutton her boots. "It's called the rendezvous-less zone."

"I bet you don't know anything about him. Did you at least get his name? You still have one more day, don't you think you should…"

"Stop talking and help me get this thing off."

Se-se had stood and walked over to Laki. She leaned over and started fumbling with the belt's knot.

"Is he a friend of yours?"

Laki had sighed. Se-se's persistence was unextinguishable. "No, I met him by accident."

"Do you think he likes you?"

"I think he likes women. Are you getting anywhere with that?"

The knot was so tiny that Se-se had trouble holding on to it. No matter how firmly she tugged at it, it refused to come apart for her fingers.

"Did you even get his name?"

Laki had slapped Se-se's hand. "That's enough. I guess I'll have to cut it off."

Se-se had gasped. "But then it'll be destroyed."

"Who cares? He's a rebel. He doesn't care about marriage; he doesn't care about rules. It's just a belt to him."

Laki had thrown off her clothing and stepped into the bathing module. She was still wearing the belt.

"Maybe it won't come off for a reason," Se-se had said.

But Laki hadn't answered. The sound of water flowing had been her only reply.

As soon as Laki had stepped out of the bathing module, a tinkling sound had wafted into the room. Both Se-se and Laki had frozen. Panic flared across Laki's face as she grabbed at her discarded cloths. She had picked up one of the cloths and hurriedly attempted to reconfigure it into a loose robe. Se-se tried to help, but she couldn't undo the seams on Laki's cloths. After Laki had succeeded at making the cloth flat again, she threw it over her shoulders, but it barely covered her torso.

Head-mother squeezed through the entrance of Laki's room. Se-se and Laki kneeled. With their heads bowed, neither of them saw five other mothers enter the room after head-mother. But they had heard them. Thousands of tiny bells embedded in the mother-unit's cloths rang out as a shimmering veil pulled them into Laki's room. The mother-unit stood in the middle of the room, bound together by a veil that cloaked their bodies and distorted their features. Each individual woman was unidentifiable, but the force of their presence was unmistakable. The air swelled with powerful emanations of love.

No one had spoken as each of the mothers surveyed different corners of the room. Within seconds, the mother-unit could step into a room and dissect the situation that had been unfolding. The sensation of being deeply seen, disrobed of all pretenses, was so overwhelming that Laki was on the verge of swooning and Se-se began to cry.

"Stand up, children," the mother-unit had hummed.

One mother had moved forward and embraced Se-se.

"Mothers, I am sorry for missing my training today. I know I have a lot to learn about the cloak, but…." Laki had stopped to gulp down the quivering in her voice.

"What is this around your waist?" the mother-unit had sung.

Head-mother had glided toward Laki from her position in the center of the room. The tiny bells tinkled as the other mothers moved with her in one undulating ripple.

Laki had fingered the belt without looking at it. "It is a marriage belt, but it was given to me as a gift, not as a proposition."

"A thoughtless gift to a girl who is two days from maturation."

Head-mother had reached out, every move an orchestra of tinkling. She palmed the belt with cloaked hands, testing its weight.

"Quite heavy, the young man is from Embankment 5?"

Se-se had perked up, thinking she might finally learn something about the mysterious giver of marriage belts. Laki was silent.

"La-Laki," a mother had sung, "Head-mother has asked you a question."

"Mothers, I don't know where he lives. I only know that his name is Fogo."

"You can't bring a marriage belt with you into your mother-unit," hummed another mother.

"You must return the belt," a third mother sang, "We wouldn't want his family coming for it."

"You have a way to return it?" head-mother sang.

Laki had fallen silent. She remembered Fogo's face, blank and disoriented, after their rendezvous. She'd had to remind him who she was. Why he had wanted to see her again was unclear to her, but he'd refused to take the marriage belt off her waist. He told her it was his insurance that she'd meet up with him again. Laki had no plans to renew their encounter. Marriage belt or not, she didn't enjoy the indignity of being inconsequential, and she wouldn't spend any time courting a repeat of the morning after.

"You must find a way to return the belt," head-mother had sung.

On that signal, one of the mothers had waved her hand over Laki's wardrobe portal, and her cloths had shot out on their rod. In a blur of twelve hands, Laki was quickly dressed in an outfit reminiscent of the mothers' clothing.

As the mothers had led Laki out of the room, Se-se had run behind Laki, grasped her sister's hand, and whispered, "I'm going to find him."

The Laki flashing her hips and flirting with the crowd at her goodbye party was completely different from the Laki glumly heading to training in her mother-unit whites. Laki had looked ghostly and ashen in her training cloths. On the dance floor, Laki was blindingly vibrant and unmistakably alive.

Se-se was still rousing herself from memory when Laki spun around and threw herself into someone's arms. She pressed against him quickly then wandered off the dance floor. Se-se lurched forward, afraid that she would lose Laki in the throng of revelers. As she rushed after Laki, Se-se's foot slipped and she lost her balance. She grabbed wildly at the nearest person to keep herself upright. When she regained her balance, she realized she was draped on a stranger's chest.

The stranger wrapped his arms around her, holding her tighter and longer than necessary.

"Don't you smell good," he laughed.

Se-se untangled herself, gave a grateful giggle, and turned to leave.

"Wait, is this yours?" the stranger asked, thrusting a black cloth at her. "You tripped on it."

"Thanks," Se-se said. She grabbed the cloth and nudged her way through the crowd. When she reached the edge of the party, she saw Laki reclining on the floor, draped across a few pillows. Se-se kneeled in front of her sister and leaned toward her. When Laki saw Se-se, she broke into a wide smile. She took Se-se's face in her hands and kissed her on the cheek. Se-se handed Laki the cloth. Laki wiped her face and sweaty torso with it.

"Don't bathe with it, put it on."

"What is it?" Laki asked, stretching the cloth out to see it better.

"Your cloth."

Laki laughed. "Thanks, sis."

"Are you going to put it on?"

Laki wrapped it around her neck like a scarf and threw one end over her shoulder. "Are you here to parent me or to party?"

"I'm here to save you."

Laki rolled her eyes.

Se-se grasped Laki's shoulder. "I found Fogo."

Laki did not react. Her expression didn't show surprise, fear, or joy. Her face locked out all emotion and refused to even hint at her feelings. Someone stumbled over Se-se, and she crawled forward to sit next to her sister.

"Did you hear me?"

"Is he coming for his belt?" Laki asked coolly.

"No, but there's someone I want you to meet."

Laki sighed. "Se-se, I don't need *another* belt."

"It's not like that. Where's your pod?"

"Why?"

"I told you, I want you to meet someone."

"And leave my party? No way!"

Laki reached out and grabbed a woman's leg. The woman kneeled, then yelled Laki's name. Within seconds, Laki and her friend were cuddling and giggling.

"We don't have time for this," Se-se said before standing up and looking around. She had never been inside Laki's pod and didn't know how long it would take to check all the labels on the gathered pods to find Laki's. She looked down at her sister, whose hands were now roaming over her friend's body. *You've come this far*, she said to herself. *Laki's worth it, keep going.*

She reached past Laki's friend and gripped Laki on the arm. "It's very important that you wait for me here, please!"

Laki nodded her head, mocking Se-se's grave tone with a falsely serious expression on her face. She watched Se-se go, then turned to look deeply into her friend's eyes.

Just as her friend was descending for a kiss, Laki heard, "Laki?"

She looked up and saw Zaha. Zaha's eyes were moist, like she had been crying. Laki's friend rolled over and Laki sat up.

"What's wrong?" Laki asked taking Zaha's hand.

"I can't find my pod." Zaha burst into loud sobbing.

Laki leapt up, swaying until she could find her footing.

"Oh no, sweetheart. It's okay, we'll help you."

"I don't know why I'm so emotional over this. I'm a wreck."

"It's the smoke," Laki said squeezing Zaha's hand. "It makes the highs higher and the lows lower."

Laki started to edge forward, but she stumbled more than she walked. Her friend stopped her.

"You sit down. I'll take her, but you better be here when I get back."

Zaha and Laki hugged each other tightly. Zaha opened her mouth to speak, but Laki silenced her.

"Shhhhh, everything is fine. Everything is beautiful. I love you."

She kissed Zaha and pushed her away. Zaha left, peeking back until the bodies of the partygoers obstructed her view of Laki.

Laki lay down again and rested her head against the pillows. She closed her eyes and felt the air around her spinning. When she opened her eyes, nothing around her had changed. The pods were still conjoined, and the party was still packed with people reveling in the glow of the nearby star bar. Laki closed her eyes again. After a few seconds, she felt her stomach drop. Everything fell silent as she suddenly found herself alone in her pod.

She opened her eyes and jerked upright. All around her, people were dancing and coupling; the blue haze still colored the air. She exhaled and lay against the pillows again. This time when she felt herself drifting, she didn't fight it. She slipped into another time, when she was alone in her pod rapidly descending before stopping with a bump. She heard a voice say: "Sorry about that."

The voice was so deep it was disorienting. The stranger who spoke those words had skin that was as dark as hers, but teeth that were more perfect. His hair was locked and tied into wild knots all over his head. He lounged with a bemused grin on his face as his pod began to fuse with hers. She opened one eye to peek out at the party once more. It was still there. Then she closed her eyes and gave herself to memory.

"I should be more careful," the stranger with the deep voice apologized. He stuck his hand into the gradually widening hole that was opening between their pods. "It seems we've fused unintentionally. I'm Fogo, and you are?"

Laki jumped to her feet and grabbed his hand. "Laki."

By the time the hole became large enough for him to step through, Laki had arranged her body in a casual but confident stance.

"Ahh," Fogo sighed, "you seem to be a little wet."

Laki shot him a look of faux irritation. "Our little accident triggered the shower module."

"Well, come over," Fogo invited with the wave of his hand. "I've got some heat and a little star juice."

"You drink in your pod?"

"Sometimes, but don't tell the regulators."

"How do you know I'm not a regulator?"

"Besides the fact that I know all the regulators in the Stretch, I can tell just by looking at you that you're a regulator's nightmare."

Fogo winked, and Laki's insides shivered. She glanced up at the ceiling of his pod and saw that his marriage belt was still there, casting a seductive golden glow. When he noticed her looking, he sighed.

"Yep, maturation 25, and I'm still hanging out in the Velvet Stretch." He waved his fingers over his drink portal. "Star juice?"

She stood facing him, looking right into his eyes, then taking in his whole face as if reading his history. He took her hand and led her to the drink portal. Laki dropped her head back and opened her mouth beneath the drinking spout.

"So," Fogo said after Laki had drunken her fill, "what brings you to the Velvet Stretch?"

Laki turned away. "It's a long and tragic story. I'd rather not go into it."

"But, you shouldn't be hanging out here. You look like you're almost to maturation, if you're not there yet. No profession as far as I can tell." His eyes roamed up to the ceiling of her pod. "No marriage belt?"

Laki walked to the center of their conjoined pods and sat on the floor. She leaned back on the palms of her hands. Her gaze wandered over the bare stretches of his neck, lingering over his throat and collarbone. She explored the cut of his arms, the length of his legs.

"You are not fond of this topic?" he asked.

Laki looked down at her waist. She rubbed her finger over the space where Pemfi's marriage belt would be resting had she accepted it, and shrugged. "Marriage belts are useless. I just turned one down."

Fogo drew back, "You aren't one of those mother-unit radicals, are you?"

Laki placed her hands flat on the floor. She stretched, lifting her hips until her legs were fully extended. She stood and walked slowly over to Fogo. She stopped when her face was a few breaths from his.

"Do I look like a fucking mother-unit radical to you?"

Fogo shook his head before speaking. "No, no you don't."

Laki put her arms around Fogo and grasped his hips. She felt the ravenous lust of her younger days rising from slumber. Maturation was at her back. *Why not?* she thought. *Why not?* She flicked her tongue over his lips.

"So are you hanging out rendezvous-less because you want to be alone or…"

Fogo drew away.

"Forgive me, but a woman of your…stature." He paused and flicked his gaze down Laki's body. "You can't think this is preferable to marriage, and you can't have much time left. You really shouldn't be here."

"Auggh," Laki groaned and threw her hands up in the air. She strode over to her pod and leaned back to begin de-fusing. "Fogo," she said, "It was wonderful meeting you." She crossed her arms and waited for the pods to separate.

"Wait," Fogo yelled. He grabbed his marriage belt and jumped into her pod. "I didn't mean to irritate you, it's just that…"

"Look," she said, "I'm three days from maturation, and you're sexy as hell. No, I don't have a profession. No, I don't have a marriage belt. In three, no, two days I'm going to join a mother-unit, but whether or not I should be here is none of your business!"

Fogo wrapped his arms around Laki's waist and squeezed her softly.

"Shhhh," he said, "shhh. I didn't mean to upset you. Put your arms up."

Laki put her arms up. "Maturation! It's all anybody wants to talk about. When did the Velvet Stretch become such a defect?" She felt Fogo lifting his hands behind her. Then he was maneuvering something over her head. "What are you doing?"

She looked down and saw his marriage belt shining gold around her waist. She felt a wild burst of adrenaline pulse through her chest.

Fogo stepped back, eyeing the full length of her. "Very sexy."

Laki opened her mouth, but could not speak — she could only sputter.

"Bet that doesn't happen often," he grinned as he tightened the belt, tying a few more knots.

"What, I get to try on some rich guy's marriage belt?"

"No, you are rendered speechless." Fogo grabbed the belt and pulled her to him. "So you want to get sent into the mother-unit with a bang?"

Laki stared into his face, then started laughing. "This is unbelievable."

She flicked her hand over the time module, but no time appeared. Fogo grabbed her hand and kissed it.

"Let's do this by starlight," he murmured.

He waved his hand behind him, and his pod went dark. He rubbed his pelvis against hers softly. Whatever reservations Laki had been harboring dissolved instantly. Laki extinguished the light in her pod, and the glow of the Stretch illuminated their pods, bathing them in starlight.

For a few brief seconds there was no movement. Laki and Fogo just stood there drinking each other in. Then Laki grabbed the front of his cloth and pulled him close. She pressed her lips against his, urgently and impatiently, but he was full of unhurried languor. When she offered him her mouth, he savored it, sucking gently on her lips while she was anxiously pushing her tongue through his teeth. Laki abruptly pulled away.

"I…"

"I know, you've got a pod full of props and a few ideas about how this should go down."

Surprise, then annoyance rippled over Laki's face. "You don't know me."

"I know you," he said. "You're used to being in control."

"You don't know me," Laki repeated.

He knitted his fingers through hers and kneeled, forcing her down to the floor with him. He pushed her shoulders back, nudging her to lie on her back.

"Let me run this one," he whispered.

Laki opened her mouth to speak, then changed her mind. Instead, she made a big show of spreading her arms over her head in surrender. Fogo ran his fingers over the closures of her vest, but it didn't open. He rubbed his hands together to create more heat and tried again.

"If you really knew me," she said running her hand along the front of his jumpsuit — the cloth parted and hung open, "you'd know that I wouldn't allow my cloths to open for anyone but me."

She brushed her hands over her vest and the cloth slid open. She lifted up slightly and waited. He maneuvered the vest off her arms. With a coy finger pressed to her lips, she slowly opened her knees to reveal buttons lining her legs from her inner thighs to her ankles.

"Nice boots." He reached out to run his hands over the buttons, then paused.

"Would you?"

With one finger extended, Laki ran her hand along the closures of her boots. Buttons, from the crease of her pelvis to her knee, popped open. Fogo rolled the leather down, then pulled off the boots. His hands hovered over her shorts.

Laki smirked and parted the shorts, slipping them off without sitting up. Fogo reached toward her throat. She shook her head.

"The scarf stays."

When she reached up to pull his cloth off, he gently moved her hands away.

"This is your moment."

"My moment?"

"All yours."

Laki raised up on her elbows. "Then why aren't you inside me?"

Fogo threw his head back and laughed. "I'm an artist. You must allow me to work at my own pace."

He leaned over and began to brush the sleeve of his pantsuit over her skin. He started slowly, rubbing the fabric softly over the sides of her torso. Then, as if gauging how much she could take, he added pressure making his caresses rougher. Some areas he rubbed repeatedly while others he barely touched. He punctuated every few touches with a stroking of her inner thighs. He rubbed his cloth down the entire length of each of her legs, then stroked her inner thigh. He brushed his cloth across her chest, across her belly, then stroked her inner thigh.

Each time he returned to her thighs, a swelling crescendoed between her legs and air escaped her in intense gusts. When Fogo's orchestra of arousal caused Laki to lose all regularity of breathing, he finally disrobed. He shrugged his cloth off his shoulders and let it drop to the ground.

"Turn over."

"Oh, so you're still running things," Laki murmured as she turned over.

Fogo began kissing and biting down her spine, veering off course to explore the contours of her back. By the time he reached the fleshy spread beneath her hips, Laki had let go of her performance. She no longer cared who was in control, she simply wanted to feel as much as she could, as deeply as she could. She reached for Fogo and pulled him to her.

"I need it now."

Fogo chuckled. "I think you should wait."

"No." Laki turned over and grasped his arms. "We can do it again later," she whispered, "But I need it now."

"I am a benevolent ruler," Fogo said as he allowed Laki to guide him to enter her. Laki had expected the shuddering and the bliss, but as soon as she and Fogo's bodies were connected there was something else—something dark and ancient that unfurled between them. She gasped, then narrowed her eyes to study his face. His expression of knowing arrogance had dissolved. Unmasked, he looked like a different person. The pleasure and surprise reflected on his face was the first true emotion he had allowed Laki to see.

An intense current of sensations began to thrum through her, pulling her outside of herself. Long-held lashes of pain unfurled and vibrated within her. Hurts began slipping out of her mouth along with a low moaning. The mysterious connection between them built, layering into a crackling climax. Time and space blurred; Laki felt as if her very being was disintegrating in air. When she was fully drowned in rapture, a chill rustled over her skin. Shivering, she opened her eyes. In that moment, a cloth fell over her body and obliterated Fogo's touch. She blinked and the rendezvous with Fogo dissolved.

The chaos of her party was just as she had left it, but she was not prepared for what she saw standing before her. She startled, then scrambled to her feet. At first she thought it was the mother-unit — her mother-unit — looking down on her. But when her mind cleared, she noticed the faces. She could see eyes, noses, lips. All the women in this unit had thinned their cloaks so that the part of the veil covering their faces had become transparent.

"M... M... M...?"

"Mahini," the mother-unit sang together.

"How did you...?" Questions flew through Laki's mind. How could a whole mother-unit fit into a pod? How did they get past the concierge? Why were they here?

"We never answer how," sang Mahini.

"You looked cold," sang one mother.

"Happy, but cold," sang another mother.

Laki bent down, scooped up the cloth, and draped it over her shoulders.

"You are the girl who is going into a mother-unit tomorrow, are you not?"

Laki nodded.

"So why are you wearing a marriage belt."

"Have you changed your mind?"

Laki pulled the cloth tighter around her body. She was having trouble accepting what she saw before her: a mother-unit with faces. She examined the expressions in their eyes, the set of their mouths.

"Can you leave the unit?" Laki burst out.

One of the mothers smiled. "I believe we asked you a question first."

"This..." Laki said, throwing one edge of the cloth open to reveal a glimpse of the belt. "...is a souvenir. I can't seem to get it off...and you, can you all leave the unit?"

The women of Mahini shook their heads. "Temporarily, in an emergency, but our cloaks are bonded."

"We are one," they sang together.

"What about your children? What happened to them?"

"We refused to accept them. They belong to someone else..."

"...and we belong to the world."

"We mother those who need it."

"We mother with our songs."

"We mother those who have never heard of us."

"We mother each other."

Laki's head bounced around as she looked into the face of each woman as she spoke.

"Where do you..." She began to ask a question, but was interrupted.

"We don't answer where," Mahini sang.

"Where is the owner of that belt?" one of the mothers asked.

"Not here. Probably somewhere in the Stretch."

"You don't want to join a mother-unit."

Laki searched their faces. "Is that a question?"

"No, that's an observation. Look at you. You're wearing a stranger's marriage belt, passed out at a wild party, yet restless as a caged animal."

"How should I be spending my last night, attaching bells to my cloths?" Laki snapped.

The women of Mahini looked at each other and smiled.

"She'll be head mother," one of them commented.

"Feisty yet docile enough to follow the rules."

"Headed off to a mother-unit like a good little girl."

"You call this mothering?" Laki asked.

"It isn't all hugs and pheromones," one said.

Laki thought about the mother hanging from the sling, giving of her body to nurture the babies. Neither hugs nor pheromones could do that. She opened her mouth to give a tart retort, but found that she didn't have the energy to respond. She was weary — weary of conversation and weary of escape. The weight of tomorrow was pressing down on her, and she had spent too much time thinking about mother-units. Tomorrow belonged to the mother-unit, tonight was hers.

One of the women began to sing the chorus from their song about the nature of mothers. It was a song that Laki had always loved but never understood. She noticed that Mahini's veil was billowing around the edges. She unwound her cloth from around her neck and rearranged the cloth Mahini had draped over her. She adjusted it so that the edges lined up in front of her body. Running her hand along the ends of the cloth, she fused it into a flowing robe. She pinched under the arms and shaped roomy sleeves. Laki listened to a few of the mothers chattering about her prospects for success in a mother-unit, then she shrugged off the conversation. She moved around to the back of the mother-unit to investigate the billowing veil. She was surprised to see that the veil was billowing because — while their sisters were chatting or singing — two of the mothers were dancing. Laki stood there, momentarily entranced by the women's faces and the grace of their movements. Then she covered her face with her hands, as if to protect herself, and joined in.

Once Laki began to move, all the women of Mahini started to dance. Movement, it seemed, was connected to singing for them. As they danced, a humming rose up — a humming that turned into chanting. Their intonations started to reach the ears of Laki's guests, and one by one, they stopped their revelry and turned to watch Laki dancing with Mahini. It was a sight that very few people had ever seen before and that very few people would ever see again. A mother-unit with exposed faces, dancing with abandon in the Velvet Stretch, veil fluttering and undulating like a living thing.

A feeling of flight, of progress after prolonged struggle, blossomed in the chests of all who heard Mahini's song. Their message was wordless, but forceful: be free, be free, be free. Mahini encircled Laki, cocooning her in their melodies and harmonies. The song dislodged her calm composure and sent her trembling with emotion.

She had been careful to avoid the embrace of Mahini's veil, but once she was undone by their song, she lost awareness of her surroundings. The sensation of their veil brushing against her skin disarmed her. She felt as if it were her own veil being thrown over her. The sensation wasn't all encompassing like the memory of Fogo. Instead, Laki felt as if she were in two places at once. She was dancing with Mahini, feeling the delicious expansion of possibility flowing through her limbs; she was in training with her mothers, feeling suffocated by the veil. She arced an arm overhead, and she was in the past, nothing more than a child grabbing at the veil, letting it tickle her tummy as her mothers dressed her for bed. She spun around, and she was imprisoned in a web of her own panic as the veil was being laid over her for the first time.

The veil was nothing like Laki had thought it would be. She had thought the veil would make the world look hazy, shrouded; instead it made everything sharper. When she was inside the veil, the things that required her attention acquired a glint, a shine. She imagined the veil would feel light and weightless, which is how it looked when the mothers were rushing down the hall to deal with something urgent. But instead of floating over her, the veil had pressed against her skin, sticking to every part of her.

The memory of that first moment with the veil washed over her. The feel of it stung, as it pushed again her skin, clinging to her. She had shut her eyes tightly and screamed in terror.

"Relax," the mothers had sung, "it won't suffocate you."

But Laki had felt suffocated. She had felt like it was plastered against her, crawling over every inch of her body. She had clawed at her neck, trying to pull it away from her throat.

"It can't be grabbed," the mothers had sung. "It can't be touched with your hands. You can only move it with emotion."

Laki had yelled louder.

"Laki, my love, the cloak is not your enemy. It can't kill you."

"Breathe, Laki."

Laki had taken deep gulping breaths. But every time she had opened her mouth to speak, the cloak flowed into it and garbled her voice.

Now Laki raised her hands high in the air and shook her head back and forth. The women of Mahini mimicked her actions. She began whirling and dipping, trying to move faster than memory, but she could not outpace her fears. They stayed with her, panting inside her ear.

She felt it again: the cloak probing her eyes, nose, and armpits. She heard her mothers trying to ease her panic.

"It won't always feel this way," one mother sang, stroking her back.

"Each cloak is unique, it becomes a part of you," sang head-mother. "It will take from you and become you."

"Then when you're in your unit it will…"

"…meld with the cloaks of the other women."

"It will be an extension of you."

"You will grow to rely on it…"

"…and it will know you better."

As she continued to dance, Laki became more aware of the sounds Mahini was making. Not the sounds of their voices, but the sounds of their breathing—and of their bells. Laki looked at their faces as she swayed with them. Each of them, she thought, had lived through their first day in the veil, and each of them had survived.

Se-se heard Mahini before she saw them. She had located Laki's pod, counted pods until she reached hers, then entered her pod. She had disconnected her pod from the party and reconnected it to Laki's. When she had done all that, she stepped into a completely different party. The abandon and frenetic energy were gone, instead everyone was swaying as if eerily entranced. For a second, Se-se thought she had made a mistake. She went over her actions in her mind, but this was no mistake; there was no other party this could be. She walked back to where she had left Laki and came to a shocked halt.

Laki was no longer lying half naked on the floor. She was clothed, and dancing with…a mother-unit. Se-se's shoulders drooped, and her knees went soft as her body prepared to bow before the unit, but then she stopped. She didn't feel the emotions she usually felt when she was in the presence of her mothers. She took a step closer and saw that these women had revealed their faces. Her mind was a jumble as she tried to understand what she was seeing.

The sight of the veil momentarily immobilized Se-se. She was transfixed as she watched it writhe with a predatory autonomy, as if it were an independent creature — haunted and hungry for new mothers. Suddenly Se-se felt the urge to grab Laki and run. She shifted forward, but when she reached for Laki, Laki slipped to the floor. Mahini reacted immediately, smoothly transitioning from chanting into a soft humming. Laki rolled back and forth with soundless sobs, while everyone in the party stood frozen in stunned stillness.

Mahini crouched over Laki and began a whispered accompaniment of sighs and hisses. Se-se crawled over to her sister and pulled on her arms, calling her softly. Laki's eyes were unfocused and vacant. Every few seconds Laki would yelp, clawing at her face and neck. Se-se grabbed Laki more firmly and shook her, yelling Laki's name. As garbled sounds started to spill out of Laki's mouth, faint trails of blue smoke wafted from her body. Se-se could see the mark of tears on her sister's face.

Although Laki seemed paralyzed, she was fighting for her sanity within. She battled hysteria by forcing herself to remember her victories. "I can thin the cloak," she murmured to herself. "I can show my face like Mahini does. I can stretch the cloak for long distances. I can do all the proper maneuvers for privacy. I can sit for hours with the cloak on, it doesn't hurt me." *But you can't get out*, a voice whispered in her head. *But you can't get out.*

The mothers described it as a particular wave of emotion — sudden fear when a child is in danger, a sharp tenderness associated with duty, or heartbreak when a child is in pain — that could part the veil. Once parted, the veil would release a mother from the unit's bond, and she could temporarily detach, with her own unique section of the veil draped over her.

Laki was full of emotions — primarily anger and rage — but those were useless in a mother-unit. At each training session, she thought of gruesome situations, awful things that would put the lives of innocent babies in peril, but it never worked. No matter what she tried, the cloak remained unmoved.

Maybe it was the pull of Mahini's voices, maybe it was Se-se leaning over her, but suddenly Laki broke through the mania of grief. She felt the sensation of the cloak falling over her again. But this time, instead of clinging to her, it laid cool and soft on her skin. It felt like the comforting presence her mothers had promised it would become, the gentle companion it had been becoming in Laki's last days of training.

The memory of the one time she had parted through the veil burst into her consciousness, and pulled her further out of her turmoil. She had been under the veil, drowning in failure, when the thought had blossomed: "I bet Se-se could do it." Her fear of never learning how to exit the veil was buried under a forceful flood of tenderness for her sister. Then it had happened — a small hole of unmoving air had appeared in the middle of the cloak's shimmer.

Laki, smiling at the memory, was suddenly buoyed by the certainty that, with Se-se guiding her, she would always learn the way out. Yes, she could not escape the veil, but holding Se-se in her heart sliced open an exit through her grief. Laki heard a whispering, felt someone cushion her head. Her eyes fluttered open. Seconds passed while she stared at the face before her, a few more seconds passed before she realized it was Se-se.

"I thought..." Laki said, swallowing back tears. "I thought I'd dreamed that you were here."

"I'm here, Laki."

Laki looked at her sister and felt both relief and a soft sadness descending. In the wake of those all-too-real memories with the veil, sadness was a sweet emotion — a reprieve from her mother-unit anxieties and a welcome respite from her rage. As everything around them fell away, she gripped Se-se's hands and smiled apologies and love at her. When their hearts had been silently emptied, Se-se and Laki snapped out of their trance.

Laki let go of Se-se's hands and looked around. "What happened to the party?"

None of Laki's guests had left the party, but there was no dancing, no laughing, and no fondling. Everyone was gathered around, watching the sisters. Everyone except Mahini — there was no sign of them.

"Can someone put the music back on?" Se-se asked.

Someone put music on, but the mood was permanently broken.

Se-se helped Laki sit up. "The pods are ready. Are you ready to go?" she whispered.

"Go? Where are we going?"

Before Se-se could answer, the party started to dissolve. A friend of Laki's came over with outstretched arms. Laki rose from the floor, fully recovered from her outburst. She was, once again, animated and enigmatic. She was passionate with her goodbyes, effusive with her embraces. A few times, she jokingly pretended to faint as punctuation in conversations, and each time Se-se jumped, arms outstretched, ready to catch Laki before she fell.

When the party had shrunken to just a handful of pods, Se-se linked her arm with Laki's and guided her toward their pods.

"Mahini was at my good-bye party!" Laki murmured.

"Am I the only one who didn't know they were a mother-unit?" Se-se asked.

Laki burst into soft laughter as Se-se pulled her away from the center of the party so they could disconnect from the other pods together. As they left behind the stragglers, partygoers who were unconscious or profoundly high, Se-se looked Laki deep in the eyes.

"I want you to follow me."

"Follow you where?"

Se-se didn't answer. She peeled a patch of material from the interior of her pod's wall.

"Where's your navigation panel?" she asked.

Laki waved her hand over a nondescript curve of her pod's wall, and the navigation panel folded out. Se-se pressed the patch from her pod onto Laki's navigation panel and waved it shut.

"Just follow me," Se-se said.

Laki sat down on the floor and watched Se-se walk to the opposite side of their joined pods.

"Tomorrow I take the veil," she said to Se-se drowsily and lay down on thc floor.

As their pods separated, Laki slipped into sleep. She remained asleep as her pod followed Se-se's around star bars and conjoined pods into the far reaches of the rendezvous-less zone.

Laki opened her eyes when she felt Se-se shaking her. She stayed awake long enough to see that they were still in the Stretch, then she put her head back down and fell asleep again.

Se-se sighed. She began waving her hands over various segments of Laki's pod, looking for the gas module. Her random searching finally coaxed a bulb-shaped protrusion from the wall of Laki's pod. When Se-se squeezed the bulb, the funky scent of ancient incense squirted into the pod. She turned the bulb and squeezed again. The sweet scent of newborn babies wafted out. She turned the bulb once more. This time a sharp menthol scent shot into the pod. Se-se coughed and rubbed her nose. She squeezed the bulb two more times and pushed it back into the wall. When the pod was filled with the tang of menthol, Laki started to stir. Finally her eyes snapped open.

"I'm up, are we home? Are the mothers awake?"

Se-se pulled Laki to her feet. Laki saw the darkness of the Stretch and groaned.

"I'm tired, Se-se. What are we still doing here?"

"You'll see soon."

She fiddled with the robe Laki had fashioned from Mahini's cloth. She pinched around the waist until it fit so tightly that the marriage belt protruded through the cloth.

"Can you shorten this?" Se-se asked, tugging at the hem.

"Do I have a date?" Laki asked. She looked around the darkness of the Stretch searching for another pod.

"Turn around," Se-se said.

Laki turned and saw a pod unlike any pod she had ever seen. The walls had a smoky opaqueness that was definitely against regulations.

"This is creepy, Se-se."

Before Laki had finished speaking, the strange pod started moving toward them. It bumped into their pods gently and began to fuse with them. The new pod's opacity seeped into their pod walls as if assimilating them. With the loss of transparency, they lost their ability to see by starlight. Both Laki and Se-se waved their hands over the light modules in their pods. When the three pods had fully fused, Laki saw a shrouded figure standing in the middle of the opaque pod.

"Enter, please," a steely voice commanded.

Se-se grabbed Laki's hand to guide her forward, but Laki held her back.

The shrouded figure walked toward them, entering their pods. The figure stopped in front of Laki and overtly inspected her.

Laki turned to Se-se, eyes glittering with anger. "What is going on?"

"Shhhh," whispered Se-se.

The steely voice spoke again.

"You were right, she is stunning." The figure threw off her cloak and stretched her hand out to Se-se. "I accept your offer."

Uncloaked, the figure was a woman. She was dressed in shimmering robes, and long strands of colored jewels hung from her ears. She had a look about her that suggested she was unfamiliar with the word *no*.

Rage rustled up from Laki's chest and flared in her throat. She glared at the woman, then dragged Se-se away.

"Who is this woman?"

"She's going to tell you if you give her a chance."

"I'm asking you to tell me."

"She's someone who can change your life."

Laki shook her head. "You never give up. Tomorrow I'm going into a mother-unit. I'm not running away and hiding out in the Velvet Stretch, I'm not marrying one of my male friends, and I'm not digging around for my hidden inheritance. It's over Se-se."

"This is not another fantasy, Laki. I swear. At least talk with her."

"May I see the belt?" the woman said cutting into Se-se and Laki's conversation.

Laki looked at the woman then shot Se-se an icy glare.

"Show her," mouthed Se-se.

Laki lifted the hem of the robe and stuffed it into the space between her waist and the belt. She pulled the hem down so that the belt now rested in plain view. She crossed her arms and waited for the woman to approach. The woman walked over to Laki and lifted the belt. She tilted it forward as if to inspect the quality of the beads. Then she twisted the belt so that she could read the markings inside. A smile spread over her face. She hugged Laki.

"You may call me Strabaha," she said to Laki.

"*Wife* Strabaha, what is the meaning of this? Why all the mystery? What do you want from me, and how do you know my sister?"

"Excellent questions." The woman grinned at Laki as if Laki were her star student. "I met your extraordinarily persistent sister only yesterday. She told me this improbable story of a young woman wearing my son's marriage belt. This young woman, she said, would soon be joining a mother-unit. She advised me to meet the young woman before her maturation, otherwise I would never get the chance."

"So this is some type of weird fetish?"

"No, this is a wonderful offer."

"I need to sit," Laki said. She turned to Se-se suddenly. "Do the mothers know where you are?"

"Of course they do!"

Se-se and Laki sat on the floor. The woman quickly braided her cloak and rolled it into an impromptu seat.

"I can see that you are tired," the woman said after she had seated herself. "I'll try to make this quick, although I do have some questions."

"Such as?"

"You are intelligent, beautiful, strong…"

"…and an orphan," Laki said.

"Well, I'm sure if you had a wife mother, she would never allow you to toil in a mother-unit. But no father, no father's sisters, no mother's father?"

"My father and my wife mother died when I was a baby. I don't remember them, and I assume their families don't remember me. The wife mothers of my brothers and sisters allowed me to stay in the birth group. The mothers raised us all the same. They were able to provide me with cloths and food, but when it came to my school fees, there was nothing that could be done."

"So they trained you to be in a mother-unit."

Laki nodded.

"Even though she's not fit for mothering," Se-se piped in.

"The mothers say no one is fit for mothering. They say I will fit to it; it will make me what it needs me to be." Laki's tone was firm as if she were disciplining Se-se.

"And you believe that?" Se-se asked, sounding more like a bitter Laki than her usual chipper self.

"You have not thought of marriage?" Wife Strabaha cut in.

"She's had plenty of offers, but she would rather go into a mother-unit than take a marriage belt dishonestly," Se-se said before Laki could speak.

"Dishonestly!?" Wife Strabaha laughed. She put her hand on Laki's. "No one marries for love. It was a romantic idea of past civilizations. It didn't work. Unfortunately, your wife mother was not around to teach you this."

"There's nothing you can say to her about it, Wife Strabaha. She can't help herself, it's just the way she was made."

"Wife Strabaha," Laki interjected, "you said you had an offer?"

Wife Strabaha cleared her throat.

"Yes, I invite you to come and live in my home as my son's wife."

There was silence as Laki tried to make sense of what Wife Strabaha had said. Then she turned to her sister, suddenly understanding Se-se's plan.

"He knows nothing of this?" Laki asked, turning back to Wife Strabaha.

"He barely remembered that he had given away the belt."

"You are asking me to help you force your son into marriage?"

"He chose to put his marriage belt on you, I did not force him to do it."

"That is true, but…"

"There is no other interpretation of what it means when someone places their marriage belt on another."

"Do you know how many marriage belts I've tried on for fun?" Laki asked.

"Well who decides when it's fun and when it's serious?" Se-se snapped.

Wife Strabaha took Laki's hands in hers. "Let's focus on the facts. Your maturation is tomorrow. You have to leave home. Are you ready to enter a mother-unit?"

Images of Mahini flashed through her mind. She saw her own mothers, felt them beaming at her with pride, remembered the hole she opened in the cloak, and smiled.

"Maybe I'm not ready but that doesn't mean it's not time for me to enter. I can wear the veil, I can be a good mother."

Se-se looked at Laki like she had grown spotted skin. Laki refused to look at Se-se. Instead she sat regally, radiating a powerful calm.

"I am offering you a different future. A future in which you will be able to see your sister, even your mother-unit again."

Laki paused. Exhaustion was pulling at her. She closed her eyes for a moment. "I understand your offer Wife Strabaha. I will have a way out of the mother-unit. You will have a wife for your son. But what will Fogo get?"

"His inheritance," Wife Strabaha snapped. "He will never marry if it is up to him. I refuse to pass the family money on to..." Wife Strabaha stopped speaking. She took a deep breath. "I see you are every bit as honorable as your sister promised. Will you accept my offer if Fogo accepts?"

"I have been trained to wear the veil of motherhood. I know nothing of being a wife," Laki said.

"I will teach you everything you need to know."

Laki's eyes slid closed again. It was becoming painful to stay awake. Her thoughts kept slipping away, and her body begged for rest. For the first time in months, the impending mother-unit was not a buzzing pain in her head or a throbbing fear jolting her with insomnia. Tomorrow was simply her future, and she had ceased to resist it.

"I'm afraid there is no time for me to change tomorrow, Wife Strabaha," Laki said, her eyes still closed.

"I will be your wife mother," Wife Strabaha burst out. "I will pay your school fees, I will help you start a business. Please allow us to visit your home tomorrow."

Laki's eyes popped open. Wife Strabaha's face was stricken with desperation. Se-se's face was twisted in tortured pleading. Was this what being in a mother-unit would be like — watching the excitable passions of her children from a calm, peaceful distance?

"I have to sleep," Laki said. She stood and stumbled to her pod. She sat on the floor and paused. Wife Strabaha's offer lay in front of her, dazzling with portent and promise. She eyed it warily. It was a magical stroke of luck that could manipulate the contours of her destiny. Yet she did not feel the desire to collapse in gratitude, instead she saw the offer for what it was — a departure from one mysterious path to another.

Laki leaned away from Se-se and Wife Strabaha. As her pod began to separate, she realized that she had not given Wife Strabaha an answer.

"Wife Strabaha, you may come to my home tomorrow, but you will have to speak to my mother-unit as I have no wife mother or father."

Wife Strabaha did not flinch at Laki's offer. She gracefully accepted it as if the idea of speaking with a mother-unit was not an insult to her.

"And Wife Strabaha, please tell your son that I will enjoy seeing him again. He will be needed to remove the belt should I decide not to accept your offer. I'd hate to destroy such a beautiful family heirloom."

Laki nodded to Wife Strabaha, as if dismissing her, and winked at Se-se. The glow of admiration spread across Se-se's face. Laki had done the impossible: she had shed the ugliness that had been weighing her down and was entering maturation luminous and triumphant. Even her pod was majestic in its shimmering crown of starlight.

As Se-se watched Laki's pod bobbing in the dark stillness of the Stretch, wisps of loss began to unfurl in her chest. She felt the echoes of yesterday tugging at her heart. She had spent an entire childhood chasing after Laki. Even now, after she had restructured Laki's future, Laki had blown her a kiss and was hurtling away without a backward glance.

Se-se's vision went blurry as the pain of it broke in her chest. She smiled a quick goodbye to Wife Strabaha then sped away. As she blazed through the Velvet Stretch, the silence of her solitude loomed, mocking her with Laki's absence. She soothed herself by pretending that she and Laki had arrived home together, and were running through the halls with twined fingers, breathless with triumph. The need to be at Laki's side, to share in the glory of the news, urged her to push her pod to move faster. But even as she raced to catch up with Laki, she knew she would never emerge from the shadow of Laki's brilliance. Laki was already gone, and Se-se was struggling to keep up with her explosive star of a sister, who was now a flash of light, plummeting toward home.

Selection from Their Dogs Came With Them

Helena María Viramontes

The hammering, someone hammering, and how could Grandfather in his La-Z-Boy recliner snooze through the noise of the hammering and the evening news? Grandfather had suffered a mysterious stroke that left him sleepy a greater part of the day, and he mostly slept all the time now except at night. He slept over TV voices and over the hammering. Fluorescent greenish tint flickered on his face while her cousin Nacho sat bored on the couch, flipping randomly through the latest issue of *¡Alarma!*, a magazine of lust and murder filled with sordid police photos and mug shots that turned up in her nightmares. All he had to do was cock an eyebrow at the sight of her, an abbreviated warning to Ermila of the inevitable eruption.

Nacho had been sent by his family five months ago to come live up north and help out since Grandfather had been disabled. Coming to the Eastside would be a good opportunity for him to learn English, have a chance at learning a trade, and earn money to send back home; but Nacho thought otherwise. Two weeks after he began his ESL classes, he dropped them; laid off from a car-washing job, he felt busing tables to be below him. He informed his parents via a letter that he proposed to paint—which was well and good, until his family found out that he intended to paint murals, not houses. Nacho boasted of painting La Virgen de Guadalupe floating above the great pyramids on the side of a corner tiendita—a strange request for the Chicano owner, who seemed prouder of being

Mexican than the Mexicans. Nacho dreamt of following in the footsteps of the three great Mexican muralists, Rivera, Siqueiros, and Orozco.

However, there was no end to their bitter correspondence. Her grandparents felt the same and waited for a time when Nacho was prepared to embark on his artistic career outside of their time and dime. Grandfather's complaints were no secret, and he took every opportunity (and opportunities became as abundant as sunrises) to reprimand Nacho for his lack of ambition, and worse yet, his downright laziness.

Surprising to Ermila now that Nacho and Grandfather could share a peaceful evening together in the same room, Nacho sat at the end of the couch, a sense of doom contained in his gaze. Ermila flipped him the bird. Lights out in the kitchen, Grandmother not in the living room. Let's get it over with, Ermila hoped. Bathroom light out, main bedroom vacant, but from the hallway she spotted Grandmother standing on her bed. Grandmother's pale skinny legs waffled on Ermila's lion blanket as she held the steel nail with pincerlike precision against the drywall above her headboard and hammered.

Oh, Grandma, what—

Ermila muffled her words, rolling them back up in her tongue. What? she shot out. Whatta you doing? When Grandmother noticed a blistering Ermila, she swung the hammer with greater force, tilting the photograph above the light switch. The two-inch tough nail had to be gunmetal-strong to hold the weight of the crucifix that Grandmother carried in the pouch of her apron pocket.

Fall down and break into tiny pieces, Ermila wanted to say, but immediately regretted the wish because Grandmother just might fall on purpose to say, *See? See? More tears are shed for answered prayers*, her little shriveled body poofing like dust particles of ancient wall plaster, just to teach her granddaughter a lesson.

Maybe this will protect you, Grandmother said, slipping the wire hoop of the bulky metal and wood crucifix onto the nail, because I can't anymore. I can't. The worn mattress springs crunched underneath.

Oh, Grandma…

There's the door, Grandmother replied. This conversation had already been blueprinted in Grandmother's mind, grievances piled so high, their tumbling inevitable. The shrill of the telephone, the muffled male voice of the television news, the mattress springs, these were the indistinguishable sounds Ermila heard, not her Grandmother's rants about Alfonso, her urine-stinking body, the risks and dangers, the lying, skipping merrily into the paths of hell like a foolish, reckless idiot.

To Grandmother, each strike of the nail held the repeated expectations of an insidious performance by her daughter whose DNA chain linked doubly to her granddaughter. Ermila was fated, punto final. And Grandmother was too exhausted by her age and Grandfather's ten years of constant nagging regarding her sole decision to bring Ermila home to rear her own "flesh and blood." A big mistake, he had predicted. Ermila's fate was something Grandmother could not challenge, and it wearied her to the point that, though she was not a churchgoing woman, she sought out God's assistance, a thing she should have done, in hindsight, when her daughter first showed signs of femaleness. All of Grandmother's rational thoughts were absorbed in preventing Ermila's sex from entering their decent household. She also knew too well that this prevention was absolutely impossible; her efforts seemed as feeble and futile as raising her palm to halt the coming of a hurricane.

Grandmother's mouth collapsed into a well of wrinkles so deep her condemnations were endless and her thready bare feet smashed some of Ermila's prized carnival dolls. Ermila made her bed each morning and leaned Alfonso's gifts carefully on her pillow shams.

I said I was sorry.

I can't believe how stupid women can be!

This is all—

Ermila hesitated because this wasn't a good time to say what she really felt but said it anyway—Bullshit! Bullshit to the second power!

You're just like your mother, and look where it got her! As if Grandmother knew from experience, as if Ermila's mother had been that wickedly crazy. Using her old rubbery arm, Grandmother lifted the hammer again and pointed to the photo, which had tilted so badly, another blow would have forced it to fall.

I'm me, Grandma, not my mom.

No more, Grandmother repeated, shaking her head. Ermila freed her waist-length hair from its rubber band and shook it loose. There's no use trying. The incessant peal of the phone, and still Nacho too lazy to answer it. She raked a few puffs of mohair in her hair and then offered a hand to help Grandmother off the bed. Grandmother's hand was bony-thin and ice-burning cold. No words of promise, no exacting behavior would ever please Grandmother again. What was the use of even trying? The ringing of the phone ended abruptly.

Grandmother slid into a pair of slippers and skimmed the floor, her old back bent from the burdensome agony of repetition. Before Ermila closed her bedroom door she watched Grandmother sadly carry the hilt of the hammer down the dark corridor of the hall. For a few generous moments, Ermila felt pity for her. It was like that from the very beginning; she loved and hated Grandmother at the same time.

Ermila tossed and turned between her sheets, unable to sleep. Drifting sinews of steam slowly entered her room from her open door. Nacho had just stepped out of the bathroom and the steam floated out and layered the ceiling, a halo of fog surrounding the hall light. Grandmother forbade them from walking around in their underwear, but since Ermila's lamp-light was off, Nacho assumed she slept. His lapse of judgment and the crack of open door afforded Ermila a glimpse of the bulbs sacked in his elastic underwear briefs. He plugged his head into the hole of his tank top, and before he covered his torso radiant from the hot shower, she saw his nipples, chocolate discs that resembled the ones she used to buy at Ray's for a penny.

Blushing, she turned her face. She had never known Alfonso fully naked except for his cock, a small anomaly of flesh that seemed strange for people to have in the first place. How it hid, then surfaced like a one-eyed pirate, the commanding growth looting, then retreating back into its own collapsible cup of flesh. The first time they did IT, it burned, harsh and bloodied. He drove her home, his arm over her shoulder as a token of recognition, his old lady, she looking out the window, surprised everything remained unchanged. Like a border crossing, sex promised a different, uplifting life and yet all she encountered was intolerable guilt, a filthy feeling that bathing couldn't cleanse, and the fear that her body would someday call for mutiny. Her girlfriends knew, could see it, smell it, but never point-blank asked her, and so she told no one and all of this grandly disappointed her. If Lollie could believe that her pretend marriage to the Monkees' Peter Tork was real, then why couldn't Ermila believe that her real sexual involvement with Alfonso was simple fantasy? She turned again to face the vertical light from the door and tried not to think of Alfonso or his cock, and then she lay on her back. Not even self-deception could force her eyes to shut, and Ermila stared up at the bulk of the crucifix for a long time trying to figure out what motivated her to do the things she did.

After the first ring, Ermila bolted out of bed so that the phone in the hallway would not wake her grandparents. She listened to the litany of Alfonso's lies, struggling to pull her arm into the sleeve of her thick chenille robe. You sound high, Ermila said, you sound wasted. She turned away from Nacho on the couch, under a floral iris-printed sheet. I never want to see you again, you asshole! she said, louder than usual, and then proceeded to whisper into the mouthpiece a time and suggest a place for Friday's date. She said she loved him, which was also a lie, and then returned to bed, immediately regretting having arranged the clandestine meeting.

The freeway bumble across First Street and the sporadic spray of bullets, too faint in the distance for concern, lulled her into a fidgety sleep. In and out of dreams, floodlights jetted through the drawn blinds, drone of engines in and out of the hours. Restless, inspired heat in the room overboiling, Ermila sensed that something wasn't right. The blind slats rippled and then settled and then rattled again and again until a force of wind billowed the pair of curtains and the hem of the curtains rose, then fell upon a small curled-up dog.

A sleepy Ermila gazed at the shadow. Huh? The shadow of the dog yawned wide, rose on all fours, then leisurely arched its back. Ludicrous on its sausage legs, the small dog seemed clownish. Grandmother had threatened her with something like this, *to protect her* because Ermila was the daughter of a mother who fled like a war refugee in the choke of night. Convinced Ermila would do the same, Grandmother must have laid a guard dog atop a rumpled pile of clothes near the open window. What other explanation would there be for the dog that raised its comically long snout to track a scent? Ermila kicked off her sheets, planted her feet on the cool hardwood floor. The dog withdrew into the shadow of the open closet door. Ermila heard paw-clicks on the floor.

Hey there, she cooed, holding out her hand. Nice doggy, stupid doggy. The dog growled low and steady as Ermila approached. The curtains camouflaged the dog's movement and it remained partially hidden in the shadow of the closet door. Nice doggy, nice. A gesture of a hand held out, an offer to the darkness.

The dog gnashed its fangs, striking her, a mighty sting. Ermila cried out, the wound throbbed around the break of skin immediately, and she cracked the blind slats for light, held her bleeding hand up to inspect the bite. The beads of blood were so lacquered red she was astonished the color belonged to her. Both the pain and surprise contributed to her bitterness. If Grandmother did things like this, little wonder why her mother had escaped into the night with her father.

Ermila backpedaled through the threshold of her bedroom door and bumped into the swelling humid heat of the hallway as if it were a low ceiling. Grandmother believed that sleeping with open windows invited burglars, and so all the hot, steamy soup of air stirred in the hallway. Nacho's floral sheet tousled about the floor, uncovering his tank top and his briefs. He lay on his back in sound sleep, one knee bent, the other stretched on their creaky couch. In order to get to the bathroom, she had to tiptoe past an arching floorboard somewhere near her grandparents' bedroom and she peeked in on the two sleeping like arthritic parentheses under the thick hand-sewn quilts, the overhead fan whumping the air.

The iodine bottle was absent from the medicine cabinet, so Ermila settled for antiseptic. With her good hand, she palmed cool tap water on her neck and water beads necklaced her breasts. How else would the dog have gotten in her room if not for Grandmother's suspicions? Ermila rinsed her injured hand, applied some antiseptic, which burned and foamed, and she winced and then awkwardly swathed it with gauze.

Back in the hallway, Ermila thought to check for unlocked doors, to give Grandmother the benefit of the doubt. Okay, so Grandmother was crazy, but a dog in the house? Perhaps Nacho had left a door open and the dog wandered in to escape the helicopters. Her absentminded cousin never thought about the rhythm of her grandparents' lives and seemed forever out of sync with their set patterns. Nacho paid dearly for this: every time Nacho left water running in the sink, drawers pulled out, lights on during the day, windows opened, toilet seat up or water boiling to evaporation, Grandmother wanted to pull his ear because this irresponsible, ill-bred young man was incapable of completing one fluid act—to open, then close a cabinet, to turn on, then off a faucet. As Nacho slumbered, a hand pillowing the back of his head, his thin lips parting to breathe, who would guess him careless enough to leave the door unlocked and open? Or could Ermila have been at fault herself for having left her own window open? Her window faced First Street and was screened, barred with wrought iron. Barely open, it was almost impossible to get a decent breeze in, much less a dog. No.

One by one, Ermila eliminated the possibilities. She gathered her hair up from between her slender shoulder blades and cat-padded delicately to the kitchen. She jingled the handle of the screen porch door, locked, and then returned to the living room. The main entrance door was locked and securely bolted. Perspiration beaded on her skin. Her bandaged hand hung lead-heavy and tingled from the dog bite and she used the other to pull back the aged sun-bleached drapes of the living room, taking a peek down First Street at midnight.

Ermila watched the Quarantine Authority helicopters burst out of the midnight sky to shoot dogs not chained up by curfew. Qué locura, she thought, the world is going crazy. The chopper blades raised the roof shingles of the neighborhood houses and toppled TV antennas in swirls of suction on the living side of First Street. Ermila's nylon underslip was pasted to her sweaty back. Above the woven arteries of freeways, a copter's searchlight swept over the roadblocks to catch a lone stray running out of the edge of light. The bitch zigzagged across the pavement of First Street, its underbelly droopy with nursing nipples. I gotta do something soon, Ermila thought, her hand swathed in gauze and dappled with antiseptic and blood. The wheeling copter blades over the power lines rose louder and closer and closer and louder, just like the unrelenting engines of bulldozers ten years earlier when Ermila was a child.

Once the copters completed their second sweep, bits of moon glistened in First Street's oil-moistened tracks. Ermila tiptoed from the window. Before going into her room, she approached the couch and bent to retrieve Nacho's sheet. In the dark, the irises looked like wine spills. He swayed his bent knee and touched his belly as if he sought out his blanket. The copters returned a third time. The walls trembled, disturbing the framed old magazine picture of John F. Kennedy, shattering a glass in the kitchen. The epicenter beneath her, the eternal moment waiting for the quaking to cease, but Nacho's abrupt movement roused her, and she felt her uninjured arm snarled in a grip. For a second she recalled how Luis the lizard boy had clamped her wrist and forced her to do something she didn't want to do. The memory of it infuriated her now.

Stop it, Nacho, she whispered angrily, I wasn't comin' on to you! Nacho propped himself up on an elbow and took the sheet she held, unfurling the flowers on his legs.

¿Qué te pasó? he asked, referring to her bandaged hand. His lengthening hair parted like dried wisps of kelp over his sweaty forehead. Did tu novio hurt it?

Let go.

Sssh, he whispered, pressing a finger to his lips. He arrived five months ago from Reynosa to torment her, and he glanced over at the grandparents' open bedroom door. She could barely see his eyes. Leave me alone. Her words dissipated. By the fourth sweep, the vibrations crescendoed, making the walls and floor unsteady. The slant of counterfeit light coming from the helicopter poured into the small living room, flooding everything around her. Light splashed on Nacho's face and the floorboards rolled beneath her bare feet once again. Ermila panicked, her slip billowed upward to her thighs. The photograph of her parents floated toward the ceiling; the stuffed dolls won in dime tosses at the church carnivals danced and dipped as buoyant as the beer caps Alfonso threw in the sea. Her slip lifted to her bare belly, and finally swelled over her two firm breasts. Her nipples felt the pinch of chill. This was happening because the world was going crazy. She could feel his moist palms inside the cool nylon of her underwear as a faint succession of bullets continued. Nacho buried his face, his lips against the slant of her belly, and she inhaled, closed her eyes because she wanted nothing to do with the light.

She exhaled. The copters lifted the floodlights and immediately the room grew gray once more. She broke his grasp, made sure her nylon slip reached her knees again.

Nacho whispered a word or two she couldn't hear and then she heard him say he planned to return to Reynosa on Saturday. In the morning.

Who cares?

What you do to me, he whispered in a concoction of English and drowsy seduction. The light in Grandmother's room flipped on. Ermila fled, slipping on a throw rug in the hallway and bumping into the phone. The large crucifix nailed above her headboard still swayed as she closed and locked her bedroom door.

The gunfire continued until dawn.

Just Killing Time

Cecilia Tan

She dreams of cordite in the air,
of anguished faces and urgent voices.
But the voices fade.

She opened her eyes on a handful of men staring down at her, amazed. The setting moon filled their eyes with shadows, dark like the knots of their ties against their white shirts. They were a mixed lot — some Asian, some White — which seemed strange, but why should that matter?

One of them helped her to sit up, muttering, "Thank the fucking lord." Then louder: "You okay now?" He draped his suit jacket over her shoulders, shooing the others back. In some of their gazes, she saw disgust, and far too much heat in their eyes.

A single white towel draped across one thigh was all she wore. She pulled the jacket around her. She didn't feel injured, but she felt like something had happened.

"Kari?"

She did not recognize the name. She did not recognize the men, either, not even the burly one with the brown mustache who called her by name and helped her to her feet. Not the kidney-shaped pool, nor the perfectly landscaped yard, eerie in the blue pool light and pinkish night-sky glow. Too tranquil for the lingering taste of violence in her mouth.

"We thought you were dead," the man continued.

"She *was* dead," said another, one of the disgusted ones. He wiped at his mouth. "I always wanted to kiss one of the boss's women, but not *after* she kicked the bucket."

She shivered. Maybe her memories got stuck in the afterlife.

"Good thing the boss missed this whole thing," Mustache said. He told the man who had revived her to get the car. "We'll take you back to the condo in town, all right?"

She nodded weakly, covering her ignorance. She leaned on him and shuffled with small steps toward the house. She was aware of their gazes on her bare legs, talking among themselves. *Best keep a low profile until this all blows over,* one said to another. *Until what blows over?* she wondered. Had one of them tried to kill her and now they were covering it up? Or was it an accident and they worried they'd be blamed?

But their voices played on; they were talking about something else. One sounded almost disappointed that the other crisis, whatever it had been, was over. *Shoulda been at the pier tonight instead, man. That's where the real action was.* Another one: *A complete sweep and clear. No one got out alive.*

At a luxury apartment in the city, they opened the door using a key from her purse. "Boss'll be back in the country soon. Don't go out. You need anything, ask Sato next door," Mustache said as he took his jacket back. He handed her a satin robe. "Here." He put the TV remote in her hand, as if she were too stunned to pick it up herself. "Could be a few weeks. Kill time until then."

Once they were gone, Kari lit the screen with the push of a button. She skipped through the channels looking for anything useful or familiar. The local news was informative. But she found movies with men in black and guns and knives and those held her attention much better than reports of the weather and traffic and waterfront buildings burning to the ground.

She swims in a shimmering pool of light, and a strong body glides up beside her, embraces her. Dream sex is instantaneous, no discussion or disrobing, just sudden thrusting punctuated by her sighs of pleasure.

Time does not always move forward or backward in her dreams. Sometimes it moves sideways, and whatever was happening no longer is. She carries a woman's body up the stairs. The woman is old and wheezes blood out of a gash, speaking in a strange musical language. But it is a dream, so she understands. She sets the old woman down in a room and bolts the door.

My loyal one, I am dead, the old woman says. Once they break down the door, we shall both be killed. No, don't protest. We have lost this fight. There are too many and they want only blood. There is only one thing to think of now. Revenge.

But how can we get revenge if they kill us?

The old woman's reply is a cackle of blood.

Kari woke to the afternoon sun in her eyes. She'd forgotten to close the curtains. After she'd had her fill of late-night action movies, she'd stood on the balcony until dawn hoping the view would jog her memory. The newscast said this was California. She sat up and rubbed her eyes. The last thing she had watched was a badly dubbed ninja movie about an all-female warrior clan. A ridiculous fantasy, but as she forced herself out of bed, images of mysterious assassins played behind her eyes. She shook her head. The mystery she needed to solve today was herself.

The face in the bathroom mirror seemed unfamiliar. Skin too brown, nose too flat? In the shower, she examined herself: there were scars on her forearms, but they didn't look recent. The tips of her hair curled in the hot steam and she combed it out straight when she emerged.

The bedroom closet was filled with dresses of the slightest type, short skirts and lingerie, lace and satin. Everything fit. In the dresser she found more lace, bathing suits, and a pair of handcuffs with no key. And money. Someone—she assumed it was herself—had hidden money all throughout the drawers. Hundreds, fifties, many of the bills crisp like new. She collected all she could find, and it came to an impressive total. She hid the money again while she pondered where it could have come from.

The kitchen cabinets held instant ramen and canned fish and packets of soup from distant places. *Am I Thai? Filipina?* Her purse yielded no ID other than an envelope of cash with the name "Kari G." written on it. What kind of name was that? *It doesn't sound Japanese,* she thought. *And yet.*

By evening, she had been over every inch of the place. She teased open a lockbox in the closet with the combination zero-zero-zero, hoping to find something important. But inside there were only more handcuffs, some shiny knives, and a set of chrome clamps on leather straps. They had a wicked look to them. Beyond that, the apartment had no more secrets to yield.

Time to try talking to Sato, whoever that was.

She put on a pair of plain cotton underwear, a plain garter with opaque black stockings and the only dress in the closet she could find that came up to her neck. After all, she didn't know how this Sato might react to a sexily-dressed woman at his door. If he was like the henchmen who'd pulled her out of the pool, there was no telling what he might do with no boss around.

She knocked on Sato's door, wondering what pretense she could invent for asking his help that wouldn't give away that she'd lost her memory. Borrow batteries for the TV remote? Ask if he'd heard from the boss? Get change for a hundred?

The door swung open on a tall Asian man, thin, just pulling a silver lighter from the breast pocket of a tailored suit. He flicked the lighter open with one hand but didn't light the cigarette dangling from his lips. His eyes traveled down her and he murmured, "I hoped it would be you."

"Yes, it's me," she said, a strangely soft sensation curling in her belly.

Sato reached for her waist. As he snaked his arm around her he said, "Does this mean you forgive me? Have you reconsidered my offer?"

Offer? "I —"

He silenced her with a kiss, and as she felt her body press against his, a startling feeling surged through her: she knew him! It was the first time anything had felt familiar. He pulled her into the apartment, the cigarette forgotten, and pressed her to the carpet. Before she knew it, he had yanked aside her panties and was inside her, thrusting hot, close, and sudden —

Almost like in the dream. Her body seemed to remember his, and she felt whole while clinging to him with legs and teeth, gnawing hungrily on his cool savagery.

When he was through, he left her lying on the carpet while he went into the bathroom. When he emerged, he zipped his fly, brushed lint from his jacket, and looked at her curiously, as if wondering why she was still on the floor. "You need me," he said, as he checked his gun.

She pondered the possibility that this was true. When she said nothing, though, he left without another word.

What "offer" had he made? What did she have to forgive him for? A lovers' quarrel? Her head hurt from trying to stretch so few facts over such a large empty space in her mind. She returned to her side of the wall, to the television. She had Chinese food delivered and searched for another yakuza or samurai movie, pondering dark-eyed Sato and his gun.

She dreams of being an animal — a tiger or a jaguar — padding through the forest. She feels drunk on life, on her own incredible power, as she bounds over fallen trees in search of prey, the rich scent of the trees in her mouth. She rolls on the mossy ground with another big cat, fur against fur, claws and teeth — is it sex or fighting? It doesn't matter.

Again the sideways shift, and she knows the bloody knife is in her hand. A tranquil calm descends. Shouts sound from the hallway but she is not concerned. She presses the point of the knife against the soft spot behind her ear while the old woman wheezes through her chants. Death will be quick and painless. She waits for the old woman's signal.

Kari woke to find a gold bracelet around her wrist. Sato had come in the middle of the night, as he had a few times that week, saying he liked to take the boss's whore right in the boss's bed. They would tumble across satin sheets as she raked him with her nails until he crushed her under him, holding her still to complete his passion. She held the bracelet up in the light and wondered why he hadn't given it to her while she was awake. Was it an expression of what he couldn't say? Some kind of apology, maybe? There was still so much to know, and she was no closer to knowing it. She liked the feeling of completeness that came from being so centered in her body during sex, from knowing herself on some instinctual, wordless level. But the hollowed-out sensation of being no one would always return.

She tried to convince herself it wasn't a bad life. Everything was provided for her. And Sato was a skillful lover, sometimes not letting her rest until she had come again and again and again. Her world felt small and small was safe, nothing but sushi delivery and action movies, gripping the comforter tight every time a sword or gun was raised for the kill. But what would happen when the boss came back?

In the wee hours, when Sato returned from his business, she asked him when the boss would return.

He was searching her refrigerator for a beer, so his face was hidden when he said, "It's not safe for him to come back yet."

"That's not what I asked."

"Soon." He straightened, holding the can by the edges. "No one can hide from me for long. I just need to track down the last one."

The last *what?* she wondered. "So…soon, then."

"Yes. And once I'm done with him…" He cracked open the beer and chugged a bit, his chin sharp as he lifted it. "You know it'll be dangerous for us once he's back."

Not knowing what else to say, she gave the smallest of nods.

Sato kissed her on the hair, but his words were far from tender. "Last time he was here for more than a week, you got sore from keeping us both satisfied."

That struck her as less than ideal.

"Are you sure you can handle it?" He ran a finger over her lower lip, teasing. "Or are you so insatiable now that it's not a problem."

She pulled away, clicking her tongue, and his tone turned serious for a moment. "You've changed, Kari."

When she said nothing to that, Sato finished the beer, crushed the can in one fist, and tossed it into the bin beside the sink. "You know how to use a computer?" Without waiting for her answer, he went on. "You need groceries. So do I. I'll bring you the laptop. Why should I do it, if you can? It should be a woman's job." He smiled like he was pleased with himself.

He retrieved the slim gray machine from his apartment and handed it to her, then waltzed back out without even a kiss goodnight.

She dreams she is a child, lost in an airport or a shopping mall, some huge indoor space full of echoes and strangers' faces. But she meanders into the burning warehouse she has dreamed of before. The battle for their lives is jumbled, flesh impacting flesh and gunfire sounding, but all she knows is that each moment she is alive, she is still alive, and she wants to stay that way.

But the enemy is winning. Then she is helping the old woman into the room at the top of the stairs. She can see the knife clearly, the script carved into its handle looking like tiny figures fighting their own battle. The old woman — Nakano-san — tells her that death magic is their only hope.

Kari liked the computer. The laptop made it possible to find movies to watch at any hour of the day or night, without even getting out of bed. They were even more addictive than before, now that she could call them up on demand. Sato would come in sometimes while she was watching, shed his suit jacket and gun, and simply push the machine aside and fuck her to the sounds of gunfire and screaming.

"You love movies about killers," he said one night. "No wonder you love me." And then, after he came, he added, "I found him, you know. The last one left."

"The last what?" she asked, before she could censor herself.

"Last enemy." He buried his mouth against her neck and bit her just to make her squirm, his hand seeking between her knees.

She let him wind her body up and release her, but she was thinking: *So. Sato has been killing the boss's enemies.*

When he got up to dress, she asked him whether he really believed he could eliminate all of them, and he laughed. "I only worry about the ones who'd kill him on sight. After the way we wiped out everyone in that warehouse, though, not many would dare." He stopped himself at the door. "My offer still stands. After I do this would be the best time."

"When will you do it?" she asked.

"Soon," was all he said.

After he left, she pulled the computer onto her chest and typed in a search. Hadn't there been some news about a warehouse…? It seemed that Sato and the boss's men had slaughtered a rival gang. That didn't happen in real life, did it? But the news was full of things that couldn't be real. A man who kidnapped a girl and kept her as a sex captive in a tent in his backyard for 18 years? Had to be fake. Or a sex addict who shot up massage parlors? That didn't even make sense.

None of it made sense, unless other people's grasp of the line between fantasy and reality was as bad as hers.

She typed in "amnesia" and started to read.

In the dream, she is in the grocery store, but as she pushes the cart toward the cashier, she realizes all she is wearing is a peek-a-boo lace piece that displays her nipples like Valentine's Day bonbons.

Nakano-san laughs, wheezing blood, and says, you won't remember. But it won't matter.

A high trill pierced her sleep, making her heart race. She'd never heard the sound before. She stared at the phone by the bed as it rang again and again. She didn't dare answer it. When it finally stopped, she decided to tell Sato.

But he was out. She never knew when he'd arrive, only that he always took his gun with him when he left. She let herself in, like she did when she put away his groceries. The two apartments were identical.

Identical. She went to the closet, curious if…yes, there was a lockbox. With the same combination. So lazy.

She gasped as she saw the passports. She flipped one open to see Sato, but that wasn't the name it showed. Neither was the second, or the third: all the same photo but different identities, different countries.

And there was one with *her* photo. And a name. Was it real or fake? She locked them away again, her mind churning. Did it even matter?

By that evening, Sato had still not returned. She resigned herself to eating alone and decided to go down to the shop on the corner to buy dinner.

But would Sato or the boss be angry if she did? She wasn't supposed to attract attention. But all her clothes made her look like a whore.

She went back to Sato's apartment, pulled on one of his finely tailored dress shirts, and rolled up the sleeves.

She ordered a bowl of soup and a plate of roast chicken. But as she stood at the takeout counter, waiting to pay, she thought, *why shouldn't I stay here to eat?* She took a table against one black granite tiled wall, where the cool air from an overhead vent blew gently and shook the leaves of potted plants hanging overhead. A bland young waiter placed her food on the table without making eye contact.

By the time she was done eating, night had fallen. She stood on the sidewalk and felt the day's heat escape into the air.

She returned to the apartment, to a subtitled samurai soap opera, and Googled "female ninja clan." So, the kunoichi were real. She fell asleep while scrolling, wondering what to believe.

In the dream, she flees through fields, but the grass drags at her ankles, until her steps come with agonizing slowness. Each heartbeat is like a hammer in her throat, but each footstep creeps forward until she gives in and falls limp. When she opens her eyes, she is once more looking into old Nakano's face as she explains: There is no time to work the magic completely, so your memories will be lost.

Then how will I know?

Death magic entwines your fate with his. Even if you do not remember, you will do as you are fated.

The sound of swords ringing and men shouting in her head mixed with the low question in Sato's voice. She sat up to find the television still on, a battle raging, and Sato brushing his fingers against her cheek.

"You were trying to talk in your sleep," he said.

"What did I say?" she asked quickly, her hands clutching at a throw pillow.

He laughed. "You said 'oh, Sato, I miss your big—' "

She threw the pillow at him, and he deflected it with one quick hand. In another instant he was on her, his hands around her wrists, his lips searching her neck for her heartbeat. She play-struggled, enjoying the friction. She felt most alive at those moments.

But then she remembered. "The phone rang today. I didn't answer it."

He stopped and looked into her face.

She stared up at the sea of tiny shadows flickering across the textured plaster ceiling. "I was afraid it was the boss."

He released her and sat on the couch beside her. "Doubtful." He lit a cigarette with his practiced moves and slid the lighter into his pocket. "I can't believe you want to stay with that pig. He sweats so much, I can smell him on you hours later."

Did I say I want to stay with him?

"I can hear you scream sometimes, right through that wall." He stabbed a finger in the air. "Tell me, Kari. Why won't you tell me what he does to you? Are you afraid of him? Or are you afraid of what I might do to him if I knew? What does he do that makes you scream?"

Her tongue grew heavy in her mouth as she tried to remember, or even imagine, but she was blank. "I can't," she said before the silence got too long.

He blew smoke into the air. "You've changed, Kari. I can feel it. You used to be as timid as a mouse. But now...you like to fight." He held the cigarette in his mouth, and one hand reached for the warm cleft between her legs. "He won't like that, you know." When she stiffened and clamped her thighs together, he pushed harder. "Not like I do." He used both hands to flatten her onto the couch, his belt buckle digging into her.

She wondered what would happen if she tried to really fight him. Probably nothing different. He would just be more savage. But what exactly had he offered? To take her away from all this? And were death and life linked like sleeping and waking?

He smoked while he fucked her, while the voices of Japanese film actresses wailed and cried in the background and her mind roamed its own expanse.

This one is a flying dream. Flying far above a shining blue ocean, white clouds swooping past as if they are the ones moving, not her. But then she trips on the edge of the horizon and falls, falls...into the water below, into dark and quiet, into nothing.

She finds herself again with the old woman. Each of them has a hand on the knife and they're praying feverishly. Nakano-san's hand feels like electricity, even though her face looks like death.

This is the only way, my faithful daughter. You have served me well, and will serve me last and best in death.

Honor feels like a warmth inside her and purpose fills her completely. They are beating down the door but she does not care, because in the next life she will have her revenge.

Kari woke to find Sato thrusting into her. The cobwebs of the dream clung to her mind, and she wanted to claw her way back into sleep, to see if there was more.

After, when he got up from the bed to get dressed, she tried to tell him. "I was asleep!"

He gave her a sideways look as he buckled his belt. "So? Did you not enjoy it?" His voice had a lilt, like he was speaking Japanese.

Two weeks had passed since the time he had told her she liked to fight. Since then she had been trying to find a way to refuse him that didn't just provoke him. And now, she realized, he would take her in her sleep *because* she had no chance to refuse. Rage boiled through her, making it hard to think. She wished she could recapture the clarity of the dream — that feeling of calm and purpose.

Her teeth clamped down as she swallowed her anger. "You *ask* first, next time."

"Or what?" His tone plummeted as he ran a hand down her arm. "You'll tell the boss?" His laugh was as dark as his eyes.

"Didn't you say 'one left' before he returns?"

Sato leaned against the headboard and shifted his balls inside his tailored trousers. "I can do it any time. But I've been waiting to see if you'd see sense." He took her hand and kissed it gently, then spun the gold bracelet on her wrist.

He'd been delaying on purpose?

"After this one, I'm leaving. I'm done." He leaned over to cup her cheek. "You're the only thing from this life I want to keep." She sat perfectly still. "There are places he can't reach. Osaka. Macau."

When she said nothing, his hand tapped her cheek, a hint of a slap. "You know it'll be better with me. If you're so worried he'll come after you —"

She batted his hand away, aggravated at his tone and his assumptions. She wasn't prepared for the slap that came in response, and suddenly they were fighting, hands flying, yelling at each other. Her nails raked his face, and he spat something in Japanese. *Stupid whore.*

She froze. *I understood that.*

He pinned her, his hair in his eyes as he bore down. "— I'll tell him you drowned."

She went limp.

He stood, anger making him abrupt, and straightened his clothes. "I'll do it tonight." The last thing he said before stalking out was, "When I get back, it'll be your last chance to make up your mind."

How can I make up my mind when I don't even know who I am? she thought. She knew she was a kept woman, but that was the answer to *what* she was, not who. Had she been trying to commit suicide in the pool, to escape this life? No, that had to be she was watching too many samurai movies. They were seeping into her thoughts. Even the dreams had a plot, now. Each time she seemed to know more about what was going on. *Some kind of turf war against an underground criminal ring…just like…*

…my life. A life that didn't seem real, not since that night by the pool. What she'd read said that memory loss could be caused by either physical or emotional trauma, and afterward, people often exhibited personality changes and experienced hopelessness and existential crises.

She flung herself back onto the bed. *If only I could go to sleep and wake up again, fresh*, she thought. *Start over.*

Flames burn everywhere, but she leaps through, barely feeling them, light as feathers against her skin. No sound is louder than her own breath in her ears. She sees Clan Leader Nakano-san pulling a knife from her side at the bottom of the stairwell. A man steps out of the shadow with a gun in his hand, aiming to kill. She needs to be faster than his finger, faster than that bullet. And she is, because Nakano-san trained her well how to kill with a single strike. He spins as he falls but more are coming. She hoists Nakano-san onto her shoulder, the old woman weighing no more than a bag of bones.

Nakano-san has held onto the knife that had been in her ribs. "Take my hand," the old woman says as they shelter in an office. She kneels and they clasp hands in a grasp made tight by desperation. "There is only one thing to think of now. Revenge. Are you afraid to die?"

"Not if it serves you."

"Then there is one last hope. The death magic. Before I die, if we can cut your soul free, I will send it to another body. A body recently freed of its soul. The perfect disguise." She coughs up blood.

They both grip the knife, as if by holding tight neither of them will need to leave this world.

"You will be drawn to the man who murdered us. Your fates will be entwined. Even if you do not remember, when the target appears, recognition will dawn."

Recognition will dawn…?

The knife is at her ear. The old woman chants the names of old gods and clan ancestors, invoking their help. She feels calm. She is going to her best destiny. The door bursts open. Nakano nods. It is time to plunge the knife into her own flesh, but before it can drive her brain into silence she sees who is in the doorway, gun in hand.

Sato.

Kari woke in a cold sweat. Never before had she died in one of those dreams. She shivered and shook, even under the hot steam of the shower. The vivid sense-memory of the knife hilt hitting her skull at the end of a painless thrust welled up. If the dream was true, it explained so much…!

No. You're mad at Sato so you made him the bad guy in your fantasy.

But so what if it was just a dream? What was it telling her? That she had died that day in the pool, but she was being given a second chance at life? That death was just a transition? That there was a way out? She could take the passport and run, she thought. But Sato could find anyone…

She stood under the water for a long time, waiting until there were almost no thoughts at all, as if after a time, repeating the same fears and doubts wore them away to nothing.

Then, calm as the water in a pool, she wrapped herself in nothing but a towel and lay down on the bed to wait for him.

Sato banged open the door and roared her name a little after midnight. He was already stripping his belt off when he came into the bedroom and he smiled to see her lying there, spread-eagled as if her hands were tied under the pillows. He whipped the towel aside and knelt between her thighs.

"Naked and ready for me. You feel better now?" he said as he stroked himself. "You just had to remember your place. Good girl."

Yes, she thought. *I remembered.* She thought about the way the knife sank into the spot just behind the ear lobe. She let him press her down and go for a while, until his awareness of his surroundings dimmed in the passion of rutting. She caressed his ear, breathing hotly into it and tugging on his ear lobe with her teeth. And then she slipped the kitchen knife from under the pillow and drove it deep into his skull.

Some part of him tried to save himself, as one hand grabbed the handle of the knife, but it was too late to even pull it free. A very quick death. She twisted out from under him.

After she washed off the blood, after she had dressed in some of Sato's clothes, after she retrieved the passport and counted the money one last time, she went back to look at the body. He seemed small now, curled up with one hand on the knife in the middle of so much blood.

The last link to my old life, whatever it was, she thought. She lit one of his cigarettes with his silver lighter and stood there a moment more. *The last link, cut.*

The money could get her far, far from there. Japan, maybe. Or anywhere. Anywhere at all.

As the Tide Came Flowing In

Sonya Taaffe

She died in springtime, out of sight of the sea. So young, her family said, such a terrible loss, and so soon after her husband's tragedy. But then she had never been strong and she had married so poorly, throwing away her youth and her prospects on a sailor man who kissed his wife twice and left her for years to the desolate company of the cold Atlantic shore and the foreign trinkets he sent home, as if Chinese lacquer and Polynesian boar's teeth could replace the solace of decent society or the warmth of a child. Small wonder if she had sunk into fancies and loneliness, watching her life drift away from her like trash on the tide, smaller wonder still if she had yielded at last to the persuasions of a man no more scrupulous than her tide-tossed husband, if closer to hand—but the dead were sinless, she was dead now and her bastard with her, and the Bridgmans of Boston wore black gloves and jet pins for their wayward daughter and said very little at the service. The youngest grandson squalled in the arms of his mother, his father the sober young banker cleared his throat above his stiff collar. In the Public Garden, the willows were yellowing like old paper and the bronzes of Washington and Sumner were tarnished with mist in the morning; the slates and granite slabs of the North Burying Ground were cold as weeping to touch. The family plot was conspicuous by the absence of her name. Perhaps there were limits to the sinlessness of the dead after all.

She was an old woman in springtime, or a woman who would have been old if she had lived to measure her life by experience rather than existence, nearly sixty years behind her eyes and more than thirty of them within the tall red bricks of Danvers State. By then there was no shortage of shaking, screaming, sleepless people, but most of them were hiding from mortar-shells, not seashells; the waves that engulfed their dreams were of shattered horses and mud-toppling men, not the Atlantic's mare-grey breakers or the Pacific's vast blue swell. They covered their eyes against blown-off faces, not weed-picked hair or sea-lichen scaled over a smile. But they would not speak much of the war to her, the nurses who combed her hair and brought her books and pinned her wrists when she still struggled after so many years, gasping with the breathless cold inside her; it was not news that would soothe a troubled woman to hear. *Our brave boys are fighting for us,* they told her, and she could not stop thinking of her own brave boy in a trench of sea-ice, glass-bubbled pale and impervious to the pounding of fists. When they left her to gaze out through the high windows that overlooked the green embroidery of the gardens and the patients who tended their elegant designs, she whispered, *I am fighting, too,* though she was no longer sure for what. Silence, perhaps, or simply solitude. Eight miles inland, she was never without the sea.

Her husband came home in summer, calling so softly under her window that at first she thought she dreamed him, his voice as natural in the night as the mewing of gulls or the heart's rush of the tide. *Elizabeth, Lizzie-o, my darling, Lizzie…* She had grown used to those dreams; they sharpened as each second summer stretched interminably toward autumn and the *Galatea*'s return, the pitiless clock of the Arctic fishery that kept her husband landlocked above the sun all winter while she mended shirts and thawed driftwood for the fire and diced the potatoes and the salt pork finer and finer, counting the days toward the opening of the ice. She had kissed him last on the docks of New Bedford when the winds were still fickle with April of '84; now it was June again, when she picked serviceberries from their windbent bushes and shelled sweet peas with her feet bare in the sandy earth, and she had been a whaleman's wife long enough to know the difference between the skin-hunger of a dream and the sound of her name in the cricket-warm night, the sea breeze rustling the tall grasses down on the dunes. Quick and caressing, a laugh in his voice with no one to wake but his wife—*Lizzie, can you hear me? Oh, come down, Lizzie-o, come down.* His mother's shawl was ghosting the back of the chair before her dressing table, its lace floating white as a gannet's wing. Elizabeth McKay took a candle, a deep breath, and went downstairs to let her husband in.

For a moment in the colorless wash of the moon, she thought she was still dreaming. His face was a figurehead's, smiling through salt ruin; she saw the flowering fire of anemones on his shoulders, a starfish stretched like a hand laid to his breast. She smelled the deep salt thunder of the sea. Then her hand trembled, slewing his shadow across the threshold and the little sprigs of dry wild rose and violets pinned for luck at the door, and in the candlelight she saw him as real and as dear as their wedding day: her Ezra, still the bright-earringed boy with his crooked grin and his hair that tousled like barley, his eyes as blue as new paint on a carousel. His peacoat was shabby with salt at the cuffs and elbows, his shirt as stained as an old map. His fingers sliding under the night-loosened braid of her hair smelled of tar and coal soap, faintly the grease of smoke that every whaleship stank of, deep-dyed into sails and decking and men's skins. She turned her face to his palm and breathed him in.

"Oh, Lizzie."

He had never had many fine endearments for her, only the soft, wondering turn of her name in his mouth, as if each time it amazed him to find her still waiting, to find *her*. Courting, he had been brash, turning new treasures out of his pockets with each call: blush-colored conch pearls and stubs of palm-pink coral, sharks' teeth, star knots, a barbed fish hook carved from tortoiseshell winking cat's-eye in his hand as he offered it to her. A little wooden walrus, such as he said he had seen the Nunatsiarmiut hunting in the summer months along the shores of Baffin Island. A jagging wheel of whale ivory, though she was a competent piemaker at best. He was a boatsteerer with a seventy-fifth of the profits to his name each voyage and her father was a Boston businessman with three daughters, the youngest alone mad enough to entertain the attentions of a chance-met sea-talker, a well-spoken harpooneer with ambitions of ship's master. He brought her a pair of brass knuckles and showed her how to weight her fist with them, a pocket sextant and taught her to steer by the stars. *When I have my own ship, you'll come with me, Lizzie, you'll see. And none of those lady ships where a master's wife has nothing to do but make soft conversation and read the Bible to green hands—I'll have you for navigator. You've the steadiest eye I know,* and she heard again the Irish in his voice like a flash of fish-silver, his American-born coffin ship's legacy. Elizabeth had waited one voyage for him, for letters from ports more remote than even her tea-trading grandfathers had spied; by the spring of '79 she had known she would not wait another. They were married in a seamen's chapel, shy and breathless, where not even her parents' hard silence echoing down from Dorchester like a winter front could dim how fiercely she felt herself smiling. Her husband held her as if a storm would take her from his arms, all his body seal-hot against hers as she gripped him in the same starving wonder. Two days later, he sailed for the Horn.

"Hello, Ezra," she said now, quite calmly. He was watching her as steadily as she remembered, his gaze roving unashamed from her hairline to the undone buttons of her nightshirt, her hand on the door and the candle paling upward in the other like a fairy tale reversed—Psyche wakened, her winged husband unmasking himself and all the tragedy over before it began. She stepped back, just enough to show him the darkened house beyond. "Will you come in?"

She had been jealous once of the women in other ports, the men who came ashore to them; she had held herself up against Inuit women with ocean-black hair and all else pale as spermaceti, Hawaiian women as strong in the water as sun-backed dolphins, and herself a graceless stick of a girl with hair as sandy as East Beach and an indifferent freckled skin, the despair of her mother's bronze taffetas and rosy silks. She could not run rigging or carve a whale's tooth. She swam better than her husband, with his sailor's superstitious unease in the sea itself, but the knots she tied were string around brown paper, not heavy rope around bollards and bitts; her fingers had been slow to learn kitchen knives and copper pans, accustomed to deckle-edged pages, embroidery needles, piano keys. She would never heave an iron into a whale's hide. But Ezra talked only of the day when she would go to sea with him, not the hindrance she must be aboard ship, of the countries he would show her and the acquaintances he would introduce her to, not their better claims on him, and when he dropped his boots at the foot of the bed and pulled her down beside him, he did not touch her like something fragile or dutiful or rare but as if the knowledge of her body, along with stars, spouts, and card-sharping, were something he carried for everyday employment. *You haven't forgotten me,* she said after the second voyage, and Ezra actually laughed, so unreservedly that he cracked the top of his skull against the headboard and had to curl into her arms, wincing, instead of kissing her. *The way a man forgets his blood, Lizzie-o,* and then it was kisses again and heat and salt and his fingers combing dreamily through her hair afterward until it shone across the bedclothes beneath them, rayed out like a lionfish's spines. After that she envied his crewmates, but it was not such a clawing, self-sick thing. *You can tell the islands a long way off from the clouds that gather over them, like pillars of white jade. Once you've seen them with the sunset underneath, all afire, redder than you'd believe… You should see the size of the moon over the sea.* Utterly confident that someday she would, only a matter of skill and savings: *And we'll never go near Southwest Jimmy's again, that stinking crimp.* Or *his shite beer.*

And he had done well for a whaleman, she knew that living in her small, slant-eaved house with a view of Clarks Cove. Instead of a rented room on Union Street and a shared parlor smelling of other men's hair oil and other women's perfume, she had the whole windswept horizon to come down to in the mornings; if she lived like a hermit without gaslight or Edison's electricity, she had not set herself alight with kerosene or whale oil yet. She had china plates on her mantel and whorled shells the same peach-yellow as a September sunset beside them and twice a week she walked to the markets of Cheapside like any housewife with an icebox to fill. She had a four-poster bed with clean-boiled sheets on it and it was not always empty, not every other fall when the *Galatea*'s fourth boatsteerer came home. Upstairs in the shifting light of the small, thick-leaded windows and flat-wick lamps, they relearned each other: scars, smiles, weight and work, stories in the skin. Ezra was not the only one carrying time like the tattoo at his wrist, gunpowder-blue under tan. Once she had reached to touch the sliced-red snarl still fading under his hair—a bottle-smashing brawl on Kekerten Island, overwintering in '81—and forgot until he exclaimed over it the long, pale weal twisting up her forearm where a cart full of empty oil casks had knocked her down on North Water Street.

Penelope waited ten years, she said simply, the year the ice was bad in the Davis Strait and the whaling worse, the men sour-tempered and the ship a creaking, smoke-ragged hulk by the time she limped into warmer waters, the year Ezra signed on to a Brava packet after two days at home—six weeks across the North Atlantic at the cusp of winter—just to hand her his advance. *How should I complain of three?*

From the other side of the pillow, Ezra said, "Did you get my letters?"

This time she was watching the lines around his eyes, the faint wheat-gold bristle along his jaw in the lamplight. "Two posted from Talcahuano," Elizabeth said. The names ran in her head like a song, cold places and hot, roaring cities and shantytowns. "One from Frisco and three from Honolulu. One from Sitka."

"I wrote you another from Point Barrow."

"You beat it home."

His earring winked at her, a plain gold spark. "I couldn't wait. Not for you."

The quilt half tangled around them was new last winter, striped calico diamonds and six-pointed stars the color of milky porridge; the air was warm enough to draw sweat where their bodies touched and Elizabeth shifted deeper into its weight, tucking her chin down into a fold as if she were chilled. Something she had said was wrong as a slack string in a piano, a quarter-tone off-key. "But the *Galatea*—"

"Oh, Lizzie, Lizzie-o. I'd come back from Hilo for you. I'd come back from Hell."

He said it as lightly and as fervently as any other love-words he had ever spoken to her and she was colder, staring at him. The letters from Honolulu had come wrapped and waxed in oil-paper, enclosing a springy rib of whalebone etched with two different type of whale, the bull-headed sperm and the bowhead with its underslung smile. *Vieira says it is as good a likeness as you will find until you see one for yourself in its native water. There was a sunset last night like a parrot's feathers and I hoped there was a sun rising like it in New Bedford. He must greet you for me when he sees you first.* He had always written more laboriously than he spoke, in a spiky, scratchy hand that lost ink around the margins of the page in little sprays and constellations; she wrote back in her slanting copperplate and sometimes their letters met. So many gone astray in gales, misunderstandings, overworked clerks' offices, crossing without making landfall. It was not the right worry; she could not put the right words around it. She heard herself say, small and dully, "Because I am safe."

"Oh, Lizzie." The featherbed humped and shifted under them as Ezra turned on his side, put his chin on his fist to look at her for so long that she began to feel like a stranger, equivocal as she had not been since the first years of their marriage when she watched the waves run white against the rocks of Clarks Point and could not imagine what they would say to one another when her whaleman returned. His mouth creased a little, not enough for mockery, unless he meant it for himself. "Elizabeth. You're not *safe*."

He was warm everywhere, his breath quick on her skin and his scent as sharp and familiar as the wind off the sea; he was sunburnt and blue-eyed and beloved, with more to say to her than they had always had time for. He was as much a stranger as every time he came home and she laughed as suddenly as she had felt desolate the moment before, feeling his fair hair sun-shot with silver frisking in the hollow of her shoulder, before he rolled her over in the sheets that smelled of salt air and sweet lavender and she took hold of him, took him in, drew him under. Breathless at the crisis, he said, "I do love you, Elizabeth." It was the last clear thing she heard. The sky beyond the curtains was banding the pearl-blue of the inside of a mussel shell, the stars going out in the clouds before dawn. Her husband's arms were fast around her and she fell into sleep like a clear black current, a bright cameo of their bedroom receding above her like a rippling lens of sky.

She surfaced without dreaming into the noise of gulls, clamoring a bedlam of grey and white feathers beyond her window as keenly as around the casks at Merrill's Wharf; there was as strong a sea-smell in the air. The quilt was too heavy and she pushed it off before thinking of Ezra who might have been dreaming of frozen rigging and cliffs of snow like whale's teeth; of the ice beginning to close as the brief Arctic summer ended, the sun dipping beneath the low wet earth again. She was tallying autumn's responsibilities in her head before she remembered. Downstairs in the kitchen were broad beans and small new strawberries, upstairs was a stickiness of heat and more windows that needed opening. She knew then what the right worry would have been.

Even then she was not afraid, only a little disenchanted—some with the dream, more with herself, scraping love together from wishful sleep and sea air. Wry-smiling, her hair loose to her waist, Elizabeth McKay sat up in bed to pull her empty blankets straight, and then she saw what lay beside her on the pillow, strewn through the sheets like storm-wrack in the unmistakable morning light, and then she began to scream.

The child came in winter, the last blustery days when even the salt cod were powdery at the bottom of their barrel and the sea smashed itself against the shore as if to scour it clean, but she had ceased to mark the seasons months ago. The east wing was for women and between the grey slates of its roof and the white plaster of its walls very little changed except for the pallor of the light and the snow thickening the panes. She hung in the light like a swelling drop of water, drawn by gravity to bulge and break, like a moon so low in the sky that it raked the jealous tides behind it. She screamed in the nurses' arms and watched her own blood running over hospital sheets and chafing hands. It would not find its way down to the sea here, drawn off by the pine-matted earth like a balked and buried stream; she could not follow it down to her love.

Over and over, they told her her husband was dead, as if she had not heard the first time when she was nearly six months pregnant with her quickening son. The *Galatea* had brought the news in October when she returned from the Arctic grounds and the cooper who bunked above Ezra could tell the story, there in the cloud-scudded sunlight on Central Wharf with Elizabeth gripping his hands as though the birth-pangs twisted through her already. But it was something else, coring as disbelief as the men came tramping down the scrubbed gangplank with their kit bags over their shoulders and her Ezra was nowhere among them, not his harvest hair, not his salt-stained jacket, not his candlelit grin. All summer she had haunted the shore, praying for her courses, scrubbing the floor with sand; she burned the curtains and the bedclothes one night on the dry granite blocks of the seawall, watching the reflections break on the scale-black water like a beacon light, and still rose each morning with their harbor-smell in her head. As her belly rounded, she went less and less often into town, clutching shawls about her shoulders when she had to, pushing her way through the crowds on Pleasant Street as if she recognized no one among them, willing even the kindest questions away: she had no answers anymore. Her dreams were full of monstrous things, half-transparent skin stretched over half-luminous bones, cold blood in colder dark. For once she was grateful for her parents' disdain; she could not imagine telling them of their grandchild.

I am sorry, Mrs. McKay. I sent his letter from Frisco, soon as we were coming home, the letter that had never reached her, the letter that Ezra had not sent before he drowned. On the docks of New Bedford, she heard from a stranger what she should have known from a dream: how the whaleboats had gone out on the ice-lashed waves off Point Barrow, the new summer sun glinting thin as isinglass on the blue-scattered dip and fall of the Beaufort Sea, and the stout bowhead had blown twice as if hailing the whalers, who laughed. They were not noisy; they drew the boat alongside the rolling, slate-shining bulk of whale, and Ezra McKay had readied his iron, as neat and handy a man as ever shed blood to the sea—but when the harpoon went home and the powder went off, instead of dying or sounding for a sleigh-ride the whale heaved itself over in the freezing water as if it knew exactly where its tormentors lay. The iron-black flukes raised high, smashed down. Five men were pulled from the blood-strung wreckage of the whaleboat, but the boatsteerer never came back up. The more romantic or morbid among the *Galatea*'s crew imagined him tangled in the line's coils, pulled into the abyss after his own iron, as if the whale had turned fisher for him; Abraão Vieira, less sentimentally inclined and with an eye to the floes crushing close around the *Galatea*'s hull, spoke only of a man's chances between the ice of the pack and the breath-snatching sea. *We looked for him, Mrs. McKay. I swear we don't leave while he had one damn chance.* Around them the traffic of strangers bobbed and butted like brash ice, though she was the one insensible as a frozen thing. *Mr. Vieira, I believe you. Your kindness—I can't say—* He was not pulling away from her, haggard as she must have looked with blue-milk shadows under her eyes and her beach-colored hair pinned badly, fraying and flagging in the raw bright kick of the wind; his eyes were green as shallows, his crisp hair fairer than the long hands steady around her own, and she knew him from Ezra's letters, Vieira who knew something about every creature they might see on their voyage. He had slept more nights within the sound of her husband's breathing than she had herself. He was not lying to her. Elizabeth wanted to weep on his shoulder, this Creole man from Cape Verde in his faded red shirt and his old brown coat; steel-straight as a daughter of Thomas Bridgman, she let go his hands and said in the voice of her mother's drawing room, *I am in your debt, Mr. Vieira. To receive dreadful news from a friend is to know at least that the shock is not singularly borne.* The hard gulp of breath that finished the sentence was not grief. Her dead man's child kicked her a second time beneath the ribs and she must have said something to the living man to take her leave of him, but all she could remember afterward was the taste of tarnished pennies in her mouth, the whirl of cracked-china sky, and the cobbles pitching up at her as sickeningly as waves through a stove boat before Vieira caught her as no one had her husband, belly-up like a storm-heeled ship, a landed whale.

She would never know if it was the young doctor summoned from his practice on William Street who betrayed her, his raw-freckled face eclipsing Vieira's like an anxious and self-important moon. She was sure only that it could not have been Vieira himself, whose short scrawled letters the attendants handed on to her as if it were an ordinary thing for a madwoman to read her own mail. Sometimes in the late months of her confinement she dreamed of him, carving a cradle from wood as white as whalebone; the shavings drifted around him like snow or the feathers of far northern birds and he smiled over his work, the scrape and tap of his chisel an icy tattoo. Sometimes she dreamed of Ezra, real dreams that left nothing of themselves in the morning but the aching gulf of grief and the slow grinding beneath that of something she could not name so easily, deeper than mere fear. She did not dream of her father railing his invocations of whoredom and disease, her mother weeping as softly as a knife. Over and over, she repeated as calmly and clearly as she knew how that she carried no one's child but her husband's, which only another lunatic would have believed.

Had she been correctly insane like her wardmates with their starvations and compulsions, their manias and melancholias, Elizabeth thought she would have taken great comfort in the Danvers Lunatic Hospital with its wrought iron roof-crowns and its granite stairs, the flowering beds of its gardens and the sturdy fields of its farm. It was airy and industrious, sometimes obtuse but rarely cruel; she had smiled to see the profusion of dahlias inside and out of Dr. Kirkbride's model asylum. It was not his fault that she raked at the well-turned earth with her nails when offered a hand in the apple harvest, as if she might scratch down to some sunken vein of sea, that she could not handle the rushes of basket-weaving without thinking of slippery kelp and knotted wrack, the seaweed she had never seen tangled about her love's head. Given a wooden puzzle, she made a long skeleton of its pieces and imagined the whale itself, like a spirit flame rising. Everywhere were things growing, things rooted, things dying back to black earth under flying snow. She could not lie easy, so far inland that her husband could not find her. Sometimes she plotted what the staff called an *elopement*, disappearing over the dry stone wall where the trains whistled past Asylum Station. Even Salem would have been close enough to breathe of the sea.

Instead she tasted the salt of her own bitten lips and the carbolic sting of sweat, her body itself the wounded, ungovernable, thrashing leviathan; she dragged breath after breath of choking thin air and screamed for Ezra until the doctor's terse orders and the sweetness of ether muffled her away. Far and blurred as the dim end of a telescope, her husband sat at the foot of the bed, casting lots with dice of red coral on the starch-white sheets. The cradle rocked beside him, whiter still in shadows of glacier-blue and aurora-green. She could not ask him if the drowned felt so curiously peaceful, tugged and buoyed by pressures so vast and distant as to feel like natural movement; she could not even see him anymore, only the rush of bubbles, silver and glass-bottle green. The dice fell through her fingers into the dark. When the world drained back in, something small and white-swaddled was being placed in her arms, a doll arranged with a smaller doll to hold. "A fine strong boy, Mrs. McKay," she heard echoing from one of the nurses' mouths, genuine warmth that she could not quite feel through her numbed and swollen flesh; her stomach rolled as though she had been too long at sea and put suddenly ashore. The calm white walls gleamed around her like close-packed snow. "Wouldn't you like to hold your beautiful boy?"

It seemed to take a hundred years to close her eyes and open them, to understand what she was being offered and what she possessed. She had never coveted children as her sisters did, though she had said all the right things over the pink-and-white faces of their infants and their dark or fair downs of hair as they drowsed or mewed in their nursemaids' arms; it had frightened her to want one from her whaleman and then frightened her more to think of some fault in herself, five fruitless years on. For all she knew, her husband's children were scattered across the coasts of three oceans, never to be known to her, or perhaps even to him. She had never been sure what it would mean to ask. The bed was hospital-cornered and empty again, but she could still see the dice falling, blood-bright with pips of bone. "Yes," Elizabeth said. Her throat felt thick as drunkenness; she tried to clear it. She could name this one for his father. "Yes, I would," and she looked down through the frozen fog of ether into her child's face for the first and last time.

She was told afterward, during the first use of mechanical restraint, that she had tried to kill her child, to wring its neck between her hands as though she broke a lobster's back. She could not make them understand that what had slid out between her thighs on a breaking wave of blood was no more her child than the mess of shells and mud and seaweeds reeking by daylight in her bed had been her husband nine months before. Her son was lost fathoms below the Arctic ice with his father—only a truly mad woman would have mistaken the sea's leavings for anything else. She had seen the red grease of its skin like stripped blubber, heard it shriek like a mobbing seabird as it was snatched from her arms. Its eyes were a glaucous blank of waters, its mouth as mindlessly gaping as gills. Even its smell was murky as low tide under the sterile washes of green soap and bichloride. How could she ever have fretted that the sea was too far to find her? Her own body's salt was its signature. How had she been fool enough to fancy it her ally? It brought back nothing it had not already disdained to keep. For the sake of one short summer night, she had let it in and now she would never get free of its hollow roar in her ears, its restless beat in the slim veins of her wrists; she tried. Stronger hands than her own wrestled her down against cool cast iron that rang like nacre with her screaming, wrapped her fast in wet white sheets like a burial at sea. She had ceased to dream of Ezra with or without cuttlefish's ink running down his face like tears, of Vieira in his well-worn leather apron casting a weather eye over clouds as pale and solid as the sunlit beach of stones, of her parents whose final visit had made her laugh, raucous and stabbing as a gull, with their useless horrorstricken courtesies. *Take him,* she had jeered, no model patient with her insomniac bruises and her ward in the outermost wing, her grin like a moray's jaws, *take him for all the good it will do you. His father'll come for him in the end.* She did not dream once of the child, abyssal or adopted. She dreamed of cowries and ivory, pancake ice and palm wine, sealskins, skuas, the great moon over the sea.

By then she had lost her parole of the grounds, for glimpsing the Atlantic from Hathorne Hill: they still thought she screamed in terror or insanity. Alone with her books and cut flowers and the writing paper for which she was sometimes permitted a pen, Elizabeth thought that even a maelstrom could not rage as she did, a tsunami, a typhoon. Even the last resort of chloral could not drown her too deep for the tide.

Her husband came back in autumn, when the rain dripped off the slates and gables and the leaf-stripped trees bent like seagrass in the wind, while far and farther off the guns stormed at Amiens and Megiddo and Meuse-Argonne and she did not hear them, though she could have stood at the height of the Himalayas and not been out of earshot of the sea. Some years she thought it grew louder as the summer waned and the Arctic season with it; then she remembered how many years it had been. She did not know if men went out any longer in ships out of New Bedford or San Francisco to hunt the whale at one cold end of the world or another; if their women still waited for them as Ezra had sworn that as a captain's wife she would not have to do. Perhaps there were neither whales nor women left anymore, only men at war on a cold, bristling ocean of sunken liners and tin fish. She had no one to ask; even the new admissions were more likely to tell stories of ferry crossings or childhood holidays and she had heard the doctor warning the younger nurses not to encourage her during her nervous times. She watched the haymaking from her windows, the harvesting of squash and corn and turnips, the healthful markers of the farming year. On very good days, she read quietly in the women's pavilion, her still thickly braided hair a beach of grey sand. She was not supposed to describe herself so, as she was not supposed to say that the clouds above the burnt treeline were white whales' bellies, the late September sky they shoaled in the hungry, reflecting blue of the water she did not need to see.

She had no other words for the moon when it fell in watery vanes through the glass beyond the window guards and mottled the floor like foam. The room's small furnishings might have been hummocks of ice or heaps of whales' bones, without motion or color, all but the man in the dark coat turning back from the night view of the well-gardened grounds. He stood in the moonlight as though in a backwash of waves, his shadow dripping from his sea-boots; his hair still fell in the same fair untidy sheaf, but it was mossy with algae and a snail moved slowly across his cheek, browsing like a beauty mark among the barnacles and small wrack. "Oh, Lizzie," she heard: something in his voice hissed and swallowed, the dog whelk's rasp against black crusts of mussels, the suck of the tide at rocks and pilings and human feet planted in sliding sand. His coat was ragged as shipwreck, or perhaps it was partly changed to weed. When he held his hand out to her, it was full of pale ambergris. "Oh, Lizzie, my Lizzie-o."

Cold in her madwoman's bed, Elizabeth knew it for a dream. Ezra McKay would never have appeared to her in this drowned half-shape, her whaleman who had loved her enough to come back from the gates of death and the grip of the back-breaking sea to lie all night in her arms until the daylight melted him like a fairy tale, forgetting in the inhuman roll of the tide how much it would twist her to lose him again, how easily the sea could steal through his longing into hers, worse than any indecent disease. Only the gold in his ear gleamed true and imperishable. The rest was echo, water-warped and mocking. "Ezra," she whispered finally, because it was the wet shadow of her husband's face looking back at her with those comber-pale eyes, the tattoo at his wrist prickling with olivine spines. His fingernails looked like stone. She was not a sane woman; she had no need of politeness, even when her voice shook. "What are you doing here?"

He took another step closer; his shadow pooled along the floorboards like polished ink. That voice she could not recognize sounded as if it were choking on sandy water, on heart-stopping ice: "I couldn't wait."

There was a great wave rising in her throat; she swallowed it before it could wake the night nurse or one of her neighbors and recognized it as rage from the way it hurt, as familiar as the waterlogged phrases across thirty-three years. She imagined her husband falling bonelessly from blue waters into black, his life's store of words like stones in his pockets for the sea to tumble and cast ashore, none of them meaning any longer what they had gone down saying. The parrot's feathers. The white jade clouds. Her name. She could not pray to a God she had long ago ceased to credit, but she thought suddenly of distant Sundays: *and there was no more sea.* In her old woman's dry night voice, "Damn you to Hilo *and* Hell," Elizabeth said to the sea on the other side of her husband's face, and struggling out of bed reached for the wall switch to dispel its specter once and for all.

In the soft bloom of gaslight, Ezra McKay looked not a day older than his drowning. His coat was weather-worn melton cloth neatly mended at the seams, his wind-creased face scrubbed clean; he looked at the ambergris in his hand as if he had forgotten the time and put it back in his pocket, out of which small crabs did not scuttle. No salt water ran from his sleeve as he reached to pull the cane-back rocker over to the bedside, though it crackled beneath his weight as he took a seat in it, leaning a little forward as he had always, eagerly done. His hair shone strand by strand like a harvest field. As if it mattered very little, Elizabeth saw that he cast no shadow except across himself, and the rest of the ward in their paralyses and psychoses and plain heartaches slept around them, and she did not know anymore if she had turned up the light, if she was dead or dreaming or he was, if the sea, unbelievably, had not cheated her after all. She did not know anything except that she had heard of ghosts with consciences, but she had so rarely seen Ezra with one, she was not inclined to believe she had invented the look of it on him, stranger than the shape-changing of death.

To her husband this time, Elizabeth McKay said, "I didn't get your letter."

"I sent none."

"You must have known where to find me."

His brows winced together; she saw the reddened fleck of a cut through one, so fresh she knew it had not quite healed when he died. "I never meant to leave you so, Lizzie. Eighteen months to the Arctic grounds and back, that was all."

His living face was sober, but his voice was still the waves' wet growl, easy to be angry with. She was bitterly conscious of her spotted hands, her sagging wrists, her parchment throat. "And yet you left me waiting twenty times that."

"I am sorry, Lizzie. I am sorry. Sorry as I can be." He had the red and white dice in his hands again, turning and clicking like loose shingle in the tide; Elizabeth wondered if they had come from some port of his last voyage or some gambling hell undersea. Perhaps he had traded with one of his shipmates for them. She would not ask if Vieira was dead. A little wryly, Ezra added, "There's no ship's chronometer," and that was another question she had to close her mouth on. He was no table-rapper's guide, even if she could picture him far more readily on the decks of a ghostly whaler than reposing among some airy haven of harps.

"Then what brought you back to port at last?"

She said it like a challenge; she saw him hear it as one, a slight, tightening wave across his face that looked mostly surprised, as she imagined it must have looked even in the midst of brawls and brothels, ever the blue-eyed innocent with blood in his hair. Or it was real surprise, because he was saying as carefully as he could with his throat of thick waters, "The tide turned, Lizzie. The heart's tide. You."

In her early years at Danvers, she had written more letters than she could count, long, rambling, sometimes ink-blotted and more often furiously steady outpourings of everything she expressed otherwise in the howls of her voice and the wrenchings of her body, all the words sane women were not supposed to know. Sometimes she had rolled them into bottles of thick-molded amber glass whose corks still smelled of medicines, sometimes folded them with great care into the small envelopes provided through the good offices of the State Board of Lunacy and Charity; she had given all duly to the ward attendants to be mailed from Asylum Station, addressed in care of *the Sea*. Had any doctor asked, she would have admitted freely that she had no expectation of reply, only the hope that her vitriol would sink into the waters, not to dissolve and be lost, but to linger and stain, like poisonous Circe. She spat onto some of the pages, bled furtively into others. She dreamed of great reefs and shoals and kelp forests streaming gold in a glissando of pearl-green and knew she had failed. Even now, she could close her eyes and feel the drum and tumble of surf in her blood. It did not seem to point Ezra-ward, only toward the shore of her body, out to the endless, indifferent sea.

The thought tasted like old iron, rusting in bitter spray. "It can't have," Elizabeth said quietly. "There was no one for it to turn to."

"Oh, Lizzie, don't I know it? When you were—when our son—" Ezra was silent, looking down at his dice with their cracked coral faces; he rolled them once on the trim white counterpane, ivory-dotted in twos and threes. "There are tides," he said at last, and looked back at her.

Not far down the hall, the radiator-hissing, clock-ticking stillness of the ward broke with a muted cry and quick footsteps; the gaslight fluttered in its mantle and she was aware that her hands resting on the covers were cold, though her pulse still raced like a riptide. She did not like to think of loose limbs hanging in the glacial dark, turning in icy currents; she did not want to imagine the pattern of gyres and streams, a lyke-road of terrible waters, that could bear a dead man from the mouth of the Arctic Ocean to the mid-Atlantic shore. Ezra was a living man where the warm light touched him, all his scars and flaws and beauties as exact as Elizabeth had not known she remembered them, and then in the colder edging of the moon she saw again the barnacle crust like a fouled hull, the rotten cloth riddled with sponge and anemone. Beneath the hospital scents of carbolic and gardenias, the room smelled of harbor mud and shoreline juniper, the oily smother of the try-works, the brine-swept wild air of the open sea, as though a wind from nowhere tacked about and about the sea-routes that had compassed her dreams and his death. Blue as a boat's painted eyes, his drowned eyes gave her no clues.

She stirred against the pillows, all the small aches and stiffnesses of a woman fifty-nine years old, never graceful and no longer slender, woken in the middle of the night. "You left me worse than a widow, Ezra. The wife of a ghost. A—" She stopped herself with an effort as strong as shouting. *A prisoner,* she had almost said, *a madwoman,* but she had been mad already in her sand-scoured house in New Bedford, mad as any sailor's wife left railing from the shore at the sea that had stolen, one way or another, her man. She had smashed the melon-colored shells and the willow-blue china before her parents' eyes, swept the cabinet cards to the floor and flung down with a clatter the painted panel where a three-masted bark black and white as a petrel had sailed stiffly and precisely over pastel-green waves; she remembered her hands bleeding from slivers of broken window, a kittiwake with trapped wings frantically beating to be free. Afterward she had known the missed opportunity had been not burning the house itself: there was salt in the bones of it now. It would never be anyone's home but the sea's. "The mother of nothing," she said instead, and watched Ezra shift but keep silent. "Or did you think the tides would bring you that back, too?"

"No, Lizzie. I didn't think that."

"Then *what*?"

"You, Elizabeth. Just you. As long as I might. As soon as there was a way. I had to see you." With his glance cast up half in shadow, she could not tell if the faintest edge of a smile moved at his mouth or merely a trickle of salt water. She heard the sea-swallowed words as if she saw them laid out again before her with clay-cold hands: "You've the steadiest eye I know."

In their silence she heard her own breath like an unsteady swell. Crouched intently forward in her rocking chair, the *Galatea*'s fourth boatsteerer was watching her with the steadiness she remembered by candlelight, the years when she had told them both into the old stories of her father's library and never imagined herself waiting longer than Penelope, for a husband who was not after all the god in monster's guising but the slip of a soul lost to the underworld, dreaming under the Styx's black water of sleep. Every movement she made, he tracked like a man attentive to the movement of his blood—no, she thought, a tide to the pull of its moon. She wondered if a satellite had ever disowned its ocean, if the great weight and restlessness of waters rejected would go slack. Experimentally, she felt in her own blood, not for direction this time but gravity. Whatever else Ezra McKay had been in life, once she had not thought him a liar.

He moved before she could speak, rummaging through his pockets as suddenly as if he had mislaid pipe or papers, not meeting her gaze now like any ordinarily embarrassed man. She watched him set out the rough fist of ambergris on the bed between them, then a square-rigged ship soot-inked into a polished tooth, then a seal of black soapstone, lounging as if hauled out on its sleekly plump side; she had not touched a piano in almost forty years and she felt, over or under the quick run of notes, the quarter-tone of something discordant, important, unsaid. Slowly, she said, "Are there stars where you are, then, Ezra?" He did not answer; he was still searching as if he could not hear her, bringing out things now that she could not imagine he had carried in his coat or his canvas trousers across any ocean but the last and least known. Here was a handful of pearls dripping with salt-black mud, there a round-bellied bottle streaked green as the plunge of a wave. Silver dollars jumbled with sand dollars, brown-inked logbook pages interleaved with dark plates of baleen. Whale stamps, stick charts, looped strands of pink jade, she felt their weight compressing the mattress springs, opening wrinkles of shadow in the tile-white sheets like leads in sea ice, and when she repeated, "Ezra," he shook his head angrily and something small and goat-eyed and whorled in mother-of-pearl moved its glimmering arms in the palm of his hand. The question was rising in her thoughts like the whale's black back, shouldering ocean and all else aside. She knew before she spoke that it was not the question of a woman in mind of her immortal soul.

"Will there be a ship, Ezra? Will there be a ship for *me*?"

His hands were still full of Bible leaves and holystone, an iceberg's blue-amber shimmer beneath flaring sun dogs; then he put them down on the reef or the pack or the foam of the bed as carefully as if he released a live thing to the waves. Full in the gaslight, his face was as young as she could scarcely imagine either of them being, except that she had been younger still when she had lain with a drowned man in a house of salt and his heart had run to her on its tide. She smelled again snow and ether, fish guts and rotted weed. Vieira's breath had been sweet-sour of a winter morning when she lay as close as she had never dreamed him, one hand against the warm brown grit of his cheek. Her face was cradled in a bright spill of hair, like a beach with the dawn rolling up it, on a clean-ironed pillow that breathed of Castile soap and drying sweat. Under the limitless blue of the ice, her mouth filled with salt, and then her lungs, and then her bones. She knew him then, the sea and the sailor, the face and the mask. "Lizzie," he said gently in his voice of deep waters, "I'll wait."

Clear as the sight of a sextant, she watched him rattle the coral dice between cupped hands, slick and limpet-studded, scarred and brown as rope; she saw the throw and his shy, startled, stranger's grin, leaping to meet the danger he had always known she was. His name in her mouth was a seabird's cry, "Ezra—" She finished it to the moonlight and gaslight, hissing faintly in the creak of the wind. The chair rocked a little, as if its occupant had stood abruptly. Neither mussel shells nor kelp nor cutting spades lay in her bed. Her hands were freezing cold.

A sane woman might have been screaming, Elizabeth thought, but she would never be sane again and she had screamed enough. Stiff in the shoulders, she put her hands beneath the covers and did not imagine that she could feel the small worn corners of coral or the sheeting ice of a glacier; when she had almost stopped shivering, she turned down the gaslight until it was too blue and tiny to disturb the white froth of the moon. "Ezra," she said aloud, knowing he would not hear her, not knowing if the sea might, rushing along the inside of her veins in sinkings and upwellings, not to be halted until, like the song, it ran dry. The night nurse's footsteps paused at her door and passed on. In the bright and war-wracked autumn of 1918, Elizabeth McKay tasted salt on her lips that she could not remember crying, spray from a shore she had not seen since the last century. "Ezra," she said again, "I'll hold you to that," and turned to her bed to see if she would wake in the morning or merely leave pearls behind.

THE FUTURE OF ANOTHER TIMELINE

Annalee Newitz

TEN | BETH

Irvine, Alta California... Garden Grove, Alta California... Tustin, Alta California (1992 C.E.)

It had been a week since I took the home pregnancy test, and three days since Hamid said he'd be home. He hadn't called yet, which was a bitter kind of relief. I didn't want to tell him anything about my plans with Lizzy and her mom Jenny, but maybe if he'd called I'd have changed my mind.

I told my parents I was sleeping over at Lizzy's house, so they suspected nothing when Jenny and Lizzy picked me up. It wasn't a complete lie, of course: I would be staying with the Bermans that night. I left out the part where we'd be driving to Garden Grove for an off-the-books doctor's appointment, paid for with a year's worth of my saved allowance.

I kept having panic flashes as Jenny drove. I was going to die. My parents would find out. A fucked-up larva covered in teeth and eyes would squirm its way out of my womb and eat the world.

The doctor was a kinetic, pale man with matted hair on every part of his body except his head. It was weird to see him sitting in the receptionist's chair when we walked in. "You can call me Bob, because we don't stand on ceremony after hours." He reached out to shake my hand, then grabbed my fingers and turned the gesture into a little bow. "Milady. Welcome to my humble chamber." I could see bright lights in the office behind him, and a vinyl-covered exam table with metal stirrups attached.

Jenny hugged me. "We'll be right out here, honey." She and Lizzy sat in the waiting room while I followed Bob to the back.

He kept up the mock chivalry routine, twirling his hand in the air as he gestured for me to sit on the table. "You're quite a young one. How old are you?"

"Seventeen."

"Naughty, naughty girl!" He waved an admonishing finger at me. "Take off all your clothes and I'll be back with my instruments."

I wasn't sure why I needed to take everything off, but I also didn't think it was a good idea to ask questions. There was no hospital gown for me to put on, so I lay bare on the sticky plastic of the table, heels in stirrups and knees pressed firmly together. Hamid was probably back at home in Irvine right now, having a nice dinner with his family.

Bob erupted back into the room, trailing a device on wheels that I couldn't properly see. After craning my neck, I thought maybe it looked like one of those hair dryers my mom used at the salon, with the silver helmet that blew hot air evenly all over her head.

"I've got some good news and some bad news for you, naughty girl." Bob adjusted a lamp nearby, and suddenly I could feel heat against my legs. "The good news is that this is a state-of- the-art machine that's sort of like a vacuum, and it does the job really quickly. The bad news is that you might feel a little cramp. Can you handle a little cramp?"

"Sure."

"Okay, open wide." He slid a hand between my knees, and I opened my legs. Suddenly I felt his gloved hand inside me, covered in a cold slime. He grunted, withdrew, and pushed in the speculum. I could hear and feel its metal paddles clicking as he cranked me open until I thought I would rip. I focused my eyes on the ceiling, covered in white tiles, and tried to decide whether they were fissured or perforated. Then I heard rattling and what I thought was the low hum of a motor. Without warning, my abdomen wrenched with pain worse than anything I could have imagined.

I clenched my teeth and fists and stared at a place in the ceiling where a water leak had left a cloudy brown stain behind. I wondered if it was normal to feel like a giant lamprey was chewing and digesting my guts.

"Almost done." Bob sounded distracted. "It's not so bad, right? Some women love it. One of my patients had an orgasm when she was giving birth." He paused, as if pondering. "Maybe one day you will too, when you find the right boy."

Everything hurt so much that his words were just sounds that meant time was passing. Soon it would be over.

When he withdrew, it felt like I was giving birth to a machine. All the mechanical parts slimed out, and I was nothing but scraped tissue and diminishing anguish. I could feel warm liquid oozing out of me, like when I got my period.

"You'll be spotting for a few days, but if it starts to bleed a lot go to the emergency room right away." Bob scooted his chair around the table so I could see his face. For the first time, he sounded like a normal doctor. "Also, no sex for a couple of weeks. That's it. Feel free to go when you're ready."

He wadded up his gloves and threw them in a silver trashcan, the kind that pops open like a mouth when you step on its foot. Then he jangled out of the room, trailing the vacuum cleaner. I sat up slowly, and another warm lump dribbled out of me onto the plastic table, creating a heart-shaped puddle of lubricant and blood. I couldn't see any tissues or cloths for cleaning up, and finally hobbled to the sink to grab some rough paper towels. I washed up as best I could and jammed some fresh paper towels into the crotch of my underwear just in case.

When I stumbled out of Bob's office, I suddenly needed to throw up. The only place to do it was in the receptionist's trash can, so he wound up with two samples of my bodily fluid that day. I didn't mind leaving the smell there for him to find.

Lizzy and Jenny jumped up as soon as I came back to the waiting room. They put their arms around me and we walked out together like that, squashing through the doorframe three abreast. It was awkward and warm and safe. I felt shaky when we got into the car, but my bleeding had slowed to a mild seep. I really was going to be all right.

The radio blipped to life as Jenny started the car, and that shitty Don Henley song "All She Wants to Do Is Dance" came on. I thought I was going to scream, but instead I started talking, my words coming faster than outrage.

"I *hate* this song. Because everybody thinks it's about a woman who is carefree and beautiful, but it's actually about how Don Henley goes to some war-torn country and meets this woman who is in the middle of the most horrible situation ever, and all he notices about her is that she's dancing. That's the *only* thing he sees. She's living in this dystopia where the government is bugging discos and mobsters are selling weapons to the military, and he actually thinks that all she cares about is goddamn *dancing*!"

My voice was a little too loud. Nobody said anything for a second, then Lizzy laughed. "I hate this song too."

Jenny smiled. "I realize that I am totally uncool because I like Don Henley. I like the Eagles, too." Then she shot me a serious look.

"But yeah, let's listen to something else. Do you approve of Tracy Chapman?" It was mom music, but I still liked it. We sang along to "Fast Car" and sailed down the freeway back to Irvine.

◆

Hamid called me two nights later. I answered on the downstairs phone next to the kitchen, where my mom was washing the dishes after dinner and listening to everything I said. That was fine, because I didn't want to say much.

"Hey, it's Hamid. How's it going?"

"I'm good. How are you?" I twisted the curly cord around my fingers.

"Pretty good. What are you up to this weekend?" He didn't offer any explanation for why he'd waited so long to call.

"I have plans with Heather and those guys."

"All weekend? You don't even have time to watch a very special video history of the Mouseketeers?" His voice hovered between needy and sad. It reminded me of when we'd talked on the beach, where he'd pulled me into his melancholy and left an alien robot baby behind.

"Yeah, sorry. I'm just super busy."

"Well, what about next weekend?"

"I have a ton of SAT prep so…"

"So you're busy."

"Yeah."

I could practically hear him getting the hint. When he spoke again, there was no emotion in his voice. "Okay cool… well, anyway, maybe I'll see you around before I leave for UCLA. Or maybe not. Whatever."

"Okay cool. Bye." I hung up and tried not to feel anything.

My mom put down the dish towel and looked at me. "Was that a boy?"

"Yes."

"You were very nice. I thought you did a good job politely turning him down."

I had one of those split-second fantasies where I smashed every single dish my mom had painstakingly dried. The room was covered in powdery shards, and then it wasn't.

"I think I'm going out with Lizzy tonight, okay?"

I ran upstairs before she could finish saying yes.

Irvine Meadows was having a summer weeknight concert with four indie bands, including Million Eyes, and we'd been planning to see it for a few days. Soojin and Heather were already in the station wagon when Lizzy picked me up.

"So what the hell happened with you and Hamid?" Heather turned all the way around in the front passenger seat, kneeling on the pleather to face me. "He said something about how you are going to be busy for the rest of the summer?"

After what happened with Scott, I figured Heather could keep a secret. So I told her and Soojin the whole story. By the time I got to the part where I'd puked in the trashcan, we were parked in Irvine Meadows's most distant and secluded parking lot.

"Please don't tell Hamid, okay?" I looked at Heather.

She nodded slowly and then let out one of her crazy cackles. "Yeah, I can see why you might be busy all summer."

"It's not that Hamid is a bad person. Actually, he's really nice. I'm just not...I know it sounds weird, but I'm not in the mood to talk to him."

"That totally makes sense. I mean, he's my cousin, so I feel bad for him. But also he's kind of a dumbass." Heather stuffed some weed in a pipe and took a long hit. "You want some?"

"I want some! I'm done driving now, hello!" Lizzy reached for the pipe, still trailing smoke.

We passed the pipe around for a while, and then headed toward our seats. After the first opening act, I heard a familiar voice behind us. "Hey, guys. Great show, right?"

It felt like the hair was walking off the back of my neck. I turned around to see our social studies teacher, Mr. Rasmann, smoking a cigarette and looking very non-teachery in a leather jacket. He'd graduated from college only a couple of years ago, and a lot of girls at school had crushes on him.

"Hey, Mr. Rasmann." Soojin smiled at him. "I didn't know you liked punk rock."

"Yeah, I miss going to shows in L.A. But this lineup is great. Have you guys heard Million Eyes before?"

I knew I wasn't going to be interested in whatever he said next. My guess was that he only asked as an excuse to barf out some giant explanation of a band I definitely understood better than he did.

But for some reason Soojin fell into his conversation trap. "I love them, but I've never seen them live."

And, as I predicted, he took her reply as pretext to launch into a long commentary about Million Eyes that he'd ripped off practically verbatim from an article in *LA Weekly*. Lizzy pulled out a cigarette to share, and Mr. Rasmann leaned forward to light it for us. It felt cool to have a teacher do that, but it also reminded me of Bob, with his "we're not standing on ceremony" routine.

Lizzy grabbed my elbow. "Let's take a little stroll before the next band."

We wandered through the loge section, and Lizzy glanced back over her shoulder. "That teacher is so gross. He's always hitting on girls in my class."

"Really? Ugh."

Soojin raced up to us, almost crashing into the railing where we leaned. "Why did you guys leave me with that pervert?" I waggled my eyebrows. "Why did you leave Heather with that pervert?"

"Heather went to the bathroom."

"What did he do?"

"Well, at first I thought he was being nice. He was like asking me to call him Tom and talking about cool music. But then he was like, hey you have skin like a china doll, and do you want to party after the show, and it was super gross."

"That asshole has been molesting girls at our school all year." Lizzy had a furious expression on her face that I'd only seen once before, on the night we never talked about.

"He's definitely got a molester vibe."

"We should teach him a lesson." Lizzy's mouth hardened into a smile. Soojin grinned back.

I thought that would be the end of it. But Mr. Rasmann was still there when we got back to our seats, and Soojin wore a fake flirtatious smirk she only used to fuck with people.

"Hey, ladies!" He was trying to riff on a Beastie Boys lyric, and it came out sounding awful.

"Hi, um, Tom." Soojin shot Lizzy a look as she spoke. "So where do you want to go party after the show?"

He bared his teeth. "You should come to my place. I have some good bourbon I got from my dad."

"Can my friends come?"

Mr. Rasmann raked his eyes over us. "Sure. What the hell. It's summer vacation, right?"

We followed his directions to an apartment complex in Tustin. It was one of dozens of suburban developments built during the 1970s to look woodsy and natural. As we wandered between amorphously shaped plots of grass and stucco walls masked by trees, I hung back for a moment to light a cigarette that Lizzy had stuffed in my pocket earlier.

"I'll catch up, you guys! I'm going to smoke for a minute."

"See you there!"

They climbed rustic wooden stairs, and I leaned against a lamp post, blowing misshapen smoke rings and wondering what the hell we were doing. I kept thinking about Hamid and how I wished he'd said he was sorry about not calling. I was raging, irrationally, that he hadn't apologized for that evening he knew nothing about, when I lay naked on a table with a pain machine inside me. Smoke and anguish pricked my eyes, making everything blurry.

Suddenly, a woman rounded the corner, walking straight toward me, her trench coat flaring open to reveal knickerbockers and a high-collared blouse that would have been fashionable during the 1980s Gunne Sax craze. Her brown hair was pulled back into a long, thick ponytail.

She stopped directly in front of me and spoke. "I need to talk to you about Lizzy."

"What?" I was too surprised to ask how she knew me and Lizzy. She looked oddly familiar, but I couldn't place where I'd seen her before.

"I want you to know that you don't have to do something you'll regret. You can stop now. Tonight." She tilted her head. "Do you understand? You can go home right now and forget about all this. Don't let Lizzy suck you into it."

Now I was seriously weirded out. "What the hell? Who are you?"

"I'm…well, there's no good way to say this."

Lizzy opened the door to Mr. Rasmann's place and called my name. In that moment, his apartment felt safer than whatever was happening here, with this familiar—yet-unfamiliar woman.

"I gotta go." I raced up the stairs and left her behind, mouth open to say something I couldn't hear.

We checked out Mr. Rasmann's living room while he rattled around in the kitchen. He had some worn sofas and easy chairs and an admittedly excellent stereo setup. There was a framed poster of Sid Vicious over the turntable and some concert flyers tacked up next to it: Black Flag, Dead Kennedys, Bad Religion. Pretty good taste.

Soojin picked up one of those fat, clothbound books full of plastic pockets for photos and opened it to a random page. She held it up to show us. It was full of Polaroids of girls, some completely naked. I was pretty sure that one of them was in my fifth-period government class.

Lizzy gaped. "Why would he leave that out?"

Mr. Rasmann made a cheerful noise in the kitchen. "Found the glasses, girls! I'm washing them just for you, because this is such a special occasion."

Soojin put the book down slowly, in the exact place she'd found it. My entire chest felt like a vector graphic from that Disney movie *The Black Hole*: a flat, glowing grid with an abstract throat punched into it. I was nothing but a sketchy representation of gravitational forces.

But Soojin wasn't. As soon as Mr. Rasmann returned, she pointed at the book. "What the fuck is that?"

Improbably, he was unruffled. He arranged some tumblers around the bourbon bottle, then smiled at us. "That's my look book. I'm a photographer when I'm not being a high school teacher."

Heather narrowed her eyes. "What kind of photographer takes naked pictures of girls?"

"Those are art. A celebration of the female form. Beautiful women like you should understand that."

The astrophysical phenomenon in my chest suddenly exploded into life, filling my ears with radioactive particles, and I heard myself yelling from far away. "This isn't art! You're a fucking pervert!"

Soojin shot me a nasty grin and snatched up the bourbon bottle. "Want to know what we like to put in our look book?"

I was gratified to see the grin evaporate from his face. "What...what do you...are you photographers too?"

"I guess you're about to find out, motherfucker." Lizzy was practically growling. She'd added a streak of red to her mohawk, and it gleamed like fresh blood. Then she grabbed the bottle out of Soojin's hand and shattered it against Mr. Rasmann's face. He made a squeaking noise and collapsed. Soojin kicked his ribs with her boots. "Call me fucking china doll, you piece of shit? I'm Korean! And I'm *not a doll!*"

I started to laugh, then felt a throb of rage working its way up from someplace deep in my intestines. My body moved before my brain could catch up, and that's how I found myself on top of Mr. Rasmann, looking into the blood and bourbon that streaked his slack face. He had a faint haze of stubble and a few scabby pimples on his forehead. I pushed one knee into his chest, holding him down even though he was passed out and definitely not going anywhere. My abdomen cramped like it had in Bob's office, and then Bob's voice was in my head, telling me that my pain wasn't so bad. His words became a refrain, a maniacal repetition: *Some women love it. Some women love it. Some women love it.*

Mr. Rasmann opened his eyes and tried to talk. "What... what the fuck...you crazy bitches..."

I leaned down close to his face and put my hands loosely around his neck. "What do you think those girls were feeling when you took those pictures? Do you think they loved it? *Do you?*" Heather, Soojin, and Lizzy had come close, standing above me on the floor, witnessing."

Answer her, you dick!" Soojin kicked him in the ribs again.

He started to whimper and struggle under my knee. "They...they wanted to!" My arms felt loose and strong. "They didn't want it!" I was howling again, and my fingers were moving up his face, across the slime and roughness of his cheeks, until I was touching the soft skin of his eyelids. I could hear Lizzy and Soojin and Heather above me, taunting him and urging me on.

I thought about Bob putting his fingers and machines inside me, and Hamid's plaintive voice on the phone, and all the girls in that look book who couldn't tell us what they wanted. And then my thumbs were in the soft, warm place that Mr. Rasmann used to look through his camera. They curled in deeper. I bet he'd never realized that eyeballs were actually holes in his face. And every hole can be penetrated. I laughed again, as I jammed my fingers in as deep as they would go, maybe touching his brain, listening to his tongue slither around his mouth and deliver a final hiss of realization.

Then there were more sounds and Lizzy was grabbing my shoulders and Heather was hyperventilating and I'm pretty sure I had shredded eyeball on my thumbs. I finally tuned in to hear Lizzy giving orders. "…take that bottleneck with us and get a towel to wipe our prints off anything you touched."

I moved in a daze through the apartment, trying not to touch anything, allowing Soojin to hold my hands under hot water.

It was only when we returned to the car that I remembered the woman I'd seen outside, the one who knew me and Lizzy. Was she a possible witness, somebody who could identify us to the police? For some reason, I felt certain she was not.

The Doctor and the Damsel: A Fairy Tale of Healing

Cynthia Gralla

Agrippina followed the doctor because he saved her from the gallows.

"I would like you to come live with me," he told her as she was fitted for a bodice in her dressing room. Because he had acted as her savior, he now appeared to enjoy privileges she'd never explicitly granted. He entered her dressing room—her *own* dressing room, at age fourteen!—with barely a knock, not caring that her breasts were uncovered. For someone whose gimmick as an actress was concealment, his intrusion was intolerable.

Agrippina began to protest.

"Do not fear. I am a doctor," he pointed out with a smile. Then he expressed his wish that she leave the city to stay with him.

"What are you going to do with me?" *To me.* In the speech of frightened women, one preposition stands in for another like an understudy for a starlet.

"I am going to cure you."

"Of what?"

"The wolf taint."

✝

The doctor had long been fascinated by the body's madness and decay.

As a child, he had lost countless hours to the observation of his father's prized automatons. His favorites were a

Harlequin-and-Columbine pair who waltzed more expertly than the tides and a Japanese doll who served tea as if enacting the universe's smallest secrets. And he was abashed to think of how many books he could have read during afternoons he devoted to contemplating the waterworks on his family's country estate. His heart skipped as he watched the thin plumes of water leap from tree to tree, the tempo quickening unbearably until a jet tapped at the green canopy of the largest. Then would come a pause that encased the doctor midair as if inside a hanging scroll. Suddenly, a waterfall rushed down the trunk and into a stream that ran throughout the garden.

Years had passed since then, but the doctor's mania for theater remained. He loved observing a body, be it automaton or human, wrapped in the illusion of autonomy, of freedom from a great design. An actress falling into a faint on stage is only doing so because the script demanded it, just as an automaton curtseys because of her swallowed gears. What if, he wondered, every decision we made were at the behest of an internal script penned by anatomy and blood?

He'd been a medical student when this question became an obsession. At the time, he was recovering from his failed courtship of a dimpled, green-eyed comedienne whom he first noticed in *Le Roi*, a hit play in Paris, where he was studying and where he was still living when he found Agrippina. His mentor, a gentle wizard with gestures as precise as those of an Indian dancer, noticed his lingering depression over the green-eyed actress. So he invited his student on a call.

"We're going to see a friend from my hometown. A woman once famed as the greatest courtesan in Avignon."

At first, the young doctor suspected that his mentor was trying to distract him with an aged but still plausible beauty. But as soon as they arrived at her damp rooms, he realized his mistake. The woman appeared to have reached Biblical age. Her mouth was toothless, her hair less visible than her scalp.

His mentor talked affectionately with the woman, who stared at him with clouded eyes and nodded as regularly as a mechanical monkey with a drum.

When they left the chilly rooms, they gasped at the fresh air. His mentor told him, "That woman was a legendary beauty in her heyday. My best friend killed himself when she rejected him. But you see that we are all subject to time's savagery. Let that be your consolation when a woman denies your desire."

A strong impression was made, but not by those words. Rather, the doctor had fallen in love with the body in its last gasps. With the once-beautiful woman in extremis.

But after a few years of haunting geriatric wards, he developed a new interest at the other end of life's timeline. He then thought of nothing but mental illness in young women.

Agrippina was an orphan born in the Paris slums. Of course, she had not always been an orphan: for twelve splendid minutes, each an apostle of hope, she'd had a mother. Then she died, and the baby was cared for by a distant cousin. When this kind woman passed away herself, Agrippina was ten years old and destined for the bordello. The theater saved her.

She loved the actresses of the Comédie-Française, whose images appeared on everything from postcards to match boxes. Agrippina had been known to swipe the latter while she cleaned tables at a local bar. She stared into their painted faces as if holding a tiny prayer card.

Agrippina worshipped one actress in particular, a tall woman with chestnut hair, gray eyes, and red lips known only as La Bouche Rouge. Her talent was more impressive than her vulgar stage name suggested. Though she had started her career by kicking up her legs at Cirque d'Été in between the equestrian acts, she quickly moved on to the plays of Molière and Shakespeare. Whenever she took her bows, she blew a crimson kiss to one man in the audience. It was rumored that several had suffered heart attacks when she chose them for the honor.

By a similarly capricious process, perhaps, La Bouche Rouge plucked Agrippina from the streets. The girl had knelt at her feet one night when she emerged from the stage door. The actress was surprised by Agrippina's huge, luminous eyes, too blue to ignore and too young to be a threat. La Bouche Rouge adopted her as one might a puppy.

While Agrippina was being fished out of the gutter, the doctor completed his studies. Through his father's connections, he was offered an honorary appointment as a royal physician. It therefore astonished everyone he knew when he announced his intention not to practice.

His mentor tried to reason with him. "You will ruin your career before it has even begun. Everyone knows the only way to gain a first-rate reputation is by attending to the aching joints of fat aristocrats."

But the doctor said only, "I want to focus on my research."

"What research?"

"Research into hereditary taints. I want to know everything there is to know about the mad female mind."

By the time the doctor discovered Agrippina, she had already developed her curious beauty: upright posture, extreme thinness, full breasts, white skin, and long, raven hair. A succubus forced into a high-society ball.

She had also manifested a surprising talent. No one at the theater, from its director to the lowliest servant, had predicted that La Bouche Rouge's whim would amount to anything. Most likely, they thought, she would tire of the girl quickly and cast her out into the streets once more. No one would mourn her. The idea that some were doomed by no greater sin than chance was ingrained in theater people.

Nevertheless, Agrippina surpassed all expectations when, in an act of pique against the director, La Bouche Rouge demanded that the little girl be given a role in her next play. Most girls in such a role — just a comic-relief walk-on — could do nothing but mimic the ludicrous behaviors that make life lively, their performance pleasing only due to familiarity. Agrippina was able to do something far better: she made the familiar unfamiliar. Every shrug of her shoulders seemed ingenious, a promise that human beings could surprise. The fans loved her for it.

At age twelve she adopted the stage name of Shōnagon and affected the pose of a Heian-era court lady and poet. No one knew how she had come to know something of the distant past in a far-off land, but the public adored the persona. Men and women alike waited outside the stage door in freezing rain to glimpse Shōnagon in six layers of heavy robes. She covered up what other actresses bared, and admirers showered her with roses and chocolates as if gifts could open-sesame brocades.

As Agrippina's star rose, La Bouche Rouge grew surly. Her roles shrank in inverse proportion to her debts. Her passion for baccarat was greater than that she bore for any of her lovers, and unlike them, the vicissitudes of its games could hurt her. When her payments came due, she lashed out at everyone around her but at her protégée most of all.

Around this time, Agrippina/Shōnagon turned fourteen and was cast as the second female lead and La Bouche Rouge as the first in a new play written by the city's most celebrated novelist. Not without a sense of humor or knowledge of the theater's backstage conflicts, the playwright wrote the parts specifically for the two actresses and cast them as rivals. In the third act, the tensions between the women come to a head when La Bouche Rouge/Celestine replaces a prop knife to be used by Shōnagon/Emmanuelle with an actual knife. When the latter uses it on the leading man, she inadvertently kills him; is arrested, tried, and hanged for her crime; and Celestine reclaims her status as the theater's uncontested leading lady. Curtain.

Except this was not just what was written but what actually happened, or almost. On the packed opening night, someone *did* replace the prop knife that would masquerade as a real knife with a true knife. When Agrippina-as-Shōnagon-as-Emmanuelle plunged the knife into the male star's heart, she killed a talented man who had just begun to study calligraphy in secret, hoping to impress her.

La Bouche Rouge scoffed at the notion that she had planted the knife to frame the girl. "Why would I do that? I have nothing to fear from that gutter rat. Besides, she knew she could just blame the crime on me. The play itself is her alibi, or so she thought."

Needless to say, it was all very confusing.

The authorities decided it was best to put Agrippina on trial. At the very least, it would provide the citizens with a good show. Such diversions were necessary to distract them from sacking the palace, which they took into their heads to do every decade or so.

After she was taken into custody, a prominent man demanded to see her. The doctor had been in the audience that night, looking for a new muse. What he found was better: the ideal research subject.

First, the doctor carefully explained to the authorities why the young girl could not have committed the crime.

"Her pupils are not dilated when she tells the story, which means she is not lying." He said it with such assurance that it must be true.

"W-well," the chief of police stammered.

"And then there's her age. Pubescent girls are among the least likely to commit premeditated murder. And you must agree that she would have had to plan the murder, replacing the knife beforehand."

"Then you think it was La Bouche Rouge?"

The doctor shook his head. "No. I think it was suicide."

"Suicide!"

"Yes." The doctor's manner was quiet and his eyes piercing, as if he were listening to the world's heartbeat. "It is obvious that the man was dying of love for Shōnagon. He put the knife into her hand so that she would deliver the blow that ended his torments."

This explanation was neat, and its elocution so faultless that the chief of police immediately anointed it fact. Agrippina was released and welcomed back at the theater by her colleagues and public alike. Ticket sales soared as the fatal play was revived. After all, a woman worth dying for was a woman worth watching.

La Bouche Rouge was replaced in the lead role by Shōnagon, because the director of the Comédie-Française knew Agrippina's arrest had raised hopes in her rival that exoneration had cruelly dashed, and he feared that the older star would now try to frame the ingénue even if she hadn't before. He kept La Bouche Rouge happy by slotting her favorite play into the next season's first night.

Everyone was happy, especially the doctor, because he had gotten away with his swindle. He was absolutely convinced of Agrippina's guilt.

It was this guilt that caused him to knock on the girl's dressing-room door and propose to take her far away, back to his family's country estate.

✢

As sure of himself as he was, the doctor never understood why Agrippina agreed to go with him. Shōnagon the actress was at the height of her fame and was destined for a triumphant career — at least until she married, hopefully well, and retired. Why go off with a stranger, even if he had snatched her from the noose?

Agrippina never told the doctor that the night before his visit, when she returned to her dressing room after the play, she had been greeted by a long red envelope, bleeding against her mirror like a slashed throat. Inside was a single slip of paper with only two words:

He knows.

Better to lead him out of the city, she figured, where there were fewer people to whom he might divulge the truth. It would just be for a while, until people forgot about the scandal in favor of a new one.

Like all medical students of his day, the doctor had studied natural philosophy as a precursor to medicine. One can't understand the body without understanding the natural world surrounding it. Still, the doctor was an apostate in his rejection of Aristotle's *scientia,* or certain knowledge, as a basis for medical theory. "There is no certain knowledge," he thought to himself. "Only what you observe or experience. But even then, you cannot rely on things to remain the same or as expected. Therefore, perhaps you can only understand a disease if you make it happen."

Agrippina was to be his guinea pig, but he didn't see the situation as exploiting her. After all, she was already mad; only an insane woman would have killed an innocent man for no reason. On their journey to his family's estate, as snow charged their sleigh, he asked her the question he would ask only once:

"Why did you do it?"

In the dark of night her skin looked like the surface of the moon. After a pause whose pregnancy promised answers, she said, "I didn't do it for the reason you think."

"And what do I think?"

"That I was trying to frame La Bouche Rouge."

"That's not what I think."

Her startled eyes appraised him. Suddenly her whole body relaxed. Agrippina still didn't trust him, of course. Trust was the one sensation she could not imagine simulating as an actress, much less feeling in real life.

"I was afraid…it would be the obvious conclusion. I don't think Philippe was in love with me. Smitten, maybe, but he wouldn't kill himself over me. But it was a tidy explanation everyone wanted to believe."

In the distance, the snow teased the rooftops of a mansion, but Agrippina could see nothing beneath it. It was as if the great house was a body, and she was seeing its floating, severed head.

She continued, "I didn't dislike Philippe. He meant nothing to me, but he was always sweet. A good actor too. But I wanted to see if I could get away with it. And once the idea occurred to me, I could think of nothing else."

"Do you hear voices?"

"I hear thoughts, but they are my own."

The doctor smiled. The girl's combination of coolness and insanity thrilled him like a caress.

At that moment, the hedge maze in front of the house swallowed the pair like sleep's nothingness painted deep green.

†

The doctor never asked her again about her motivations for murder, but he levied many other questions. She only asked him one, on several occasions: "Why are you doing this?" But never in the plaintive voice of a lamb about to be sacrificed because her heart had been chilled like a bowl of berries. There was now only coldness in her, even when questioning her dark fate.

He never answered, but occasionally he would reveal to her a little of his past in reply, as if confession were the same as explanation. On one such occasion, he told her how his mother contracted syphilis from his father, who had contracted it from a tart. It ravaged her far more quickly than it did him, and she was dead before the doctor was ten and she thirty, but not before it had blinded her. "I still see her moving through the house with one arm outstretched. It looked like she feared not bumping into furniture but cruel entities coming at her."

Usually a few sentences at a time were all the doctor shared, but on this occasion, after a pause, he kept speaking. "I was afraid I had inherited syphilis too. When I was in her womb. Often the symptoms lie dormant for years.

"So when I first fell in love, with the daughter of our caretaker, I was afraid to make love to her. Instead, I proposed a suicide pact. Really, I was just looking for an excuse to die, convinced that my blood contained horrors. We both took an overdose of sleeping powders. But she died and I woke up."

As he talked he prepared a syringe; it was time for Agrippina's daily injections. After he plunged it into her arm, he admitted one thing more.

"Since then, I have kept my distance from women as much as possible. That is partly why I choose to admire actresses. They are made to look at, to worship, but not to touch." And he swabbed her puncture wound.

✢

What exactly did he do to her? Later in life, Agrippina tried to remember. But a haze hangs over all cures.

She recalled piles of books. *De humani corporis fabrica* by Andreas Vesalius, which the doctor said challenged the knowledge of human anatomy that Galen of Pergamon, a physician and philosopher of ancient Greece, had amassed by dissecting monkeys. A copy of *British Pharmacopoeia* enlivened by termites. An ancient *Bibliotheca Anatomica*. If the doctor consulted these tomes, he did it in her absence, but he prodded her, for hours on end, in rooms honeycombed with their insights and damnations.

When she concentrated hard, the past leapt up inside her, inflamed like a story told by campfire. The doctor looming over her, a shaman intoning prayers in an unfamiliar language and smearing her forehead with blood. The image flickered, and he was then sitting primly on a bed, the teenage Agrippina kneeling at his feet. The two of them were praying, but the crucifix swaying in his hand looked like the watch on a chain he used to hypnotize her.

In another scene, the doctor was attaching greedy leeches to her white skin; she screamed, he laughed, and the monsters sucked bad blood. Then he was talking patiently, explaining the theory of humorism; she looked down at her dark dress as he parceled out her blood, phlegm, and yellow and black bile. The instruments changed with the memories — scales and incense becoming forceps and needles — but the doctor was always, always talking. About autopsies and dissections, plagues and contagions, the resurrection of Greek medical models in the Renaissance and the embrace of empirical science that followed.

Agrippina began to wonder if the doctor healed only as an excuse to talk.

In her memories, the chronology was confusing, but it seemed that as the months passed, the doctor began to elicit speech from her. By that point, she had been silent for so long she could only speak the words of others, so she offered him monologues from the plays she had performed. But no, he wanted something else, something deeper. Yet how could she share with him what she did not know was there?

"It's in you to access," he insisted, and she sank under waves as he ordered her to sing out songs beneath that sea.

This mania for catharsis was followed by a rage for vaccines, and Agrippina was pricked so many times she dreamt she was full of holes. The doctor began to ply her with pills when she was sad and speak of her genes as if they were a piano to be tuned. She didn't understand what he was talking about, but it made no matter, for when she turned eighteen, he expelled her from his care.

⸸

Agrippina never knew if he had always planned to kick her out once she reached a certain age. Certainly, the doctor had grown irritated during her final two years with him as she began to display a dark forest of symptoms he got lost in. Joint pain floated around her body, afflicting first her knees, then her elbows, then wrists and knuckles. The pain was always symmetrical, the balance of its design mocking the body's malfunction. Then came periods of fatigue, slight fever, and an occasional blush across her cheeks and the top of her nose. The last passed over her every once in a while, too seldom to be tied to her menstrual cycles, but the doctor blamed her hormones all the same.

"Your womanhood wreaks havoc with my work," he scolded. But he knew her gender made it more fascinating too.

At times, she felt pain even when she took a deep breath, but terrified of his anger, she didn't tell him. Sometimes the disease is easier to take than the stab at its cure.

Despite her efforts to hide her troubles, one morning the doctor coldly diagnosed the situation. "You are incapable of adapting to a cure."

"Have I done something wrong?"

"You must leave."

She was surprised that she hesitated, but then, she had nowhere else to go. So much time had passed. She doubted the theater would take her back. How to even get there? And she was now sick. After all his talk, after all his injections and pills, she was now sick.

But she sought out the nearest village and searched for pity disguised as lust. Agrippina found a husband soon enough. He was sturdy and laconic. She was still crazy, maybe, and she still fell prey to pains and fevers, but the seasons' march left little time for thoughts of murder.

✝

She gave birth to a daughter named Giselle, and her husband died. Rumors of her black arts circulated. From the start, the villagers had noticed that Agrippina harbored a grave respect for wolves at odds with their own fear and hatred. The pale, dark-haired woman even left the wolves offerings of food on new-moon nights. Three days after Giselle's birth, as Agrippina resumed her round of chores, she discovered that they had returned the favor, depositing, in the same spot, a stag's bleeding carcass. While several men retrieved and cooked it, she stood by watching, Giselle a cupped moon in her arms.

As Giselle grew, Agrippina realized that she hated her daughter. This was not true, could not possibly be true, she thought at first. Could it? Something did shift over time, though, and eventually a maternal indifference mutated into hatred.

She smelled wildness on her daughter. The taste of summer fruits in winter and sunrise at dusk. The wildness she'd had when young. The wildness that wasn't bad in itself until she expressed it by murdering an innocent man.

Giselle never walked when she could run, never ran when she could send a horse charging. Often, she went out riding in the morning and returned long after dark, even on starless nights when nothing lit her way. She ignored the village boys who hounded her steps like puppies. But she kept a sharp eye on the moon and once a month let loose a howl, its cry as icy as New Year's moonlight.

As days slipped into the river and Giselle began to bleed with the moon, the girl smelled more and more like wolf. Agrippina couldn't get away from her scent. The scent of closeness, underbrush, rain, and spices she hadn't tasted since she was pretending on the stage.

In another moon's turn, Giselle would turn fourteen, be betrothed, and marry the same day. The decision of bridegroom was neither the girl's nor Agrippina's. It was the village elders' choice, and they were known to pair the wildest young women with the harshest, oldest men. They forced girls into bondage when the wolf taint, for those who had it, was most ferocious.

Fourteen. The age of the mother's murder, and the age her daughter's will would die.

Meanwhile, the physical symptoms that Agrippina's pregnancy had halted returned with a vengeance, and they worsened as her daughter aged. As she grew feebler, she recalled the doctor's prognosis when she left him:

> "You may be okay for a time. But the wolf taint will always return. You are damned by it."

And then she knew that the doctor had only saved her shell from the gallows. The rest of her — the once-was-wildness, cured like meat — was still hanging from it.

Giselle's birthday always brought heavy snows. It fell in February, during the breeding season of the wolves.

Shortly after dawn, the villagers gathered in the square as if for a stoning. Most of the girls, their long hair tightly plaited, walked to their wedding nervous but excited. They knew they were steps away from a husband, childbirth, and all the secret knowledge the grown women braided between them as they worked.

But Giselle wasn't nervous. She was defiant. Her hair unbound and tumbling to her waist, she looked more beautiful beast than blushing bride. As she stepped onto the raised platform where she would vow her obedience for eternity, she shouted,

"I will marry no one but the wolves."

The town's healer, an elder who could have been either man or woman, rushed forward and bound Giselle's hands behind her back. The girl was clearly mad, and madness could not be allowed to roam among the people. Agrippina watched as three grown men dragged her daughter to the healer's hut.

That night, Agrippina heard shrieks from the healer's hut. The night was so thick with the howls of nearby wolves that sorting Giselle's pain from the pack proved impossible for any villager but her mother.

The sound seared Agrippina, its true blade striking a false heart.

By midnight, everyone was sleeping soundly, the villagers having drunk all the mead meant to toast nuptials that had not taken place. To tread as quietly as she could, Agrippina ran barefoot across the snow. The cold burned like coals beneath her feet.

The ageless, nameless, genderless healer was asleep on the floor, forehead smeared with blood. On a cot, Giselle was bound from head to toe in white cloth. She was to a bride what a child's stick toy is to the proud animal it figures.

Agrippina at last understood what the doctor could not.

She understood the difference between a madness that maybe cannot be cured, like hers, and a madness that needs no cure, like Giselle's.

She understood, too, that it is madness to try to cure without consent, and it is madness to attempt to cure what we do not want to understand.

Giselle was still unconscious as Agrippina unwound the cloth from her limbs. She'd been bled to pallor, and her mother worried that she couldn't walk. But at that moment, the wolves' clamor grew louder. At its insistence, Giselle's eyes opened.

She and her mother saw each other for the first time.

"Go," one whispered, or both of them did. Mother watched from the village edge as daughter loped into the woods to join her kind.

At the next full moon, Agrippina heard howling in the distance. During the hour of the wolf, she knifed the dark with her happy cry.

Welcome to Your Lifting

Tara Campbell

My sister sat across the table from me in the hotel restaurant, holding the brochure by its edges as though it were infectious.

"'The Samami Center is a place of freedom,'" Mia read. "'Millions of persons around the world have chosen to manage their fertility with us, and we hope you will choose to exercise this right with us as well. Our Sisters have drawn upon centuries of Samami wisdom to bring our method of fertility management to the United States in a manner that is both reliable and humane.'"

"'Persons'?" she repeated, handing the pamphlet back to me over her half-eaten pancakes. "Why 'persons'? Why not just say 'people'?"

I shrugged. "I don't know." I had no idea why she would choose to obsess over that word, given the range of objections she'd lobbed my way over the past few months. I was just grateful we'd gotten past the *Why not just say "women"?* part of the discussion.

Mia hmpf-ed. "At least you're doing this before any 'persons' move into yours."

"You mean fetuses," I corrected her. "You mean before a fertilized egg implants and ownership of my body somehow transfers to *it* rather than *me*."

Her lips twitched to the side, and she picked at her hashbrowns. I was exaggerating, of course. Personhood at conception hadn't quite become the law of the land, but not for lack of trying. I wasn't going to sit around and wait.

My stomach rumbled; I wasn't allowed to eat the morning of the surgery. I'd hoped Mia could at least have gone without one meal in solidarity, but of course she'd ordered an outsized breakfast, probably hoping I'd dig in and derail my procedure. When she'd offered to drive out to the Center in Maryland with me, I'd wondered whether she was coming to offer grudging sisterly support or to talk me out of my plans. The past two days had been a passive-aggressive combination of both.

"Anyway, it's time to go." I took a sip of coffee and gestured for the check, reminding myself that she was only trying to help — in her own way.

"Want me to drive?" she asked.

"No, I'm good. It'll keep my mind off food."

Besides, we were almost there, and I wasn't about to risk having her go rogue and drive me anywhere else.

An hour later we rolled up to the Samami Center, an enclave of sleek low buildings featuring smoked-glass windows and shining white surfaces, their glare softened by overcast skies. The main facility in the middle was connected by hallways to smaller buildings around it, which I assumed were the suites for clients like me. It would have been nice to stay here last night as well, to be able to sleep in, but insurance wasn't covering any of this, and the two-night minimum stay was all I could afford.

As soon as we stepped out of the car, I got a whiff of the citrussy scent I'd read would permeate the air.

Sniffing the air, Mia seemed pleased too, despite herself. "Do they have fruit trees around here?"

"No, those are essential oils," I said, grabbing my backpack out of the trunk. "Lemongrass, orange, peppermint. They're supposed to have antibacterial and antifungal properties."

"Oh, right, I read about that new age stuff."

I let it go. It didn't matter how normalized this was in the rest of the world; Mia chose to read its newness here as suspect. But at least she'd looked at the website.

We walked past a man with a clipboard inspecting a series of slim, cylindrical metal posts topped with flat metal discs, maybe ten feet tall, lined up between the parking area and the front door.

Mia looked at me with her *what-the-heck-is-that* face.

I shrugged. "Sculpture?"

The lobby was impressively clinical-looking, everything stainless steel and spotless white — even the metal detectors had been retrofitted in white, blending in for a less jarring experience. The Samami woman behind the counter was barely older than I was, but her hair gleamed silver, just like in the pictures. Real hair, but almost the same shade and sheen as Christmas tree tinsel, a striking contrast to her olive skin.

"Ms. Irving, welcome to the Samami Center. I hope you had a smooth trip here." I nodded, and she turned to my sister. "And you must be Ms. Waters?"

"*Mrs.*"

"Mrs. Waters, we so appreciate your presence here to support your sister's reproductive choices." After checking our IDs, she handed me a packet with keycards and a facility map. Her smile was genuine, and her eyes were kind, despite their glacial blue.

"You're in Suite Seven; there are two keys there. You've got just under an hour to settle in before your pre-procedure consult. You'll check in for that off to the right here," she said, pointing toward a set of clouded-glass doors.

"Do I come with her for that?" asked Mia.

"You can, but you'd just wind up sitting out here. The first part of prep is a mental cleanse, which the client does alone."

I could feel Mia's eyes rolling from where I stood.

"But your support is crucial in post-op," the woman continued. "We'll notify you when the procedure is over and take you to the recovery room. We'll advise you on how to keep her comfortable the rest of the day and tonight—and we hope you'll be there for the Lifting tomorrow?"

Mia sighed. "Yes, I'll be there."

↔

No one knew where the Samami women originally came from, or how many there actually were. For over a hundred years, their enclaves had been popping up around the world, but there didn't seem to be one country, or even one continent, that could clearly be defined as the first.

What we did know:

> They all identified as women, calling each other Sister, no matter their age. They all wore the same full-length, long-sleeved tunics made of delicate white cloth; and all had the same long, silver hair.
>
> They worked in threes: an elder guiding the Lifting and Keeping, together with a young girl, and a third Samami woman of some age in between. There were many more women in the compound, however, and they rotated into the circle of three to spell each other, preventing any one Sister from Keeping to exhaustion.
>
> Although they didn't seem to have relationships with people of other genders, even fleeting ones, there always seemed to be at least one pregnant Sister in each Center. Regeneration was important to them, with new babies and children growing up in the Centers to take their places in the triads of women holding the uteruses aloft.

Something else we knew:

> The Samami women aged more quickly than the rest of us. Their work regulating the floating of our uteruses, slowing ovulation, preserving our fertility—all of this allayed our concerns about racing the clock, giving us more time to decide what futures we wanted. At the cost of theirs.

Nevertheless, it was work they said they were happy to perform.

↭

My phone rang while Mia and I were settling into our suite.

"Hey Mom."

"Hi honey. You at the Center now?"

"Yeah, we just got here."

She lowered her voice: "How was the trip?" She knew Mia was coming with me, and like me, she wasn't sure when or how my sister had become so conservative.

"Well, we made it."

She chuckled. "You must be starving, honey. When's the procedure?"

"Soon." I held the phone out to check the time. "I have to go in a few minutes. I want to visit the ovary bank before my consult."

"Okay." I heard her breathe in the way she did when deciding whether or not to bring something up.

"Mom, what is it?"

"Did you see the news?"

I shook my head as though she could see me.

"That Maidens of God group tried to barricade a Center out in California. They had to arrest about a dozen of them to get them out of the way."

I exhaled, exasperated.

"I know," she said. "They're getting more aggressive. You didn't see any of them over there, did you?"

"No." Though thinking about it, maybe we had. There'd been a couple of people with signs near the turnoff, but their signs were too small to read. And, of course, my thoughts had been otherwise occupied.

"Good. Okay, well, I don't want to make you late. Everything will be fine, honey. Tell Mia to call me. Love you."

"Love you too." I hung up and looked over at my sister rummaging through her overnight bag. "Hey, did you see protestors outside when we drove in?"

"How's Mom?"

"Fine. She says to call her later."

She pulled her charger out of her bag. "Yeah, I saw a couple."

I nodded, debating what the point would be of going any further with her. I knew where she stood on the Samami method: it's not natural, it's against His will, they're just harvesting women's organs, etc. At least Mia toned it down face to face. But her social media posts were another matter…

"Time to head over," I said.

Mia had offered to walk me to my consult. I guided us toward the ovary bank on the way, hoping to convince her I wasn't just "throwing away our legacy" as she put it, which didn't even make sense to me because she'd taken her husband's last name, and their future children would all have his name too. And anyway, since she *wanted* to have children, did the world really need *me* to reproduce as well?

Nothing here was likely to change her mind, but I needed to do something to occupy my thoughts — it wasn't every day I banked a part of my own body. I'd read up on hysterectomies, but this wasn't the same thing. Somehow your body held space for the missing organ, and you didn't need hormonal supplements. It seemed too good to be true.

And yet, somehow, the Samami method worked. According to their materials, over a million people were living perfectly healthy lives while their uteruses floated in the Sisters' care. Hundreds of thousands of women around the world had come back to retrieve their uteruses and successfully given birth; thousands had donated their organs to others who needed them. The term "Samami babies" was becoming as antiquated as "test-tube babies" — at least, in other countries.

"Well," Mia said. "Are we going in?"

I blinked. I was standing in front of the frosted-glass door of the ovary bank, unsure whether we were supposed to knock or just go in. Mia reached past me and pushed the door open.

The Samami woman inside greeted us so warmly, I felt compelled to apologize for not having an appointment. "That's quite all right," she assured me. She was almost as pale as her tunic, a nimbus of light behind a sleek white desk. "How can I help you?"

"Well, I'm — Opening today." That's what they called the whole procedure, the extraction and Lifting of the uterus, the banking of eggs: Opening up your options. "I just wanted to see where they'll be. The eggs."

"Certainly, Ms…"

"Irving. Lisa Irving."

"Welcome Ms. Irving. And you?" she said, turning to my sister. "Are you also Opening with us?"

"No," snapped Mia. "Just her."

"Well, thank you for being here to support Ms. Irving today." Clearly accustomed to gliding through hostility, she invited us to have a seat on the white chairs in front of her desk. "I'm happy to help you better understand the process. First of all, you should know that for the vast majority of clients, the eggs remain in their ovaries, together with the uterus. We track their numbers here, ensuring that each client's wishes for their use are maintained."

She placed a form on the acrylic desktop in front of me. "You've received this in your information packet via email, I hope."

I nodded. The menu of options had been included, but I hadn't really been able to properly visualize it.

"There *are* a lot of options," she said kindly. They all spoke with the same, unidentifiable accent: slightly Nordic, somehow West African too? "You'll go over all of this in your individual consultation, but basically: you can donate any number of eggs you wish to make available to others who may need them. You can set a minimum number to retain for yourself, or waive a limit and let fate decide. The difference is, by slowing down the menstrual cycle — by which we mean the follicular, ovulatory, and luteal phases — we increase your window of viability. We decrease the speed of the cycle by about half, giving you in theory twice as much time to decide what's best for you."

"So, it's just the accounting here?" I asked.

"No, no, we do keep certain deposits here as well, eggs as well as the complete uterine/ovarian system, in cases where they require special handling due to illness or injury or other needs." As she spoke, she motioned toward the frosted-glass wall behind her, through which I now noticed shapes moving back and forth. More Sisters at work.

"Isn't that great," I said to Mia, unable to resist. "Preserving all that life."

Mia's mouth was a tight line.

The Samami woman kept her smile neutral. "The process does enable one to unequivocally consent to conception. Eventually we'd like to bring down the costs for clients, so everyone can have that choice, but it's proven very tricky in this country."

I sighed. That seemed to be the whole point of government lately: to resist anything that gave women a choice. Abortion was banned in my state, and there was talk of targeting contraception next, all in the name of "the children" and "family values." It made no sense to me, but it did to people like Mia. When I first told her my plans to come here, she'd accused the Samami women of "stripping women for their parts." At least she was looking at the form now, reading it, informing herself. Maybe she would finally understand why I wanted to make this choice for myself—while I still could.

"Can I keep this?" she asked.

"Well, this is for the patient. But here," she said, sliding a different paper toward her. "This FAQ sheet provides a pretty detailed introduction."

Mia flashed a polite smile and took the pamphlet. I folded and pocketed my form, aware of my sister's eyes on it. On the way back to our suite, I noticed more of the silver posts out the window, their brushed steel gleaming in the sun now that the clouds had cleared.

Mia saw them too. "What passes for art nowadays," she snorted.

I stopped and crossed my arms. "Do you have to keep sniping at everything here? I didn't ask you to come."

"I—" She continued looking out the window, but her face softened. "You're right. I said I was here to support you, even if I don't agree with it."

I let out a sharp breath. "Look, we've talked about this: it's not abortion, it's not Plan B, nothing's even getting fertilized—"

"You know what these things remind me of?" she asked, nodding at the steel pillars. "Remember string art?"

My mouth hung open for a moment. Not in a million years would I have put it together, but now I could see it—the giant posts set up around the Center like pins, waiting for thread to be wound around them, back and forth across the facility to create some intricate pattern you could only see from the clouds.

"Wow, that's one from the archives," I said. She'd tried to teach me when were in our teens, but I didn't have the patience for it. "Where did that come from?"

She shrugged, a small smile on her face.

"You were so much better at it than I was." A laugh bubbled out of me. "Remember my deformed dolphin?"

She chuckled. "Poor DD. I tried to get you to so slow down."

"Oh my god, it was awful." A swell of nostalgia hit me. "I wonder if Mom still has the horse you did." I could see it clearly in my mind: evenly placed silver pins outlining the form of a horse, white threads crisscrossing a maroon felt background to fill in the stallion tossing its mane.

"Probably." We looked at each other, smiling — of course, Mom kept everything.

Then Mia's expression changed and she grabbed my hand. "It's not too late to change your mind, you know."

I squeezed her hand. "I won't."

She let go of me then, and I watched her walk away.

↭

I was glad Mia wasn't with me during my consult. It left me a little rattled, and she was the last person I wanted to see while I was feeling any kind of shakiness about the whole thing.

The Samami counselor had been completely transparent, almost to a fault. She showed me photos of exactly what they would be removing, and the images weren't easy to look at. Real uteruses aren't that sanitized, pristine pink they show you in the textbooks in school. Real uteruses are bloody and red, the ovaries and fallopian tubes encased in globs of protective tissue, attesting to the fact that human bodies are not naturally severable. We are not like those neatly packaged Invisible Man and Woman dolls, all of the organs clean, separate, and dry.

She also showed me an image of a uterus and ovaries after they'd been sanitized and prepped for Lifting. I marveled at how small the uterus actually was. This thing, seat of life and subject of so many battles over power and control, looked like nothing more than a palm-sized chicken heart. My own heart pounded at the thought of mine being outside my body.

And, the Samami woman reminded me, that was still my choice to do or not to do. Even after I signed the forms and she showed me to another room for personal reflection, she assured me I had the right to refuse the procedure. If I chose, I could simply walk out of the reflection room and sign another form retracting my consent, then check out of my suite, and only have to pay a fee for the consultation and late cancellation.

If, on the other hand, I wanted to proceed, I would merely need to change into the purple robe and press a button for them to fetch me. The room was comfortably warm and lavender-scented, and the robe hung right there; and yet, this thing I'd been saving up for, and had doggedly asserted the right to do, suddenly seemed so…radical.

Was there no other way to have control? Could it really be that the only other choices were taking hormones, or having a foreign object lodged into my uterus, or hoping a diaphragm stayed in place, or relying on condoms (as much as one could with tearing and stealthing), or being the saintly, virginal woman the Patriarchy wanted me to be—until the Patriarchy felt horny.

And until they outlawed even those options?

For now, at least, it was still up to me.

I imagined my uterus in the hands of the Sisters, floating serenely, waiting for me to take it back whenever, *if* ever, I should want it; my eggs plentiful and perhaps helping someone else until—and again, only *if*—I was ready to use them myself.

I breathed in. And out.

And I reached for the purple robe.

↭

The next morning I was up early, still sore—and hungry. All I'd managed after the surgery was some applesauce in the afternoon and soup in the evening, so I was in the mood to make up for lost time. I picked up the phone and ordered waffles, eggs, bacon, hashbrowns, things Mia would like too, since I knew I couldn't possibly finish it all.

It was just the lazy morning I needed, nibbling from a bedside tray and reading until I dozed, then nibbling some more. I was saving as much energy as I could for the Lifting that afternoon. The rapid turnaround wasn't ideal, physically — staff would have to roll us out to the field in wheelchairs — but doing it this soon ensured the organs remained fresh.

While I ignored work emails and social media, Mia was restless, constantly on her phone, texting away, excusing herself for calls.

The one call I took was from Mom.

"Honey, are you okay?" she asked, her voice tense.

"Yeah, I'm fine. Just a little sore, but nothing more than expec —"

"I mean the protestors."

"Where?"

"There. At your Center."

I put the call on speaker and thumbed to social media, where it didn't take long to find posts about a dozen Maidens of God picketing across the street from the main gate. I stretched to look out a window, but my room was facing the wrong direction. "I can't hear a thing from here," I said.

"But nobody said anything?"

"No. I guess it's not a real threat."

"At least not yet. Is Mia there with you?"

"No, she just stepped out." Like she had for so many calls today. "When we're done I'll text her to call you."

Mia texted back: she'd heard the protestors, loud but not dangerous; yes, she'd call Mom.

I searched for more information on my phone, but the pain meds made me drowsy. The next thing I knew, I was waking up from a dream where Mia was pinning my uterus to a square of maroon felt. A moment later my alarm went off, meaning I only had an hour before the ceremony.

Wincing at the ache in my lower abdomen, I rubbed my eyes and reached for the pain pills. I almost dropped them when I noticed Mia sitting in an armchair, intently staring at me. After I fumbled with the cap for a bit, she seemed to snap out of whatever was going on in her head to come help me.

"Are you sure you want to do this?" she asked, dropping a pill into my palm and handing me a glass of water.

"Well, they already have my uterus so…" I sat up to swallow the pill, then handed the water back to her. "They'll be here soon to get us."

"No, I told them I'd wheel you out."

I raised an eyebrow at her, a bit surprised she'd want to play any kind of active role in the ceremony.

"I mean, with the protestors…" she began. She sat back down and folded her hands in her lap. "I asked one of the Sisters about those metal posts. Turns out it's a new security system."

"Well, at least they're being proactive," I said.

She shook her head. "It's still being installed. They haven't turned it on yet, and I'm afraid someone's going to try to get in before they do."

I blinked and focused on her. Her concern was genuine enough to make my pulse spike. "Did they say something? Was there a threat?"

"No. No, honey." She reached over and held my hand. "I'm just… I just want us to stay close. In case. Let's be sure to stick together, okay?" She tried, unconvincingly, to smile past her nerves.

She helped me to the bathroom, where I changed my post-op pad and did what I could with my hair and makeup. I wrapped a fresh purple robe over the lilac nightgown they'd provided, trying to rekindle the joyful anticipation I'd felt earlier, but the moment was soured. On the one hand, it was nice to see Mia's concern for me, but on the other hand, I wondered how much of that concern was merely a reflection of her own anger and paranoia.

And on the other-other hand, we did enter the facility through metal detectors.

Once I was ready, I couldn't help but notice how Mia clenched the wheelchair's handles. I reached for my phone as I sat down to be wheeled out to the Lifting field, but then I remembered the rule against any kind of camera-/video-capable devices at the Lifting site. I put it back down and told her I was ready to go.

When she pressed the button to open the doors to the back of the facility, I heard the faint noises of shouting from a distance, though I couldn't make out any words.

"It's all right," said one of the Sisters. "We normally have a few protestors outside. Today just a couple more than usual."

Mia followed the other Sisters, pushing me up a winding path to the field out back. The wheelchair proved incredibly light and easy to steer, outfitted with some complex array of wheels and pulleys. It figured, given the Sisters' emphasis on sustainability, that they would incorporate human-powered devices wherever they could. Indeed, the Lifting was entirely powered by the Samami women, and despite the shadow of Mia's concerns, I was eager to finally see it up close.

I breathed in, letting the citrussy air lift my mood. A slight breeze rippled native grasses on either side of us, and the sun warmed my face as I closed my eyes and tilted my head back to greet it.

"Thank you for being here, Mimi." I hadn't used her nickname for years; now I wondered if we could maybe be that close again, or at least begin to. She was here, after all, putting aside her own beliefs to support me in my own.

Mia wheeled me into a clearing set up like a natural amphitheater. A Sister showed us to one of a dozen spots marked out in a wide semicircle around a low hill in the center. Three Samami women stood in a circle on the hill, oblivious to us, their arms raised into the air, their white robes and silver hair wafting gently with the twirling funnel of air they generated amongst themselves. It was a clear, controlled tornado, a swirl of air that rippled like heat off summer asphalt. But it wasn't heat. It was the Lifting.

A middle-aged Samami woman with tawny brown skin wheeled the last client into place, then stepped between our semicircle and the ring of three Sisters. When she smiled and folded her hands together in front of her, all murmuring faded away, leaving only the twittering of birds, the tiny saw of insects, and the gentle whir of the air spinning behind her.

"Welcome to your Lifting," the woman said, nodding to each one of us in turn. I glanced back at Mia. Her expression was one of guarded curiosity.

"The Samami Center is a place of freedom," the Sister continued. "Persons of all genders come to us to manage and safeguard their reproductive lives, entrusting us with their hopes for the future. These hopes take different forms for different persons: Some of you may plan to use your uteri and ovaries, but later. Others may not be entirely sure if you'll ever use them. Still others of you have consented to release your reproductive organs to whomever might need them."

As she spoke, I looked around the semi-circle from a young blonde woman, to an Asian woman somewhere in her thirties, to an androgynous-looking person, to another one who presented male, all of us with our own stories and our own reasons.

"We thank you for your trust and your courage — for it takes courage to take control."

Twelve Sisters filed toward a steel cabinet, the gauzy white fabric of their tunics floating as they moved, making them look like angels. Each woman retrieved a silver box from the cabinet, then turned to approach the twelve of us. My heartbeat sped up as a smiling Sister walked up to me, my box resting on her palms. She held it out to me. It was about the size of a jewelry box, and my name was inscribed on the lid. I exchanged a respectful nod with her as I accepted it and placed it on my lap. The box was heavier than I'd anticipated, and I felt its chill through the fabric of my robe.

"From beginning to end, this process happens only with your consent. My fellow Sisters will open the door, but only you can decide to release what is yours into it."

She turned toward the trio of Sisters with their arms in the air, then raised her own. The twelve Samami women who had handed out the boxes followed suit, raising their arms and moving them apart as though opening heavy curtains. The funnel of rippling air before us began to take on more density, coalescing into a wisp, then a haze, then a swirling, conical fog. From above, a dark line began to form, spidering downward toward the earth while thickening at the top. Something was opening up.

The movement of another Sister hurrying over caught my eye. She spoke into the ear of the woman leading the ceremony, who then told the other Sisters something I couldn't hear. Together they all mimed a closing action with their arms.

My chair jolted as Mia clutched the handles. The dark line down the center of the funnel disappeared while the cloudy fog faded back into clear, rippling air. While the original three Samami women maintained the funnel, the ones who had been conducting the Lifting ceremony quickly conferred.

"What's going on?" I asked; but instead of answering, Mia swung my chair around and started wheeling me back toward the facility. I clutched my silver box to stop it from sliding off my lap.

"Excuse me, everyone," said the Sister who had begun the ceremony. "We've had some unsettling news."

A murmur rose behind us, and I turned in my chair to see what was happening, but Mia kept rolling me away.

"We are safe," the voice behind us continued. "There is no active threat here, but for your safety we must postpone your Lifting. Please listen carefully—"

"Mia, stop. I can't hear what they're saying."

"We're fine," she insisted.

Then we abruptly stopped, and I heard something clatter to the sidewalk. I caught a glimpse of Mia's phone on the ground before she picked it up.

"Excuse me."

I turned to find a short, plump Samami woman standing in front of us. The woman held out her hands. "I'll need to take that."

"What?" Mia asked.

I was surprised too. Rules were rules, but why would they confiscate someone's phone during an emergency? "I'm sorry, she just forgot—"

Then I noticed the woman was looking at the silver box in my lap. "I'll need to take that from you," she repeated. "For safe storage."

"What's going on?" I asked, handing the box over.

"There's been an attack on another Center," said the Sister. "We're okay here at the moment. We haven't received a threat, but we're taking precautions until we have more information. Shelter in place in your suite; we'll keep you informed."

By then other wheelchairs had begun to overtake us on the path. The Sister gestured for us to follow them before she hurried in the other direction to secure my uterus and ovaries.

My head felt light as Mia maneuvered me back into the building, threading past Sisters pushing carts and equipment and guiding clients back to their suites. Their actions were quick but smooth — they'd trained for this. They'd had to.

As soon as Mia wheeled me into our suite and shut the door behind us, she started packing.

"What are you doing?"

"Get your stuff," she said, throwing her clothes into her suitcase. "We're leaving."

"But we're supposed to stay here," I said, clutching my chair's armrests. "Shelter in place."

Mia wheeled me into my bedroom and put my backpack on my lap. "Gather your things, we've got to go."

"But —"

She bent down and put both her hands on mine. "Please. Trust me." The look in her eyes frightened me. All I could do was nod.

She rushed out, and I heard her clanking around in the bathroom as I packed. "I'm grabbing both our things in here," she yelled out. "We'll sort it out later."

This was not my meticulous sister. A cold feeling settled in my gut. She knew something. She'd asked around about the security here…

No. She'd said some pretty inflammatory things online, but she wouldn't actually hurt anyone. Hurt me.

Would she?

I pulled out my phone. A quick search pulled up breaking news about an armed attack on a Samami Center in Seattle. Shots fired.

"Lisa, you almost ready?" she called from the living room.

According to the report, the assailants knew exactly where to go. They went directly to the Lifting field and —

"Lisa!"

I started and looked up from the article. Mia stood at the threshold of my bedroom.

"What are you doing, we have to go."

I swallowed. "What's going on?"

She hesitated.

"Mia…" I held my phone out to her. "They're saying it was the Maidens of God."

She was still silent, but the way she gripped the door jamb…

Mia set her jaw and rushed in, reaching for my phone.

"Stop!" I stuffed my phone inside my backpack and pushed her hands away. Pain spiked where my uterus used to be, squeezing my eyes shut and curling me over into myself. "Are they coming here?"

She sank to her knees in front of me. "I don't know." I heard her breath shudder, like she was trying not to cry.

"Mia, what do you know?" I opened my eyes and scrutinized her. "You have to report it."

"There's nothing to report," she said, brusquely wiping her tears and yanking my backpack closed. "Let's go."

There was still a dull ache in my pelvis. "Let me go check myself, at least."

She slung my backpack over her shoulder and wheeled me into the bathroom.

"I might need something from there," I said, reaching for my bag.

She didn't hand it over. "There's pads in the drawer. I'll be right outside." She closed the door behind her. "Just be quick."

I had to think. I had no time. I backed the chair up to the door, looking around the room as though I'd find an answer written somewhere.

There was an emergency phone next to the toilet.

But what if she went to jail? I'd be the one who sent her.

The pain had faded enough for me to stand. I checked my stitches and post-op pad for fresh blood. None.

I had to think.

Mia knocked. "Lisa?"

"Just a minute."

The article said the assailants headed directly for the Lifting area. Here, Mia would know where to send them. But she wouldn't.

Would she?

I activated the brake on my wheelchair, then opened and closed a couple of drawers, pretending to look for pads to conceal the *click* as I locked the bathroom door.

Mia knocked again. "Lis, need some help in there?"

Her voice. It was the old Mia, the one who patiently straightened my crooked needles in the felt, who tried to show me how to guide the thread around them.

"Mia?" But I didn't know what else to say. She couldn't be part of this. Even if she hated the Samami women, she couldn't possibly do this to me and all those other people.

She rattled the doorknob. "Hey, Lis, open up."

"Mia. What do you know about this?"

This time she banged on the door with her fist. "We don't have time for this. Open up."

Leaning on the counter, I took one slow step after another toward the emergency phone.

Mia banged again, insistent. "Hey, are you okay? Lisa, come on, talk to me." Her voice wavered between anger and concern.

I clutched the receiver, but I couldn't bring myself to pick it up and call anyone. Not yet. Not until I understood.

"No, Mia," I said. "You need to talk to me."

A pause. A long sigh. "It wasn't supposed to be like this."

I waited.

"I was just…" She paused. "It was all just supposed to be protesting. Just signs. No weapons."

My head felt light. "Well, that didn't happen in Seattle, did it? So, what about here? What about those people outside?"

"I—"

The phone rang under my palm and I jumped.

My heart thundered.

The phone rang again.

I put the receiver to my ear.

"Ms. Irving?" It was a Samami woman's voice. "Are you and your sister all right?"

I hesitated. "Yes."

"Good. We're calling to update everyone. Our facility is still safe; the protestors are being cleared; we have additional security on the way. We're asking everyone to stay put until we know more."

On the other side of the door, Mia began to cry.

"What should we do…" I asked. "If we — if someone had information. About the Maidens of God?"

"That would be very helpful."

I swallowed. I didn't know anything, really. And Mia said it was just a protest.

"For everyone's safety," prompted the woman.

Then I heard a click. And a shaky breath. It was Mia, picking up the phone from the other room.

"Ms. Irving," the Samami woman asked, "is there something we should know? Something that could prevent further harm?"

"Yes," said Mia, her voice stuffy with tears. "There might be."

↭

Police, FBI interrupt armed plot against Maryland Samami Center

Law enforcement raided a Leesburg, VA, home late Sunday night, seizing a cache of weapons and bomb-making materials they believe were intended for an attack on a Samami Center in nearby Potomac, MD. Social media posts link the homeowner to the Maidens of God, an unofficial network of opponents of the Samami Sisters' technique of reproductive management…

Comments:

*Holy sh*t, those MOG b*tches are bonkers!*

That's supposed to be "pro-life"?

Until you disagree with them, sure!

ok they were out of hand but so are those clinics, tearing those women up and hanging their organs up like some kind of meatlocker

So blow them up?

Under His eye, motherfuckers! Blam blam!

This isn't God's will.

Epidurals are? Where is the section on IVF in the Bible?

Oh, the real theocrats don't want you to have those either

God: "I didn't ask for you to do this..."

But like, how do you amass that many weapons and stuff and nobody catches you?

Free country. We have a right to arms, not to abortions

This isn't even abortion. This ensures you won't need one.

This is what happens when we eliminate sex ed from school.

Don't bother arguing with them, some people refuse to understand.

"Welcome to your Lifting."

Weeks later, I am hearing this for the second — and hopefully last — time. It's the height of summer now, and we're all wearing sunglasses against the glare, even the Sisters. This concession to practicality creates an odd disconnect with the diaphanous white gowns, the flowing silver hair, the Samami women with their arms raised toward the whirling cone of rippling air.

Or perhaps the strangeness lies with who *isn't* here, and why.

"The Samami Center is a place of freedom," says the Sister leading the ceremony. "We have faced many challenges, but we persevere; and we are grateful to all of you who continue to come to us to manage and safeguard your reproductive lives."

Mia isn't allowed to be here, of course. She told the FBI she was supposed to be gathering information for an exposé, not an attack. She'd been promised there would be no violence.

The Sisters come around to us, one by one, with our silver boxes. I hold out my hands, nod when my box is placed into them. Everyone else whose Lifting was delayed that day has already been accommodated. I, on the other hand, took a little longer to be cleared, my organs safeguarded in the ovary bank until today.

The Sister speaks about choice and power, and I am left to ponder how little of either remain for my sister.

The Sister instructs us to open our boxes and look at the beautiful decision we are making. I open the lid and stare down at the pale-pink, pear-shaped organ in its bath of nutrient gel. My eyes trace the swell of my uterus, the elegant curve of my fallopian tubes, my plump, oblong ovaries. I look around at all twelve of us, holding our uteruses: such small, delicate things, unaware of all the outrage they're creating just by being outside our bodies.

"We will now commence the Lifting."

The Samami women raise their arms and move them apart, and I realize that the speech and the opening of boxes and the opening of the air are happening in a different order this time. They must have made changes, for security purposes. So much of having these organs revolves around security — even choosing to give them up.

The funnel of air coalesces into a whirling haze, and the familiar dark line forms and lengthens, threading down the length of the funnel. The top of the dark line thickens and splits, like someone curling back the pages of a book. All I can make out inside is brightness.

"Even now, the decision is yours," says the Samami woman. "You can close the lids of your boxes, if you choose, or you can let your uteri Lift into our care."

It is a strange feeling to hold part of your own body in your hands. It is even stranger to see it lift itself, still glistening, and float toward a glowing crevice of light spliced into the air. It rises until it becomes a hazy silhouette against the brightness, a dark spot floating with eleven other dark spots into the radiance beyond.

Would seeing this have helped Mia believe?

My chest feels full, and I blink against tears. I feel joy, yes; relief, yes; but mixed with a new anxiety. I don't know how long I'll be able to afford this. Mia's legal bills will be immense. But she's my sister, and that's my choice. This is all my choice.

I look around at eleven other faces tilted up into the light.

May this always remain our choice.

The Last Witch of the Ewes

Anya Johanna DeNiro

For so long I had taken what was given to me, and I had accepted it. This, I had thought, was a form of strength and patience. In Oer-Vestal, the only place I had ever lived, I thought I knew the boundaries of who I wanted to be: a mother, first and foremost, and a survivor lucky to be alive from a husband who was hundreds of leagues away from me.

I certainly didn't consider myself a witch.

For certain, I was good with plants—I collected them and sold them in the village, and I was known for that. That was my escape nearly every day, to the meadows and the abandoned orchards, a far walk from Oer-Vestal. When my son Raiben was small, I would sling him on my back and meander. He would reach up as I walked and try to grab the branches, and I would laugh and tell him, no, no, Raiben, and I would duck lower. I would let him play in the meadows as I bundled the herbs with cords. All of this passed as a dream, and I was happy, even when I was otherwise alone.

I could feel the earth below my palms hum a little, but honestly I thought nothing of it. I thought *everyone* could feel that.

There were many little things that might have led me to become a witch, but I suppose I had eased into it, like a bath whose water was too hot, but in which one keeps sitting, in hopes that it will cool a bit.

When I became a witch, I was thirty-five and had no idea of what I had coming to me. All was not as neatly ordered as I had sometimes imagined my life to be. *East of the moon, west of the chaos,* people used to say about those people who needed to leave the village. I never did. But all the same I never quite found what I was looking for here in Oer-Vestal—a true home with other witches—either. No, they were all dead, or cast out decades ago by the Triumphal. I had no real reason to continue, because I was picking up scraps of a tradition—the tradition of the Ewes—that had been burned out of living memory.

But I did continue. More than that—I fought and clawed to make the secret world more visible, and perhaps more importantly, to know who I was.

Because it turned out I didn't have any idea.

I watched about a dozen rokhs pass over our village, flying in an arrow formation towards the black smoke far to the east, the high badlands where nothing really grew and the war raged on. Why would I—why would anyone ever want to go there? The rokhs passed on until they were dots, and then they were gone. These rokhs would have no reason to come to Oer-Vestal. These were not the rokhs who dropped off supplies for us, rather those flying above me were full of spiked barding, instruments of war against the harpies. Meanwhile the Aelyf who lived in the hut by the river on the other side of the palisades wanted to cheat me again for the wightwillows I had gathered, by the Ka'rth graveyard. Fae was my only customer who did not come to me; the Aelyf by custom was not allowed in the village. My son Raiben, so tall and solemn at all of his ten years, came with me this time in hopes that his presence would soften the Aelyf, but it was not to be. The price was poor—just a couple of black scripts that fae curled on faer long finger before handing them to me—but I took it anyway.

"Why didn't you fight for more?" Raiben asked as we walked back up to the open gates of Oer-Vestal, surprising me. The town watcher nodded at me as I passed through. She was already into her cups.

I shrugged. "I suppose I don't have very much fight left in me," I said, and that much was true. His father was off in the City of Chrysolytes, which sloped into the Sea of the Mare's Song, with the towers that caught the sunsets and reflected them back onto the moon, or so I'd heard.

The farther away, the better, when it came to him.

The Aelyf was the only one of faer kind that I knew, and fae had to have been ostracized at some point from faer own kind, but I didn't ask. Fae had runes etched up and down faer arms, but I couldn't read them. They were neither old or new script, but something else. I couldn't tell if they were a punishment or not. They probably were. I got Raiben to bed that night in the little cottage that my former husband's family used to own and no one else had sought to claim, and I curled up by the fire and cried until there were only embers. Not for my former husband—the cottage was no place of love, except for my mother's love for Raiben—but rather for whatever dreams I might once have had.

When I was young, I was told by a traveling wonderworker, that I would have an uncanny ability, should I choose to develop it, to divine time and nature with smooth pebbles, the sea's shells (though Oer-Vestal was nowhere near the sea), and the wind. And that, given enough time, I could make the wind and water do what I wanted them to do—provided an appropriate sacrifice was made to the Ewes. My family, of course, did not believe in the Ewes, only the Empire Without Sorrows, and these thoughts were soon banished from me by a byrch rod my father had cut with his fleshing knife, and the casting away of my little collection of pebbles that I hid under my hide mattress into the River Oer.

That was the end of it.

The Aelyf stirred up these memories, and I did not like it.

✦

Oer-Vestal had about five hundred people inside its wooden walls, and a few who lurked outside of them, like the Aelyf. And like Halex. Whom I would not think about, since she was away from me. Lord Willingness' shabby, rambling castle was perched on the high hill called the Cairn above the town, and the Vest River snaked between the town and the hill. Oer-Vestal was a port, although not a very popular one anymore, now that the rokhs brought their own imperial commerce. Still, growing up, when the docks were busier, I saw the azure caravels from river ports farther up the Vest, and the trade barges that went upstream with the Ewes' cantrips from farther down, towards the sea.

I had always called it home, for better or worse, and had never traveled farther than a day's walk from Oer-Vestal; to the Wintering Market in the North; or the village of Vorpal Sink, even sadder than ours, in the south.

In the early morning, the smoke atop the eastern mountains hadn't cleared, turned more orange. My son was sleeping still. Soon—not that morning, but maybe in another year—he would have to sign a script to enter the fields. Or apprentice himself to another trade—anything except tanning, my father's profession, for I would not allow it. If he did apprentice himself, it would be extremely unlikely he would be able to stay in Oer-Vestal, as none would want to take my son. Not because he wasn't well-liked—he was—but because many in town were afraid that my husband would return any day from soldiery and debauchery, and seek to claim what he called his, and put his thumb on Raiben like a scale.

Perhaps he would return. But I was not afraid of him. I would slit his throat. Or I would poison him with a death nettle. At any rate, I watched my son as I let him sleep, cooking pearl lentils over the fire. I was never a good cook. They popped and sizzled a little. The sparrows had a nest in the hole in the roof. Needed to be patched but the daubed nest would seem to do the job for a while. He finally woke up, stretching his arms and staring into the fire.

"Did you sleep good? Did you dream?" I asked him, like every morning.

"I dreamed of snakes," he said, shaking his head. "I think it's the schoolwork with the script."

"Maybe lift your head up from the script," I said, running my hand through the hair on that very head.

I added a few dried cyanberries and put the bowl in front of him. He wrinkled his nose. His father would say that I doted on him, but his father was nowhere to be found.

"Mom," he said, sitting up and brushing his mop of hair out of his eyes. I was happy. By the Ewes, I was happy, for one gleaming minute. He was learning to read, and though he found it taxing, I figured that it would serve him well with any trade he took on. The lector, a woman named Sandryn who was my age but acted much more wizened, was with the Order of the Liventine, which supported the Empire Without Sorrows, spreading across every little village that used to have nothing but little lordlings who didn't pay much mind to whatever duke in the cities claimed their lands. The scripts were both money and worship, and at times a whispered form of divination, for those who were called by the Empire Without Sorrows. That was the New Script. Raiben's had a good head for numbers and words, but I hoped that was not his path.

I had learned to read when I was a girl—not from the wonderworker, it should be stressed—but that was a different story altogether.

I hated the Empire Without Sorrows—the dire, austere festivals, the nosy parsons, the fact that no one would explain in a couple sentences who or what the Empire Without Sorrows *was*, except that it was centered in the faraway capital—but in many ways I had no good reason for my hatred, except that my former husband worshiped them boisterously and with too much show. Sandryn was firm though kind with my son and absolutely thorough in her instructions. But I still didn't trust her. I didn't trust any of them.

Every month the Liventines would distribute food to everyone in the village: grain, sweet butter that was still cold, oils from the olive trees of Sjaricka, dried fruits, white and blue linen for spinning, and if winter was coming, furs. The goods came on the backs of rokhs from the capital. We grew plenty of our own food, of course, and tended our own animals and tithed much of it back to the Liventines, but we had enough in excess of everything else that this did not seem like much of a burden. It was not a time of leisure, but we had enough. We all had enough.

"Those filthy Ewes never did this for us," one of the younger women named Felwaa (who was a new-wife from the mountains and honestly sounded like she was trying too hard) said to one of her friends while passing out of the grocer's cottage. I wondered if Felwaa *wanted* me to hear this. "It was always, like, what could *we* do for *them*?" She trailed off. She was, it had to be said, born after the Empire Without Sorrows came to power, so what did she know.

With that said, the Ewes were difficult to understand, much less worship. In many ways they didn't seem to be pleased by any sort of contact whatsoever. And when I was too young to remember, all of the witches were driven out or killed when the Land Ordinations happened, and the war with the harpies began in the mountains. Or at least, that was where it was closest to us, though still quite far away. Though many of the cairns and field lines of the Ewes had been destroyed by the Orders, I knew a few things about the Ewes, mostly from Halex (I have not discussed her yet).

There were three Ewes: the Green, the Pearl, and the Roan, which might not have been entirely a Ewe at all—or rather, a Ewe, but also something else. Anyway, Halex would tell me that they would bring good fortune by burying tufts of wool, prepared in ceremony at different points in the lines that crisscrossed the landscape, tilled or untilled. The Green Ewe would make sure everything grew; the Pearl Ewe would make sure everything would be used according to need; the Roan would make sure everything died so life could begin again. Sometimes when I wandered the meadows to look for medicines I would see traces of the lines, though the Orders really did well to scorch them away, or uproot them en masse. When I wandered the Kayaarth Graveyard, looking for witherweeds and its pale, almost-gray orchids, sometimes I felt the lines were drawing me in, or sending me traveling on a most ephemeral path. But then I would lose the trail. The gravestones' runes had been faded for centuries, and the expanse was little more than a wide field of broken stones.

But this was where I found the plants that I could sell.

Once I had thought that the graveyard was a secret, but I realized that no one from the town *wanted* to go here. They said that it had *wendt-elderinne*—an old phrase that meant "memories of memories." And they were not pleasant. They would overtake and consume a person. I didn't care though, and the town needed me, they fucking needed me, and the Aelyf needed me for his poisons, and the parsons needed me for the healing teas she would make from the gryphweed, and the wives needed me for the little pink deathflowers that they would eat at midnight in order to keep themselves from having a baby they didn't want.

Halex also needed me. (Halex kissing my neck, Halex whispering secrets in a language I didn't understand while she slept and I curled next to her like I was a cat and she was a warm stove.)

This was what I told myself too.

✦

It was noon in the graveyard, but the air was getting unseasonably chill, and my fingers were getting numb. A wind to the west. I sat down on a boulder that I was sure used to be part of a tomb and rested for a few minutes, watching the sky for rain. The last few weeks of summer were good for the white marigolds that would twist, softly, towards my hand when I'd hold my palm next to them. (This was not magic; they would do this for anyone.) I plucked the blossoms and placed them into my blue bag, the one with the yellow drawstring.

I heard someone walking towards me, and my heart melted. Halex. Halex!

"You bitch!" I said without turning, laughing at the sound of my love's footfall. "You've been gone a week and you didn't tell me where you were going—"

I turned around and almost leapt from my resting place, ready to jump into her arms, ready to forgive though I wasn't really mad in the first place, but then I saw it was the Aelyf, loping around, not especially noticing me. I froze and my heart sank. Fae *did* notice me of course.

"Oh," I said. "I thought you were someone else."

Fae gave a little smirk, but it wasn't necessarily unkind. Impossible to read. Fae wore a wide-brimmed straw hat, which almost looked fanciful. This was the only Aelyf I knew, and there weren't terribly many in the world anymore, at least in the Empire Without Sorrows. Because no creature was more sorrowful than an Aelyf. Fae towered over me.

"Do not trouble yourself," fae said. "I have no wish to pluck flowers and weeds. It's valuable what you do, for I would never do it myself."

I didn't think it was either a compliment or a put-down, so I didn't acknowledge it. Instead I said: "I didn't realize you—Aelyfs, I mean—could go out in the sunlight."

The sunlight was weak, it was true, but I had always thought it would have burned fae to a crisp. He looked up wanly towards the sky, then back to me, and said, "No, no, that is a lie." Fae paused. "The world is full of lies. Still, I don't quite enjoy it all that much. But I am all right with a little armor." Fae tapped the brim of faer hat.

I tied a clutch of marigolds together as fae talked. "What are you doing here?" I was beginning to flush from my awkwardness, which had replaced all of my certainty just a minute before.

Fae outstretched faer arms. I saw etched runes on faer bone-white arms, the sleeves billowing. I grew even more flustered. I turned my head as faer laughed.

"Did you not know? This is my family's gravesite. I am here to care for it."

"Oh," I said. Fae wasn't doing a very good job, but I wasn't about to say that.

I realized with a little shame that I thought—everybody thought—this cemetery had been abandoned, that it was a hair's breadth from being subsumed back into the wild woods and brambles, as so often happened in the Hither. And this Aelyf was here to care for what could really not be cared for.

"I do not do much," fae said. "I mostly ensure that the graves themselves far below are not disturbed." Fae knelt and touched one of the gravestones with the tip of his finger. "Do you not hear them singing below?"

"Who?" I managed to say. I felt my spine tighten.

Fae stood to faer full height. "My ancestors," fae said. "I am surprised you do not hear them. You're sigil-born after all."

I started and almost fell back, as if hit by an arrow made of faer words. Panic welled up inside of me like sludge. I knew fae was saying something important, but I had no idea what it was. But just as I was going to ask my breath caught in my throat, and fae ambled away, along the edges of the woods and the gravesite.

✦

When the Aelyf was out of sight, I headed home, almost running, even though I hadn't collected as much as I wanted to that day. It began to rain, and I nearly lost my footing a few times. I had no idea, really, why I was panicking. I thought about going to Halex's cozy house up in the trees, but I knew she was still gone; I knew it, and I didn't want that to panic me anymore. What was I afraid of? *Sigil-born.* But what did that *mean*?

I slowed my walk as I made it to the walls of Oer-Vestal. At the Boar Gate was Geris, a boy about my son's age who held his father's pike. Vlon must have gone to the tavern for a drink.

"It's really raining!" Geris said to me as I walked by. I managed to nod. Once I reached home I restarted the fire from the embers and hung my plants up to dry, my hands shaking. The rain pattered on the roof, drip-dropping past the poor barrier of the sparrow's nest. When I was done tying them, I knelt by the fire and buried my face in my cold hands for a few seconds. I heard someone approaching. I stood up and took a deep breath and imagined myself as perfectly fine, a normal woman who cleaned her house and collected plants and raised a son.

It was Veryk, the tavern-keeper's husband. Right, he'd be wanting the order of talyn which his wife used to make rue-spirits. He looked at me quizzically. "Everything all right?" he said quietly. He was usually quiet.

"Of course," I said, handing him the little bundle of the silken black leaves, which they would ferment in the basement of the tavern. He looked hard at me, but then gave me his customary script.

"Don't let them get wet!" I called out after him. The storm was not abating. Why I was such a wreck? Perhaps it was the sight of the Aelyf faerself, wandering in one of my only sanctuaries, a sanctuary that fae claimed to be faers. Maybe that was a part of it. But the Aelyf had left a jeweled barb for me to step on, and I was unable to get it out of my skin.

The rain had lessened, but not enough. I would have to go to the keep of Lord Willingness, who was once the protector of Oer-Vestal from his estate.

The Empire Without Sorrows had ripped away that facade a long time ago.

✦

The cold rain kept coming down, and the main road through town, such as it was, had turned to a soft mud. I pulled my cloak and hood tighter, past old man Corder's chicken-house, and the family of elder and younger Arithisa, who crafted jewelry and curios and portraits in polished amethyst. When I crossed the sagging bridge and reached flat ground again, I saw the Ever-Watchful—Liventine's shining tower, enameled blue—at the southern edge of town, and I thought of visiting my son at school, but I needed to visit Lord Willingness's castle before anything else—not for Lord Willingness himself but rather for someone in his retinue.

Lord Willingness was not called that before. To tell you the truth, I forgot what his name might have been. People did not like speculating on it. An ordinator, if they were passing through town, might have considered such remembrances worth chiding, or even correcting sternly. His castle was at the end of a steep, winding road with a switchback that looked over the village. I sighed and held onto the slick rope that led up to level ground, trudging up the best I could up the Cairn. Going to the other way, a white donkey, now strewn with mud, nearly slid down the path, knees buckling.

In order to distract myself, I allowed myself to think about Halex and almost immediately regretted it. I had not seen her in a week, and I had an unshakeable worry that I would never see her again. She had disappeared before, but this time felt different, and I didn't know why. She lived deep in the woods next to the boar dancers, though not really. Her treehouse was in the outskirts of the outskirts, deep in the Hither. The first day we met, she had come across me first in much the same way that the Aelyf found me—wandering in the graveyard while I worked. It was a dry summer day, and I had taken off my cloak and was toiling in a loose tunic. She was just coming out of the woods, a gyrfalcon on her arm. She had red hair and blue eyes, and I was lost, just absolutely lost, immediately and without any warning to my heart. I nearly dropped my paring knife. Memories of memories. She started laughing, and I started laughing, and she whistled and let the falcon fly.

"What are you doing here?" I had asked her, shaking my head to clear the last of the laughter. We had an easy familiarity from our first words.

"I live in the woods," she told me. Within a few hours I was in her treehouse, as she pinned me against the wall, kissing my neck hard.

In our eight months together, when we were curled together in her treehouse (always in the day, so I could be back in time for my son), she never told me much about herself. And she didn't ask me terribly much about my own life. I could tell from the weathered books in her treehouse that she knew a great deal about the Ewes, yet when I asked, seemed indifferent to them spiritually and politically. She was even more disinterested in the Empire Without Sorrows. Her gaze was always elsewhere, in other corners of the world that I could not begin to see.

When I pressed her, she just kissed me on the forehead and told me that though she was going far away, she would be back soon.

She always brought her falcon.

Four days gone, I was heartsick.

Halex would know what I needed to know. Of that, I was sure. But she was not here. I had to rely on far less reliable help.

✦

I found Corlynx, the old parson, working in the wind and rain. He was an old man at this time, but still he worked. He had to, in order to eat. When I was a young girl, he probably still had vestiges of status on account of his shepherding of the village with the Ewes. The Empire Without Sorrows were in charge, but they still hadn't uprooted everything old yet. That would soon change.

He was a boisterous man in my childhood, often to be found in the tavern, but of late—in the few times I had seen him, I had very little reason to head up to Castle Willingness ever—he was gaunt and sullen. Having your entire status ripped away from you and being forced to work as an assistant gardener would do that to a person. Perhaps he had protested too loudly about the Ewes getting erased from all things. Lord Willingness, for his part, had capitulated easily when the Empire Without Sorrows came. He and his family had protected the village, often unevenly, in the few times that it needed protection, for centuries. But in turn for his obedience to the Empire, he had relinquished all control of the village—as well as any tithes—except for his own private lands; he had been turned into a figurehead only. He dutifully appeared at the Empire Without Sorrows' monthly festivals for the twelve hues of light, but engaged with the village in few other ways.

Corlynx was resting on the end of his shovel for a few seconds when he saw me walking towards him.

"I have no time," he said, out of breath.

"Sorry!" I said. "Sorry for disturbing your work." I managed to force a smile, trying not to let pity overwhelm me. He stared at me through the rain and clearly didn't recognize me.

"I'm Maran's daughter," I said quietly. I didn't want to say my father's name out loud.

"Oh!" he said, shaking his head. He was about to go back to his work and said, "And how is she?"

I clenched my jaw but managed a slight smile. "Oh dear, she died about ten years ago, parson."

The word slipped out of my mouth, and I didn't even know why. But this was first time he truly became animated. His eyes widened, and he almost growled at me: "Do *not* say that out loud! I am not a parson. There are none of the parsons of old left."

"Apologies," I said, holding out my hands. After a second of cold silence I pulled a little pouch out of my cloak. "Here. I wanted to give you a gift. I know you work hard."

He looked around, as if he was being spied upon—no one was around in this gale—and took the pouch. "What is it?" he said.

"Gallus seeds," I said. "A couple in a tea and—"

"I know what they do," he snapped. They were a powerful analgesic. Take a few and you could be a numb, floating cloud for days.

"Of course," I said.

"Thank you," he muttered, taking them, hands shaking a little. He was not ashamed about needing them. He was about to turn back to his work, but I cleared my throat.

"I *did* want to ask you about one other thing..." It came out in a whisper. I barely managed to catch his attention.

"Well?" he asked, as if I had been stalling to ask him for long minutes. "What is it?"

I took a deep breath. "I just wanted to ask about what it meant to be...sigil-born? Is that something you—"

He nearly threw his shovel at me, though he barely had the strength to hurl it more than a couple feet. "Again with these old, dead things, child! I promised your mother I would never tell you, and I don't intend to do that now. If you want to know, you will have to ask *her*."

I stood there in shock, but then said quietly, my heart sinking at the lie I was about to tell, "Actually, my mother told me to come to you. She thought…she thought that it was best to hear directly from you."

He stood there confused, and I wanted nothing more than to wrap him in a blanket and get him out of the rain, get him into a warm bed of straw. "Well, in that case…." He put a hand on his forehead. "In that case, well." He coughed. "I had very little to do with those transfigurations. That was the *splendor solis*. Women's work, you understand. I would never hear the end of it from the Shepherdess if I butted in." He managed to laugh, lost in a daydream for a few seconds.

"The Shepherdess? Is she still…alive?"

He shrugged and was suddenly clear-eyed. "She certainly is not in the village anymore," he said. "Those Empire Without Sorrows bastards—those…." He held his hand to his mouth, as if an imp had forced him to clamp his very thoughts shut. He swallowed and managed to say: "I am very grateful you had the sigil-work done. Otherwise life would have been very miserable for you."

He turned back to his work. I never spoke with him again. In fact, he was found dead on the castle grounds two months later.

I was shaken, needless to say, but I returned in time for Raiben to get home and to cook for us: fried dough and cured meat (though I knew not from what animal, to tell the truth), and the dark cherries of the scattered groves that I had picked. He told me about his day with the Liventines and how he was learning about the scripts and the stories of the Empire Without Sorrows' capital, Liventia, which was thousands of miles away. He was reading scripts about the five golden rokhs, legendary visages of the Empire. But my mind was restless. I kept trying to parse what the old parson had told me. *Otherwise life would have been very miserable for you.* I had no idea what that meant. Something happened when I was born or right after I was born, and the desire to know what it was now only grew and grew with every breath.

After Raiben went to sleep, I knew what I had to do. The rain had at last stopped, and the village was quiet except for the braying of an occasional dog or a couple arguing loudly in the distance. I put on my cloak again—I knew the boy would be all right by himself, for a little while—and headed out of my cottage door.

I wended through the village, avoiding both the people stumbling in and out of the tavern as well as the glowing orange light from the crown of the Liventine's tower. It still wasn't terribly late, and the gate was open a crack. Even though it was still Lord Willingness' responsibility to pay the guard, he did so only occasionally, and thus the guards were often absent. I managed to slip out and go towards the Aelyf's hut near the river.

I couldn't hear any noises inside, though there was a rich smell that I recognized as cardamom, one of the herbs that I have procured for faer. My curiosity getting the better of me, I slipped inside. The hut, at nighttime, was warmer and almost livelier than in the light of day. There were flagons with viscous liquids in black and blue on a center table, and five daggers arranged in a circle around them. I couldn't tell if this was a magical ritual or a chemical rendering. Maybe it was both.

"What are you doing here?" Faer voice shot across the dimness. Before I could blink, much less say anything, fae stood inches away from me, with a small, obsidian blade at my throat.

"I'm sorry, I'm sorry!" I hissed, breathless. "I need to talk to you."

Fae towered over me. Instead of faer usual array of tatterdemalion garb, fae only wore wide legged pants. Without faer shirt on, I could see all of the spiraling and crisscrossing of the runes on faer body. The runes told a story, one that was perhaps only meant for faer.

I managed to suck in a breath. "Please," I whispered.

Fae snorted a little and took his blade away from my face. "I'm working, you see," fae said in faer more customary soft voice, almost but not quite apologetic. "These are dangerous chemicals, as you should well know."

"Believe me, I know." I had never wanted to know what fae was doing with the plants I sold him. I had heard in whispers in town that he made blade-poisons for the Empire Without Sorrows. This was supposedly why they tolerated faer presence in town, but people would talk even if fae did nothing except sit in faer hut all day and sing hymns. People would talk.

"Tell me what you want to know," fae said, a little gentler this time. "So I can get back to my work."

I took a deep breath. "You mentioned that I was sigil-marked," I said. "Up at the cemetery. What is that? I need to know."

Fae almost laughed to faeself. "I should have known. Sit."

I sat. And fae began to tell me the story of myself, or at least one part of it.

"Now, the Ewes were wrong about many things, but they were not wrong about this: each human child is born with two souls. The true soul and the false soul. It's in the discerning of which is true and which is false that itself brings life."

"Do the Aelyf have two souls as well?" I managed to whisper.

Fae was not pleased by my interruption. Fae said: "We have five. Now, listen. These two souls could be a male soul and a female soul. Or a female soul and...well, something older. Without a name. Each soul was detritus from Pallas, which is beyond everything. And so normally, the true soul would defeat the false soul. And the child would be able to find their place in the world." Fae let these words hang in the air. I heard his phosphor crackle.

"But not always."

"No, not always. And it is difficult to say why. It could be the weather on the sun, or a pinprick of fate from Pallas' children, the Sullen. But—" Fae spread faer long fingers and looked at me. "Let's suppose that the male soul was false and yet managed to destroy the true, female soul. What then?"

What then. "I don't know," I said.

I could tell that the Aelyf was choosing faer words extremely carefully. "The parson would know this when the child was still in the womb, and know that no good could come from a child with a false soul. So, they would do the sigil-work, and venture to the land of dead souls, and bargain for the true soul with the Sullen. The true soul would be augmented with the sigil, and the false soul could be extinguished."

"And the Triumphals do not believe this."

"My child, of course not. For them, the soul is unitary. Singular. Souls are shot through with the Triumph. It's rubbish, of course but ... empires have been forged on less."

"What is the sigil then?" I tried to keep myself from shaking.

The Aelyf shrugged. "Fragments of words captured from the throats of the old goddesses. But powerful ones. And thus, the child would enter the world with a true soul. But a changed one."

"Are you saying—" I trailed off. "Are you saying this happened to me?" I said in a quiet voice. I didn't want it to be quiet. I wanted my voice to be as loud as the world, but there was no way to make that happen there, in the Aelyf's hut.

"Quite so," fae said. "We can sense these things, these afterimages of your soul."

"And so my false soul was that—was that of a man? And the parson and witch-wives changed it? In my mother's womb?"

"It would appear that way." Fae leaned forward. "I am sorry, but I only had seen this as a curio. You are clearly attaching a great deal of import to this revelation."

"I would say so," I said. "I would fucking say so." And yet, I knew what fae said was true.

The Aelyf sighed. "Are you not happy? Would you have wanted to live a life with the wrong soul?"

I could not imagine this. I could not. It would have simply been untenable.

"No," I said. "No. But tell me, tell me if you know—why did they do this in the first place?"

Fae spread faer long fingers. "Altruism, by the dictates of the Green Ewe. But also..." Fae hesitated, which surprised me.

"What?" I said, leaning forward.

"I cannot say for sure, and dead witches cannot speak for themselves. But sigil-born are known to be attuned to the ley-lines and the winds. You see—" Fae paused. "Once recovered, the sigils, hooked and connected to the true soul, give it heft and texture. Whether that turns into magic...is up to the person to decide."

Fae looked at me then as if to say, *clearly this is for you to decide, human.*

I staggered to my feet and put my face in my hands. This was all too much. Too much.

"I apologize for bothering your work so late at night," I managed to say, before dashing out of faer cottage, almost falling forward. The Aelyf said something to me, but I was rushing away too fast to catch it.

I barely remembered the walk back to my cottage. The gate was still open, and I slipped inside. I heard shouts from somewhere near the Liventine's priory, but figured it was mere drunkenness. I retreated into my cottage and settled down to sleep next to Raiben.

Only I couldn't sleep. How could I. Everything I thought I knew about myself had been premised on an untruth. And yet, what remained could be nothing less than the truth. *My* truth. And it terrified me, and emptied me of any joy or pain. There was only my soul, my sigil-soul, resting deep within me, newly named.

I had no idea what to do with it.

✦

I awoke to the bell from the Liventine's priory ringing. I was confused as I sat up, groggy, because in the past the bell had only pealed for the light festivals. I heard shouts and murmurs from elsewhere in the village.

Something was not right. I had slept like shit from all the things the Aelyf had told me.

"Raiben, wake up," I said, turning around. I put my hand on the rumple of blankets where he slept.

But he was not there.

The bell kept ringing.

"Raiben!" I called out. No answer. I began to feel the old panic come over me. I didn't know what else to do, so I threw on some new clothes, went outside, and followed the sound of the bell to the priory, like everyone else.

"Do you know what's going on?" I asked Veryk, catching up to him on the path. He shook his head silently. I could tell that he was afraid. That was a bad sign, because he was usually too drunk to be afraid of anything. If only Halex was here; she would know what to do.

The dread felt two steps ahead of me. But when I reached the square in front of the tower, it caught up with me.

"No," I said.

Halex *was* here. In the center of the square. Tied to a tall elmen post—sacred wood from the Empire Without Sorrows capital.

A black rokh circled her. Halex's hands and feet were bound by silver chains. Those were only used for harpies (and the Aelyf, for that matter). I wanted to run right toward her and free her, but the entire village was there. Everyone. And if I did that, I would soon be on a stake next to her. She had bruises on her face, a cut lip. I trusted that she would be all right when she had went away. My dear, dear Halex, my sweetness—

The bell stopped ringing.

I almost expected her to change into a bird and fly away, away from the clutches of the rokh. Or reveal her true form as a harpy and bite at the chains holding her down. But neither of those things happened.

With a start, I scanned the crowd for my son. I at last found him close to the base of the Liventine's tower with the other students, all in their rose-gold robes. I had never ventured close to the tower and had never seen him in such fineries before. He met my gaze for a second, and I tried to smile reassuringly at him but he turned away.

Sandryn, herself in these robes, with an eye amulet at her neck, turned to face the village. Lord Willingness sat at the base of the tower but seemed distracted and disinterested, checking his nails. The rokh stopped moving. These were not the rokhs that brought supplies but rather the kind that brought the war to the harpies.

"A harpy spy!" Sandryn shouted. "On the edge of your village, your homes. Dwelling here, plotting, no doubt reporting back to their unholy aeries." She took a deep breath. "Since we have eradicated the wicked Ewes from your land, we have provided the Republic's bounty, we have taught your children the New Script." Her tone has become even angrier, like a mother to a petulant child. "But this demands vigilance on your part. We are not far from the war, from the mangled bodies of both rokh and people. If you have seen this woman before, you need to confess." She raised her staff and a faint din washed over the crowd. I felt a tightness in my head. People cried out, and I tried to breathe, not very well.

Somehow she will know, if she doesn't already. The noise inside of me pierced my skull. I had to tell her in order to stop the noise. I had to—

I took a deep breath and something else, something deeper, said *No. Do not say a word.*

Maybe the voice came from my sigil-soul. I could not say for sure. But I felt the earth ground me. I felt the firmament there, stretching far beyond my little village and crisscrossed with the little trails and worn stones connected to each other, and to me. The din didn't fade, but I managed to push it out.

"I saw her once," a voice said. Candel stepped forward. He was a middle-aged man who lived alone and grew barley. His wife had drowned several years back, and I remember gathering garlands for the funeral. He was sweet and harmless.

"She was…she was laying traps for grouse in my fields," he continued, hopelessly.

"And you said nothing?" Sandryn said. "You did nothing?"

"I…figured she was a beggar," he said. "I never saw her again." The sound dimmed and Candel seemed to pass out of its spell."

"I see," Sandryn said. She motioned to the black rokh, who in a fast, seamless motion darted towards Candel. With a swipe of its ferociously toothed beak, it tore off his left arm.

Everyone started to shout and shriek, but the yelling rapidly died out. The fear came quick. I was as terrified as everyone else, but my anger washed over the fear. I looked over at my son. The students were struggling to keep it together, but Raiben was stone-faced, staring ahead of him.

My poor boy.

I looked at Halex. She was not staring at me, but she was not afraid. She had an almost placid smile on her face.

"Halex," I whispered. Everything was wrong—here, in the only home I'd ever known. My son distant and unreadable, my love in chains in front of me, a gentle innocent man stumbling on the ground in shock, trying to find his arm. Everything was wrong. But for the first time I knew what was *not* wrong. I was sigil-born. I was, in some small fashion, a witch of the Ewes, and whatever their faults, they would not abide this cruelty. I fell to my knees. No one noticed. Sandryn tried to quiet the crowd, to no use. I put my palms on the ground. More than ever before, this centered me. I felt the ley lines crisscrossing close to me. And I became a node to all of them. I took deep breaths.

I didn't know what was happening.

On the other hand, I knew exactly what was happening.

I looked up, with a twinge.

The Aelyf was standing there, perched on the city wall, tucked away in a shadow, gazing straight at me. He knew what was happening, even if I didn't entirely know myself. He smiled though, almost sadly, though not without compassion, and shook his head.

I knew what he was trying to say.

Not yet.

"Mom!" my son shouted over the crowd. Sandryn picked up Candel's arm and held the nape of his neck. She whispered something I couldn't hear and there was a flash of light from the crown of the tower. When my eyes adjusted, I saw that Candel's arm was reattached, though twitching a little. The village gasped but then quieted when Sandryn held up an arm.

"Know that the Glory is merciful," she shouted. "But mercy has limits. I know you are penitent, Candel, and you will choose not to test those limits in the future."

He shook his head fervently. My own heart felt sick, even though Candel had his arm back. I felt a crackle in the air that made the hairs of my neck stand on end, as the light in the tower began to dim.

I focused on Halex. While everyone was occupied with Candel, I stared at her. She was whispering something under her breath. I didn't quite know what was happening, but all the same I gasped. The ground which had once seemed so solid now buckled from me. She looked at me one last time and gave me a smile, though I had no way to understand what it meant. She then screeched. Sandryn turned around.

"No!" she said, raising her staff.

But it was too late. Halex's body disappeared in a pillar of black smoke, and in its place was a bird. A falcon to be exact—the largest I had ever seen. It took all of my effort to keep from crying out her name as it swirled around the crowd once, and then flew east, towards the mountains.

I blazed inside. I had nowhere to put that fire, but it would not go out. I didn't want to listen to the Aelyf's *not yet.* I blazed, and I blazed, and I blazed, and the light I had would not go out, and soon everyone was not looking at Rossalyne, or at where Halex used to be, but at me.

Soon, the tower was on fire.

The Things Melati Learns

Jaymee Goh

i. How to Make Friends

The woman has a thin line across her neck, a stark white against her warm brown skin. She makes no effort to hide it: no tudung veiling her hair and shoulders, no concealer makeup, not even a plain scarf. Melati is shocked, but also impressed; her tudung hides more than just aurat, and she is not even that spiritual. A perfunctory nod, and slight but friendly smile, and the woman is already walking away. Melati says nothing; she wants to respect the rules of hiking, which is to let the other person enjoy their solitude unless they indicate otherwise.

But something in Melati blooms. Perhaps the trail was so isolated that having such open scars is okay. Melati doesn't have to cover herself — who is going to judge her for exposing herself in the emptiness of the woods?

She does not mention this to Sham, because he would go ballistic. Her hair is for him alone, to look at, to touch, to pull. She hates the pulling, but according to her mother, it is part of marriage. Not that she agrees — she's got several friends who are married, and none of them seem to get their hair pulled, even if they don't wear tudung.

When Melati sees the woman again, it is on the same route, the same general vicinity, perhaps even under the same tree. She maybe wears a different shirt, but otherwise looks about the same. There is a faint sour smell coming off her, like formaldehyde.

This time, she musters up the courage to say, in a small voice, "hello."

The woman's smile is wider than usual, and she actually slows her pace. "Second time yah?"

Melati nods, hope brimming in her that she'll have someone to talk to other than Sham and her plants.

ii. How to Be Married

The woman's name is Hawa. She works in the nearby town as an undertaker, which accounts for the smell. She hikes across the rolling hills of Bukit Jejarum often. She is not married.

"And your family doesn't mind?"

Hawa's smile is needle-sharp and doesn't quite reach her eyes. "I have no family."

"Oh."

They hike together for the rest of the day. Melati is bursting with excitement when Sham comes home that night, preparing his nightcap and his hookah. "I made a friend today," she gushes as he starts smoking. She hates how he likes to blow smoke her way, but tolerates it because he says it turns him on.

"A friend?" He frowns. "What kind of friend? A man, is it?"

"No! A woman."

"What kind of woman goes hiking by herself out in these hills? So dangerous!"

Melati is confused. "I do," she tells him. "I hike by myself all the time. The forest isn't that dangerous as long as you pay attention."

But while Melati knows to pay attention to the patterns of weather and animals in the forest, while she knows to pay attention to news from the papers and fellow villagers for potential man-eating tigers, she does not know men very well.

That night, Sham yells at her: a long tirade that rains insults on her intelligence, accuses her of neglecting the house, demands that she only do the simple, basic tasks of a wife who has everything she could possibly ask for. Melati understands in theory that he is not really talking about her, but her face is hot and wet with sweat and tears by the time he is done. It is as if her knowledge of the truth has taken form outside of her body and sat next to her, a shield she cannot reach to protect herself from the force of his rage.

He apologises later. "I'm sorry — the hills are dangerous and I was worried — people go missing around here all the time — don't believe me I show you the reports — I can't stand the idea of you going missing —"

They make love, and Melati stays awake a little longer, wondering if she just doesn't understand marriage, wondering if the gnawing inside her was normal for new couples.

iii. How to Lie

Hawa is the first to bring up the bruises. Melati is surprised, because firstly, she has no visible skin besides her hands and face, and secondly, the bruises have mostly faded.

"When you move you have a weird gait. Like you're trying to avoid bumping into things."

As Melati thought: Hawa is more perceptive and articulate than her sour smell belies. "I fell down," she said, somewhat embarrassed to make up such a lie. They have been hiking buddies for some time now, and Melati has been hoping this made them friends. But she cannot gauge whether they really are, and she cannot bring herself to confide in Hawa.

There is a pause, over a gnarly set of tree roots, before Hawa says, "Oh. You're okay?"

"I'm okay!" Melati babbles some story about how she had been mopping and then her heel hit an odd angle causing her to slip and fall on her side right on the staircase. "Stupid right? My husband couldn't stop laughing."

Hawa gives her an odd look — slightly widened eyes, an eyebrow going up a tick, lips pursing just a bit — and says, gently, "it's a common accident. But please be careful."

Melati feels terrible, for lying to a nice person like Hawa, for laughing at what was a bad accident. If a friend had told her she had fallen like that, Melati would not be laughing like a donkey.

"Why didn't your husband help you? What's his name? Hisham?"

"Sham wasn't home at the time."

"And you have no one to help? Don't you live in that big house on Jalan Rusa? If you can afford that house, you can afford a helper, right?"

Melati shakes her head. "I can handle it. I don't work, so I can take care of the house myself."

"Couldn't you have called your husband, when you fell?"

"Of course not!" Melati is appalled. "Small thing, no need to bother him about it!"

"Melati, some of my clients died like that, you know? It's not a small thing."

Melati opens her mouth, but Hawa is already continuing the hike, which is a relief, since Melati doesn't really know how to respond to that. She knows what might happen if she were to tell Hawa, and she does not want to confront either possibility. Not now. Perhaps not ever.

iv. How Human Anatomy Does, and Doesn't, Work

At a waterfall, the two women stop to take a dip. They sit with their feet submerged, water lapping around their shins, and they talk about birds and flowers they have seen on the hike so far. They discuss the books on birdwatching and botany that they've read, as well as the latest novels. Melati likes tragic literary fiction, and she is surprised at Hawa's reading choices: trashy romance novels, particularly those involving uztazas and imams. The trend ended about ten years ago, but Hawa can talk about them like they're still the hot topics that make books fly off shelves.

Hawa has more than just a thin line around her neck. It meanders down her back and chest unevenly, like a rivulet guided only by gravity. Down the front it loops unsteadily around her belly button. Down the back it is a jagged zigzag, like carelessly torn paper.

Melati flushes when Hawa notices her staring, and the other woman smiles.

"It's okay, I know it looks unusual. Do you want to touch?"

No would be a lie, so Melati nods. Hawa bends towards Melati, and the latter gently traces a fingertip along the side of Hawa's neck.

She jerks back when she realizes that the thin line is actually a crevice. "I thought it was a scar."

"No."

"Is it...a birthmark?"

Hawa grinned. "Kind of, yes. Want to see something neat?" And she spreads the sides of the line a little wider.

Melati stares, a little horrified at the sight and the sound. The mark, scar or whatever it is, spreads open, unnatural as a wound, but lined with clean pink walls like the eyelid just past the lash line. It makes a soft squelching sound.

"That's not normal," Melati whispers, and she can't move, because she's fascinated by Hawa nonetheless, despite the gruesome secret, or perhaps because of the gruesome secret. She's not sure which, and she doesn't think it matters. "How, uhm, deep does it go?"

"How deep do *you* go?" Hawa retorts, and Melati gasps at the audacity of the question. She blushes too hard to answer, and Hawa spends the rest of the hike giggling every time they make eye contact.

But Melati keeps thinking about the question, about the way Hawa's skin felt under, and around, her fingers. Wishing they were more than casual friends. Melati wonders if they could trade secrets — Melati's fears of her marriage for Hawa's truth of what kind of ghost she really is.

v. How to Cope with Death

Sham is always complaining about the foreign workers on his development site. Someone or another is always running away. Sometimes it's not even the Bangladeshi workers. Sometimes it is a manager. One has already scammed tens of thousands out of Sham, and another disappeared with no resignation notice, at a critical point of the building project. There have been accidents, and suspected acts of sabotage. Melati only knows about this because Sham spends hours ranting about it on the phone when he gets home.

Melati has never been to the building site herself. She asked once if she could come along to look, and Sham gave her such a cold glare she excused herself to get coffee for him. Later he explained that he didn't want everyone else to see his lovely wife, not the dirty Banglas, or dirty Indons, or dirty Myanmar—it didn't matter which nationality the workers were; they were all dirty to him.

His jealousy is cute. Melati would rather have his jealous fits, however ugly they look, because indifference would be worse.

One day, Melati hikes alone, because Hawa is busy with work. Hawa's embalming sessions take anywhere from two to four hours, and that does not count the travel time. She sometimes stays to comfort the family of the deceased; she often stays to help with arranging the affairs of the dead. The Chinese, she says, do not have an imam who can rally the community around their loved ones, to wash their dead bodies, to carefully wrap them in the funeral shrouds. They display their dead at funerals for relatives to speak their final goodbyes. Their customs sound a little morbid.

It is this day she decides to break off from the usual hiking path into the lubang babi she has passed several times but never deigned to try. If the wild animals find it safe enough to pass through that rough break in the tree line, then she should find it safe too. The path beyond is not very well defined, but she sets her walking stick down firmly and forges ahead.

She almost falls into the gully, catching her heel on a root down the unexpected slope before she loses her balance.

Then the rotten smell hits her full in the face, and she falls backwards, her tailbone hitting a tall root but slightly cushioned by her backpack. It is the worst smell of her life, and she scrambles to get away from it before she retches.

The worst smell of her life is followed by the worst sound of her life, because nothing can happen one bad thing at a time. It's a slick, wet sound of gnawing. Melati carefully crawls away, trying to be as noiseless as ants, measuring her breathing the way she sometimes does when she does not want Hisham to hear her.

The chewing sound ends, and there is a high whistle and a whoop overhead. Melati sees out the corner of her eye a long-armed creature swinging among the branches, not unlike a monkey, but entirely unlike a monkey in that it is only a torso. Skin flaps in the wind.

Like carelessly torn paper.

vi. How to Keep Secrets with a Comrade

Despite her bad decision to marry Sham, Melati is not stupid. In fact, the fact that she is not stupid is probably why Sham married her, because she is at least clever enough to not enrage him into a heart attack. She said this to her mother once, and the old woman promptly hung up on her. She said it to Hawa too, and Hawa had the slightly panicked smile of someone who knew she ought to nod and laugh along but was actually very alarmed at the subject matter.

When they next bathe together in the waterfall, Melati gently touches Hawa's scar-not-scar. She knows she should be scared, but the knot of fear, usually so present in her when she is about to bring up an uncomfortable topic, is silenced — by curiosity? By trust? By foolhardiness? She is not sure.

Melati decides to just delve right into it and caresses the thin line around Hawa's neck. "Did it hurt?"

Hawa is a little startled, and there is a tight wariness around her eyes before she answers. "A little, at the beginning."

"But now?" Melati asks, because surely such dark magic must exact a sacrifice.

"All the time."

"Then why did you do it?"

"Because it was my chance to live free."

Dying is not freedom, Melati thought, but kept it to herself. "So…did you kill those men?"

Now Hawa grins, but there is no warmth in it. "Not all of them. Bukit Jejarom is cursed, you know. All sorts of things live here."

"Is that why you live here too?"

Thoughtfulness relaxes Hawa's face. "No. I didn't realise it before I came here. I simply wanted to get away to somewhere more natural."

"More like somewhere more SUPERnatural."

Hawa stares at Melati, wide-eyed in disbelief. "What was that? A joke? A bad joke? You think this is a cartoon?"

"It's funny," Melati protests, but then bursts out laughing, unable to hold in the nervous tension anymore.

"Oh, no. No, no, no." Hawa groans dramatically, covering her eyes with the balls of her hands. "I can't believe this is what our friendship has come to."

Melati devolves into giggles and leans against Hawa, who indulgently rolls her eyes and goes back to scrounging the in-betweens of her toes.

"Can I see?" Melati asks later, as they sit in the shallows of the river, the water up to their waists, kicking their feet in the slightly deeper waters to rile up the sand and fish.

Hawa takes a long time to answer. Melati is allowed to touch, to trace the lines, to sometimes slip her fingers in and feel Hawa's shudder, but she keeps her hands in her lap now, nervously twisting her sarong.

"Not today," Hawa finally says.

Melati nods her assent. She's not disappointed; she's glad that she didn't cross a boundary.

They hold hands as they walk towards the exit of the forest. Melati feels like they are holding something so much more, and the togetherness of it warms her inside, like an embrace.

vii. How to Deal with Surprise

When Melati throws up three mornings in a row, she finally plucks the courage to sneak out of the house to the pharmacy for a pregnancy test. It is only when she is halfway through the forest, running to where she thinks she can find Hawa, that she realizes she should have called her husband first. But then it doesn't matter in the next second, because instead she encounters Hawa bending over a freshly-dead body.

Hawa swings around. "It's not one of mine!" Hawa yells as soon as she sees who it is, but drops the phone in her hands when Melati doubles over in shock.

As Melati dry-heaves over a low bush, Hawa pats her back gently. "Sayang, 'yang, you're all right, whoever did it is long gone, and this one won't turn into…into something else."

"It's okay."

"No, it's not okay, you're vomiting because you saw it."

"I didn't even see it. It smells extremely bad, Hawa."

Hawa sniffed the air. "I didn't think it smelled that bad," she admitted.

"It's okay, I'm just being sensitive. I heard pregnant women's sense of smell is very strong, so maybe that's it." Also, Hawa works with dead bodies, so maybe her sense of smell is gone. Melati gags again. "Can we get away from here?"

"What?" Hawa's mouth drops open, which was very funny in the moment to Melati, though not so funny she forgets to dry heave again. "Oh, shit, quick quick quick." Hawa quickly retrieves her phone before she runs over to pull one of Melati's arms around her shoulders. "Let's go, let's go, let's go. You didn't tell me this. How long has it been? Are you okay? Did Hisham force this on you?"

"What? Sham doesn't even know."

"Are you sure? That's good then. There might be something around here to help with the problem." Hawa casts a searching gaze across the forest floor.

"What! A baby's not a problem," Melati exclaims. "What do you have against kids?"

Hawa is surprised. "Nothing."

"What do you mean, nothing? You …you became a thing that can't have babies, right?"

"That doesn't mean I have anything against children. I just don't want to have any, myself." Hawa squints up at the sky. "I was from a poor family. What kind of life could I have given a child?"

"You could have married," Melati points out.

Hawa rolls her eyes over to Melati, who flushes in embarrassment.

"You sure have a difficult life," Melati mutters.

"Not anymore," Hawa replies cheerfully. "But I promise, if you need help, I will have something for you. Now let's go somewhere with better phone signal so we can call the police."

Melati frowns, dissatisfaction settling into her stomach. "I want to see a doctor. A real doctor. A obby-jen."

"A what?"

"A obby-jen!"

"OB-GYN?"

Melati sticks her tongue out, and Hawa sings "obby-jen, obby-jen" the rest of the way down the hill. It is ghoulish to do so, given there is a death that needs investigating, but it is better than Hawa discussing possible home abortions.

viii. How to Have Uncomfortable Conversations

When Melati tells her husband, he gives her a blank look and says, "Oh." And then he eats his dinner like nothing monumental like a pregnancy has been announced.

When Melati tells her mother, she gets a lecture on childcare and natal care, mostly prohibitions. Pantang this, pantang that, pantang, pantang, pantang.

When Melati tells her secondary schoolmates in their WhatsApp group, there is a long line of congratulations, confetti emoji, and well wishes, immediately buried under the news of a more popular friend moving to another country.

Hawa, however, treats Melati just the same. The same meeting time, the same spot, the same bland conversations that remind Melati that there is the rest of the world beyond her pregnancy.

But when Hawa does bring it up, Melati wants to shrink away. There is something strange about discussing pregnancy with a mortician, a life-bringing process to someone who tends to dead bodies, and advisories on bodily safety to someone who has mangled her own. For months, they have a stalemate: Hawa insisting that Melati attempt an abortion, even after the first forty days, and Melati stubbornly sticking to the pregnancy, her last chance at having a normal life.

She swallows it all down, though, because Hawa, unlike Sham, still holds her hand as they walk together.

ix. How to Leave

Her contractions begin during Friday prayers, and she initially pays no mind to it. Contractions are a normal thing, she has read. As is a normal trickle of water between her legs, and she knows she is not urinating. At some point she sends Hawa a text about her contractions, just to let her friend know why she will not be answering her phone, and not just because she is still afraid of Hawa. Then she goes to the outside kitchen and carefully pounds some fresh curry paste, because she is craving something hot to go with the day.

When Sham comes home, calling for her, she is still pounding, and when he sees her squatting over the mortar, his frown twists. "Are you crazy?! Why are you sitting in a puddle of piss? Is this how you greet your husband?"

Melati takes a long sigh before she levels an irritated expression at him, patience running thin. "I'm in labor. I was waiting for you to get home to take me to hospital."

"Hospital?" Sham's screams go higher, in volume and in pitch. "I just came from town, and you want me to drive you all the way back there?"

"I'm giving birth," she grits out. "I told you I want to go to hospital for it. You deaf?" She can see the vein in his forehead throbbing, but she doesn't care at the moment. She carefully stands up, pushing her knees down for leverage. She is about to reach down for the bowl of paste when the doorbell rings.

Sham and Melati exchange glances, and Sham huffs and goes into the house.

The doorbell rings again, because Sham did not answer the door.

It's Hawa. She has a little concerned frown furrowing the space between her bushy eyebrows but her eyes are bright with excitement. Melati feels a sudden peace wash over her. Even if Hawa thinks Melati ought to have aborted the baby, she at least knows how to *look* happy for Melati. "I got your SMS — I'm so sorry I didn't reply sooner — are you okay? Do you need anything?"

"A ride to the hospital?" Melati asks hopefully.

Both women are crestfallen the next moment; it just so happens that Hawa's car is at the workshop.

"Where is Hisham? Can't he drive you?"

Melati pinches her face. "He says he won't drive me. Too tired." Then she doubles over. "Oof. That was a hard one."

Hawa leads Melati to the nearest couch, patting some cushions for Melati to lay her head on. "Let me make a few calls and see if I can borrow a car —"

A loud stomping interrupts them: Sham coming down the stairs. "Oh, you must be Hawa!" he says loudly in false cheer.

"Encik Hisham, how are you?" Hawa's smile and voice are tight, with no warmth. "Give me a few minutes and let me see if I can get Melati to the hospital, save you a trip?"

"My wife will give birth here," he snaps, pretense at friendliness suddenly gone. "There is nothing wrong with her, and home births are perfectly normal." Melati is surprised; he usually keeps his cool for longer. Also, the home birth plan is new to her.

Hawa glares. "Your wife wants a hospital birth," she says in a low voice. "And since she has no midwife, she will be safer there, unless you are going to assist her."

"It's a natural process. She's a healthy woman, and she'll be fine. The gas price is too high."

"You could at least lie and pretend you're going to help." Hawa puts her hands on her hips, ready to fight.

"Sayang," Melati says weakly from the couch. She's not sure which one she's referring to at this point, because the pain makes her dizzy.

"Sayang!" Hawa leans over her, and Melati smiles, reaching out.

"Sayang?" Hisham roars. "This is your sayang? Not I? So you have sinned twice over?" He grabs Hawa's hair and yanks her back. Melati starts at Hawa's yelp, and struggles to get up on the couch seat to see what is happening. Hawa is on the ground, hissing, and there is something strange about her neck, where the line looks bigger than it usually is, thicker, like her neck is longer—

A sharpness cracks across the side of her head and her left earrings. "No, Sham, it's not like that," she begins to say, but there is now a heavy sound—inside her head, or outside, she is not sure, but she cringes and crouches to protect herself, and her child inside her, which is also, she is sure, squalling in its watery bed as it demands to be born.

x. How to Love

When Melati opens her eyes, the pounding has stopped, and she sees Hisham on the far end of the living room, his own eyes glassy like a fearful fish that has suffocated on air. There is the wet chomping, a slick shk-shk-shk, because looming over Hisham is half a body, a spine balanced on the floor supported by intestines. Hawa holds herself up on one hand, and the other plunged into Hisham's belly to pull out the long cords of gut.

Melati watches as Hawa digs with one finger to pluck out a small intestine — "the Westerners call this duodenum" — from under Hisham's sternum. He emits a gasp and a rattling moan, and Melati sees that he is awake through it all, just like she was awake through all his beatings, how he would wait until she was conscious before continuing. And his eyes beg, help me, help me get away from this monster, but for what? He is dying, no matter what Melati does.

Hawa begins to sink down, and Melati can see the penanggalan's stomach expanding as it takes in its nourishment. The hands that have held Melati tenderly grips at a large intestine, pulling it up to a mouth once hungry for kisses. It is one thing to be aware of this other side of Hawa; quite another to see it in action up close.

But they are the same hands, and that is the same mouth — the things that spoke passion now visiting violence, and they are on the same body, belonging to the same person.

Melati is ready now, and she creeps over to Hawa, still hunched over the dying Hisham. She could trap the creature somewhere and throw it out to die in the rising sun. She could snap its spine. She could pull its gut viscera out and see whether it would survive without its digestive system. She could also just run, now, while it was still devouring what was left of her husband. He is only half-eaten now, after all, and there seems to be plenty of time to make her way out.

Melati's womb seizes again, and she gasps at the rude yank back into her body. Then she is ashamed, because this is not just a random mindless creature she is looking at — this is Hawa. And she must trust that her lover will remember her even in the throes of monstrous hunger.

She approaches the hungry figure, the snapping sounds, the slurping of blood and bodily slurry. Up close she can truly appreciate the grotesquerie of Hawa's form: the jagged line on the neck where skin has stretched itself free from its torso, the feathery lines of nerves fanning out from the spinal cord and wrapped around the gut viscera that has accompanied the long trachea line, the lungs unnatural with their perfect symmetry, and the stomach and intestines hard at work already, digesting the hapless man meat passing through them.

And there, strangely pink like jambu air, nestled between lungs and stomach and pancreas, Hawa's heart throbs in a rhythm Melati remembers well.

When Melati first runs the back of a finger along the intestine trailing on the floor, Hawa stirs, slowing her chewing, as if to see what Melati is doing, but not alarmed enough to stop. Emboldened, Melati brushes her fingertips along large intestine, and at the penanggalan's grunt, she slips in her hand into the writhing mass, and they twitch at her touch, inch after inch tenses up as if embracing her fingers, and quiver as she moves past in complaint of neglect. She caresses the curve of the pancreas, and reaches up with both hands to rub the length of the lungs, working her way between them, until at last, she reaches the heart, and Hawa has stopped eating, is now trembling, because perhaps even monsters can feel fear of betrayal.

"I have your heart in my hands," Melati whispered.

"You may keep it." Hawa's voice is a ragged susurrus.

For a moment, Melati wonders if Hawa means it literally, that Melati has permission to pluck it off, if Hawa is offering to slice open Melati's chest and place in a new heart, if Melati is allowed to eat it.

But she only bends forward to kiss it gently. "I already have a second heart to care for."

Hawa says nothing for a long moment, but the second Melati tumbles backwards from another contraction, she rises into the air, tendrils of hair and viscera roping around Melati. "Then we must take care of both hearts."

And cradled in Hawa's depths, Melati finds herself borne up and through a window, towards a cool night sky with cicada choirs emanating from below, and the moonlight cast on Hawa's face makes a second moon.

Melati does not remember much after, because her contractions begin coming faster and harder and she has never been in so much pain. She will later recall being gently deposited by the emergency entrance of the nearest hospital with a nurse rushing out to help her, and being warded. She will give birth safely to a healthy baby boy. When Hawa comes, she will report that Hisham's body has been discovered in the forest, where a vigilante has been dumping the bodies of poachers and known criminals. Melati will be free of suspicion because at the time of Hisham's death, she had been on the road in the Ford Ranger driving towards the hospital.

Against Melati's ear, the skin of Hawa's chest whips free and fragile, like carelessly torn paper, and Hawa's heart, still in Melati's hands, beats steady as a well-kept promise.

Bullet Point

Elizabeth Bear

It takes a long time for the light to die. The power plants can run for a while on automation. Hospitals have emergency generators with massive tanks of fuel. Some houses and businesses have solar panels or windmills. Those may keep making juice, at least intermittently, until entropy claims the workings.

How long is it likely to take then? Six months? The better part of a decade?

I stand on the roof deck of the Luxor casino parking garage, watching the lights that remain, and I wonder. I don't even know enough to theorize, really.

I'm not an engineer. I used to be a blackjack dealer.

Now I am the only living human left on Earth.

It's not all bad. I don't have to deal with:

- Death (except the possibility of my own, eventually).
- Taxes.
- Annoying holidays with my former extended family.
- Airplane lights crossing the desert sky.
- Chemtrails (okay, those were never real in the first place).
- Card counters.
- Masie the pit boss. Thank God.
- My ex-husband. *Double* thank God.

Well, of course I can't know for sure that I'm the only living person. But for all practical purposes, I seem to be. Maybe

Las Vegas is the only place that got wiped out. Maybe over the mountain, Pahrump is thriving.

I don't think so. I hear the abandoned dog packs howling in the night, and I've watched the lights go out, one by one by one.

I feel so bad for those dogs. And even worse for all the ones trapped in houses when the end came. All the cats, guinea pigs, pet turtles. The horses and burros, at least, have a chance. Wild horses can survive in Nevada.

There are so many of them. There's nothing I can do.

If there are any other humans surviving, they are far away from here, and I have no idea where to find them, or even how to begin looking. I have to get out of the desert, though, if I want to keep living. For oh, so many reasons.

I can trust myself, at least. Trusting anybody else never got me where I wanted to be.

Another thing I don't know for sure, and can't even guess at: Why.

Not knowing why?

That's the real pisser.

⁂

Here is an incomplete list of things that do not exist anymore:

> Fresh-baked cookies (unless I find a propane oven and milk a cow and churn some butter and then bake them).

> Jesus freaks (I wonder how they felt when the Rapture happened and it turned out God was taking almost *literally everybody*? That had to be a little bit of a come-down).

> Domestic violence.

> Did I mention my ex-husband?

There's more than enough Twinkies just in the Las Vegas metro area to keep me in snack cakes until the saturated fat kills me. If I'm lucky enough to last long enough that that's what gets me, I might even find out if they eventually go stale.

A problem with being in Las Vegas is getting back out of it again. Walking across a desert will kill me faster than snack cakes. And the highway is impassable with all the stopped and empty cars.

Maybe I can find a monster truck and drive it over everything.

More things that don't exist anymore:

> Reckless driving.

> Speeding tickets.

> Points on your license.

> Worrying about fuel efficiency.

Las Vegas Boulevard is dark and still. Nevertheless, I can't make myself walk on the blacktop, even though the cars there are unmoving, bumper to bumper for all eternity. The Strip's last traffic jam.

There might be bodies in the cars. I don't look.

I don't want to know.

I don't think there's going to be anybody alive, but that might be worse. More dangerous, anyway.

I mean, I *think* I'm the last. But I don't *know*.

That was also the reason I couldn't make myself walk along the sidewalk. It was too exposed. The tall casinos were mostly designed so that their windows had views of something more interesting than hordes of pedestrians — hordes of pedestrians now long gone — but somebody might be up there, and somebody up there might spot me. A lone moving dot on a sea of silent asphalt.

Lord, where have all the people gone?

So I stick to the median. With its crape myrtle hedges and doomed palm trees already drooping in the failed irrigation to break up my outline. With the now pointless crowd control barriers to discourage jaywalkers from darting into traffic.

Two more things:

> Traffic.

> Jaywalkers.

Hey, and one more:

> Assholes.

⁂

I am half hoping to find people. And I am 90% terrified of what they might do if I find them. Or if they find me first.

I'm pretty sure this wasn't actually the Rapture.

Pretty sure.

I keep trying to tell myself that there's not a single damned person from the old world that I really miss. That it's time I had some time alone, as the song used to go. It is nice not to be on anybody else's schedule, or subject to anybody else's expectations or demands. At least my ex-husband is almost certainly among the evaporated. That's a load off my mind.

I moved to Vegas, changed my name by sealed court order, abandoned a career I worked for ten years to get, and became a casino dealer in order to hide from him. Considering that, it's not a surprise to find myself relieved that whatever ends up causing me to look over my shoulder from now on, it won't be Paul.

I got the cozy apocalypse that was supposed to be the best-case-apocalypse-scenario — wish-fulfillment — complete with the feral dogs that howl in the night.

But it doesn't feel like wish fulfillment. It feels like…being alone on the beach in winter. I'm lonely, and I miss…well, I already left behind everybody I loved. But leaving somebody behind is not the same thing as *knowing they are gone.*

There's potential space, and there's empty space.

Maybe that's why I'm still here. Nobody thought to tap me on the shoulder and say, "Hey, Izzy, let's go," because I'd already abandoned all of them to save my own life one time.

Hah. There I go again. Making things about me that aren't.

I thought I was used to being lonely, but this is a whole new level of alone. I feel like I should be paralyzed by survivor guilt. But I am a rock. I am an island.

> Simon

> Garfunkel

Lying to yourself is, however, still alive and well.

⟷

The gun is heavy. Cold, blue metal. It feels about twice its size.

I find it under the seat of a cop car with the driver's door left open. The keys are in the ignition. The dome light has long since burned out, and the open-door dinger has dinged itself into silence.

It's a handgun. A revolver. Old School. There is a holster to go with it, but no gunbelt. There are six bullets in the cylinder.

> The Las Vegas Metropolitan Police Department.

> Crooked cops.

> Throwaway guns.

I unbuckle my belt, thread it through the loops on the holster, and hang it at my hip.

There *are* plenty of rattlesnakes, still.

⟷

> Antivenin.

> Emergency rooms.

There *are* plenty of antibiotics. And pain medication. And canned peaches.

And a nice ten-speed mountain bike that I liberate from a sporting goods place, along with one of those trailers designed for pulling your kid or dog along. I've never been much of an urban biker, preferring trails, but it wasn't like I would have to contend with traffic. And it seems like the right tool for weaving in and out of rows of abandoned cars.

I pick up a book on bike repair too, and some tire patches and spare tubes and so on. Plus saddlebags and baskets. And a lot of water bottles.

It turns out that one thing the zombie apocalypse movies got really wrong was the abundance of stockpiled resources available after a population of more than seven billion people just…ceases to exist.

There's plenty of stuff to go around when there's no "around" for it to go. Until the stuff goes bad, anyway.

That's the reason I want to get out of the desert before summer comes. Things will last longer in colder places, with less murderous UV.

↭

Things that apparently *do* still exist: at least one other human being.

And he is following me.

He picks me up at a Von's. I'm in the pasta aisle. The rats have started gnawing into boxes, but the canned goods are relatively fine. And if you can ignore the silence of the gaming machines and the smell of fermenting fruit, rotten meat, and rodent urine, it's not that different than if I were shopping at 2 AM in the old world.

I'm crouched down, filling my backpack with Beefaroni and D batteries from the endcap, when I hear footsteps. It's daylight outside, but it's dark inside the store. I turn off my LED flashlight. My heart contracts inside me, shuddering jolts of blood through my arteries. The rush and thump fills my ears. I strain through them for the sounds that mean life or death: the scrape or squeak of boot sole on tile, the rattle of packages.

My hands shake as I zip the backpack inch by silent inch. I stand. The straps creak. I can't be sure if I have managed not to tremble the bag into a betraying clink. One step, then another. Sideways, slipping, setting each foot down carefully so it doesn't make a sound.

As I get closer to the front of the store (good) the ambiance grows brighter (bad). I hunker by the side of a dead slot machine, shivering. From where I crouch, I can peek around and see a clear path to the door.

The whole way is silhouetted against the plate-glass windows. The pack weighs on my shoulders. If I leave it, I'm not really leaving anything. I can get another, and all the Chef Boyardee I want. But it's hard to abandon resources.

And hey, the cans might stop a bullet.

Don't hyperventilate.

Easier said than done.

Sliding doors stopped working when the store lights did. Too late, I realize there's probably a fire door in the back I could have slipped out of more easily. In the old world, that would have been alarmed...but would the alarm even work anymore?

There is a panic bar on the front doors. I crane over my shoulder, straining for motion, color, any sign of the person I am certain I heard.

Nothing.

Maybe I'm hallucinating.

Maybe he's gone to the back of the store.

I nerve myself and hit the door running. I got it open on the way in, so I know it isn't locked. It flies away from the crash bar — no subtlety there — and I plunge through, sneakers slapping the pavement. The parking lot outside is flat and baking, even in September. The sun hits my ballcap like a slap. Rose bushes and trees scattered in the islands are already dead from lack of water. The rosemary bushes and crape myrtles look a little sad, but they are holding on.

I sprint toward them. Now the pack makes noise, the cans within clanking and thumping on each other — and clanking and thumping against my ribs and spine. I'll have a suite of bruises because of them. But I left my bike on the kickstand in the fire lane, and — wonder of wonders — it's still there. I throw myself at it and swing a leg over it, pushing off with my feet before I ever touch the pedals. I miss my first push and skin the back of my calf bloody on the serrated grip.

I curse, not loud but on that hiss of breath you get with shock and pain. The second time, I manage to get my heel *on* the pedal. The bike jerks forward with each hard pump.

I squirt between parked cars. As my heart slows, I let myself think I've imagined the whole thing. Until the supermarket doors crash open, and a male voice shrill with desperation yells, "Miss! Come back! Miss! Don't run away from me! Please! I'm not going to hurt you!"

And maybe he's not. But I'm not inclined to trust. Trusting never did get me anywhere I wanted to be.

I push down and pedal harder. I don't coast.

He only shouts after me. He doesn't shoot. And I don't look back.

❧

Now that he knows I exist, he's not going to stop looking.

I know this the way I know my childhood street address.

And why *would* he stop? People need people, or so we're always told. Being alone — really alone, completely alone — is a form of torture.

To be utterly truthful, there's a part of me that wants to go looking for him. Part of me that doesn't want to be alone anymore either.

The question I have to ask myself is whether that lonely part of me is stronger than the feral, sensible part that cautions me to run away. To run, and keep running.

Because it's the apocalypse. And I'm not very big, or a trained fighter. And because of another thing that doesn't exist anymore:

> Social controls.

Dissociation, though — that I've got *plenty* of.

↭

He is going to come looking for me. Because of course he will. I hear him calling after me for a long time as I ride away. And I know he tries to follow me because *I* follow *him*.

We're the last two people on Earth, and how do you get more Meet Cute than that? We've all stayed up late watching B movies in the nosebleed section of the cable channels, and we've all read TV Tropes, and we all know how this story goes.

But my name isn't Eve. It's Isabella. And I have an allergy to clichés.

↭

> Dating websites.

> Restraining orders.

> Twitter block lists.

> Domestic violence shelters.

↭

I stalk him. I'll call it what it is.

It's easy to find him again: he's so confident and fearless that he's still wandering around in the same neighborhood *trying* to get my attention.

I mean, first I go back to my current lair and get ready to run.

I load up the bike trailer with my food and gear, and flats and flats and flats of water. My sun layers and my hat go inside, and I zip the whole thing up.

Then I hide it, and I check again to be sure my gun is loaded.

And *then* I go and stalk him.

⁂

He's definitely a lot bigger than me. But he doesn't look a damned thing like my ex, which is a point in his favor.

And he isn't trying in the least to be sneaky. He's just walking down the sidewalk, swerving to miss the cars that rolled off the road when their drivers disappeared, pulling a kid's little red wagon loaded with supplies. He's armed with a pistol on his belt, but so am I. And at least he's not strung all over with bandoliers and automatic weapons. Plus, there are enough of those hungry, terrified feral dog packs around that a weapon isn't a bad idea.

I wonder how long it will be before the cougars move back down from the mountains and start eating them all.

The circle of life.

Poor dogs.

They were counting on us, and look where that got them.

⁂

The only other living human being (presumed) is wearing a dirty T-shirt (athletic gray), faded jeans, and a pair of high-top skull-pattern Chucks that I appreciate the irony of, even while knowing his feet must be roasting in them. I make him out to be about 25. His hair is still pretty clean cut under his mesh-sided brimmed hat, but he's wearing about two weeks of untrimmed beard. Two weeks is about how long it's been since the world ended.

He calls out as he walks along. How can anyone be so unafraid to attract attention? So confident of taking up all that space in the world? Like he thinks he has a right to exist and nobody is going to come take it away from him.

He's so *relaxed.* It scares me just watching him.

I *do* notice that he doesn't seem threatening. There's nothing sinister, calculated, or menacing about this guy. He keeps pushing his hat up to mop the sweat from under it with an old cotton bandanna. He doesn't have a lot of situational awareness, either. Even with me orbiting him a couple of blocks off on the mountain bike, he doesn't seem to notice me watching. I'm staying under cover, sure. But the bike isn't silent. It has a chain and wheels and joints. It creaks and rattles and whizzes a little, like any bicycle.

Blood has dried, itchy and tight-feeling, on the back of my calf. The edge of my sock is stiff. I drink some of the water in my bottle, though not as much as I want to.

It's getting on toward evening, and he's walking more directly now, in less of a searching wander, when I make up my mind. He seems to be taking a break from searching for me, at least for the time being. He's stopped making forays into side streets, and he's stopped calling out.

I cycle hard on a parallel street to get in front of him, and from a block away I show myself.

He stops in his tracks. His hands move away from his sides and he drops the little red wagon handle. My right hand stays on the butt of my holstered gun with the six bullets in it.

"Hi," he says, after an awkward pause. He pitches his voice to carry. "I'm Ben."

"Hi," I call back. "I'm Isabella."

"You came back."

I nod. Never in my memory—probably in living memory—has it been quiet enough in this city that you could hear somebody clearly if they called to you from this far away. But it's that quiet now. Honey bees buzz on the crape myrtles. I wonder if they're Africanized.

"Nice bike, Isabella."

"Thanks." I let the smirk happen. "It's new."

He laughs. Then he bends down and picks up the handle of his little red wagon. When he straightens, he lets his hands hang naturally. "Have you seen anybody else?"

I shake my head.

"Me neither." He makes a face. "Mind if I come over?"

My heart speeds. But it's respectful that he's asking, right?

I don't get off the bike or walk it toward him. I cant it against one cocked leg and wait.

"Sure." I try to sound confident. I square my shoulders.

You know what else doesn't exist anymore?

> Backup.

⁂

We head off side by side. I've finally gotten off the bike and am walking it, though I casually keep it and the wagon in between us and stay out of grabbing range. The step-through frame will help me hop on and bug out fast if I need to.

Ben offers me a granola bar. I guess he learned early on, as I did, that once the power went off, there wasn't any point in harvesting chocolate. Well, I mean, it's still calorie-dense. But if it's daytime, it's probably squeezable. And if it's not melted, it has re-solidified into the wrapper and you'll wind up eating a fair amount of plastic.

"Terrorists," he hazards, with the air of one making conversation.

I shake my head. "Aliens."

He thinks about it.

"We probably had it coming," I posit.

"I don't think it's a great idea to stay in Vegas," Ben says, with no acknowledgment of the non sequitur.

"I've been thinking that too."

He glances sidelong at me. His face brightens. "I was thinking of heading to San Diego. Nice and temperate. Lots of seafood. Easy to grow fruit. Not as hot as here."

I think about earthquakes and drought and wildfires. My plan was the Pacific Northwest, where the climate is mild and wet and un-irrigated agriculture could flourish. I figure I've got maybe five years to figure out a sustainable lifestyle.

And I don't want to spend the rest of my life living off ceviche. Or dodging wildfires and worrying about potable water.

I don't say anything, though. If I decide to split on this guy, it's just as well if he doesn't know what my plans were. Especially if we're the last two people on Earth.

Why him? Why me?

Who knows.

"Lot of avocados down there." I can sound like I'm agreeing to nearly anything.

He nods companionably. "The bike is a good idea."

"I'd be a little scared to try cycling across the mountains and through Baker. That's some nasty desert."

Mild pushback, to see what happens in response.

"I figure you could make it in a week or ten days."

That would be some Tour de France shit, Ben. Especially towing water. But I don't say that.

> Tour de France

"Or," he says, "I thought of maybe a Humvee. Soon, while the gas is still good."

He loses a few points on that. I wouldn't feel bad at all about bullet pointing Hummers, and I don't feel nearly as bad about bullet pointing the sort of people who used to drive them as I probably ought to.

"Look," Ben says, when I've been quiet for a while, "why don't we find someplace to hole up? It's getting dark, and the dog packs will be out soon."

I look at him and can't think what to say.

He sighs tolerantly, not getting it. I guess *not getting it* isn't over yet either.

"I give you my word of honor that I will be a total gentleman."

You have to trust somebody sometime.

I go home with Ben. Not in the euphemistic sense. In the sense that we pick a random house and break into it together. It has barred security doors and breaking in would be harder, except the yard wasn't xeriscaped and all the

> Landscaping

is down to brown sticks and sadness. Which makes it super easy to spot the fake rock that had once been concealed in a now-desiccated foundation planting, turn it over, and extract the key hidden inside.

We let ourselves in. There used to be a security system, but it's out of juice. The house is hot and dark inside, and smells like decay. Plant decay, mostly: sweetish and overripe, due to the fruit rotting in bowls on the counter. Neither Ben nor I is dumb enough to open the refrigerator. We do check the bedrooms for bodies. There aren't any — there never are — but we do find the remains of a hamster that starved and had mummified in its cedar chips.

That makes me sad, like the dog packs. If this *is* the Rapture, I hope God gets a nasty call from the Afterlife Society for the Prevention of Cruelty to Animals.

We find can openers and plates and set about rustling up some supper. All the biking has made me ravenous, and when I finish eating, I am surprised to discover that I have let my guard down. And that nothing terrible has happened.

Ben looks at me across the drift of SPAM cans and Green Giant vacuum-pack corn (my favorite). "This would be perfect if the air conditioning worked."

"Sometimes you can find a place with solar panels," I say noncommittally.

"Funny that all that tree hugging turned out useful after all, isn't it?" And maybe he sees the look on my face, because he raises a hand, placating. "Some of my best friends are tree huggers!" He looks down, mouth twisting. "*Were* tree huggers."

So I forgive him. "My plan had been to find someplace that was convenient and had solar, and if I was lucky its own well. And wait for winter before I set out."

"That's a good idea." He picks at a canned peach.

"Also, the older houses up in Northtown and on the west side of the valley. Those handle the heat better."

"Little dark up there in North Vegas," Ben says, casually. "I mean, not that there's anybody left, but it was."

I open my mouth. I close it. I almost hear the record scratch.

I'd have thought it was safe to bullet

> racism.

But I guess not.

I don't say, *So it's full of evaporated black people cooties?* I get up, instead, and start clearing empty tin cans off the table and setting them in the useless sink. Ben watches me, amused that I'm tidying this place we're only going to abandon.

Setting things to rights, the only way I can.

He's relaxed and expansive now. A little proprietary.

I am not *quite* as scared as I ever have been in my life. But that's only because I've been really, *really* scared.

"It's just us now. You don't have anybody to impress," Ben says. "You're free. You don't have to play those games to get ahead."

I blink at him. "Games?"

He stands up. I turn toward the sink. Knives in the knife block beside it. If it comes down to it, they might be worth a try. I try to keep my eyes forward, to not give him a reason to think I'm being impertinent. But I keep glancing back.

I look scared. And that's bad. You never want to look scared.

It attracts predators.

"Nobody can hurt you for saying the truth now. And obviously," he says with something he probably means to be taken as a coaxing smile, "it's up to us to repopulate the planet."

"With white people." It just comes out. I've never been the best at self-censorship. Even when I know speaking might get me hurt.

At least I keep my tone neutral. I think.

Neutral enough, I guess, because he leers again. "Maybe God's given us a second chance to get it right, is all I'm saying. Don't you think it's a sign? I mean, here I meet the last woman on earth, and she's a blue-eyed blonde."

The little tins fit inside the big tins. The spoons stack up.

> Ice cream.

Though I could probably make some, if I found that cow. And snow. And bottle blondes are still going to be around until my hair grows out. I don't have any reason to try to change my appearance now.

Ben moves, the floor creaking under him. "If you're not going to try to save humanity, what's the point in even being alive? Are you going to just give up?"

I turn toward him. I put my back toward the sink. I half-expect him to be looming over me but he's standing well back, respectfully. "Maybe humanity has a lifespan, like everything else. You're going to die eventually."

"Sure," he says. "That's why people have kids. To leave a legacy. Leave something of themselves behind."

"Two human beings are not a viable gene pool."

"You don't want to rush into anything," he says. "That's all right. I can respect that."

And then he does something that stuns me utterly. He goes and lies down on the sofa. He only glances back at me once. The expression on his face is trying to be neutral, but I can see the smugness beneath it.

The fucking *confidence*.

Of course he doesn't need to push his luck, or my timeline. Of course he's confident I'll come around. He's got all the time in the world.

And what choice have I got in the long run, really?

There will always be assholes.

I leave that house in the morning at first light. I lock the door behind me to be tidy.

Only four bullets left. I should have anticipated that I might need more ammo. But this is Nevada. I can probably find some.

Maybe I can find a friendly dog, also. I love dogs. And it's not good for people to be too alone.

There might still be some horses out in the northwest valley that haven't gone totally wild. It'd be nice to have company.

I can get books from the libraries. I've got a few months to prepare. I wonder how you take care of a horse on a long pack trip? I wonder if I can manage it on my own?

Well, I'll find out this winter. And if I get to Reno before the snow melts in the Sierras…I'm a patient girl. And I'll have the benefit of not having slept through history class. What I mean to say is, I can wait to tackle Donner Pass until springtime.

The lights that are still on stay on longer than I might have expected. But eventually, one by one, they fail. When I can't see any anywhere anymore, I make my way down to the Strip with Bruce, my brindle mastiff, trotting beside.

Before I head North, I want to say goodbye.

That night the stars shine over Las Vegas, as they had not shone in living memory. The Milky Way is a misty waterfall. I can make out a Subaru logo for the ages: six and a half Pleiades.

I stand in the middle of the empty, dark, and silent Strip, and watch the lack of answering lights bloom in the vast black bowl of the valley all around.

I cannot see so far as Tokyo, New York, Hong Kong, London, Cairo, Jerusalem, Abu Dhabi, Seoul, Sydney, Rio de Janiero, Paris, Madrid, Kyoto, Chicago, Amsterdam, Mumbai, Mecca, Milan. All the places where artificial light and smog had, for an infinitesimal cosmic moment, wiped them from the sky. But I imagine that those distant, alien suns now shine the same way, there.

As if they had never been dimmed. As if the Milky Way had never faded, ghostlike, before the glare.

I reach down and stroke Bruce's ears. They're soft as cashmere. He leans on me, happy.

That night sky would be a remarkable sight. If I had a soul in the world to remark to.

Abyssinia

Raven Belasco

It was one of those impossibly, intolerably muggy Philly summer nights.

There's no breeze on nights like these, but just in case the air might move the tiniest bit, she was sitting out on the battered square of a back porch, drinking a pilfered bottle of Babbo's grappa.

She could steal his grappa because Babbo didn't really like the stuff. He had to pretend to because it was Italian, and Babbo was as proud of being Napoletano as a person could be. At every gifting occasion, neighbors and the men from the union would proudly offer him bottles of grappa smuggled in from the Old World, and he would welcome them with cries of joyful thanks. And then later they would collect dust in the back of the liquor cabinet, while the bathtub gin and moonshine never needed wiping off.

Prohibition might be the law of the land, but dry laws never seemed to have impacted anyone she knew. No one in the neighborhood was narking to the flatfoots because *everyone* boozed, male and female alike. Indeed, there was a chapter of Women's Organization for National Prohibition *Reform* that met at the Baptist church down the corner.

The first time she'd stolen a bottle, she'd thought grappa tasted like gasoline. But at least it was *free* gasoline. And now she even liked the harsh bite — it made you know you were drinking something. And it was even better with a cigarette, when she could afford to splurge on a pack of Luckys or was offered a loosey. It had to be offered though. She was too proud to ask.

And tonight she *needed* the giggle juice and a snipe. It had been a hard, damn day. And then a hard, damn night. Her hand shook a little when she picked up the bottle to take another swig.

She'd taken another gal to see Emma after work. It wasn't an easy one. After she'd helped that poor thing home, she'd barely been able to get herself home. She didn't like to cry where people could see. You looked like a *pathetic frail*, like you had no pride. She didn't have much, but she did have plenty of pride. Babbo had taught her that. If you were born with the name Vitale, you had the Vitale pride. One of her teachers — before she'd left school to get the National Biscuit Company factory job to help out because Mamma was having another baby — had told her that her name had come down from the ancient Romans, and it meant *life*. "*Certo!*" Babbo had boomed when she'd told him, but she could tell he hadn't thought of it before, and it made him even more proud..

"And you *are* vital, so full of life," came the softest whisper from the darkness of the alley, and she almost knocked the bottle of grappa down the steps. She had to take a second to decide if she was hearing things.

"I got a knife!" she called out and reached for the switchblade in the pocket she'd sewn into her dress.

"You do not need a knife with me, sister," came the voice, still low as if gentling a scared animal, but also low for a woman, a warm contralto.

It made her want to relax into it right away, but that feeling scared her even more, so she thumbed the little round switch. The blade sprang out.

"No, no," the voice assured her, as the female shape, which until this moment had merely been a darker shadow, slid close enough to make out details. The shadow woman was what men would call a "butter and egg fly," filling out a thin-pleated black dress with perfect round curves. Her skin was a rich honey bronze, and her glam pin curls were the same honey shade.

"I am impressed with your defenses," the dusky dame promised in her low tones, "but I am no threat to you, Palmina."

"How do you know my name?"

"Everyone in the neighborhood knows you. I simply had to ask."

"Well, why d'ya ask then?"

"Why would I not want to get to know such an impressive woman as yourself?"

"Ahhh, stop! Why're you saying these things to me? Nobody from here talks like you. What d'ya want? *Really*."

"You are astute as well as brave. There is indeed something I want from you—"

"I knew it!"

"But now that I have met you, I want your friendship, as well."

"That ain't how friendship works, lady."

"I know how friendship works, sweet girl. Give me a chance to earn your friendship, please."

Palmina looked at the stranger. From the shadows, she was *shady* in every sense. But she was compelling too. The pleated dress and matching boxy jacket were probably silk, the way they glistened in the low light from the windows above the sides of the alley. The woman didn't wear a hat or gloves, but her shoes were brand-new, black leather Cuban-heeled oxfords with a delicate pattern of perforations. She was well-to-do, but she wasn't stuck-up fancy. A woman could tell so many things about another woman from her clothes and shoes. Makeup and hair also told stories. While the woman had perfectly waved hair, she wore almost no face paint. Her skin was so flawless that Palmina had to assume she wore foundation, but her eyebrows were not plucked Hollywood thin, nor drawn in, and she wore no eyeshadow. She *must* have put mascara on, but just that and perfect carmine lips. She still looked like a movie star, regardless, not like anyone she'd ever met before.

Palmina found herself wanting to hear this woman's story, so she pushed aside what was otherwise perfectly reasonable mistrust. "I never had a friend whose name I didn't even know."

"Ah, a very good point. My name is Astryiah."

"Ahh-stree-yah?"

"That is it exactly. However, most Americans do not seem able to say it. I have been telling people my name is Alyssa. They seem more capable of pronouncing that."

"Astryiah's beauteeful! Where's it from?"

"Thank you, sweet one. And what a subtle way to find out about me. Your diplomacy shall be rewarded. I come from a country that in your Bible is called Judah. It is now called Palestine, and against all reason or logic, it is ruled by the British. In essence, I have no home."

Palmina had known the woman was foreign, but this was vastly more exotic than anything she would have guessed. This Astryiah had seemed coolly unemotional, despite her stated, and obvious, desire to make friends with Palmina. But when she'd said, "I have no home," Palmina could hear the depths of emotion under the simplicity of the words.

"I'm sorry to hear that," was all she could say, but she could also hold out the grappa bottle as a tangible form of comfort.

"This is very kind of you." Astryiah took the bottle, and somehow in the process, Palmina found herself scrunching over to make space for her on the top step. It would have been too much to call the cramped space a *porch*; it was just five rickety steps up to the back door with a railing on one side that you grabbed at risk of splinters at best and complete structural failure at worst.

As the shadow lady settled so close beside Palmina that their hips were touching, she handed the bottle back. Palmina took a swig and put the cap back on before she realized the woman hadn't bothered to take a sip. Well, that wasn't a surprise. Many people found grappa to have a taste reminiscent of paint thinner, her Babbo included. She put the bottle down between her feet.

"Astryiah," she said, the name still tasting so strange in her mouth, "I kinda wouldn't mind knowing why you're sitting on these steps with me. *Besides* being my 'friend.'"

"It is because we are friends that I will tell you, *chamuda*. I am unused to telling my business to anyone…but I do desire to share with you.

"I have been in this country…some while now." Astryiah waved an elegant hand to dismiss the value of mentioning any specific length of time. "Since I am a woman without a home, I thought it good to come to a country that thinks only of the future. This new Philadelphia is a vibrant place where a stranger can fit in to the bustle and thrum of human life."

That was an odd way to phrase things. But then again, this woman was unlike anyone she'd met before. And she was *foreign*. Foreigners could be expected to say things strangely, English not being their first language and all. Why, her Nonna and Nonno could barely even speak English. Astryiah spoke it better than they did, by far. She talked better than some of the kids she'd grown up with, American-born and all.

The pause in the conversation gave Palmina a chance to enjoy the warm glow of the grappa in her mind and body, relaxing for the first time all day. She was also acutely aware of Astryiah's hip and thigh pressing against her own. The sultry night air seemed right for this moment, despite the trickle of sweat down her back, despite the damp stickiness of her bra against her skin.

"As your friend-to-be, may I ask what has been troubling you on this hot summer night, so like the nights in the land of my birth? Summer is the time to be carefree in this country, is it not? Dances, cookouts, and I do not know...parades?"

Palmina laughed. "Parades mostly happen during daytime. Don't they have those things where you come from?"

"Cookouts were nothing special to my people; we cooked outdoors generally. I have been to parades, but they were always — shall we say — *military* in nature. I haven't danced in... many, many years."

"But that just ain't right! Dancing is...I dunno...you just can't *not!* Hold up!" Palmina ran into the house and started the record player. She'd had enough extra pennies last week to buy a 45 of Artie Shaw's "Begin the Beguine." She left the back door open, and made brave by the booze, as she ran down the wobbly steps she grabbed Astryiah's hand and pulled her out into the alley.

"I...I do not know how to dance to this music —" Astryiah began.

Palmina just laughed, settled one elegant bronze hand onto her shoulder, and held the other outstretched with her own. Taking the lead, she spun them through the torrid shadows.

Her unexpected visitor brought an equally unexpected new pattern to Palmina's life, which had felt full enough already. Every day she got up too early for the bus ride that ended when the conductor yelled, "Pick Me Up Central! All you *working* men and women get out here!" with a leer on his face. It was assumed that because the National Biscuit Company employed women as well as men, that affairs between employees were inevitable. Whether it was a self-fulfilling prophecy or not, it wasn't wrong.

Then it was a full day boxing Lorna Doones, Oreo Cookies, and Fig Newtons — and staying out of the river of drama that flowed through the factory. After all that, she had her...

other job. And then when she got home from *that*, most evenings she'd find Astryiah waiting for her.

She took Astryiah to some jolly-ups, for her shadow lady turned out to be a natural jitterbug, a jive bomber. Palmina derived great satisfaction watching the boys who fancied themselves real cool cats trying to impress a dame who so clearly outclassed them. Astryiah treated them all with good-humored dismissal, not hostile, but clearly not welcoming to unwanted attentions. Palmina took notes, because she'd always found men far more of a hassle than Astryiah seemed to. Although after the first attempt to introduce Astryiah by her real name, she quickly fell back on "Alyssa." No one else seemed to be able to handle it, although that could be because it was hard to really hear anything anyone said when the joint was jumpin'.

On other nights, they just stayed in, spun some platters, and talked. Astryiah was a true world traveler, although many places she had visited — "oh, quite some time ago" — with that same airy, elegantly dismissive wave of the hand. But she would still answer Palmina's eager questions. Not all of them, but enough.

"You have never left this country, not even to go to the land of your ancestors? But no, so few people get a chance to travel, most especially not women. You would make an excellent traveler, *chamuda*. I would love the chance to show you around the world."

Astryiah would often say ridiculous things like that. Palmina ignored the obviously impossible as a matter of course.

Astryiah apparently never slept. Palmina had never minded the occasional late night in the past, but as the weeks went on and her conversations with her late-night friend ending regularly sometime around sunrise, Palmina began to feel the lack of sleep taking its toll. To her surprise, she had an attack of the whips and jangles.

"Astryiah — I love our talks. But can we skip 'em for a bit?"

"If you are enjoying them, why stop?"

"Because I'm joed! Uh, that's slang. I mean I'm just too worn out these days to handle everything I gotta handle."

"You have talked *around* all the things you must handle. I know about the factory. I know about how much your family demands from you. But there is a third thing, a very big thing, and it drains you more than just staying up talking with me. Have we not grown close enough that you might share it with me…?"

"You don't wanna hear about this. It's not nice."

"*Chamuda*… I have seen far more terrible things in this world than you can imagine. Tell me. Maybe I can help."

"How could you help with this? You're a stranger. I mean, you're not from the neighborhood. The gals wouldn't know they could trust you. They trust me because they know me."

"I see. And this is a problem where only women can help women?"

Palmina paused. She didn't talk about this part of her life. Not with anyone who wasn't already involved. Would speaking of it to Astryiah be a betrayal? But Astryiah seemed to be understanding it already, so she said, "Yes."

"Oh, my dear one. This is no new problem for women. We have always had to help ourselves with this, for men are never help."

"You dig what I mean?"

"Of course I understand. Listen. The city I come from — in ancient times there were whorehouses. Not like they are today, dirty and shameful. No, the women were respected as providing an important service. In times further past, they had been admired as acolytes of the Goddess, and some of that respect still was attached to their trade.

"But when women and men have pleasure together, there will be results. And these women were not desirous of raising all these results. These women did not have time to be mothers, at least not at this stage in their lives. They were what you might call 'businesswomen,' and they had their careers to attend to.

"There was a bathhouse attached to their establishment. The women and their clients enjoyed the warm bath, hot bath, cold plunge, and steam room. There were masseurs and even barbers. But there was also a woman who sold certain herbs for women who found themselves…in that condition. She would give you the herbs, and then if you grew very sick from them, she would nurse you.

"And it was not just the women of this house who used her services. Women from all classes, all ranks of life from the richest senators' wives to the lowliest serving girls, all found their way to this woman, because there is a right time for love to turn into new life, but there are also times when it would be very bad indeed."

Palmina sat through this outflowing of words, frozen by their unexpectedness.

Astryiah continued, "So, you see, *chamuda*, I understand this matter well. There has never been a time when a woman could fail to understand it. And seldom indeed have there been times when men have kept their desire for power and control — and their unwanted noses — out of this private, personal business of women."

"Oh." It was all Palmina could say. Why was she so shocked to hear Astryiah's words? Of course every woman around the world had this in common. She'd never thought about women in other countries, but then she really didn't have time to think, because she was always so busy trying to keep her gals safe.

No, it was silly to be shocked. And it would be foolish to see if Astryiah didn't have some knowledge that would help her.

"I'm not…the woman with the herbs, like back in your old days. I just help fems who need it. They know to come to me. And I set up a time and place, and the woman who has the know-how to fix it meets us there. I hold my gals' hands while it happens. I hold 'em while they cry. I make sure they aren't too sick to make it home. Sometimes they doss here overnight. Sometimes they cry all night, and I stay up with 'em. I cry with 'em."

The outpouring of words choked to a stop in Palmina's throat. She'd never said those things out loud before. She just *did* them. Lived them. Got through them — and helped her gals get through them. That was the most important part. Palmina's own needs became seemingly insignificant in the face of the constant need of these women; in the hardest, most terrible of circumstances where either choice meant a different risk of death for life, different hazards of physical pain and heartbreak.

But now, telling Astryiah these things, suddenly Palmina felt need too. A deep need for the wounds this work had inflicted on her soul to be soothed — to be heard, to be understood, to be forgiven, to be accepted. Simply, to not be alone.

She didn't know how to ask for all that, but Astryiah seemed to know without words what Palmina needed. They were on the too-small bed with the brutally lumpy mattress that had come with this apartment, for Palmina had only a table and one chair in the tiny kitchen that, along with the water closet you could barely turn around in, made up the three "rooms" of her lousy apartment. The only place for two people to sit down together was the back stoop or the bed.

Astryiah sighed, the deep sigh of a woman holding another woman's pain, and folded Palmina into her arms. Palmina had been in those arms plenty of times, dancing, or tripping home from a hop, swacked, in the wee hours of the morning. But this time it was different. It was "all us gals" camaraderie before. Now it was a safe place where she could let go of all she'd been holding on to. It was a *homecoming*.

As her gals had cried in her arms, Palmina let go and cried in Astryiah's arms. Out it all came in sobs and choking gasps. And a startling amount of snot, for which Astryiah silently produced a handkerchief.

At first she was drowning in the immediacy of the pain shaking loose. Then it became a floating in release, safe in warm, strong arms. For a little while, maybe she dozed off; she hadn't been that relaxed in so long. And then with a nasty start, she came to herself, embarrassed for putting her problems on someone else like that. And, equally, for letting anyone see so deeply into her private emotions.

"I…I'm sorry! I been real punchy these days! Please — I'm so sorry —!"

"Hush, *chamuda*, hush. It was a gift you gave to me, your trust. And it was a gift I could give to you, some peace. It is what we *friends* do for each other."

Palmina still felt the hot flush of shame on her skin, despite Astryiah's soothing words, despite her hands softly stroking down Palmina's back. The Vitales were stoic. Well, they were loud enough in anger, and there was no lack of public wailing for the acceptable kinds of loss. But these shameful, private emotions — weaknesses — these were not meant to be shared with *anyone*.

"*Beseder, teraga.* It is well. Relax. Everyone needs to share their woes and receive comfort now and then. You are not made of stone."

"I didn't mean to burden you."

"Be quiet now. I asked for this trust; it is no burden at all." They were silent for a minute, and then she asked, "*Chamuda*, I know I ask much now, but…have you ever needed this… service you provide for women?"

Palmina shuddered, and the tears nearly started again. She'd not let herself even think of that for so, so long. Briefly she fought it. But it rose unstoppably from where she had hidden it down inside.

"Ye-yeah. It's how I found out about it. There was a moment. One of my brother's friends. He said such nice things. We were slap-happy. It felt good. I didn't think that just one time…could lead to…I'd always heard that nothing could happen the first time. Or if he pulled out, and I *did* make him pull out. But in a month, there I was. In that *condition*. And I didn't want to *marry* Jack. He's nice enough, but I don't *love* him —"

Palmina discovered she was talking so fast that she'd forgotten to breathe. She stopped, caught her breath. Astryiah didn't interrupt the silence.

"So. I couldn't have — not right now. I have no money — the factory don't pay much! And I won't — I won't! — move back home. So I couldn't — I just couldn't…!"

"No, *chamuda*, you could not. And I regret that you live in this time and place where you could not have had a safer, healthier experience." Astryiah started to say something else, broke off. She pulled Palmina in, held her tight, as if now she had something *she* was afraid to say. Palmina had never seen Astryiah look the least bit scared of anything.

"Palmina…there is a gift I can give you. It would keep you safe from ever getting pregnant again if you want that freedom. Is that…something you would wish?"

"Not ever getting knocked up, ever? Yeah!"

"Not *ever*."

"Not even if I was married and wanted kids?"

"That is the cost of the gift. You would not be able to be impregnated ever again."

"That's a…real large order."

"It is not an easy decision, no."

"But then…I'd be safe from havin' to go through that all over again?"

"Yes. And you would be…healthier, stronger, safer from disease as well."

"Whatcha talkin' about? A drug? Some kind of operation?"

"No! Nothing like that! Just a…sharing. An intimate sharing."

"That don't jive. Sharing what?"

"Ach. This is the hard part. Let me first ask an unspoken question…."

Palmina was going to ask her what she meant, but Astryiah slowly leaned her face closer, and then closer, and then their lips met. Palmina closed her eyes from habit, and without the distraction of vision, she suddenly was not aware of anything except how incredibly soft those lips were, how good they felt against her own. She put all of her surprised self into returning the kiss, and that led to Astryiah wrapping her oddly strong, lithely feminine arms around Palmina and pulling her close for a deeper kiss.

When they finally broke apart, Palmina felt faint. "I never kissed a girl before," she confessed breathlessly to Astryiah.

Her shadow lady smiled. "How did it compare?"

"Oh! You can't compare it! Apples and oranges!"

Astryiah chuckled. "I myself might call it *pomegranates*. Did you like the new fruit?"

"*Yes*. Yes, I did. But—what does that have to do with keepin' rabbits from dyin'? I mean, obviously you can't knock me up. But you don't just mean *only* makin' whoopee with minnows. I have a feelin' it's real nice, but I don't think it would scratch all my itches."

"No, indeed. And men can certainly be useful for those vexatious itches. What I am offering…is part of the, eh, *process* for making you safe from the negative side effects of scratching that particular itch. It is very hard to describe this process. I do it infrequently, and when I do, I do not need to explain anything…but with you I want to be very clear and candid. I want you to understand and consent—or not, and we go no further.

"My blood has special properties. If I drink blood from you, and you drink from me, that will share those powerful qualities with you. I believe if we do this twice, you will be protected for the rest of your life. For certain, if we did this thrice, you would always be protected...but twice might be enough."

Palmina looked at Astryiah, who looked steadily back, deadly serious. After a few minutes of this, Palmina got up, snagged the grappa bottle, took a deep swig, offered it to Astryiah. When the latter shook her head, Palmina said, "Right, you don't like this stuff. Not many people do, to be honest."

"It is not that. It is that I drink *only* blood. You have noticed that I eat nothing and drink nothing—you've just been too polite to ask why. I am now telling you why: I am what is called an 'am'r,' and we drink only blood."

"Oh! Like *Dracula* with Bela Lugosi! I loved it! Are you... like that?"

"It was a terrible motion picture. The am'r are nothing like that. Except that, yes, we drink blood."

"I thought that Bela Lugosi was a pip!"

"Dracula is nothing like him."

"Dracula is *real*?"

"That is a long story. For another time. We have gotten off the point, which is: I am offering you some of the protection of am'r blood. I am offering you a most intimate gift. It is a complex decision to make."

"Seems like the only decision that matters is if I wanna get in the family way, ever."

"You are not afraid of me drinking your blood? Or of drinking mine?"

"That's all you eat, right?" Astryiah nodded, so Palmina continued, "So I figure it can't be that bad, and you gotta be pretty good at it."

"Oh, *chamuda*, I am very good at it indeed." Astryiah purred this with such assurance that Palmina felt turned on... but also unnerved. Well, this whole talk was so cockeyed that no wonder she felt unsettled.

"What...what'll it do, besides preventing eating for two?"

"Ah, you will like the other side effects. Your skin and hair will be so fine. You will feel strong, and you will not get sick as easily. I can promise those things, and if you drink only twice, I think they will last you many years until you are old enough that bearing children is no longer a concern."

"You *think*?"

"Well, I have not really, ahhh, experimented. With all who have shared blood with me, we have carried it through to the full three times. After that, things are...more certain. But also, ah, there are more consequences."

"What kinda consequences?"

"If we share blood three times, then once you die you will arise back to life, but a life like mine. You will live in the nighttime hours because the sun will be too strong for you. And you will require to feed upon blood as I do. There are many wonderful things, like becoming stronger than mortal humans—we call them "kee"—but those are mere details, which I will tell you when you want to know more."

Palmina thought for a while. Astryiah let her do so, in her perpetually calm, unbothered manner. Except Palmina thought maybe she was not perfectly serene underneath it. "So, if we only do the blood thing twice, I just get starlet looks and no fella can knock me up? But it might not last? But if we do the blood thing three times, then I become Dracula?"

"Dracula is already Dracula; you would not become him. You would become am'r, like me. Eventually. Also, if we exchange blood three times, well, it would be a bit like getting married. It would be a *commitment*. I do not believe you are ready for this. But I do believe if we share blood only two times, I could give you some protection. I would like to give you that gift."

"Could I, uh, have time to think about this? It's kinda big."

"*B'hechlet*. Certainly. I will return here tomorrow after sunset."

"Uh, later than that. In fact, not tomorrow. I gotta bring a gal to Emma. It might take a while, and maybe she'll sack out here. So, uh, Thursday?"

"Very well, *chamuda*. Thursday."

"Abyssinia!"

"What? What does the land of Egypt have to do with this?"

"Egypt? Huh? Nah, it's slang. It's 'I'll-be-seein'-ya' all smushed into one word."

"I see. Well then, Abyssinia, dear Palmina, Abyssinia."

Palmina didn't sleep much that night. She could've awfully used the sleep. The next day at the factory dragged interminably, and she could barely force herself to joke around with the gals.

After work, Betty was waiting for her, looking pale but determined. Palmina took her to a diner on the far side of town, following Emma's instructions never to go to her place directly from work or home. Betty couldn't bring herself to eat, but Palmina made her drink a cup of hot coffee with a generous nip of some moonshine she kept in a flask for these purposes.

Emma got the job done, as always. Palmina held Betty's hand through it and held her after as she cried. The cramping and bleeding were bad this time. Betty hadn't figured things out real soon, and it was always so much easier on the girls if they did. The later you left it, the worse it was. But Betty was married and didn't want to spend the night at Palmina's. "Frank won't like it," she kept saying and insisted on getting up as soon as she could stand. Palmina saw Betty home and gave Frank the excuse that Betty had felt sick at work and gone to rest at her house after, as it was closer to the factory. It was an excuse that had worked with many a husband or father. Mothers could be better — or worse. She waved good night to Betty, who looked haggard enough to support the excuse of feeling poorly.

Palmina got to bed at a decent hour for once.

The next morning at work, all the ladies were whispering. Ethel, who worked beside her on the line, rushed over, pulling on her work smock. "Didja hear 'bout Betty?"

Palmina felt a cold stillness descend over her. "No. What —?"

"She's *dead.* Kicked off in the night. Her man, that Frank, says he has no idea why, that she was right as rain, and then, boom! Gone!"

Linda, on her other side, tutted knowingly. "Betty got herself in a fix. Clear as day."

Palmina made herself reply — didn't know what she said. The gossip moved in a susurration up and down the production line, flowing over her. She did her job automatically, numb to thought or feeling.

Lunch break was a dreaded pause. This was often the time when women who'd gotten themselves in a bad way would sidle up to her and ask about Emma: how to contact her, what the procedure was like, was it really safe? Today nobody came to her for that. Ethel, who was practical and older, unlikely to ever require Emma's services, sat down deliberately beside her.

"So, ya think Betty died from having *it* done?"

Palmina didn't ask how Ethel knew. She wasn't dumb. "I-I dunno. No one's died from it. Not that I know of. Emma's technique's *real* safe. It's from Europe. Actual docs even refer women to her on the Q.T."

"Still. It's a risky thing, something like that. And Betty was never healthy as a horse, was she?"

Palmina thought about how many times Betty had worked through the day hunched over in pain or exhaustion. It was incredible that she'd managed to find the time and energy for an affair, given how often she was ill and with Frank demanding his dinner as soon as he got home.

Should she have urged Betty not to get the procedure, knowing that her health wasn't great? But she and Emma had both told Betty the risks. And Betty knew well enough the *other* risks, the complications from pregnancy and birth and the complications of an angry husband. Betty was a grown woman who had made her choices and weighed the stakes. Palmina was not at fault for this death.

But thinking that didn't help her feel any less to blame.

When Astryiah let herself in the back door, as she'd become accustomed to, Palmina raised herself up from where she was crying on her bed with a start. She'd forgotten all about her shadow lady.

"*Chamuda!* What is wrong?"

Astryiah normally hesitated before touching her, Palmina had noticed. A slight, subtle pause before any sort of physical contact. And she never touched anyone else; more than that, Palmina had noticed that strangers, even drunk ones, maintained a respectful distance *from* her. But now Palmina found herself being cradled in those sturdy arms without a second's pause. After the first question, Astryiah asked no more, and Palmina sank into the quiet peacefulness of the other woman.

Not just "woman." An "am'r," whatever that *really* was. Really a vampire, like in the pictures, was it possible?

Astryiah *was* like Dracula, now that she thought about it. Never eating or drinking, arriving only at night, and powerful in the most unexpected ways.

Powerful. And safe. Safe from illness, Astryiah had promised her, and from *pregnancy*.

If she did that blood thing with Astryiah, it would be like Astryiah's arms were around her all the time. She would be protected. And strong. Strong on her own, as Astryiah was, moving through the world as effortlessly as a man, free from the fears and weaknesses of being a *frail*.

In that moment it was all she wanted, strength and freedom. If drinking blood was how she could achieve it, well, she drank grappa, didn't she? Blood couldn't be *worse*. Maybe it was an acquired taste as well. Although she only had to do it two times.

"Astryiah." Her voice was muffled by speaking into a silk-clad shoulder, but the quiet reply was instant.

"Yes, *chamuda*?"

"I'm ready. I want to do the blood thing."

Astryiah laughed softly. She squeezed Palmina tightly, too tightly for an instant, but just as quickly relaxed, and with a wordless motion in her shoulder, suggested Palmina raise her head.

"I am so glad." Astryiah spoke so low it was almost a whisper. It perfectly captured the intensity of her words.

That was only the start of the intensity. It took quite a while for Astryiah to get to biting Palmina and for Palmina to find out if drinking blood was worse than drinking grappa. Along the way, she found that what she had thought of as "sex" was just a sad approximation of the sensations she could — she *should* — have been feeling. Again and again she was plunged into sensuality beyond anything she had ever expected. By the time Astryiah sank her fangs into Palmina's neck, it held no shock for her, and even the immediate pain got lost in continuing pleasure. By the time Astryiah ripped open her wrist for Palmina to tentatively sip from, she was not truly surprised to discover that that brought its own new, deeper blisses.

Drinking blood left grappa, bathtub gin, moonshine, even that bottle of champagne she once had, in the dust. Even giggle smoke was nothing compared to it.

Afterward, she lay in Astryiah's arms, just as strong as any man's, and luxuriated in how *good* she felt. She had not felt so healthy — so full of joy yet also at peace — in so long she couldn't remember. Perhaps ever since she'd stopped being a kid.

"Is drinking blood always like this?"

"Oh no. Not always. This is a special kind of blood exchange; my people call it "vhoon-vayon." For the am'r, this is the best kind. But as with kee — that's normal people, to you — with kee sex, it is not always this loving or this beautiful."

"You shred it, wheat! Beauteeful is the word! I never felt *anything* like this!" Palmina paused, afraid to say something wrong in the intensity of the bliss that filled her. "Uh, thank you…for all'a this."

"Oh, *chamuda*, it was my pleasure — you cannot know how much pleasure you have given me. But sleep now. You may feel very well indeed, but you need rest after this. And make sure to look in the mirror tomorrow morning. No, I will not tell you why — no more talking! Sleep!"

When Palmina woke up, she could not for a moment remember why she felt so swell. She'd had such a hard day and then a very late night with Astryiah — Oh! She had done *that thing*. And it had not been in any way what she'd expected, and the results were equally nothing like she'd expected. Every movement she made proved this as she bounced off the lumpy old mattress with energy, ease in all her limbs, and a rush of delight in the birdsong outside the window.

Remembering Astryiah's cryptic (even for Astryiah) comment, she rushed to the bathroom. The dark undereye circles that had only been getting darker were gone. Her skin, which had been looking dull from continuous exhaustion, was glowing.

Murder! That blood thing really was *something*.

"You look very well indeed. How have you felt today, *chamuda*?" is what Astryiah said when she came in the back door that evening. She took Palmina's face between her hands and examined her minutely.

"Ring a ding ding! I been aces all day long! Feel like a kid again! All the gals were asking me what new makeup I was using! I can't believe just knocking back a bit of blood could do all that!" Palmina overcame a kind of shyness she'd never had with boys and pushed her face forward through Astryiah's hands to give her a smack on the lips.

Astryiah smiled with such warmth that it transformed her habitually distant expression until she almost seemed a different person. She kissed Palmina back, deep and thorough, a real honey cooler.

"I am pleased that you have taken to it so naturally. But my vhoon, my blood, is not the same as if you had just drunk from any mortal person, any kee. You understand that, *ken*?"

"Uh, guess so. I mean, you've told it to me, but I can't really dig it."

"But you are comfortable with it?"

"Well, I feel real killer-diller! That's comfortable enough!"

"Are you ready to do vhoon-vayon with me again?"

"Have all that fun again? Sure thing!"

"It *is* fun. But it is more than that. This time we will make you so you cannot be impregnated by a man, not ever. I must remind you of this, *chamuda*."

"That's one of the perks. After what happened to Betty...I don't want that to happen to me, not ever!"

"No, I do not want that either. But I feel I must repeat—must remind you that a child could someday be a thing you wanted as well. My vhoon does not just prevent unwanted pregnancies, but *any* pregnancy...."

Palmina shook her head. "Even when you *want* a baby, if something goes wrong, you'll be pushing up daisies. This sets me free from all that."

"*Lo*, it does. I have seen so many women die from complications in pregnancy, during childbirth, or be crippled by inept delivery. It is a thing undertaken so lightly but often at such cost. Well, you shall pay another cost then. Come to bed. Let me set you free."

❧

As the blood she'd gulped from Astryiah's wrist made its way into her body, she felt truly freed. For a moment she felt like she had become a bird, and she could use brand-new muscles to take off into the air, nothing holding her down ever again.

After she had soared through sensation for a while, suddenly it seemed very silly to her, and she muttered, "Fluttering dickey-birds," one of her favorite swears, and then she was laughing at all of it, and Astryiah was holding her and laughing with her, kissing her with sharp nips of teeth, and she wished the joy of it would never end.

❧

The next morning, she felt as if energy ran through her instead of blood, which would have been a funny ol' thing. Her skin seemed poreless and perfect. Her eyes were bright with health, and the world seemed to sparkle. She sang along with the birds. The night before was still inside her, an echo of euphoria.

It was the weekend. She went shopping for groceries, and on the way stopped in the record store and treated herself to a 45 of Ellington's "Mood Indigo." She should have stopped in to see Babbo and Mamma…but they might have noticed something different about her, and she wasn't ready to answer their questions. She didn't really know how to answer her own questions, the ones that bubbled in the back of her mind, waiting to be considered when the exhilaration wore off.

She was starving; she couldn't get enough food to eat. She made up a huge batch of pasta fazool, which normally she'd share with friends whom she felt didn't get enough hot meals. Today she ate almost the whole pot, one bowl after another. She didn't get indigestion, but did eventually find relief from the intense hunger.

There was a hop that night, and she dragged Astryiah to it, and they danced to every song. Palmina felt the same endless energy moving through her that she'd seen in Astryiah. The hot jazz pumped through her like an external, communal heart.

As Astryiah saw her home, with the sky softening to a lighter purply-blue where the sun was going to rise, she was still feeling the rhythms moving her muscles, and she took Astryiah's hand and spun them along the empty street. Astryiah laughed with her and didn't let go of her hand.

"Why didn't ya share your, uh, vhoon, with me before this? I coulda been feelin' this sweet all this time!"

"I am so very pleased you are happy with your choice, *chamuda*. But it is a very intimate and intense thing. It is a risk I take, to reveal that aspect of myself to you. Many kee could not handle such information. They would want to kill me for being a monster. As in your *Dracula* film."

"Risk? But *you're* not scared of anything! And you're nothing like Dracula! This, what I feel, this is nothing like that. You're not a monster. You—you're a lifesaver! I feel so full of life. *Dracula* was all about *death*."

Astryiah stopped. She took Palmina's other hand and looked down at her, more seriously than Palmina had ever seen that solemn face. "I'm afraid I have failed to convey to you what gift you have accepted from me." She looked around and led Palmina to a small park between buildings, just a few benches and some grass and trees. With no streetlight, the shadows made it a space of enveloping privacy. Palmina realized she'd normally never have felt safe in an unlit part of the city, until she'd walked at night with Astryiah.

Astryiah sat them down on a bench and started speaking with low urgency. "*Chamuda*, I do not know if you are just giddy with my vhoon — it does take some kee like that — but I fear that your lack of understanding may bring you pain or worse hurt.

"I bring death, like your Dracula. That is what you said you wanted. With only two sharings of blood, I have rendered your body unable to bring forth life in the normal, kee way. This strength you feel rushing through you is not the strength of life, not in the way you know, but a strength that doesn't meet its full potential until your own kee death. You have drunk of death, *neshama shèli* — my soul, and I have not saved you. You are right that there is strength from *sheol*, and we may harness it to make our time in this world, however long, a more loving and powerful life.

"By going only this far with me, I think I prevent you from finding the disadvantages of my existence; you get only a small taste of the advantages. But do not doubt that the changes you feel within you are from brushing too close to death, not from some bright flame of life."

In the deep shadow of the park, Palmina could not see Astryiah's face, not well. She could see the outline of her head and a little light catching on nose and cheek, a low gleam from the shiny honey-colored marcel waves, perfectly styled as always. Palmina wondered if she could see a little better in the dark than before, but it wasn't enough to read her dusky dame's face; only the tone of voice and the pressing of Astryiah's urgent fingers against hers gave her the true impression of how serious this was.

"You're right; I don't dig it, not all the way. I know I feel just *aces*. I know how safe I feel around you and how safe I feel with your vhoon inside me now. But how can I *really* understand it? I don't hardly know *anything* about you, about your life. I don't even know why you're here in Philly. You could be anywhere in the world. Whatcha doin' *here*?"

"I am here with you. For now, I am your lover and protector."

Palmina shook her head in frustration. "No — what for didja come here, before you met me?"

"I was traveling around the States. It is a very young place with many problems, but in some ways reminds me of my home, which is a very old place, but with problems which are ever renewing."

"OK, but what for were ya in the alley behind my place that first night?"

"Ehhhh. Well." Astryiah paused. A long pause. Palmina bit her tongue to keep from asking any other questions, thereby giving Astryiah a way out of answering.

"Well, I had heard of Emma. And that you were the best connection to her. I found you first."

Palmina's head spun.

"What could *you* have possibly wanted from Emma? *You* can't get in that kinda trouble."

"Ehhhh. *Lo*. Well, in a different way than I have helped you, I could help Emma, and you, and all of Emma's clients."

"'Help'." Palmina's voice was flat.

"*Ken, ken!*" Astryiah sounded almost-nervous for the second time Palmina had ever heard. "I could be of great help! But then I met you, and I did not know how to make the offer without perhaps causing offense. And then…I did not want to risk offense even further and losing you from my life. This time with you…has been a rare delight for me."

Palmina pushed the compliment away with a wave of her hand. "How do you think you can *help*?"

"Ehhhh. Well…if I drink from a woman who is pregnant and who does not want to be, and if I give her just one small mouthful of my vhoon, her body will abort. It is much safer for the women, even than Emma's modern methods. I wanted to offer that medically safer option."

"But. You didn't. You just did a different thing with me."

"Well, I developed feelings for you, a connection with you. It made it harder."

"Harder to help other women?"

"*Lo*...! Just. Clouded. Complicated."

Palmina felt a surge of anger, brighter than any anger she'd felt before. Everything was so much more intense now. She fought to keep her voice level; even in this rush of emotion, she could tell that Astryiah wouldn't put up with any beef.

"Please. Square up why your plans changed when ya met me."

"I cannot explain. Please accept this. It is about emotion, and it is hard for me to talk about. I believe I have made it quite plain how I feel about you. I was...concerned that I might... scare you away...if I made my original offer to you, once our friendship had begun."

Palmina pushed down the cascade of emotions that threatened to come out at top volume. Her family dealt with emotions loudly and at length. She was comfortable with that. She *really* wanted to blow her wig right now. But — and here was a voice inside her that she tried to ignore — while being around Astryiah made her feel safe from others, a part of her was intensely aware that Astryiah was dangerous like a gun, like fire: something that *could* protect you but wasn't guaranteed to be something that *wouldn't* hurt you. Kill you, even.

"Well. Now I know. So what's this offer, exactly?"

Astryiah could not miss the lack of emotion in her voice or the way she held herself so still and distant. She felt Astryiah's body echo hers, pulling away from her on the bench. She almost reached out after her, but then she heard Astryiah's voice, so cold it hurt to hear, replying, "It is a simple offer. Instead of bringing the women who need help to Emma for the procedure she uses, they could be brought to a nice warm hotel room where I would be. Or someone's back bedroom. Not the dangerous spaces you have found for the procedure. They would be given just enough information to consent that they would lose some blood and drink a small amount of 'medicine,' and then they would not have any danger, just a heavy menstruation, some cramping. I am very far from being in a kee body, so I do not remember anymore what all is involved, only that it would never cause injury and never create a situation like poor Betty. They would just need a good hot meal, and then they could go back to their lives unharmed. Well, except for what emotions they must endure from the loss."

Palmina thought for a long while. Astryiah waited like a statue.

"I'm not sure I'd'a believed you or what you'd've had to *do* to get me to believe you if you'd talked to me about alla this that first night. I think I dig why you did whatcha did...but I still don't *like* it. Makes me feel like you were using me."

"This is unfortunate. I was trying to keep you from assuming I was only interested in you for vhoon; *that* is why I changed my plans."

They sat in the silent shadows, neither sure where to go from there.

"Maybe you oughta—" Palmina started as Astryiah began, "Perhaps I had best—" Both came to a screeching verbal halt. Astryiah eventually finished her sentence. "Perhaps I had best go away for a while to give you time to think."

She didn't want that, but she made herself say, "Yeah... maybe you better."

And then she was alone in the dark.

When Astryiah left, she took joy with her, more joy than Palmina had realized was in her life. She'd been so exhausted and worn down for so long she hadn't realized how Astryiah's wry observances of life had bolstered her up. Even before the vhoon-vayon, she'd come to count on that fixed presence in her nights, the intimacy in words long before intimacy of bodies.

Words, words spoken in the dark where they could safely be said.

Bodies, bodies intertwining in the dark where fingers and teeth could break through barriers that would have been too impermeable in daylight.

As soon as Astryiah had left the painful void in her wake, Palmina was able to entirely understand and excuse her actions. Once it was too late to take back her words.

Maybe she'll come back? She said, "Go away for a while." That means she'll come back.

Life went on. At least it did for everyone else. At the factory, the biscuits went along the production line, as did the intrigues and gossip. Palmina smiled, but it did not touch her; it did not feel as *real* as anything Astryiah had brought into her life. At the dances, the jazz was hot, but the music did not touch her pulse. The girls would say she'd "run out of gas," and it sure felt like that, all right.

As life went on, the problems of life continued as well. It was not a week after Astryiah had left only terrible emptiness in her wake that a gal whispered to her at the end of the lunch break, "I need to see Emma. *Please.*"

The weeks went by. Another lady needed Emma's services. Each was sick afterward. Nobody shared Betty's fate. But as she escorted the shaken women to their homes, eyes red and skin drained of color, she thought about how much easier and safer it *could* have been for them. *I denied them that. My high-hat made it harder for 'em.*

Guilt was the only thing that she felt acutely through the numb ache of loss and regret. The rest of her existence seemed far away, the sound muted, her senses dulled.

Her vhoon-boosted health was so robust that she shouldn't have been able to feel down. She got compliments — and demands for her beauty secrets — every day. Men flocked to her, and it took everything she'd learned from Astryiah to fend them off. It seemed she would not need Astryiah's exotic birth control; she felt no desire to put up with fumbling hands on her body when she remembered her shadow woman's skillful, intuitive fingers. She had no urge to play the flirtation game with anyone less coolly ironic or excitingly worldly.

She tried not to think about how the other women could have benefited from Astryiah's powerful blood, even as she connected them to Emma and took them to and from their procedures.

ɞ

She didn't go to the New Year's hop or any parties her friends were having. She went to bed early and the next day cooked several batches of spaghetti so she could give out dishes of it to various friends who were down on their luck. Her appetite had gone back to normal over the months, so cooking for others was doable again. Since it was a day off from work, she distracted herself by cooking and delivering bowls wrapped in towels to keep them warm.

With the remaining sauce simmering and the cooking water just poured off the last batch of pasta, the tiny kitchen had become too hot, so she went out to sit on the back stoop for a minute. She'd cool down real quick in a Philly January.

"Have you perhaps any grappa to share?" The voice had been too longed-for, too anxiously anticipated, for her to recognize it at first. Her head came up sharply, and there in the twilight's purple gloom was her lady of the shadows.

"Nah. I didn't feel like getting sauced alone today." Her month's-long blues helped her to answer coolly instead of running up and throwing her arms around Astryiah. Getting her hopes up seemed too hard, even with the woman she'd pined for standing right there in front of her.

"I could keep you company," Astryiah offered. It was the only vulnerability she would show, Palmina knew; this one advance, this one risk of rejection. And if it was turned down, Astryiah would disappear out of her life forever.

"There's room here for you to sit," she answered carefully. She was afraid. Afraid to say something wrong: to try too hard or be perceived to not be trying hard enough. Astryiah could be spooked so easily, and she felt no confidence that she could stop or repair it.

"Well," Astryiah said when she had settled down beside Palmina. Their thighs had a hairbreadth of space carefully held between them. "You needed time to think. Have I given you long enough to consider everything?"

"Yes! Yes. You did. I have." Palmina found it hard, in the moment, to say things she'd so desperately wished she could have said before. "Look — I'm sorry."

"You need not apologize. The am'r world is different from the one you are used to. Different principles. Different purposes. Different focuses and importances. You are not of that world, so things I say can shock your sensibilities. I am long since departed from your kee worldview. I pushed you too far, too fast."

"You gave me time! I know you tried to tell me. I just couldn't hear it, not right away. But I dig it now. I do. I promise."

"You are really come to an understanding?" Astryiah did not look hopeful, just serious.

"I am! I wantcha'ta help as many women as possible. I wanna help *you* help as many women as possible."

Astryiah paused and looked dead in Palmina's eyes. "I must clearly ask you now. I must know that you do truly accept all that that means. I will drink the blood of those women, giving them a small portion of mine in return."

"Yeah, yeah. That jives."

"And you and I...*we* cannot do vhoon-vayon again. Not unless you choose to leave your kee life and enter my am'r one, leaving your friends and family behind."

"I...understand. At least, I *believe* you since I can't really understand."

"*Tov!* We will work together to help these women. I am very glad you want this. Very glad, *chamuda*."

"Can we...uh...can we, just, you know, *cuddle*? Be in bed, without the blood?"

Astryiah got a complicated but not unhappy look on her face. "I do not normally 'be in bed' with one with whom I am not vhoon-sharing. However...I have missed how you feel in my arms, dear Palmina. You are exceptional, so I will make an exception for you."

Palmina found herself in Astryiah's arms, smelling the slightly musky-seawater-metallic scent of her, feeling the firmly muscled body melt around her to fit together best.

If anyone had been keeping track of such things, they would have noticed that for some decades, few women in Philadelphia and its immediate environs died of certain "unexplained causes," and fewer unplanned babies were thrust into an unwelcoming world.

"Nothing lasts forever — at least not the good stuff," Palmina would reflect years later, in the community for the elderly where she'd found a comfy little cottage she could maintain by herself as the aches and pains of age slowed her down. "But for a while we did some good, we did."

She said as much to the woman who held her in her arms on the final day. She had given up eating a week ago; a graceful exit from a graceless disease like cancer. When life lost its joys, it was time to go. She was at peace, she was ready, and the pain was bad enough that she was more than ready. She would have liked to see her shadow lady one last time, but that partnership had ended long ago. Astryiah had gone back to her am'r world, and Palmina had continued onwards in her very human life, with human problems and human loves. No children, but a wide network of loving connections. She was a woman well-loved, who had loved well. Except for her dusky dame — who she knew she'd never see again — that network had gathered in her final days to say goodbye, and to fill her final days with laughter and loving memories.

She told them all to leave for the night — no sense in anyone sleeping in a chair, waiting around for death with her. She could go to sleep in peace — and better if she didn't wake up in the morning to have yet another "final day."

But she did wake up, in the middle of the night. To find familiar arms around her, so familiar that for a confused moment she didn't know which decade it was. "Ah — Astryiah?"

"Shhh, *chamuda*. I am here, here for the last night, here to take away the final pain. I missed how you felt in my arms, and I could not let you go without feeling that one more time."

Palmina laughed with delight. "I'm like a bag of sticks now! I sure don't feel like I usta!"

"You still feel like my dear Palmina."

"I'm so glad you're here. You were the only one I couldn't say goodbye to. Didn't wanna to go without that — though I never expected to get the chance."

"But here I am, *chamuda*. Feel my arms around you. Let me help you say goodbye."

"Abyssinia...."

"*Ken*, *ken*, I remember. We said this back then, didn't we? Abyssinia, Palmina, my love. Abyssinia."

Author Biographies

Maggie Mayhem (she/her) is an activist and full spectrum doula based in San Francisco, California. She has served on the Board of Directors of the Sex Worker Outreach Project-USA as well as the Leadership & Training Council of the Bay Area Doula Project. Her abortion activism has been featured in *The Atlantic* and she has been profiled by the *Huffington Post*. Her website is maggiemayhem.com.

Nisi Shawl (they/them) is the multiple award-winning author, co-author, and editor of over a dozen books of speculative fiction and related nonfiction, including (with Cynthia Ward) the standard text on diverse representation in literature, the Aqueduct Press Conversation Piece titled *Writing the Other*, which is the basis of the online workshop of the same name. Shawl's best known work of fiction is the Nebula Award finalist novel *Everfair*. Their Aqueduct Press short story collection *Filter House* co-won the 2009 Otherwise Award (formerly the James Tiptree, Jr. Award). Among their editing credits are *Stories for Chip: A Tribute to Delany* (with Bill Campbell); *Strange Matings: Science Fiction, Feminism, African American Voices, and Octavia E. Butler* (with Rebecca J. Holden); and the first two volumes of the New Suns anthology series. They've spoken at Duke University, Spelman College, Stanford University, Sarah Lawrence College, and at many other learning institutions. Recent books include a new Aqueduct Press story collection, the horror-friendly *Our Fruiting Bodies*; and the Middle Grade historical fantasy novel *Speculation* from Lee & Low. Shawl likes to relax by pretending they live in other people's houses.

Ellen Klages is the author of three acclaimed MG historical novels: *The Green Glass Sea*, which won the Scott O'Dell Award and the New Mexico Book Award; *White Sands, Red Menace*, which won the California and New Mexico Book awards; and *Out of Left Field*, which won the 2019 Children's History Book Prize and the 2019 Ohioana Book Award. Her adult novel, a historical fantasy, *Passing Strange*, won the World Fantasy and British Fantasy awards in 2018. Her short fiction has been translated into a dozen languages and been nominated for or won multiple Hugo, Nebula, Locus, Mythopoeic, and World Fantasy awards. Ellen lives in San Francisco, in a small house full of strange and wondrous things.

Kathleen Alcalá was born in Compton, California, to Mexican parents and grew up in San Bernardino. She has a BA in linguistics from Stanford, an MA in Creative Writing from the University of Washington, and an MFA from the University of New Orleans. She has also attended Clarion West and Macondo workshops. The author of six books with stories in over 30 anthologies, Kathleen is co-editor, with Norma Cantú, of *Weeping Women*, an anthology of work about La Llorona forthcoming from Trinity University Press. Kathleen has received the Western States Book Award, the Governors Writers Award, and two Artist Trust Fellowships. Kathleen sometimes teaches creative writing on or near Bainbridge Island, where, a member of the Ópata Nation, she makes her home within the ancestral territory of the suq̓ʷabš "People of Clear Salt Water" (Suquamish People).

K Ibura is a writer, editor, and artist from New Orleans—the original home of the Chitimacha Tribe. She writes essays about identity and gender, and fantastical fiction about ancient histories and future imaginings. She is the author of two speculative fiction collections: *Ancient, Ancient*—winner of the James Tiptree Award, and *When the World Wounds*; and a novel for children *When the World Turns Upside Down*. Her *Notes From the Trenches* e-book series examines the emotional underpinnings of the writing life. Learn more about her at kibura.com and kiburabooks.com.

Helena María Viramontes is the author of *The Moths and Other Stories*, and novels *Under the Feet of Jesus* and *Their Dogs Came with Them*. She is currently working on a novel in triptych form entitled *The Cemetery Boys*. Viramontes is Distinguished Professor of Arts & Sciences in English at Cornell University and former director of Cornell's Creative Writing Program.

Cecilia Tan is an award-winning author of science fiction/fantasy, romance, and erotica. Her short stories have appeared in *Asimov's, Strange Horizons, Absolute Magnitude*, and many other places. She is the founder of Circlet Press, publishers of erotic science fiction and fantasy, and has edited over 100 anthologies of fiction, as well as the being author of many books, including the ground-breaking erotic sf/fantasy short story collections *Black Feathers* (HarperCollins) and *White Flames* (Running Press), and the Magic University series (Riverdale Avenue Books).

Sonya Taaffe reads dead languages and tells living stories. Her short fiction and poetry have been collected most recently in *As the Tide Came Flowing In* (Nekyia Press) and previously in *Singing Innocence and Experience, Postcards from the Province of Hyphens, A Mayse-Bikhl, Ghost Signs*, and the Lambda-nominated *Forget the Sleepless Shores*. She lives with one of her husbands and both of her cats in Somerville, Massachusetts, where she writes about film for Patreon—https://www.patreon.com/sovay—and remains proud of naming a Kuiper belt object. Find her at https://sonyataaffe.com.

Annalee Newitz writes science fiction and nonfiction. They are the author of three novels: *The Terraformers, The Future of*

Another Timeline, and *Autonomous*, which won the Lambda Literary Award. As a science journalist, they are the author of *Four Lost Cities: A Secret History of the Urban Age* and *Scatter, Adapt and Remember: How Humans Will Survive a Mass Extinction*, which was a finalist for the LA Times Book Prize in science. They are a writer for the *New York Times* and elsewhere, and have a monthly column in *New Scientist*. They have published in *The Washington Post, Slate, Popular Science, Ars Technica, The New Yorker*, and *The Atlantic*, among others. They are the co-host of the Hugo Award-winning podcast *Our Opinions Are Correct*. Previously, they were the founder of *io9*, and served as the editor-in-chief of *Gizmodo*.

Cynthia Gralla is the author of *The Floating World*, a novel published by Ballantine, and *The Demimonde in Japanese Literature: Sexuality and the Literary Karyukai*, an academic monograph from Cambria Press. She has also written fiction and nonfiction for *Michigan Quarterly Review, The Mississippi Review, Salon, Electric Literature, storySouth, The Conversation, Asymptote Journal, Ruminate, Witness, Iron Horse Literary Review*, and many other publications. She teaches literature and academic writing at the University of Victoria and Royal Roads University on Vancouver Island.

Tara Campbell is an award-winning writer, teacher, Kimbilio Fellow, fiction co-editor at Barrelhouse, and graduate of American University's MFA in Creative Writing. She teaches creative writing at venues such as American University, Johns Hopkins University, Clarion West, The Writer's Center, Hugo House, and the National Gallery of Art. Her publication credits include *Masters Review, Wigleaf, Electric Literature, CRAFT Literary, Daily Science Fiction, Strange Horizons,* and *Escape Pod/Artemis Rising*. She's the author of a novel, two hybrid collections of poetry and prose, and two short story collections from feminist sci-fi publisher Aqueduct Press. Her sixth book, a novel featuring sentient gargoyles in the 22nd century American West, is forthcoming from SFWP in fall 2024. Find her at www.taracampbell.com.

Anya Johanna DeNiro is a writer and trans woman living in Saint Paul. She's the author of *City of a Thousand Feelings* (Aqueduct Press, 2020), which was on the Honor Roll for the Otherwise Award, and the forthcoming novel *OKPsyche* (Small Beer Press, 2023). Find her at www.anyajohannade-niro.com.

Jaymee Goh is a Malaysian-Chinese writer, reviewer, editor, and essayist of speculative fiction. Her work has been published in a number of magazines and anthologies, such as *Lightspeed Magazine, Beneath Ceaseless Skies,* and *New Suns: Original Speculative Fiction by People of Color*, and reprinted in *LeVar Burton Reads* and *Best American Science Fiction & Fantasy.* Her reviews and nonfiction have appeared on *Tor.com, The Los Angeles Review of Books*, and *Strange Horizons*. She co-edited *The Sea Is Ours: Tales of Steampunk Southeast Asia* (Rosarium 2015), and edited *The WisCon Chronicles Vol. 11: Trials by Whiteness* (Aqueduct 2017). A graduate from the Clarion Science Fiction and Fantasy Writers Workshop in 2016, she received her PhD in Comparative Literature from the University of California, Riverside, where she dissertated in science fiction studies and critical race theory. She is an editor for Tachyon Publications.

Elizabeth Bear was born on the same day as Frodo and Bilbo Baggins, but in a different year. She is the Hugo, Sturgeon, Locus, and Astounding Award winning author of dozens of novels; over a hundred short stories; and a number of essays, nonfiction, and opinion pieces for markets as diverse as *Popular Mechanics* and *The Washington Post*. Elizabeth is a frequent contributor to the Center for Science and the Imagination at ASU, and has spoken on futurism at Google, MIT, DARPA's

100 Year Starship Project, and the White House, among others. Find her at https://www.elizabethbear.com.

Raven Belasco (she/her) is the pen name of Lisbet Beryl Weir, for the ease of readers to easily distinguish the genres she's playing with. By now she will answer to either name. The Blood & Ancient Scrolls series whose vampire characters have a rapidly growing dedicated fan base. Prior to writing novels, her articles and short fiction have been published for over twenty years. She loves cooking, yoga, and her small indignant terrier (who takes her out for walkies when plotting gets tricky). Find her at https://ravenbelas.co